Who the
BISHOP KNOWS

BOOKS BY VANNETTA CHAPMAN

THE AMISH BISHOP MYSTERIES

What the Bishop Saw

When the Bishop Needs an Alibi

Who the Bishop Knows

✠

PLAIN AND SIMPLE MIRACLES

Brian's Choice
(ebook-only novella prequel)

Anna's Healing

Joshua's Mission

Sarah's Orphans

✠

THE PEBBLE CREEK AMISH SERIES

A Promise for Miriam

A Home for Lydia

A Wedding for Julia

"Home to Pebble Creek"
(free short story e-romance)

"Christmas at Pebble Creek"
(free short story e-romance)

Who the
BISHOP KNOWS

Vannetta Chapman

HARVEST HOUSE PUBLISHERS
EUGENE, OREGON

Cover by Bryce Williamson

Cover Image © Elysiumm, jlophoto / iStock

Published in association with the literary agency of The Steve Laube Agency, LLC, 24 W. Camelback Rd. A-635, Phoenix, Arizona 85013.

WHO THE BISHOP KNOWS

Copyright © 2018 by Vannetta Chapman
Published by Harvest House Publishers
Eugene, Oregon 97408
www.harvesthousepublishers.com

ISBN 978-0-7369-6651-1 (pbk.)
ISBN 978-0-7369-6652-8 (eBook)

Library of Congress Cataloging-in-Publication Data

Names: Chapman, Vannetta, author.
Title: Who the bishop knows / Vannetta Chapman.
Description: Eugene, Oregon : Harvest House Publishers, 2018. | Series: The Amish bishop mysteries ; 3
Identifiers: LCCN 2017036958 (print) | LCCN 2017040453 (ebook) | ISBN 9780736966528 (ebook) | ISBN 9780736966511 (softcover)
Subjects: LCSH: Amish--Fiction. | Clergy--Fiction. | Murder--Investigation--Fiction. | BISAC: FICTION / Christian / Suspense. | FICTION / Christian / Romance. | GSAFD: Christian fiction. | Mystery fiction.
Classification: LCC PS3603.H3744 (ebook) | LCC PS3603.H3744 W495 2018 (print) | DDC 813/.6--dc23
LC record available at https://lccn.loc.gov/2017036958

Printed in the United States of America

18 19 20 21 22 23 24 25 26 / LB-GL / 10 9 8 7 6 5 4 3 2 1

For the fine folks of the Texas Hill Country

ACKNOWLEDGMENTS

This book is dedicated to the residents of the Texas Hill Country—where two lanes are still plenty, and it's commonplace to find yourself driving behind a cattle or horse or sheep trailer. Ten years ago my husband and I left the big-city lights of Dallas and moved to small-town Texas. We found the people friendly and the sunsets long. We rediscovered games of 42, the thrill of nature, and the fun of high school sports. In other words, we rediscovered our roots. Thank you for that.

I'd also like to once again thank the Harvest House staff, who have been a dream to work with through the last 12 books. My agent, Steve Laube, is a continual source of wisdom and humor, plus he answers emails promptly. My pre-readers, Kristy Kreymer and Janet Murphy, are incredibly talented and encouraging. I love you both.

My husband, Bobby, is unbelievably patient with me while I'm "in the cave." My mom takes care of post office runs and animal care when I'm away. And my son reminds me I need to occasionally take an afternoon off and go see a movie. You all help me keep it together, and I love you more than I can say.

Who the Bishop Knows is my twentieth full-length novel and the last in the Amish Bishop Mysteries. I hope you've enjoyed this journey into the Colorado Amish. With every book I write about the Amish, I discover new things about their community, their lifestyle, and what we have in common—which is what reading and writing are really about.

And finally, "Always giving thanks to God the Father for everything, in the name of our Lord Jesus Christ" (Ephesians 5:20).

Suffering passes, while love is eternal.
That's a gift that you have received from God.
Don't waste it.

LAURA INGALLS WILDER

☩

We have different gifts, according to the grace
given to each of us.

ROMANS 12:6

One

San Luis Valley, Colorado
July 27

Bishop Henry Lapp ordered two hot dogs, two bags of chips, and one large drink. He waited for his purchases somewhat impatiently, having received his change and hoping he wouldn't miss the last of the local amateur events. Local boys were competing—even Amish boys— and he wanted to be in the stands to cheer them on.

He was thinking of that, of how the Amish and the *Englisch* so often stood together as one community, when the unmistakable crack of a rifle rang out.

"Rodeo clown?" the woman behind him asked.

"Sounded like the real thing." This from the teen working the hot dog counter at the Ski Hi Stampede, Colorado's oldest pro rodeo.

Then the screaming started.

Henry dropped the napkins he was holding, turned toward the stands, and took off at a sprint toward his seat. In the back of his mind, he needed to reach Emma, but that was ridiculous. Who would shoot Emma? Who would shoot anyone at a rodeo?

A river of people poured from the arena stands.

"Someone has a rifle!"

"Get out of my way!"

"Call the cops! Has anyone called the cops?"

Henry pushed against the crowd, dodging to the left and right, fully

9

realizing he was headed the wrong direction but knowing he had no choice. He had the sensation that everything was moving too fast. At the same time he seemed to be stuck in slow motion. He turned the corner into the arena, his heart pounding and sweat trickling down his back. Emma was still in the stands where he'd left her, surrounded by her family, who had huddled up like a high school football team. The bleachers were more than half empty now, though they'd been packed to capacity five minutes before.

Henry rushed up the stands, pausing only long enough to make eye contact with Emma, to assure himself she was uninjured.

Once he reached their row, he turned to stare at the tragedy before them. Around the arena stood cowboys and cowgirls, young and old, *Englisch* and Amish. Henry allowed his gaze to slide past them, toward the middle of the arena, where a young man lay motionless in the dirt as medical personnel rushed toward him.

"Who is it?" Henry asked, breathless from his dash up the stands.

"Jeremiah Schwartz." Clyde scowled at the ever-growing crowd gathering in the center of the arena.

Jeremiah had been competing in rodeos since he was a lad of sixteen. Now he was nineteen. Technically, he was visiting from Goshen to help his widowed grandmother with her farm chores for the summer, but everyone knew his passion was steer wrestling. The real reason he came was the chance to compete in the 97th Annual Ski Hi Stampede.

He was Plain, but he hadn't yet joined the church. It was past time that he made that decision, and Henry had spoken about it on more than one occasion. Jeremiah was enjoying his *rumspringa*, or at least he had been up until a few minutes ago.

Emma's family looked on in alarm as the medical personnel attended to the young man.

Stephen and Thomas, Emma's youngest grandsons, pressed in close to their father. They were only eleven and twelve, and their expressions revealed shock mixed with a little fear.

Rachel grasped Clyde's hand and reached out to touch Emma. She was a good woman, and Emma had shared on several occasions that she thought of her as both a daughter-in-law and a friend.

Katie Ann stood frozen, eyes wide, both hands clasped over her mouth. At eighteen, she'd already seen too much death.

Silas, the oldest of Emma's grandchildren, bounded up the steps. "Sheriff Grayson is setting up a perimeter. No one's to leave the arena."

"Half of the people have already fled," Henry pointed out.

"Unless they're walking home, they won't get far. Monte Vista PD posted officers at the parking lot gates. No one in and no one out."

"Even buggies?" Clyde asked.

"*Ya*. Even buggies."

Emma made her way around her family, touching each of them as she did, and stopped next to Henry.

"You're okay?" he asked, though he knew she was. He could see she was, and yet his heart needed to hear her say so.

"*Ya*. Of course."

He clasped her hand in his, sending up a silent prayer of gratitude for this woman who had changed his life. She had brought back color and joy and laughter. She'd taught him to embrace his gift.

"Do you think you should go down there?" she asked.

"Not much I can do."

"Maybe not for Jeremiah, but..."

Henry didn't want to involve himself in this tragedy. Images of Betsy Troyer, Vernon Frey, and Sophia Brooks darted through his mind. He thought of himself and Emma and Sophia's sister huddled beneath the sand dunes as a killer stalked them. He didn't know if this was another murder, but he did know he'd rather not be involved.

"Too many people down there already." He understood better than most that they were looking at a crime scene that would need to be contained.

"Surely they would let you through."

"But what good could I do? The professionals are seeing to him."

"You could pray."

"Which we can do here."

But then he saw that Ruth Schwartz had almost made her way to the bottom of the stands, fighting the crowds, her hands in the air and her *kapp* strings flying behind her.

Henry looked at Ruth, glanced at Emma, and nodded his head. Jeremiah was Ruth's grandson. She shouldn't be dealing with this alone.

He picked his way back down the stands, circumvented the folks who were gawking by the railing, and walked up to the police officer who was intent on keeping people off the field.

"No one else is allowed out there. Sorry, Henry." Ricky Moore was the newest addition to the police force. A personable fellow, he had a sister married to a Mennonite pastor. He'd always been pleasant and agreeable to Henry, but he was trying to handle a crisis—one hand was on the butt of his gun, the other hovered near his radio. His expression, usually smiling, was grim, and his eyes continuously scanned the crowd.

Instead of arguing, Henry waited until Moore glanced his way again, and then he inclined his head toward Ruth Schwartz. The crowd of officers and first responders had parted for her, and she'd collapsed to the ground at Jeremiah's side. A wail that cut to Henry's bones pierced the evening.

"Is she one of your congregants?"

"She is."

Moore didn't hesitate, and Henry thought that said something about the man. He stepped aside and mumbled, "Try not to trample on any evidence."

Two

Emma watched Henry as he stood next to the police officer, waiting to be let near Jeremiah's body.

"I can't believe this is happening again," Rachel murmured.

"Who would do such a thing?" Clyde asked, not expecting an answer. But Silas seemed to take the question seriously.

"Jeremiah was running with a rough crowd."

"*Englisch*?" Clyde raked his fingers through his beard, tugging the corners of his mouth down and into a frown.

"*Ya*, rodeo types."

"Do you know who would want to harm him, Silas?" The question flew from Emma's mouth before she considered whether she should ask such a thing with others standing so close. The last thing she wanted to do was start rumors while Jeremiah was lying on the ground.

"*Nein*." Silas crossed his arms and stared at the growing presence on the field. "I can't imagine anyone wanting to do such a thing, being angry enough to do so. It's beyond me."

"It sounded like a rifle," Clyde said.

"How would anyone smuggle a rifle into an arena?" A heavy weight had settled on Emma's chest, along with an ache at the back of her throat. She wanted to sit down and weep. This was supposed to be a family outing, a night Jeremiah had looked forward to for many weeks. She knew that because Ruth had told her so. And now, once again, they were facing a tragedy. "Why would anyone do such a thing?"

"We've seen this before. Like with the Monte Vista arsonist." Katie

Ann didn't look at Emma, but she stepped closer and dropped her voice to a barely discernible whisper. "And Sophia's murderer."

"Let's not assume the worst," Emma said, but even as she said it she knew the worst had happened. From their vantage point more than half-way up the stands, they could see Jeremiah. He hadn't moved since falling from the horse, since being shot from the horse. The steer he was supposed to have wrestled had been corralled in a far corner of the arena.

Stephen and Thomas were trying to be stoic, but they looked as if they might burst into tears at any moment.

"Katie Ann, maybe you could take the boys up a few rows and engage them in a game of I Spy." Katie Ann looked as if she were about to argue, so Emma stepped closer to her and said, "Maybe distract them away from the field."

"*Ya, gut* idea. Let's go to the top, boys. Maybe if we look hard enough we can see Cinnamon from there." The boys started talking about their buggy horse as they turned away, and Emma mouthed a *thank you* to Katie Ann.

When they were gone, Clyde motioned them into a tighter circle.

"Did any of you see anything?" he asked.

Rachel, Silas, and Emma all shook their heads.

"I was watching for Henry," Emma admitted. "He'd gone to get us both a hot dog."

Rachel hugged her arms around her body as if she were cold. "The boys were pestering me for money. I didn't realize anything had happened until I heard the screams."

"I was thinking about tomorrow, what I need to do at the farm." Clyde ran a hand up and around the back of his neck. "I wasn't really paying attention at all."

"Well, I was," Silas said. "Jeremiah had just come out of the gate. He was gaining on the steer when a shot rang out, and then he flipped backward off the horse. I remember thinking he could be trampled by the steer if it turned back toward him."

"He fell backward? You're sure?"

"*Ya.* The horse shot out from under him like an arrow from a bow." They all turned to stare at the horse, now being handled by two of the rodeo clowns.

Clyde's brow wrinkled as he looked back at the chutes and then toward the opposite side of the arena. "All right. So if he was coming out of the chutes from the northwest..."

"Then the shooter had to be to the southeast, or maybe a little more east if he wanted a straight shot as Jeremiah moved around the arena."

"And it happened just as the sun was setting, so the light wouldn't be a problem."

"Stop," Emma said. She couldn't stand one more minute of this sort of talk. "This isn't another mystery we're becoming involved in. This is a member of our church..."

"Actually, he hasn't joined yet," Silas said, reminding them.

"And he wouldn't join here anyway." Emma sank onto the bleacher, but her gaze remained on the field, on the calamity taking place there. "Ruth told me he planned to go back to Goshen at the end of the summer."

"Just trying to figure out what happened, *Mamm*." Clyde offered her a weak smile. "We're not trying to involve you in another mystery."

"*Gut*, because I'm done. I don't want another thing to do with the police unless it's thanking them for watching over our town." She sat down next to Rachel and finally echoed what her daughter-in-law had said a few minutes earlier, what had been running through her mind since the shot rang out. "This cannot be happening again."

"I'll go talk to some of the others. See if they've heard anything." Silas darted off toward a group of Amish teens.

"Um, *Mamm*." Clyde leaned forward, peering toward the crime scene. "Maybe you need to go down there."

"Me?"

"It looks like Henry's making his way to Ruth."

"Why would he need me?"

"She might respond better to a woman." The crowd had grown quieter as Ruth's wails seemed to increase in length and intensity.

Rachel supplied the obvious answer. "You'll soon be our bishop's wife, and poor Ruth doesn't have any other family here."

Ruth's husband passed after they moved to Monte Vista. Her closest friends were Nancy Kline and Franey Graber, two women with whom she'd opened a local bakery. Emma knew for a fact that Nancy and

Franey weren't there tonight—they were busy with extra baking for the crowds that flocked to the rodeo. The three hotels in Monte Vista were full for the entire week, and the restaurants struggled to feed everyone in a timely fashion. Bread 2 Go was making a killing.

Ruth Schwartz was indeed her friend, though they weren't as close as the three widows who ran the bakery were to each other. But Rachel had hit on the real reason she should be kneeling next to Ruth—Emma was about to become the bishop's wife.

She longed to be married to Henry Lapp.

They'd decided the year before to marry, which should have been simple at their age, but life had intervened. She'd had to travel back to Goshen to be with her sister, who'd undergone chemotherapy. Fortunately, her cancer was now in remission, and she seemed to be well on the road to recovery. Emma was glad to be of help, but she'd also been eager to be home, to move on to the next phase of her life. The past few months had been difficult for both her and Henry, but through their many letters she understood better what Henry needed in a spouse, what it meant to be a bishop's wife. She knew her family was right—she should go down and be by his side, to help Henry help Ruth.

She stood, smoothed out her apron, and threw a look back at Stephen, Thomas, and Katie Ann. The boys had their heads together and were pointing at something in the direction of the carnival. Katie Ann stood close beside them.

"We'll be fine," Rachel assured her.

Emma's heart sank as she made her way down the bleachers. When she'd nearly been killed the year before, she promised herself she would never again become involved in solving any type of crime or murder. But this was different. This was her friend weeping over the body of her grandson. She really had no choice at all.

She straightened her posture, raised her head, and walked toward the Monte Vista police officer, determined to find a way to comfort her friend.

Three

Henry was held up as more law enforcement officers made their way into the arena—stringing up crime scene tape, pulling out equipment, and marking off the area. He used the time to assess what was happening around him. The horse Jeremiah had been riding stood at a distance, throwing its head, snorting, and pawing the ground with its right hoof. Two men in clown suits had rushed toward it, attempting to calm the beast. The steer Jeremiah was to have wrestled to the ground had already been corralled in a far corner of the arena.

Henry wasn't an expert on rodeo events, but since moving to Monte Vista, their community had regularly attended the Ski Hi Stampede. Everyone did, including officers from both the police and sheriff's departments.

Henry saw attending the rodeo as one more way to build bridges in the community, and it was natural for Amish *youngies* to be interested in the horse and cattle events. Team roping, barrel racing, and goat tying were some of the more popular events for local youth. There was rarely any risk of injury, and practicing provided fun, safe entertainment.

Steer wrestling was another matter entirely. It required a horse-mounted rider to chase a steer, drop from the horse while it was running full speed, and then wrestle the steer to the ground by grabbing its horns and pulling it off balance.

The risk of injury to the rider was high. The chances of the steer suffering any harm was much less, though that didn't stop animal rights activists from claiming the event constituted cruelty to animals. Most rodeos used longhorns that weighed 450 to 650 pounds. From what Henry had seen, it irritated the steer more than anything else.

But Jeremiah hadn't been injured by the steer. He'd been shot.

Finally Officer Moore nodded, indicating he could pass.

Henry moved quickly across the area, and the officers and officials stepped aside to make way for him. He slowed as he processed what he was seeing.

Two paramedics were attending to Jeremiah. Another team of paramedics stood by in case they were needed, but plainly they didn't expect that to happen. They glanced at the ground, at the victim, and then their eyes darted away.

As Henry approached the center of the crowd, he understood Jeremiah was past their ability to care for him. His eyes were open, locked on the stars that were only beginning to appear in the sky above. If Henry had to describe his expression, he would say it was one of mild surprise.

Someone had opened his shirt, revealing a crimson stain on his chest, just left of center. They were applying compresses when one of the paramedics glanced up, shook his head twice, and the other glanced at his watch. Then he wrote on a clipboard. Henry was sure he was noting the time of death. Then they both moved back, giving Ruth a moment of privacy.

When Henry took the final steps to reach Ruth's side, he realized there would be no evidence to trample on. The person who killed Jeremiah Schwartz had to have been up in the stands. There would be nothing in the surrounding dirt other than the bullet. Whoever had done this was probably long gone. Otherwise, he'd already be in custody. Jeremiah's murder had been committed with a rifle, from a safe distance, and any evidence found wouldn't be next to his body.

Ruth was now kneeling beside her grandson, covering her face with her hands and rocking back and forth. Henry knelt in the dirt beside her.

"Ruth, perhaps we should let the paramedics do their work." It was a ridiculous thing to say. There was no doubt that Jeremiah was dead, had probably died instantly, but Henry needed to move her away so the officers could begin the process of photographing and then transferring the body.

Ruth seemed not to hear him at first. She continued rocking and weeping and wailing. Henry put one hand on each of her shoulders and turned her gently so that she was facing him. Slowly her hands came away from her face. The heartbreak Henry saw in her eyes was nearly his undoing.

"He's gone, Ruth."

"Jeremiah?" The question was a plea, a last, desperate attempt to deny the reality in front of her.

"*Ya*. I'm sorry, Ruth."

"He...he needs me."

"He's with the Lord now. His life is complete."

Henry rose, bringing Ruth with him, and then he guided her away from Jeremiah's body. She made it to the edge of the arena and then collapsed into his arms.

By this time, Emma was standing next to Officer Moore, trying to convince him to let her join them. He wasn't budging an inch, but Emma didn't retreat. Henry called out, "Let her come. I think maybe she can help."

Moore looked around as if he might find someone else to make the decision, but another look at Ruth convinced him to wave Emma through.

Emma was practically Henry's wife, a bishop's wife.

More importantly, Ruth needed her.

She stopped mere inches from Ruth, reached out, and touched her face with her fingertips. That seemed to bring Ruth back from some dark abyss. They huddled closer then, their heads together, Emma's arms around the dear woman as her body shook with sobs. Henry stood close enough to see that Emma was not talking to Ruth so much as sharing the burden of her grief, and then Emma motioned for Henry to join them.

He didn't ask questions. Instead, he put one hand on Ruth and one on Emma. They made a sort of circle. He began to pray, asking God for His presence and mercy and grace. The words flowed from his heart and from dozens of other experiences with people who were grieving, though none of them had perished from a gunshot wound during a rodeo.

When he was finished, Ruth continued to weep, Emma rubbed her back, and Henry waited.

He didn't have to wait long.

He noticed Sheriff Grayson with the body, spending only a few minutes there. Then he glanced around the arena as he plodded toward them.

"Henry."

"Sheriff."

"Mrs. Fisher."

"Sheriff Grayson." Emma continued to rub Ruth's back. "Does she need to stay here, or could we...maybe take her to sit down?"

"I need to ask a few questions first." He turned to Ruth. "Mrs...."

"Schwartz," Henry said. "This is Ruth Schwartz, and the young man on the field is Jeremiah Schwartz."

Hearing Jeremiah's name caused Ruth to tune in to the three people standing in front of her. "My grandson. He's my grandson." She made to wipe her eyes with the sleeve of her dress, but Henry quickly pulled out a clean handkerchief and handed it to her.

"I'm sorry for your loss, Mrs. Schwartz. I realize you're probably in shock and no doubt grieving..."

She nodded, her eyes round and trying to focus on Grayson's face.

"Did you see what happened?"

"*Nein.*"

"Anything at all?"

"He...he came out of the chute. I saw him raise his right hand. He always held on with his left so he could handle the steer with his right. He was...he was practically even with the steer when I heard a pop, like when...like when the men shoot doves."

"What happened next?"

"He was on the ground. I thought the horse had thrown him, or maybe he'd jumped wrong. People started screaming, 'Gun! Someone has a gun!' and I didn't understand. I only knew Jeremiah was on the ground and not moving. I only knew I had to get to him. But the crowd..."

"Any idea which direction the shot came from?"

Henry understood that Grayson knew the answer to this question. The arena was an oblong structure, with the short ends on the northwest and southeast sides. The chutes were located on the northwest end of the arena. Jeremiah would have come through the gate, and based on what Ruth was describing, had been shot almost immediately. The shot had to have come from the southeast.

But Grayson, Henry was sure, wanted to keep Ruth talking in the hopes that she would remember something. He tried a few more questions, tried the same questions in a different way, and finally handed her his card. "Please call me if you think of anything else. I'll be in touch again in a few hours when we know more. In the meantime, one of my officers will give you a ride to the hospital."

Monte Vista was a relatively small town with fewer than five thousand people. The closest hospitals were in Del Norte and Alamosa. Del Norte was the county seat and housed the morgue used by all three towns. It was sixteen miles to the west of where they were—too far for Ruth to travel in her horse and buggy.

Ruth nodded as if she understood what Grayson had said, but she didn't move or turn away from the scene playing out in front of her. The crime techs continued to work, though they had finished placing markers, crime tape, and camera stands around Jeremiah's body. The last thing Ruth needed was to see her grandson photographed.

Grayson glanced at Henry, and Henry turned to Emma. "Maybe you could accompany us…"

"*Ya*, I'll be happy to."

Henry turned then to go with them, but Grayson reached a hand out to stop him. "If you could stay for a minute."

Emma nodded, indicating they would be fine. She put her arm around Ruth and escorted her toward the nearest bleacher seat.

"Did you see it, Henry? Did you see what happened?"

"*Nein*. I was in line for hot dogs when I heard what sounded like a gunshot."

"Looks like a rifle to me." Grayson tucked the pad he'd been writing on back in his shirt pocket. "Someone had to see something."

"*Ya*, you would think so."

"Takes arrogance to smuggle a rifle into an arena."

"Perhaps the person hid it here beforehand."

"I was thinking the same thing. Are you sure you couldn't..." He made the motion of someone drawing.

"I wish I could. I'd like to help, but I wasn't even in the main arena at the time."

"Too bad." Grayson pulled off his sheriff's hat and resettled it on his head. "I established a perimeter as soon as I realized what happened, but no doubt some people slipped through. Could you ask around? Maybe someone from your congregation saw something."

"If they saw something, I won't have to ask. They'll come to me."

Grayson nodded as if that made sense. They'd been through two murder investigations together, and in both of them Henry's special talent for drawing had helped to solve the case. This time, his gift would be of no use to them. Instead, it was going to come down to old-fashioned detective work. On the plus side, Henry could focus on ministering to Ruth and others affected by Jeremiah's death. It was a truly terrible thing to have occurred on a beautiful summer night, and at one of Monte Vista's most popular events.

Perhaps whoever planned the murder had hoped to hide under the cover of the crowd.

But people saw things, remembered details they didn't realize they knew. It was usually a matter of asking the right questions to uncover that information. Henry, however, could draw. He could never explain the things he was able to draw, but his mind recorded every detail of what he'd seen in the same way people processed and stored memories, especially of traumatic events. Henry knew this because he'd made studying memory something of a hobby.

Grayson thanked him and trudged back toward Jeremiah's body.

Henry walked slowly toward Emma and Ruth, praying he'd be of some comfort to Ruth as she walked through the valley of the shadow.

Four

Emma explained to Clyde and Rachel where she was going before hurrying back down the bleachers, making her way out of the arena, and climbing into the police cruiser with Ruth and Henry.

The ride to Del Norte passed in silence. As they drove through Monte Vista's downtown area, she couldn't help but notice the banners hanging over each intersection.

San Luis Valley

Ski Hi Stampede

Colorado's Oldest Pro Rodeo

The pro events hadn't even started yet.

Jeremiah had competed in the amateur events, which preceded the professional events. The entire rodeo was then followed by a dance. Usually their families left well before the band struck its first chord.

To the left of the wording on the banner was the outline of a man riding a bucking horse—a cowboy, enjoying the prime of his youth, alive. And yet Jeremiah's life had been cut short. Henry would say his life was complete, and she believed it was true. *All the days ordained for me were written in your book before one of them came to be.* Hadn't Clyde preached on that very topic the week before? Yet the words from the Psalms wouldn't pierce the grief her friend was experiencing, not right away. Perhaps in time...

Henry seemed lost in thought as he stared out the window, or maybe he was praying.

Emma was struggling with the fact that this was her third murder investigation. She didn't want to be a sleuth. She didn't want anything to do with unnatural deaths. Their lives were simple by choice, but neither could she abandon a woman who had been her neighbor for nearly fifteen years.

The officer followed Highway 160 west through town and then angled northwest toward Del Norte. The sun hung low on the horizon, and the Rockies rose in the distance.

She glanced at Henry as they passed into the shadow of the mountains.

He nodded once, as if he understood her thoughts.

Ruth had fallen into a stupor. She seemed oblivious, even unaware she was in the vehicle and traveling toward the hospital. Her hands lay motionless in her lap, her gaze fixed on something in the gathering darkness. Occasionally she would shake her head slightly, as if she could deny the reality of what had just happened. No doubt the poor woman was in shock.

Based on her previous experience, Emma knew it would be hours before Jeremiah's body was delivered, and a day or more before Ruth could take him home for burial. Perhaps Grayson wanted her out of the way. Maybe it was a kindness to suggest she wait at the hospital. At least she wouldn't have to watch the crime scene techs at work or see the crowd gawk at her grandson.

When they walked into the hospital emergency room, Ruth looked around as if she were momentarily lost. Running her fingertips across her forehead, she said, "Do you think there's a phone? I should call Clara and Gideon."

"I can do that for you." Henry had taken off his hat and held it calmly in his hands.

Emma realized in that moment how much she loved the man standing in front of her. They'd rescheduled their wedding for August, and she had every intention of keeping that date. Henry was kind, compassionate, and wise in the way of one who had suffered much. She adored him as a friend and wanted to be his wife, his helpmate. Their entire family was looking forward to the union, and Clyde and Silas were working on a *dawdi haus*, complete with a new workshop for Henry.

All those thoughts, those happy images, passed through her mind as they stood waiting on Ruth's answer.

"*Nein*. I'll call them. It should be me. Jeremiah—" Her voice caught on the name, but she pulled in a deep breath and pushed on. "Jeremiah came to spend the summer with me, to help me..."

"You can't blame yourself for this," Henry said.

"I don't. Truly I don't. I think I'm in shock." Her hand went to the top of her head and she tugged her prayer *kapp* more firmly into place, pulling out one of the bobby pins and replacing it. "He was here to see me through the summer, to help me with the crops, and now he's gone. I should be the one to tell his parents."

"Can I get you anything?" Emma asked.

"Coffee. Coffee would be good. I suspect we have a long night ahead." She turned to go but then pivoted back. "Thank you. Thank you both for staying with me."

And before they could answer, she was gone.

They followed the signs to the vending machines and waited for the coffee to drip into a paper cup.

"How can this be happening, Henry?"

"It's a shock."

"Why would someone kill him? And in front of a crowd?"

"I can't begin to fathom a reason."

"What did Grayson say to you after he questioned Ruth?"

"Not much. But he said it was a rifle. It had to be a rifle."

"Silas and Clyde said the same thing."

"Maybe someone saw something." Henry offered to purchase her a cup of coffee, but she settled for a bottle of water. The last thing she needed was jangly nerves.

"But you didn't see anything?"

"*Nein*. I was getting our dinner."

"I suppose that's something of a relief to you." When Henry looked at her quizzically, she pushed on. "You didn't want to be involved with Betsy's murder back in Goshen."

"Indeed I didn't."

"You certainly had no intention of tangling with Vernon Frey's killer."

"Glad to have that behind us."

"And who would have ever imagined that we'd both end up stalked by Sophia's murderer?"

"My life, our lives, have taken some strange turns, it's true."

"And yet *Gotte* used you during those times." They walked slowly back to the waiting room and sat down in a corner where they wouldn't be disturbed and could watch for Ruth. "It's interesting that at a time when you've learned to embrace your gift—"

"Thanks largely to your encouragement."

"Something happens where you can't use it at all."

Emma sipped from her bottle and then offered it to Henry. He waved away the offer, but he turned his gaze to her, studied her a moment, and then said, "My gift—this strange talent I have—it's a blessing. I understand that now, but you are a bigger blessing, Emma Fisher. Your friendship, and now your love, mean more to me than my ability to draw what I can't remember."

Emma didn't know how to answer that, but Henry's words eased the trouble ricocheting through her heart. There was no way to know what this was about or what lay ahead of them, but she knew they'd make it through together. They'd done so in the past, and they would in the future. That was the confidence and trust God had built in her heart over the last year, and she would hold firm to it as they ministered to Ruth, Jeremiah's parents, and anyone else in their congregation who needed special attention.

It was a bishop's job to guide members of the church through both happy times and sad. Emma trusted that the former waited for them, and that it was only a matter of getting through this present darkness to the light beyond.

Five

Naomi Miller searched for her best friend, Katie Ann, and finally spotted her at the top of the bleachers with her two younger brothers.

Katie Ann pulled her into a hug and then tugged her a few feet away from Stephen and Thomas, who were now watching the lights of the carnival rides set up at one end of the Stampede's parking lot—a carousel, bumper cars, a flying scooter, a kamikaze, a tilt-a-whirl, and of course the Ferris wheel.

Naomi was supposed to be riding those...with Jeremiah. He'd promised that after the rodeo, after he won, he'd buy all the carnival coupons she could spend. He'd laughed when he said that and slung an arm around her shoulder.

"Where have you been?" Katie Ann held her at arm's length and studied her face. "I was so worried."

"I was with the other girlfriends, down near the chutes. The police wouldn't let me leave. I told them I had to find my family, had to find you. It's not as if I could have left the arena. All the exits are blocked. Finally they agreed after taking down my name and address."

"Are you okay?" Katie Ann asked.

"I don't know. It hardly seems real."

"When did you last talk to him?"

"This afternoon."

"And your *aenti* and *onkel* aren't here tonight?"

One violent shake of Naomi's head, and then tears began to pour down her cheeks.

"I'm so sorry, Naomi. I know you cared about Jeremiah."

"I did, but…Oh, it doesn't matter now, does it? He's gone, and we'll never know. Maybe I should have…maybe if I had…he could still be…"

"Don't do that to yourself."

Katie Ann gave her a few minutes to calm herself—clasping her hand and sitting beside her, not saying a word. That was one of the things Naomi dearly loved about her friend. She didn't push, and she didn't judge. Naomi didn't judge Katie Ann for choosing to be a veterinarian's assistant, a quite unusual job—unusual for an Amish girl, at least. And Katie Ann didn't judge her for keeping her nose in a book, for pausing to write down a phrase that came to her mind, for courting someone her *aenti* had never approved of.

Which didn't matter now. She'd wanted to clasp her hands over her ears when Jeremiah's grandmother had begun to wail. She'd stared on in disbelief as Henry and Emma had comforted Ruth and then led her to the police cruiser.

Naomi scrubbed her cheeks dry, noticing they felt hot and chapped. "Maybe I should talk to someone, tell them what Jeremiah's plans were. I'm not sure he shared them with anyone else."

"*Ya. Gut* idea, but who?"

"The police?"

"I don't know. Maybe…"

They sat there a moment, staring at the aftermath of what could have been a natural disaster, only it wasn't. This tragedy had been conceived and implemented by an evil person. Naomi couldn't imagine who would do such a thing, or what could possibly be a strong enough motivation for taking another life.

Most of the people had returned to the stands and were clustered in small groups.

Some of the children were crying, no doubt not understanding what had happened or why they couldn't go home.

Parents looked concerned—Amish and *Englisch* alike.

Jeremiah's body was still lying where he'd fallen. Giant floodlights had been brought in. Even brighter than the arena lights, they were set up around Jeremiah, and someone was photographing his body from various angles. What could they possibly tell from that? It seemed to Naomi that they were wasting time, that they should be out looking for the person who had done this.

And in that moment her resolve hardened. It didn't matter that she had continued being Jeremiah's friend despite her *aenti*'s warnings that such a relationship would only lead to trouble. It didn't matter at all what people thought of her. What mattered was that she might be able to shed a little bit of light on what happened.

"I'm going to do it. I'm going to go and talk to that officer down there."

Katie Ann reached out and snagged her arm. "I'll go with you. If you're sure you want to. But maybe…maybe it would be a better idea to talk to Henry. After all, it's not like you saw the person or have a clue as to who he or she is."

"They'll be looking into Jeremiah's life, though. Looking for clues, like your *mammi* did with the Monte Vista arsonist."

Katie Ann visibly flinched, but she didn't deny it. Everyone in their community knew about Henry and Emma's involvement in catching not one but two murderers. Naomi had even heard some of the *youngies* refer to them as a Plain Holmes and Watson. Naomi hadn't known what that meant until someone showed her a video clip of the movie *Sherlock Holmes* on their phone.

"I owe it to Jeremiah to try to help catch whoever did this."

Katie Ann kept her eyes on her brothers while she considered Naomi's words.

"I guess you're right."

"You know I am."

"What are you going to tell them?"

"His plans. What he was going to do after tonight. His crazy scheme to run off and—"

"*Ya*, but I'm not sure how that will help. What Jeremiah was planning to do next…it didn't happen. So how can someone's plans shed light on what *has* happened? How can it reveal anything about the person who killed him?"

"I don't know."

"Can you think of anything else?"

"*Nein.*"

"Anyone he argued with recently?"

"Nothing like that."

"Anything at all?"

"If you're asking me if I know who could have killed him, the answer is no."

"No enemies you know of?"

"Jeremiah had secrets. And we'd only been courting since summer began. Even that had become...well, awkward. And now...now...Oh, Katie Ann, I'm going to wake up tomorrow and find I've dreamed all of this, that it was a horrible, terrible nightmare."

Katie Ann scooted closer to Naomi and pulled her hands into her lap, their shoulders touching and Naomi's cheek resting against Katie Ann's *kapp*. The presence of her friend helped. She wasn't in this alone, whatever this was. Together they would figure it out. Together they would go to Henry and then to the police.

Somehow they would navigate a way through this terrible nightmare.

But Naomi understood, as she watched the officers walk up and down the stands handing out statement forms and pens, that this wasn't a dream. This was real, and she wouldn't wake up to find her life as it had been a few hours before.

Six

Ruth returned to the waiting room, her cheeks flushed from crying, her eyes red and swollen, but more in control of herself. She'd slipped into the role of parent, of the eldest in her family, and now she would focus on taking care of the others. Her own grief would be pushed aside. Emma knew all of this at a glance, maybe because she'd been through the same thing when her husband died.

"Did you have to leave a message?" Emma asked.

"*Nein*. They have a phone out in the barn—something Gideon didn't want, but Clara insisted on because he was having to walk to the phone shack several times a day." Ruth glanced from Emma to Henry.

"I may have told you my son is an auctioneer now," she explained. "He took it up after he hurt his back farming. He's quite good at it, but it does require quite a bit of communication to set up each auction."

"Did you reach them on the phone?"

"Jeremiah's sister answered. She fetched both Clara and Gideon." Ruth closed her eyes, taking a moment to allow a wave of grief to wash over her. A shudder and a deep breath, and then she opened her eyes and continued. "They'll make arrangements to come here on the bus from Goshen."

"I'm sure their bishop would allow them to fly," Henry said.

"I suggested as much, but Gideon wouldn't hear of it. He's quite conservative." Ruth laughed, but there was no amusement in it. "He still fusses about the phone, though of course it's allowed for business."

"How did they take the news?" Emma asked, because it seemed that Ruth wanted to say more.

"Clara was beside herself, alternately weeping and questioning me...as if I might have the wrong Jeremiah in mind."

"And Gideon?" Emma knew a little of the problems Ruth had endured with her son.

"No emotion. Nothing, really. I think he's in shock."

"Let's pray for them," Henry said. "Pray for all involved."

His voice seemed to calm Ruth, or perhaps it was God's Holy Spirit, who was with them in their hour of grief.

"The Lord is close to the brokenhearted..." Henry murmured. "He saves those who are crushed in spirit."

Emma squeezed Ruth's hand more tightly.

"He heals the brokenhearted and binds up their wounds."

How she prayed it was so, that God would heal Ruth's broken heart, that He would bind her wounds.

"Our flesh and heart may fail, but God is our strength."

The words in the Psalms had been written so many years ago, and yet Emma felt their truth anew. It was true that their flesh and their heart would fail. This was part and parcel of being human, but God would never leave nor forsake them.

When Henry finished, Emma fetched Ruth another cup of coffee. The one they'd purchased had turned cold.

The three of them passed the next hour in silence. Henry found the remote for the television mounted in the corner of the waiting room. Because no one else was there and they certainly had no interest in watching it, he turned off the contraption. Emma tried to smile her thanks, but she was afraid it came out wobbly. In truth, her emotions were still all over the place. Though she'd barely known Jeremiah, the night's events were dredging up memories she'd worked hard to forget, memories from those other murder investigations.

The hands on the clock were creeping toward ten in the evening, and the sky outside the hospital windows had long since turned dark, when Ruth began to talk.

"Jeremiah was having trouble in Goshen, you know. That's why

Gideon agreed to his coming here. My son...he's nothing like his father. He's nothing like me, if I were to be honest. I can't begin to understand why he's as unyielding as he is."

"That must have been hard for you," Henry said.

"*Ya*. It was a good reason for us to move. When we still lived there, I would have to watch him interact with the children, with my *grandkinner*, and it broke my heart. He was never abusive, but his attitude and his words left a mark nonetheless. I would try to talk to him, tell him to be less hard on the children—they have five. Four boys and a girl. Jeremiah was the youngest. I'd talk to Gideon, but those conversations never ended well. The last time Leon stepped in, Gideon became so upset he didn't speak to us for a month. That was when we decided it would be better for the family if we didn't live so close."

Emma glanced at Henry. She was thinking about the Monte Vista arsonist, about his mental instability. She lowered her voice and asked as gently as possible, "Do you think Gideon might be suffering from depression or some other mental illness...like bipolar disorder?"

"Depression, maybe. What I know about bipolar, which is limited, is that people suffering from it have ups as well as downs. Gideon doesn't seem to have ups. I've spent many hours praying on it. I could never figure out where we went wrong with that boy."

"Now, Ruth, we are only responsible for raising our children in the faith, with love and the wisdom we have. As to the twists and turns of Gideon's life, you're not held accountable for those."

"I suppose." Ruth offered a weak smile. "We decided we could be a better influence from a distance, and for a time it seemed we were. Gideon was less volatile to suggestions we put in letters, possibly because he had time to process them. Or maybe he was maturing. At least, that's what I thought."

"I remember he couldn't make it for Leon's funeral."

"*Ya*, it's true, though he did ask me to come back and live with them, but by that time I'd fallen in love with the valley and with this community." She squeezed Emma's hand before standing and pacing over to the window.

"Maybe because Jeremiah was the youngest of the *grandkinner*,

Gideon held on even tighter than usual. The other three boys all eventually left Goshen."

"The boys left because of their father?" Henry asked.

"I think so." Ruth ran her fingers up and down the strings of her prayer *kapp*. "They would never speak disrespectfully of Gideon, but their letters to me...well, what they don't say is as telling as what they do."

Emma couldn't imagine her son moving away from her, not wanting to be close.

"How does your granddaughter handle it?"

"Lydia was relieved when the boys moved away." Ruth returned to sit across from them. The rows of chairs were so close together their knees practically touched. "Oh, she missed her brothers. Don't get me wrong, but she thought they'd be happier if there was distance between them and their father. She still lives on her parents' farm with her husband, but in a separate house they built on the property. Perhaps that little bit of privacy helps."

Henry sat forward, his elbows propped on his knees and his fingers laced together. "You said there was trouble with Jeremiah?"

"Nothing with the law, not like that. But he didn't want to join the church."

"I spoke with him about it as well. He seemed open to the idea, only not yet." Henry sighed.

"Four years is too long for *rumspringa*."

"There's no set amount of time, and his hesitance wasn't too unusual for his age. They eventually come around."

"Gideon was afraid he wouldn't. He pushed, and Jeremiah responded by rejecting even more of our Plain ways and turning toward the *Englisch* life."

"The rodeo."

"*Ya*. Though in truth, the boy loved to be on a horse as soon as he could walk." Ruth folded her arms and stared out into the darkness as if she might find answers there, or maybe she was simply looking for comforting memories from the past. "He was good with them—both the buggy horses and the Percherons. I thought he might become a farrier or even a breeder."

"I had the impression he was doing well here," Emma offered.

Ruth shrugged. "I fed him. I made all of his favorite meals so he'd eat. At the first of the summer he was as thin as a reed, but he seemed to be filling out and sleeping more. His moods were less volatile, and the rodeo...well, it meant the world to him. Maybe more than it should have."

"What do you mean by that?" Henry asked.

"I don't think he planned to return to Goshen, and I'm not even sure he intended to remain Amish. The *Englisch* world was calling him, and though he appreciated some aspects of our life, he was dazzled by the possibility of success on the rodeo circuit. He told me he would prove his father wrong or die trying. That's what he said."

She closed her eyes then, and Emma knew she'd once again slipped into despair.

Seven

Sheriff Grayson didn't show up at the hospital until nearly one that morning. By that time, Henry, Emma, and Ruth had all succumbed to the need for caffeine. The vending machine coffee was only palatable with the help of small packages of cookies. Even to Henry they tasted like sawdust. Not that he was a baking expert, but he'd done his fair share of eating.

At ten minutes before one, the automatic doors to the hospital's emergency room opened, and Sheriff Grayson stepped in with a gust of wind. He walked straight to them, removing his hat as he did so. He repositioned a chair so that he was sitting at the end of a U shape, with Ruth on his right and Henry and Emma on his left. Fortunately, they were still the only ones there. Other than Jeremiah's murder, it was a quiet night in the valley.

Grayson directed his first comments to Ruth. "Your grandson is being delivered to the morgue now. You'll be able to go back in a few minutes if you'd like to."

"I would."

"All right. I've already cleared it, and of course Henry and Emma can accompany you."

"*Danki.*"

"You're welcome." He pulled out his small notebook and stared at it, running his left thumb over his eyebrow. "If you feel up to it, I'd like to ask you a few more questions."

"Of course."

"We found a cell phone on your grandson, but it's passcode protected. Would you have any idea what that passcode might be?"

"*Nein*. I knew he had a phone, but he never brought it into the house, so I let it slide." She stared down at her empty hands, as if the phone might suddenly appear and answer all of their questions.

"All right. Judge Alvarez has signed a warrant for the information on the phone, and I've scheduled it for data extraction, but it may be a day or two before we have results."

"What do you hope to find?" Henry asked. He thought he understood well enough what data could be stored on a cell phone, but he wanted Ruth to hear it from Grayson. He suspected that in the coming days she would learn things about her grandson she couldn't have imagined. Henry had never owned a phone, but he understood that teenagers and young adults left a digital record that closely resembled a diary.

Grayson sat back, tapping the small pad against his knee. "I don't really know. It's possible that he knew someone who was upset with him, someone who would want to kill him. We'll be able to see who he communicated with, what friends he had who might know something. And we'll also be able to monitor his computer activity, including what social media sites he visited."

"I don't understand," Ruth said. "What does his phone have to do with a computer?"

"The type of phone he had—a smartphone—also provided Internet access."

"Oh."

Grayson glanced back down at his notebook and flipped it open. "How long had Jeremiah been involved with the rodeo?"

"For years. Even back in Goshen, though his father, my son, forbade it."

"It was a source of contention between father and son?"

Ruth glanced at Henry and Emma. "*Ya*, but then nearly everything was."

"He was staying with you. What can you tell me about his friends? Did anyone come over to your house—Amish or *Englisch*?"

"He was seeing Naomi Miller. I don't know if they were courting exactly, but they seemed to be...friends."

"Anyone else?"

"Now and then someone would pick him up in an automobile."

"Can you describe it to me?"

"Truck—always dirty, so the color was hard to tell. Gray or white."

"Did you ever see who was driving?"

"A teenage boy, I think. Long hair, wore a baseball cap. He never came up to the house."

"Any other girls he might have been involved with?"

Ruth hesitated, stared out the window at the darkness, and finally looked over to meet Grayson's gaze. "I think so, but I don't know who it was. I don't even know if she was *Englisch* or Amish."

"Can you recall anything that upset him recently?"

"He was excited about the rodeo and in an unusually good mood. I remember thinking that maybe...maybe the rodeo around here would be a good experience, and then afterward he would be willing to settle down."

That statement sat between them for a moment.

Finally, Grayson turned back a few pages in his notebook and began reading. "We won't have all of the forensic evidence processed for a few days, but preliminary reports indicate your grandson was killed by a rifle, shot from more than a hundred yards away."

"From across the arena," Henry said. To him, it seemed the only logical explanation.

"It would have to be. We've interviewed every person working with the rodeo contestants in the arena—all of the workers, in fact. Even the ones in the food booths. So far we have no reports that anyone saw a person with a rifle."

"Was the man who did this lurking in the stands?" Emma asked. "It seems there would be witnesses if he was."

Grayson didn't correct her on the assumption that the shooter was a male. Henry supposed that in all likelihood it was. He also understood that the sheriff wouldn't be discounting any possible suspects—male or female—at this point.

"It's something we're working on."

"How?" Ruth asked.

"Ma'am, we're going over statements and collecting forensic evidence, and I'll be conducting interviews of any possible suspects. Rest assured we want this case solved, and we want it solved quickly."

Ruth studied him a moment and finally nodded her head in agreement. "Thank you for all your efforts. It seems...it seems you would have a small list of suspects, of people who could possibly do such a thing."

It occurred to Henry that Ruth might be on to something. "Wasn't it an awfully long shot? To shoot from that distance, with Jeremiah a moving target? Do you think you're looking for an expert marksman or...or a military person?"

"In the past, yes, but nowadays one hundred yards is the minimum distance for modern rifle shooting and hunting. Many gun, scope, and cartridge combinations are capable of two to three times that distance."

Technology seemed to affect every aspect of their lives no matter how much they sought to separate themselves from it. Now someone in their community had been killed, and the way it happened was possible because of advances in the making of firearms. Though Amish practiced nonresistance, they still hunted, and the animals they harvested provided meat for much of the year. Henry had only ever used his father's rifle, made back in the 1920s, but he'd seen some of the newer rifles. They were quite sophisticated.

"Witness reports?" Emma asked.

"Still working on them. We handed out forms to everyone in the arena. As you can imagine, it's going to take some time to work through that amount of information."

"When will Jeremiah's body be released?" Henry knew firsthand that the investigation could go on for days, weeks, or even months. But the process of grief was the same, and that was what he was interested in guiding Ruth through. "Jeremiah's parents will be traveling here from Indiana."

"Will he be buried there?" Grayson asked.

"*Nein*." Ruth rubbed at her eyes. "We'll lay him to rest here, beside his grandfather."

"His body will be released as soon as they're finished with the autopsy."

"Is that really necessary?" Henry asked. "You know the cause of death."

"I'm sorry. It's required on all homicide victims."

Henry nodded as if he understood, though in truth he didn't. There were times when the reasons for *Englisch* ways completely eluded him, but the law was the law, and there was no use fighting it.

Grayson shifted in his chair. "Forty-eight hours, at the most."

"Then the body would be released on Monday. We could have the visitation and burial on Tuesday. Ruth?"

"*Ya*, that sounds right."

Ruth Schwartz was a strong woman. She'd stayed at her husband's side the last year of his life, nursing him and tending to many of the farm chores, though neighbors often offered to help. Since his death, she'd gone into business with two other women, and then she had provided a home for her grandson. It shouldn't have surprised Henry that she was coping so well, but it did. The human heart's ability to persevere was a miracle.

Eight

Transcript of interview between Monte Vista Sheriff Roy Grayson and Justin Lane regarding the July 27 homicide of Jeremiah Schwartz. Audiotapes and a transcript of the interview are included in the permanent case file.

Sheriff Roy Grayson #3604
INTERVIEW WITH Justin Lane
Case #4751.06
3:15 a.m., Saturday, July 28

Sheriff Grayson (SG): Could you state your name for the recording?
Justin Lane (JL): Justin Lane.
SG: Middle name?
JL: Tanner. Tanner Lane. I always hated that. Sounds like a road or something. I go by Justin T. Lane.
SG: Okay. And you live at 14771 North Avenue, Del Norte, Colorado?
JL: (inaudible)
SG: I need you to say yes, for the recording.
JL: Yes.
SG: Your birthday is 12/03/96?
JL: (inaudible) Yeah.
SG: Do you know why we've brought you in tonight?
JL: It's not because of the weed in my truck. (inaudible) That was a joke. There's no weed in my truck. Honest. You want the keys? You can go check.
SG: You're not under arrest at this time, Justin. You're free to leave or

contact a lawyer at any point in this interview. We just want to ask you some questions since you were friends with the deceased.

JL: You mean Jeremiah.

SG: Yes.

JL: I wouldn't call us friends.

SG: How would you characterize your relationship?

JL: I don't know.

SG: Acquaintances?

JL: Nah.

SG: Enemies?

JL: Nothing like that.

SG: Then what?

JL: We hung out sometimes. I guess because we were both steer wrestlers.

SG: How long had you known Jeremiah?

JL: A couple weeks? Maybe longer. I guess he moved in with his grandmother first part of the summer. He worked at her farm during the week and then bulldogged on weekends.

SG: Bulldogged?

JL: That's what we call steer wrestling.

SG: Was he any good?

JL: (inaudible)

SG: I need you to answer verbally for the recorder.

JL: He was okay. Nothing to write home about.

SG: So you're the better bulldog?

JL: Sure, but ask around. Don't take my word for it.

SG: Actually, it seems you and Jeremiah were pretty even as far as steer wrestling ability goes.

JL: I wouldn't call us even.

SG: You won the first three stops on the circuit—Elizabeth, Cortez, and Evergreen.

JL: I'm pretty good at what I do.

SG: But you didn't win by much, and Jeremiah won the last three—Alamosa, Greeley, and Gunnison.

JL: These chairs aren't very comfortable, are they? This is like some old movie where you stick me in a small room with nothing to eat or drink, hoping I'll grow uncomfortable enough to confess.

SG: Do you have something to confess?

JL: No.

SG: We have vending machines if you'd like a candy bar or a beverage.

JL: Nah. I'm fine. Just messing with you.

SG: Back to you and Jeremiah. You'd each won half of this year's regional events.

JL: He was on a lucky streak, yeah. A lot of it's skill, but some of it's which steer you draw.

SG: Is it fair to say that the Ski Hi Stampede was an important event...say, if someone were considering going pro?

JL: (laughter)

SG: Why do you find that amusing?

JL: You sound just like him.

SG: Like who?

JL: Jeremiah. He was always talking about going pro, but we all knew that wasn't going to happen.

SG: Why is that?

JL: Look, Jeremiah was a nice kid, and he had some skill—yeah. But he was Amish.

SG: He couldn't be a pro because he was Amish?

JL: Amish kids play around on the circuit sometimes. We've all seen it. They're good with the animals and seem to have this uncanny understanding of what they're going to do next. But an Amish guy or girl is never going to win the big one. They don't go pro.

SG: And why is that?

JL: Because they're not competitive enough. It's just not in them. You ever see them play baseball? They don't even keep score.

SG: Were you watching when Jeremiah was shot?

JL: Sure. Everyone was watching.

SG: What did you see?

JL: Not much. Saw him fall off the horse. Like I told your deputy, no one knew he'd been shot, and we sure didn't see where the shot came from. You know how loud an arena is? I didn't even hear the pop of the rifle.

SG: Do you know anyone who would want to kill Jeremiah?

JL: No. I don't.

SG: Is there anything else you'd like to add?

JL: I think you're looking at this all wrong.

SG: How so?

JL: It wasn't someone with the rodeo. We're like a family, you know?

SG: Even families have trouble—jealousies, rivalries, bitterness.

JL: But it couldn't have been a rodeo person. We don't kill each other. You have a beef with someone else? Then you ride better than them the next time out. You prove you're the better man.

SG: Do you have a theory as to who might have wanted Jeremiah dead?

JL: Maybe it had something to do with that Amish girl he was hanging around—

SG: Naomi?

JL: Yeah.

SG: Why would you say that?

JL: Aren't most murders crimes of passion?

SG: Were there problems between the two?

JL: He's a man. She's a woman. There are going to be problems.

SG: Anything specific he mentioned to you?

JL: No. We didn't talk about stuff like that.

SG: We have statements that say you and a Daisy Marshall double dated at least a couple of times with Jeremiah and Naomi.

JL: Not against the law last time I checked. Just because we grabbed a burger together doesn't mean he spilled his guts to me. Look, like I said, Jeremiah was a good kid, but he was still a kid.

SG: Nineteen isn't exactly a child.

JL: When I was nineteen, I still thought I could win the gold before I was twenty. Now I understand it takes years and determination to perfect your skill. Jeremiah had natural talent, but he wasn't really dedicated to winning.

SG: Can you think of anyone else I should speak with?

JL: I don't know. Maybe that chick from Alamosa he hung out with sometimes when Naomi wasn't around.

SG: Do you know her name?

JL: Nah. He never introduced her, and she didn't hang with him at the rodeo because...you know, he was with Naomi. But I'd see her there, watching.

SG: Description?

JL: Dark haired. Indian, I think—like Native American Indian. Not like the foreign kind. She's little.

SG: Anything else?

JL: Tattoos on her left arm.

SG: Tattoos of what?

JL: I don't know, man. I didn't date her. I just saw her a few times.

SG: Thank you for coming in. I'll be in touch if we have additional questions.

Nine

The sun was peeking over the horizon when the Monte Vista police officer drove Henry and Emma and Ruth back to the rodeo grounds. Henry was worried that Ruth might want to go inside the arena to see the scene of her grandson's death once again. She didn't. Instead, she stared at it for a moment, her shoulders slumped and her fingers pressed to her lips. Finally, she straightened and turned toward her horse and buggy.

But they weren't where she'd left them. Someone in their community no doubt had driven the buggy to her house and had driven Henry's buggy and horse, Oreo, to his house as well.

The officer offered to take them to their homes. They all piled back into the vehicle and proceeded to Ruth's house.

"Would you like me to stay with you?" Emma asked.

"No, but thank you, Emma. You've been a *gut* friend—you and Henry both. What I would like most now is some time to rest and pray."

When they arrived at her home, she gave Emma a brief hug, squeezed Henry's hand, and then tottered off to her house.

"Will she be okay?" Ellen Cunningham had been with the police force a little more than a year. Grayson had once shared that she was only twenty-five years old and still a bit wet behind the ears, but she was a good officer he hoped would stick around.

"Someone will have already left her food and seen to her animals," Henry said. "Hopefully, she'll be able to get some rest, and later this afternoon some of the women will stop by to sit with her."

Officer Cunningham's eyes sought his in the rearview mirror. "That's good. No one should be alone after such a thing."

"Is this your first homicide, officer?"

"It is, and I don't mind saying I moved to Monte Vista because I didn't want to be a cop in Denver, where I grew up."

"Are things bad there?" Emma asked.

Cunningham shrugged. "Property crime is down, but violent crime is up."

"I can't imagine such a thing," Emma said.

"Amish communities are usually in rural areas for several reasons— we can purchase the necessary farmland, we can watch out for one another, and we have a better chance of living a life separate from the rest of the world…as we feel called to do."

"You're not too separate." Cunningham nodded back toward the facility they'd just left. "Going to the rodeo and all."

"We try to be good neighbors, to involve ourselves in the community to the extent that seems healthy. But living in a city…no, that's not the Amish way." Henry let that sit between them for a moment, and then he added, "Are you enjoying life in the valley?"

Cunningham gestured toward the mountains on the horizon. "Wide open spaces and the work are to my liking. Mainly we deal with domestic issues, speeding tickets, a few drunk and disorderlies—that's enough action for me."

Emma smiled through her weariness. "And usually that's all you'd find in Monte Vista."

"Maybe a few cows loose on the road," Cunningham said.

"Or a donkey munching the flowers on the town square." Henry smiled at the memory. Oh, that their problems could always be so commonplace.

Cunningham drove Emma home next. Henry stepped out of the cruiser in order to walk her to the porch steps.

"Would you like to come in for breakfast?"

"I would, but I should get home to Lexi." He'd had the beagle for nearly two years and was still surprised by how attached he was to her.

"Someone will have checked on her."

"*Ya*, but she gets anxious when I'm gone too long, especially if I haven't warned her beforehand."

"Henry Lapp, you talk as if that dog understands what you say."

"At times I think she does." Henry leaned forward, kissed Emma on the cheek, and promised to stop by the next day for Sunday dinner. It was their off week, so they had no church service. Instead, they would meet in small groups throughout the community—a few families that lived near one another gathered for a meal and fellowship.

"We can drive over and check on Ruth after lunch."

When he went to climb into the back of the police cruiser, Cunningham motioned him to the front.

"I didn't know if it was proper," Henry admitted.

"At the officer's discretion." Cunningham grinned, revealing a small gap between her two front teeth. Henry liked her for that. She wasn't so vain that she needed to have it cosmetically fixed. She didn't take herself quite as seriously as many young *Englisch* women her age seemed to.

"I appreciate your carting us around. I realize the Monte Vista police department isn't a taxi service."

"And yet we're here to serve."

Henry could have walked home. Emma often walked to his house, and he occasionally snapped a leash on Lexi's collar and walked to hers. He yawned largely. Probably it was best to be grateful for the ride. It had been a long night, and he needed to conserve his energy for the days ahead.

As soon as they'd pulled out on the two-lane road, Cunningham brought up Henry's past. "Is it true? What they say you can do?"

"You're referring to the drawing?"

"I am."

"Depends on what they're saying."

"They're like a photograph, only more detailed."

"True."

"They're always accurate."

"Also true."

She hesitated, and then she added, "Some people say you can draw things that haven't happened yet."

"I'm not a prophet, only a bishop." Henry said it lightly, but Cunningham's brow crinkled as if there was something there she didn't understand. "What I mean to say is I don't have the gift of prophecy, of seeing the future. The drawings, that ability...well, it's a result of a baseball accident when I was a young boy. I was only twelve years old."

"I read about that."

"Then I suppose you know I spent two weeks in ICU after Atlee Stolzfus smacked what would have been a home run if the ball hadn't come into contact with my head."

"Are you still friends?"

The question made Henry smile. He'd shared his story many times over the years—usually with families that thought they wanted to move into their district. He didn't want anyone under his spiritual guidance who didn't fully understand his past. He wasn't ashamed of it, but he was aware that his ability made some people uncomfortable.

"I'm not sure anyone has ever asked that before, but *ya*. We've remained friends through all these years. Atlee turned seventy last month, and we still occasionally exchange letters."

Henry indicated his small acreage coming up on the left. Cunningham slowed, flipped on her blinker, and then turned down his lane.

"The article I read said you have a photographic memory because of the accident."

"Doctors assure me there is no such thing. Some refer to my condition as accidental or acquired savant syndrome."

"Either way it's unusual."

"Very."

Cunningham stopped a few feet from his house and slipped the transmission into park. Henry had seen his *Englisch* friend Stuart do the same many times. He thought if he had to, he could drive an *Englisch* vehicle, but he preferred Oreo and his buggy.

"The article said only a few others are like you, and that their abilities are different."

"*Ya*. Brain injuries affect different people in different ways."

"It must be hard, being different." Cunningham's tone told Henry she was speaking from experience.

"Sometimes. I once thought of what I can do as a curse, an accident that happened while *Gotte was* distracted with other things."

"And now?"

"Now I realize it's a blessing."

Henry was reaching for the door handle and was about to thank her again for the ride, when she asked what had probably been on her mind all along. "Will you be able to help with the investigation? Like you did before?"

"*Nein.* I can only draw what I've seen. I don't actually remember the details, but my mind somehow records the images, and then my hand...well, my hand can draw them. Because I was in the food court when Jeremiah was shot, I didn't see anything. Unfortunately, in this instance, my ability won't be of use to anyone."

Ten

Henry loved Sunday worship. He couldn't remember a time when he hadn't enjoyed the gathering of everyone in the community, the hymns he could remember his grandparents singing. Everyone participated whether or not they had a good singing voice. And, of course, even as a youngster he had looked forward to the fellowship afterward, when they'd eat until it felt as if his suspenders would pop, play games, and temporarily forget the hard work living on a farm entailed. He also remembered thinking the sermons would go on forever, and that the sun might set before he had a chance to enjoy a game of baseball.

After becoming a bishop, he'd learned to appreciate the off Sundays as much as the ones where they met in worship. With smaller groups, he could spend more time with each of his congregants, and people sometimes opened up to him more in the casual setting. He tried to rotate which house he went to, but more and more often he went to Emma's. Already he was thinking of the place as his home.

He would move to the Fisher farm after they were wed. His place had very little land—only enough to pasture his horse, grow a small garden, keep a small barn, and have his workshop, where he made the wood items he sold in local stores. Keeping the land after he wed Emma would be an unnecessary expense when Clyde and Rachel had a good-sized piece of property that easily allowed for another small house, so he'd sell it. The walls of their *dawdi haus* were already up. Clyde, Silas, and Henry worked on the inside whenever they could. The home should be completed before the wedding—just a few weeks away—but if they ran into any problems, the congregation would schedule a workday.

For the adults today, a somber pall hovered over the day's luncheon because of Jeremiah's death. The children had seemed to pick up on the melancholy mood throughout the meal, but once they were in the pasture, their youthful exuberance returned. It was good and right that it should be so. The young had a way of leading them forward, even when life's path was full of obstacles.

Henry was leaning against the pasture fence, thinking about the impending move and changes in his life and watching the *youngies* engage in a game of baseball, when his new neighbor, Seth Hoschstetler, walked over and joined him. Seth and his wife, Roseann, were in their late forties, childless, and had come to Colorado because they felt hemmed in by the growth in Indiana. He was a big man at over six feet and a hard worker. In two months he'd managed to plant and tend to all of his crops, as well as shore up his barn and make repairs to his house. Moreover, he was a good neighbor with a pleasant outlook.

"Fine day for a luncheon," Seth said.

"You'll find most days in the valley are. We have *wunderbaar* weather all year long."

"You're forgetting we moved here in late May. We still had lows in the twenties."

Henry smiled as he crossed both arms on the top rail of the fence. "*Ya*, May was unusual."

"Actually, Roseann and I don't mind the temperatures. I *am* relieved that she's no longer having the headaches."

"It can take some time to adjust to the elevation, for sure and certain. Remember, our valley sits at an elevation of 7664 feet, which is a wee bit higher than Shipshewana, Indiana."

Lexi had been playing with the children, but when she spied Seth, she headed toward him.

"What's up with the vest?"

"Purchased it a week or so ago, and I'm trying it out. I like it better than clipping a leash to her collar. One book said choke collars can be hard on their necks, and she just slips out of a regular collar."

"Well, she looks quite proper in it."

Lexi was sniffing at Seth's feet. She dropped into a seated position and gave him a beseeching look.

"I think my dog has taken a liking to you."

"Roseann keeps a piece of leftover bacon or sausage for her every morning."

"That explains it."

"I hope you don't mind."

"Actually, I was worried she was bothering you. I found the hole in our fence line where she's getting through. I've been thinking about mending it, but I keep putting it off."

"Don't bother. We enjoy her visits. I might get a little one for Roseann next time Abe's dog has a litter." Seth slapped him on the back. "We're headed home, but I wanted to come over and speak. Though we live side by side, we don't see each other often enough."

"We need to remedy that. Take the girls out to eat or something."

"After your wedding. But maybe you can come over for dinner much sooner than that."

As Seth walked away to say his goodbyes to the rest of the group, Katie Ann and Naomi approached the bishop.

"Henry, could we talk to you for a minute?" Katie Ann asked.

"If you're not busy," Naomi quickly added.

Henry studied them curiously. Katie Ann seemed nervous, and Naomi had none of her usual energy. Normally the girl couldn't tolerate sitting still unless she was writing in one of her tablets. They'd all celebrated when Naomi was accepted as a scribe for the *Budget*, a distinctly Amish publication. Now she stood beside Katie Ann, clasping her hands at her waist and staring at the ground.

Something was definitely up.

"I'm not busy," Henry said. "Only full from all the luncheon foods and needing to walk about a bit."

"We could go to the barn," Katie Ann suggested.

Katie Ann worked for their local veterinarian, Georgia Berry. Henry wasn't sure how God would use Katie Ann's love for animals, but he had no doubt she would settle into an important role in their community.

At eighteen, she was growing in her faith, more mature each time he saw her, and a real joy in Emma's life. It startled Henry to realize she would soon be his granddaughter.

The thought filled his heart with joy, and he found himself wishing the time until his wedding to Emma would pass more quickly.

They walked in silence toward the barn, Lexi dashing in front of them and then falling behind to stop and investigate something. A tri-colored beagle, she was no longer a puppy, but Henry still thought of her that way. Her coat was white with large black and brown patches. She was smallish for a hound, both because of her breed and because she'd been the runt of the litter. But her sense of smell was great, she'd become fiercely protective of Henry, and she'd proved her worth on more than one occasion.

Henry watched her dash past them. She'd reached a height of fifteen inches and weighed twenty pounds at her last checkup. Large, dark-brown eyes matched her floppy ears. Both girls laughed when she stuck her nose under a clump of wildflowers and then jumped backward to bark at it.

They were nearly to the barn when Katie Ann glanced at the horse pasture and was quickly distracted by the sight of a young colt feeding next to Clyde's newest mare. They changed their course and stood appreciating the beauty of the foal on this sunny July afternoon.

"She's a beauty," Henry said, crossing his arms and leaning on the fence.

"We named her Ginger because she's such a pretty, soft brown."

Henry waited, but Katie Ann continued to stare at the colt, and Naomi had taken to picking at her fingernails.

"Who would like to begin?"

The girls looked at each other and then at him.

"Naomi wants to speak to you because she's worried that she knows something about Jeremiah."

"Possibly I know something. It could be that I don't."

"And if she does, she wouldn't want to keep it to herself and hinder Sheriff Grayson's investigation."

"I'd thought of going to him directly, but Katie Ann suggested I speak with you first."

They fell silent, waiting.

"Well. All right. I appreciate your trusting me with your concerns. You were Jeremiah's *freind*?"

"*Ya*, and possibly...possibly more."

"You were courting?"

"We went out a few times. I don't know that it was officially courting." Naomi's words tumbled over one another like a river stream headed downhill. "He'd come from Goshen less than two months ago, and you know my *aenti* and *onkel* live in Goshen, so we had a lot to talk about. We knew the same kids from when I've been to visit there. I let him walk me home from a few of the singings."

"I thought Jeremiah seemed quite taken with you," Katie Ann said. "Though sometimes you'd go a few days without hearing from him."

Henry considered carefully whether he should ask Naomi the question bouncing around in his mind. He brushed away any reticence because, in the end, he decided it might make a difference to what else she'd say. "Naomi, did you love Jeremiah? Did you plan on marrying?"

"He mentioned marriage a few times, but sort of in a laughing way. I wasn't sure how I felt." Her face reddened at the confession. "I cared about him, I did, but Jeremiah was a little...well, a little wild. And while that can be fun for a time, I knew that in the end I wanted to settle down, raise *bopplis*, and write for the *Budget*. I didn't want to move to the West Coast."

Henry stared at her in shock. Finally, he asked, just to make sure he'd heard correctly, "The West Coast?"

Naomi nodded mutely, her confession spent.

"Why would he do that, Naomi? Was Jeremiah thinking of leaving the faith? Is that what you're saying?"

Tears spilled down Naomi's cheeks, and Katie Ann quickly moved closer and took her hand.

"He said he was going and that he'd take me with him, or that he'd come back and get me. I tried telling him I didn't want to go, but he wouldn't listen, and we...we argued about it more than once, and then...then...then he was shot."

Henry gave her a moment to compose herself, and then he asked, "Where, Naomi? Where was Jeremiah planning to go?"

When she finally managed to find her voice, her answer wasn't what Henry would have guessed if he'd had a hundred years to do so.

"Hollywood. Jeremiah was determined to go to Hollywood."

Eleven

Emma sat at her kitchen table with Henry, Sheriff Grayson, and Ruth Schwartz. The sheriff had picked Ruth up on his way over, after Silas had run to the phone shack to call the police department.

Naomi had answered all of the sheriff's questions, and then she and Katie Ann had asked to be excused. One look at Ruth told Emma the poor woman was in a state of shock. She'd gone from disbelief, to grief, to surprise, and now to amazement.

"Jeremiah...on an *Englisch* television show. I can't imagine why he'd want to do such a thing."

"Most of the reality shows have some sort of monetary prize," Grayson explained. "I've never heard of *Boots, Buckles, and Broncos,* but new shows pop up all the time. Some barely make it through a season."

"Why would they want an Amish person?" Emma asked. She honestly couldn't imagine. Their life was so simple—the same from day to day, nothing anyone would want to watch unless they found milking a cow or doing laundry exciting. She did lots of laundry.

"A few shows featuring Amish did well, at least for a time." When they all stared at him blankly, he said, "Seriously? You haven't heard of them? *Amish in the City, Breaking Amish, Amish Mafia?*"

"I've heard of that last one," Henry admitted. "Actually, I read an interview with Ira Wagler once. Do you know Ira? He wrote a book called *Growing Up Amish.* He's since left the faith, but he has a good perspective, I think, on things that bridge the Amish and *Englisch* world. Anyway, some news reporter asked Ira what he thought about *Amish*

Mafia, and he said the whole concept was just silly. That's pretty much my take as well."

"What does it mean to the investigation?" Ruth asked. "Does it help you at all in finding the person responsible for killing my grandson?"

"It might." Grayson ran a hand up and down his jaw, and it occurred to Emma that the job of protecting the residents of Monte Vista was taking its toll on the man. He hid it well, but the strain showed more quickly with each murder investigation. "We'll contact the producers of the show, see if this was even real, and if he was scheduled to go out for an audition. If nothing else, it broadens our list of suspects."

"Someone wanting him on a show wouldn't kill him," Emma said.

"No, but someone else might have been bumped. Maybe they thought they had a spot, but then the producer finds this Amish kid who is a hotshot rodeo star..." Grayson stopped and shook his head. "I'm only thinking aloud, mind you."

"Naomi seemed upset, as if she could have stopped the turn of events that led to Jeremiah's death." Ruth rubbed the heel of her palm against her chest. "I'll speak with her. Not now, but after she's had some time to rest and pray. I don't want the poor girl thinking she was in any way responsible."

Grayson cleared his throat. "It's a big break that she was able to tell us the passcode for his phone. It probably saved us a couple of days on the data extraction."

"And that's important?" Ruth asked.

"The phone will have a lot of information, as I explained at the hospital. I have a tech going over it now. It's definitely a good, solid lead."

Grayson stood, and Henry did as well. "I'll walk you out."

Which left Emma and Ruth alone, for the first time since the shot rang out in Ski Hi Park Arena.

"How are you holding up, really? And don't tell me you're fine."

"*Nein*. Fine isn't how I would describe myself at the moment."

"Did you sleep any last night?"

"A little." Ruth rubbed her eyes as if the question had made her realize how tired she was. "I would nod off and then jerk awake, remember what happened, and feel the loss of it all over again."

"He was a *gut* boy," Emma said. "I don't pretend to understand all that he was going through, but it's plain as can be that he treated Naomi well. And he was a real help to you this summer."

"That's true, and it's part of the reason I didn't fuss over the nights out and weekends away, or over the *Englisch* boys he spent time with. It seemed that he was fulfilling his part of our bargain, and so I thought he would grow out of it."

"Which they usually do. We've all had similar issues, Ruth. Albert Bontrager nearly drove his parents crazy with the way he pushed against the *Ordnung*, and look at him now. He's successfully running his own farm."

Ruth smiled, maybe for the first time since Jeremiah had been killed. "Rumor is he ordered a wind tree."

"A wind tree?"

"You hadn't heard?"

"*Nein*. I don't even know what that is."

"Like the big windmills, only smaller. It charges a portable generator, which then provides enough power to run small items such as fans, radios, and the like."

"Oh dear. Does Henry know about this?"

Ruth shrugged. "Abe stopped by for something else and saw Albert installing it."

"Installing it? Do you bury a wind tree? Prop it up in the dirt? Place it in the middle of your garden? Do you have to water it?"

"I'm not really sure, but Abe's wife mentioned it to Franey, who was talking about it at the bakery on Friday. Now that seems like a lifetime ago."

Emma could just see out the kitchen window over the sink. Silas walked by with one of the teenaged Amish girls. She never knew from one day to the next whom he was courting. It seemed to her that he'd been through every girl in their community and was now headed back for a second round. Most of the time, the relationship didn't make it past the first two weeks. She'd asked him about it once, and he'd clumsily patted her shoulder and said, "Don't worry, *Mammi*. It'll work out."

"We never really know their lives," Emma said. "We think we do, but we only know what they want us to see."

"It was the same with our generation."

"Do you think so?"

"I do. We thought our parents wouldn't understand, so why tell them?"

"Sometimes we assume everything has changed since we were their age."

"And yet much of life stays the same. My children and now my *grandkinner* seem to face the same struggles. It's as if each generation has to learn on its own."

"I know you worry about Gideon and Clara."

"Indeed. It's better now, I think, with the children grown and the boys moved away. My son isn't a bad man, but it may be as you suggested. Perhaps he is depressed. I'm going to suggest that he see a doctor."

"And you think he will?"

"Probably not." Ruth stood, rinsed out her coffee mug, and then turned back to Emma. "I'm not saying my son caused Jeremiah's death. He wasn't there. He didn't pull the trigger, but I do think an unhappy home life pushed Jeremiah toward the *Englisch*, and I won't tolerate it any longer. He either agrees to see a doctor or I'll speak to his bishop."

"Perhaps it would be better to wait until after the funeral, until he's back home."

"You could be right, but I won't wait long. There's a chance that in his grief, in the depth of his despair, he'll be willing to listen to reason."

"We'll pray, both of us, that he will."

"Thank you, Emma. This life is certainly full of grief and uncertainty."

"At times it is, but there will be happiness in your life again, you can be sure of that." They'd walked out onto the porch, and in the distance she could make out the new colt. When Ruth saw where she was staring, she stepped closer to the railing. Emma knew when she spied the little animal, because a smile tugged at her lips.

Life *was* full of grief and uncertainty. Hadn't the writer of Ecclesiastes said as much? But it seemed there was a balance to life if one could hold on long enough. *A time to be born and a time to die...A time to mourn and a time to dance...A time to tear and a time to mend.*

She prayed that her friend would find the strength to hold on to her faith until life took yet another turn.

Twelve

Henry and the sheriff were stopped three times as they walked toward the police cruiser.

Each time, Grayson assured the person everything was being done to find Jeremiah's killer, and he didn't believe the community was in any danger.

Grayson's presence might have looked odd to an outsider, or even to an Amish person from another community. Normally the Amish mingled very little with police officials. In fact, they often went out of their way to avoid them. But Henry felt that, as the community's bishop, it was his job to create a channel for communication between the local authorities and the people of his church.

Certainly one could argue that special circumstances surrounded the community in Monte Vista. They'd been through hard times together. Not just the two previous murder investigations, which had both involved the Amish community, but also at least half a dozen damaging storms throughout the years. Each time the families in his church did what they would in any similar situation, in any other location. They helped one another and they helped their neighbors, whether they were Amish or *Englisch*. This had gone far to build goodwill between the two groups, until they'd finally reached the place where they were separate, but they could work together when the situation required.

In return, the local shop owners had embraced the cottage businesses established by most Amish families. Over the years it had become difficult to make a living off the land anywhere, but especially in this place that averaged only eight inches of rain a year. Most families sold quilts or blankets or, in Henry's case, items made from repurposed wood. Those ventures were marginally successful when sold from a roadside stand. However, items offered in the little boutique and gift shops in town reached far more customers. The shop owners took their percentage, which in Henry's opinion was fair, and quickly reimbursed the remaining amount. They'd forged an economic coalition of sorts, and it seemed to be benefitting everyone.

That ability to coexist amicably was evident as they walked toward Grayson's vehicle. The people who stopped them were respectful and offered to pray for the sheriff and the investigation.

Henry was proud of what they'd built in the valley, and while pride might be a sin and certainly did often precede a fall, he prayed that wouldn't happen. It wasn't him he was proud of, but the people he led, in the same way a father could be proud of a child. Certainly that wasn't a sin, though a good dose of humility was needed in every situation.

"We're going to find this person, Henry. I wasn't just mouthing platitudes." Grayson stopped at the door of his vehicle but made no move to open it.

"I believe you will."

"It's not what I was expecting to be dealing with this summer."

"Still planning on retiring in the fall?"

"I am."

"Fifty-one is young."

"Except I started at twenty-one, so I have thirty years with the department. It's enough, and I promised Melanie I would. She wants to travel, see the grandkids, spend time together."

"There's more to life than work."

"And yet it's important work. Whoever had the gall to shoot a boy in a public arena, in front of hundreds of people, as his family was watching...well, that person shouldn't be walking around free. Mark my words, if they get away with it this time, they will strike again."

"Unless it was a personal vendetta."

"Even then, it's as if once the monster is unleashed, it grows bolder. Suddenly, a small slight by the clerk in the grocery store may take on monumental proportions." Grayson opened the door to his vehicle, but he didn't get in. Instead, he stood looking out over Emma's farm—at the cattle and the garden, the new foal and the children playing ball. "But there's another side to it. Someone that bold? They're going to make a mistake. They probably already have."

"You and your department will find that mistake. You'll do your job well. You always have."

"Thank you for the vote of confidence. I've never dealt with a murder investigation where hundreds of people were present during the murder. It's a bit overwhelming."

Henry understood that the confession was a testament to their friendship. "We will help in any way we can."

As soon as Grayson had driven away, Henry's deacons joined him—Clyde and Abe and Leroy. They were good men, every one of them, though quite different in their own ways.

Clyde was Emma's son, the youngest of the three at forty-two, and fairly new at being a minister. No one had been surprised when the lot fell to him to replace his late father as minister. God's ways were mysterious, but Henry had known, from the moment Clyde opened his Bible to find the marker, that the younger man would make a good leader.

Abe was in his mid-forties with dark hair and glasses. He'd matured spiritually and emotionally over the last ten years, though much of that had been because of tough times in his family. His brother, who had originally moved with them to Monte Vista, had left his wife, sued for divorce in *Englisch* court, and eventually married an *Englisch* woman. It was up to Abe to care for Franey, Alvin's first wife. In Amish communities, women weren't eligible to remarry unless they were widows. In the eyes of the church, Alvin and Franey were still married. She was often referred to as a widow, and the women who owned and ran the bakery were often called *the three widows*, but for all practical purposes she was still considered married. It made for an awkward situation, but Abe navigated it well.

Leroy was an unlikely candidate for deacon, but again the lot had fallen to him, and he'd taken up the mantle of service without complaint. He had a dour disposition, which kept the others' optimism in check. In addition, he was the wealthiest of their group, owing to a fine business sense and a real skill with numbers. Those abilities had come in handy when keeping track of how much they had to spend on benevolence as well as on missions, which were their only two expenses other than a small stipend for the schoolteacher.

Now the three men stood around him, and it was plain from the look on their faces that they were trying to think of how to begin. Finally Leroy said, "This is a terrible thing for our community to endure—again."

"Very few burdens are heavy if everyone lifts."

"*Ya*, the proverbs are good, but I doubt they were inspired by murder investigations."

Henry smiled at his deacon and tried another tack. "James wrote that where jealousy and selfish ambition exist, there will be disorder and every vile practice."

"Is that what this was? Jealousy? Ambition?" Abe pushed up on his glasses.

"Hard to say."

"But what can we do?" Clyde asked. Henry could always count on Emma's son to be the practical one of the group.

"For the moment, we need to focus on ministering to Ruth. Her son and his wife will arrive tomorrow. The funeral will proceed on Tuesday as we planned."

"We'll have the plot dug in plenty of time. I've already marked out the spot beside Leon, just like Ruth asked." Leroy had donated a corner of his property for their cemetery. He and his sons took care of digging the graves by hand, as was their custom.

"Albert has begun work on the grave marker." Abe pushed up his glasses again. "It'll be a proper funeral, Henry. No need to worry."

"You can do one other thing for me. Sheriff Grayson could use our help."

"Did he say that?" Leroy asked.

"He didn't, but I've worked with the man before, and I can tell. This case is weighing heavily on him. He thinks he'll find answers on Jeremiah's phone, and he may. But we all know much of what Amish do is off the grid, so to speak. And Jeremiah, even though he may have been flirting with an *Englisch* lifestyle, was still very much Amish. I suspect if clues are to be had, they'll come from our *youngies*."

"What would you like us to do?" Clyde asked.

"Start with your own children. Talk to them privately. Ask them to talk to others. Let's find out exactly what Jeremiah was involved in. When we do, maybe we'll find the person who felt justified in taking his life."

Thirteen

Naomi and Katie Ann had walked over to the barn and then out to the back pasture, where a picnic table sat underneath a large aspen tree. The day was warm, and since they were alone, Naomi pulled off her *kapp* and shook out her hair. The sun felt good. It reminded her she was alive, that the world would keep spinning, that some things continued the same day in and day out regardless.

"Your hair is so wavy," Katie Ann said. "Mine is straight as a board, like a boy's."

"Straight hair can be a blessing. It stays in place better." Tears pushed at Naomi's eyes and her arms began to tremble. She closed her eyes and focused on pushing past the grief.

"What is it? You thought of something."

"Jeremiah and I never did more than kiss, you know? But he loved it when I'd take my *kapp* off. He'd run his fingers through my hair and tell me it reminded him of golden wheat."

"I know you told Henry you weren't sure, but did you love him?"

"*Nein.*" Naomi met her best friend's gaze and then looked away, ashamed to have admitted such a thing. "I should have, but I didn't."

"You can't help how you feel about a person." Katie Ann moved behind her and began to massage her scalp. The slight breeze was just enough to keep it from being hot, and Naomi began to relax for the first time since Friday night.

"My *aenti* says you choose someone you respect to marry, someone you know will care for you and provide for you, like a partner in a job."

"Only the job is for life."

"Exactly. She says the feelings come later."

"Maybe for some people it is that way. Remember Erin? She married that man in Montana, someone she'd never even met. They'd only exchanged letters. Yet according to *Mammi*, her mother says she's quite happy."

"How would they know?"

"Letters they receive, and I guess the occasional phone call."

Naomi shook her head, causing her hair to shift back and forth. Some days she wondered what it would feel like to cut it short, to be rid of the weight of it, though of course such a thing was unheard of among Amish women. They would get a slight trim now and then perhaps, but she'd never seen an Amish woman with short hair. "Sometimes, though, you tell people only what they want to hear. Sometimes it's easier to hide the part that hurts."

"Is that what Jeremiah did? He hid his feelings?"

"I believe his family life was difficult."

"I think you're right. I heard *Mammi* tell *Mamm* that Ruth mentioned his father was quite harsh." Katie Ann lowered her voice. "Maybe he tried to ignore the hurt, and it...festered. Maybe that's why he was thinking of leaving the faith."

"I guess it's possible, and maybe that's why I never fell in love with him."

"You knew you wanted to stay."

"There's that, plus he only showed me a part of himself. He was always holding back about some things."

"Like what?"

"Anything specific about his family. He would never talk about his life in Goshen unless I prodded him, and then he'd only tell me about the crops or jobs in town or new Amish tourist sites."

"He never mentioned his problems with his father?"

"*Nein*. But I could see it in his expression if I brought up his *dat*."

Two other girls passed by them. They were younger, but they called out, "Old folks headed this way. Better braid that up."

Naomi rolled her eyes, but she didn't resist when Katie Ann began braiding her hair. It was easier that she was facing away from her friend, that she didn't have to see the look on her face as she spoke.

She lowered her voice and said, "Actually, I think he was hiding things from me."

"Why would he do that?"

"I don't know. Jeremiah mentioned marriage a few times, but I didn't feel that I knew him any better after two months than I did the day he moved here."

"Give me an example."

"He'd go to the phone shack and ask me to wait in the buggy. I could sometimes hear him raising his voice, but then when I asked him what was wrong, he'd say 'Nothing.'"

"Why would he use the phone shack if he had a cell phone?"

"I don't know."

It felt good to be sharing the thoughts that had been circling in her mind. She couldn't bring herself to voice her worries about what Jeremiah was involved in earlier, not with Ruth sitting there. It seemed cruel to speak ill of someone who had passed, but she wasn't speaking ill. She was only being honest. Plus, she trusted Katie Ann to keep what they said private. "There's more. He let me...let me use his phone."

"To make calls?"

"*Nein*. I didn't have anyone to call, but you can shop that way."

"Shop?"

"Not that I ever bought anything, but I'd look."

"It would be nice to have more selection than we have in the few stores here in Monte Vista—not that I have so much extra money."

"Also, there are magazines you can read."

"On the phone?"

"*Ya*, and news sites that tell about movie stars." She hesitated and then added, "Even some web pages where you can learn about writing."

"Pretty much what we can find at the library."

"Exactly, except I didn't have to drive into town. I could look something up while Jeremiah was finishing some work at his *mammi*'s or caring for her horse. It's very convenient."

"I imagine it is." Katie Ann finished winding the braid on top of Naomi's head and reached for her *kapp*.

"Do you think I'm terrible for having used it?"

"'Course not. You and I haven't joined the church yet."

"But we both plan to."

"We do, but now is our time to try *Englisch* things. *Mammi* says it's so we'll know what we're giving up."

"Thank you for not judging me." Naomi stood, smoothed out the apron over her dress, and then looked at Katie Ann. "You're a *gut* friend."

"As you are to me."

They began walking back toward their families.

Naomi slowed her pace. There was still something she needed to say, to confess. "The thing is...I checked his browser history."

"Browser?"

"It showed what sites he'd looked at on his phone. I wasn't snooping. I just wanted to know what he was interested in."

"And?"

"Nothing. He always deleted any evidence of what he'd done."

"Why would he do that?"

"I don't know. It was his phone. He had a passcode protecting it. His parents weren't even here, and if his *mammi* knew he had one, she never mentioned it. Certainly she never used it. She wouldn't know how. The only reason to delete the history was so I couldn't see what he'd been doing."

"That doesn't make any sense."

"I know. It makes me think I didn't really know him at all."

Fourteen

Transcript of interview between Monte Vista Sheriff Roy Grayson and Dana Kennedy, regarding the July 27 homicide of Jeremiah Schwartz. Audiotapes and a transcript of the interview are included in the permanent case file.

Sheriff Roy Grayson #3604
TELEPHONE INTERVIEW WITH Dana Kennedy
Case #4751.06
6:30 p.m., Sunday, July 29

Sheriff Grayson (SG): Could you state your name for the recording?
Dana Kennedy (DK): Dana Kennedy
SG: Middle name?
DK: Elaine.
SG: And what is your position with Cowboy Television?
DK: I'm the producer of several of their reality shows.
SG: Including the upcoming *Boots, Buckles, and Broncos.*
DK: Correct.
SG: Thank you for returning my call so quickly, Ms. Kennedy.
DK: I had just heard about Jeremiah's death. It's quite...quite a shock. People think anyone in Hollywood is incapable of feeling, but that's not true. We're quite saddened by his passing. He seemed like a fine young man.
SG: Can you tell me how you first met Jeremiah?
DK: I was scouting for talent earlier this year, at the Elizabeth, Colorado, rodeo event.

SG: And that was when Jeremiah caught your eye?

DK: He was a natural, good with the horses, had a stellar smile—and let's be honest. The Amish bring in viewers.

SG: *Amish Mafia*?

DK: Exactly. Only this would be more authentic, and that's what we're shooting for on *Boots, Buckles, and Broncos*—authenticity. That's what today's viewer craves.

SG: Did you speak to Jeremiah while you were scouting in Elizabeth?

DK: I did. I didn't want the competition to snatch him up.

SG: You approached him about being on the show.

DK: We conducted a preliminary interview and shot a short video to see how he'd translate to the screen. Some people might look authentic riding a horse, for instance, but they can come across as too stilted or even too perfect on video. Jeremiah was every bit as good on screen as he was in person.

SG: And what was Jeremiah's response?

DK: He was excited. Who wouldn't be? It's a wonderful opportunity, especially for someone with so few options.

SG: So few options?

DK: No schooling and all that. I mean, I suppose it's fine if you're going to be a farmer, but Jeremiah had a lot of potential.

SG: Was Jeremiah interested in your offer?

DK: Yes, of course he was.

SG: Do you think he planned to travel to Los Angeles?

DK: We already bought his ticket. (inaudible) Yes, I have the paperwork right here. He was to fly out on August 6.

SG: A week from tomorrow?

DK: That's what it says.

SG: And you had already delivered those tickets to him?

DK: E-tickets. He should have an email from my assistant with the ticket link attached.

SG: Did you look at anyone else while scouting in Elizabeth?

DK: Yes, but they didn't work out.

SG: Can you be more specific?

DK: Sometimes personalities just don't click. There were a couple of possibilities in Elizabeth. Otherwise I wouldn't have bothered to fly out. Usually that's something I leave to my staff.

SG: But you felt the need to see these young men yourself?

DK: And women. It's an equal opportunity world, Sheriff Grayson. We'll have cowboys and cowgirls on *Boots, Buckles, and Broncos*.

SG: Was there anyone who thought they had a slot but were bumped because you decided on Jeremiah?

DK: How can I know what anyone thought?

SG: I'm trying to solve a homicide here, Ms. Kennedy. Any information you can provide—no matter how seemingly insignificant—would be appreciated.

DK: (inaudible) There was a young man named Justin Lane and a girl (inaudible). The girl's name was Piper Cox.

SG: So you auditioned three prospects for your show while in Elizabeth, Colorado—Jeremiah Schwartz, Justin Lane, and Piper Cox. Is that correct?

DK: Yes. Yes, it is.

SG: But you only offered Jeremiah a spot.

DK: A formal audition. We offered him a formal audition. Of course, we would pay all of his travel expenses as well as his food and hotel while he was here. Nothing was guaranteed, though. The final choice is the director's.

SG: You offered Jeremiah a formal audition, which he accepted, but you told Justin Lane and Piper Cox they didn't make the cut.

DK: No. It's not my place to deliver that sort of news.

SG: So how did they know?

DK: My assistant phones them and thanks them for auditioning.

SG: Can you tell me when those calls were made?

DK: (inaudible) Here it is. It looks like she left a message for each of them on Friday at 2:00 and 2:05 p.m. That would be West Coast time.

SG: Last Friday?

DK: Correct.

SG: Only a few hours before someone shot Jeremiah Schwartz.

DK: Doesn't mean the two things are related.

SG: It doesn't, but the timing indicates one could have precipitated the other.

DK: We can't anticipate how contestants will respond. You see that, don't you? I mean, if someone was upset and decided to run over Jeremiah with a car, that wouldn't have been our fault. We can't account for the twists and turns of human nature.

SG: Twists and turns.

DK: Hollywood isn't all glamor. I've seen my share of the dark side of human nature.

SG: I imagine you have.

DK: Is there anything else I can do? I honestly would like to help.

SG: You could fax me the entire file you have on Jeremiah, Justin, and Piper.

DK: Of course. Your assistant left a fax number when she first contacted me.

SG: Thank you for your time, Ms. Kennedy. I'll be in contact if we have additional questions.

Fifteen

Henry arranged for Stuart to pick him up Monday afternoon, and together they drove to Alamosa to wait on the bus that would deliver Ruth's son and daughter-in-law. They would have spent nearly twenty-four hours on the bus, having boarded at noon the previous day, and Henry expected them to be quite tired.

"You were able to get your wife's car." Henry glanced behind him at the rows of seats. They should fit easily, even if some of Jeremiah's siblings came.

"It's a van, technically. I didn't want to put your out-of-town visitors in the bed of the truck, so it seemed best."

"*Danki*, Stuart."

"Don't mention it, Henry."

Stuart and Henry went way back. Stuart had retired a few years earlier. Since he liked to read and didn't mind waiting, shuttling the Amish had seemed like a perfect part-time job. He'd confessed to Henry that a few people took advantage of this, asking for rides they didn't offer to pay for. Each time Stuart patiently explained that being an Amish taxi driver wasn't a hobby but a way of supplementing his retirement income. The response to that had been good, though a few people had quit calling him. "Didn't hurt my feelings a bit," Stuart had said. "I am, after all, semiretired."

The short of it was that Stuart adjusted to his part-time work/retirement, and the Amish community was grateful to have his services for any trips farther than a few miles.

"How's retirement working out for you?" Henry asked.

"It's easier than I thought it would be." Stuart laughed. "I haven't tired of reading, of course. And in my free time I work on our garden."

"Ah. We're being a good influence on you."

"No doubt, and I've also started collecting records."

"Records?"

"LPs, vinyl..."

"Music?"

"Yes! Come on now, Henry. I know you're Plain, but you don't live in a bubble. Certainly you remember vinyl."

A slight smile played across his lips, and Henry tapped a rhythm against the armrest. "When I was young, some of the girls bought a record player at a garage sale. Even then, some Plain people had generators. We'd plug the record player into the generator and enjoy the music, though it was forbidden, of course."

"You were one of those wild Amish youth."

"I remember Simon and Garfunkel, George Harrison, and even the Beatles."

"Confessions of a bishop."

"Indeed. I hadn't thought of that in years."

They were nearly to the bus station parking area when Stuart said, "I meant to tell you I'm sorry about the boy who was killed. Terrible thing to have happen."

"Yes, it was terrible."

"And this is his parents we're picking up?"

"*Ya.*"

"Gosh, Henry. You have a tough job."

"It's not always like this. Remember last spring when we had the big wedding party arrive from Indiana?"

Stuart started laughing. "Kept me busy for three days. I was beginning to wish I had a bus to haul them all in."

"We celebrate together and we mourn together. It's what being in community means."

They found a parking space where they could see the buses arriving and departing. Each bus had where it was coming from and where it was going displayed on a digital scroll bar across the front windshield. When the bus from Indiana pulled in, Henry hopped out of the van. Stuart had his book in his hand before Henry shut the door. An old man was on the front cover, and Henry saw the word *Ove*. Stuart's reading tastes were broad. The week before it had been something about a girl on a train.

It had to have been at least fifteen years since Henry had seen Ruth's son and daughter-in-law. Many families in the Monte Vista community resettled there from Goshen, so they shared a common history—cousins, weddings, funerals, births, and deaths. Henry vaguely remembered Gideon marrying Clara, and he could recall counseling Ruth's husband, Leon, on more than one occasion when he was worried about the young family.

As the couple stepped off the bus, Henry carefully composed his features so his expression wouldn't betray his thoughts. Gideon Schwartz couldn't have been fifty years old, and yet he looked much older than Henry felt. His hair was completely gray, and a scowl pulled down the corners of his mouth, causing his beard to droop. He was tall and thin to the point of leanness. Clara, conversely, looked like the typical Amish grandmother—round and impeccably dressed, with her *kapp* carefully pinned to cover nearly all of her hair. Her face seemed to melt into relief when she spotted Henry. She was grasping an older suitcase by its handle, but she dropped it and began waving as soon as she saw him, as if afraid he might not notice them.

"Gideon and Clara, welcome to Monte Vista. I'm very sorry you had to come under such circumstances."

"I can't imagine coming here under any other circumstances."

Which was when Henry remembered that Gideon hadn't visited when his father had died. It wasn't unheard of because travel was difficult when long distances were involved, and yet most children found a way to attend their parents' funerals.

"Did any of your other children come?" He didn't want to appear rude, but he didn't want to leave anyone behind either.

"No. They wanted to, but they couldn't." Clara's words sat between them for a moment.

Henry didn't know what to say to that, so he remained silent. Often silence conveyed the sentiments of his heart when words couldn't—or at least that's what he hoped and prayed.

"We're so glad to see you." Clara clasped his hands, and Henry noticed the haggard look around her eyes—from lack of sleep and mourning and worry. "This is such a terrible time, but knowing you were here, that you were looking over our son's funeral, has been a real balm to my soul."

Gideon grunted and said, "Don't see your buggy."

"It's too far for that. I hired a driver."

"A waste of money if you ask me."

"Stuart's rates are quite fair, and the distances between towns here in the valley are greater than in Goshen. We hire *Englisch* drivers when we need to go anywhere farther than Monte Vista."

By this time they'd made it to Stuart's van. Only Clara returned Stuart's greeting as she continued to drag the suitcase. Gideon climbed into the back and scowled out the window. Clara sat next to him, attempting to pull the suitcase in behind her. Stuart was out of the van by then. He picked up the suitcase, tossed a questioning look at Henry, and slipped the bag into the back of the vehicle.

Henry sat in the front, buckled his seat belt, and then turned so he could speak with Gideon and Clara.

"We can stop for a bite of lunch if you're hungry."

"Didn't come here to eat."

Clara ignored her husband. "What would you like to do, Henry?"

He glanced at his watch. "If you're not starving, I'd say let's go on to Ruth's. People have been delivering meals since Saturday, so she has quite a spread."

"Everything's set for the funeral?"

"*Ya.* Jeremiah's body was delivered this morning. The visitation period will begin at nine tomorrow morning at Ruth's, of course, followed by a brief service at Leroy's place, and then a luncheon back at Ruth's." He knew Ruth had shared all of these details with Clara already, but it seemed to calm the woman to hear them again.

They rode in an uncomfortable silence for the next ten minutes. It was when they passed a Monte Vista police cruiser headed in the opposite direction that Henry thought to update them on the investigation. "Sheriff Grayson is in charge of the inquiry into Jeremiah's death. He's coming by this evening to update you on the latest developments."

"That won't be necessary," Gideon said, still staring out the window. When Henry didn't respond, he turned his gaze to him. Henry realized in that moment that Gideon had totally blocked himself off emotionally from what was happening. It wasn't only that he hadn't processed the manner and untimeliness of Jeremiah's death, but he wasn't even acknowledging on an emotional level that it had happened.

"Not necessary at all." And with that Gideon returned his gaze out toward the high desert valley they were driving through.

Clara stared at her hands, but Henry noticed the tears slipping silently down her face.

He resisted the urge to reprimand Gideon. Such a thing should be done privately if at all possible, and he'd rather not embarrass the man by doing so in front of his wife and an *Englischer*. No, best to wait. In the meantime, he'd pray that God would soften this man's heart, that He'd minister to his hurting spirit, and that He'd bring the entire family closer together.

Sixteen

Several hours later, Emma, Ruth, and Clara sat in Ruth's kitchen. Each woman clutched a cup of coffee, but no one was drinking.

Jeremiah's body had been laid out in the living room on a makeshift table. They had worked together to dress him in white clothing, as was their tradition. Clara wept through the entire process. Ruth told stories of things that Jeremiah had done since moving to Monte Vista, small things she hadn't asked him to do and so had been surprised by them.

Fixing the gate to the horse pasture. It had always hung crooked, and lately it had been difficult to open and close.

Planting flowers around her mailbox, which was out by the main road.

Filling her hummingbird feeder at least once a week.

The coffin he was to be buried in was made from Colorado pine and handcrafted by Lewis Glick. Lewis had moved to their community a few years before. He'd finally married, a woman he'd been sending letters to for more than a year. Now he and Josephine were expecting their first child. Lewis wanted to give back to the community, and so he'd offered to provide the coffins when needed if someone else could supply the wood. It was a work of love, what he did, and Emma knew Clara had appreciated it as she'd run her hands tenderly over the soft wood. The scent of pine filled the house, offering a comforting reminder of the trees and nature and life—God's abundance—that went on outside those four walls.

Gideon had stood at the foot of the coffin, gazing down at his son.

The look on his face was one Emma wouldn't forget anytime soon. It was a combination of surprise and grief and anger. Those emotions seemed to war within him, until he finally turned and walked out of the house. That had been thirty minutes ago, and he still hadn't returned. The sky outside was still light, though the clock said it was nearing seven in the evening. Days in the valley could be long, especially in July.

Grayson had come and gone, leaving more questions than answers. Henry had left, promising to return early in the morning.

Now everything was done except enduring the next twenty-four hours.

"Oh, I almost forgot, Ruth." Clara let out a weary sigh. "Lloyd Yutzy's mother asked that I inquire as to how he was doing."

"Lloyd?" Emma glanced at Ruth, who shook her head once.

"Yes, Lloyd." Clara glanced at Emma and then back at her mother-in-law. "He came...he came to watch Jeremiah in the rodeo. She thought...that is, we both assumed he would be staying with you, *Mamm*."

"*Nein*. I haven't seen Lloyd. Haven't seen him since my last visit to Goshen." Ruth glanced at Emma. "Lloyd and Jeremiah went to school together. They were in the same grade. They were...friends, I guess."

"I know Lloyd. He's staying with Chester and Mary Yoder. I saw Chester and Mary at the rodeo, though Lloyd wasn't with them. I don't even know why he came to Monte Vista. I suppose I thought they'd asked him to come help with the crops."

"His mother thinks he was just coming for the rodeo. She thought it a bit odd, but then you know how *youngie* can be..." Clara's words drifted off, dissolving in the air between them like the hopes she must have had for Jeremiah. Quietly she added, "Perhaps I misunderstood."

Silence once again permeated the room. Emma was okay with the quiet. It gave each of them time to order their thoughts.

"I know he wasn't perfect." Clara began digging in her apron pocket for a tissue. "You both know that as well, I suspect, but Jeremiah had a good heart—a tender heart."

"None of us is perfect," Emma pointed out.

"And he was coming along." Ruth shifted in her chair. "He really was. I saw a maturity in him the last few weeks. As far as what Sheriff Grayson said, about the Hollywood show, well, it's just difficult to believe."

"Not really, *Mamm*."

Emma loved that Clara called Ruth her mother. She knew the two women exchanged letters quite often, more so since Clara's own mother had died of cancer the year before.

"Jeremiah had the ability to keep parts of his life separate," Clara said. "I walked into the discount store in Goshen once. We were out of soap, shampoo—things like that—but when I walked in the door, Jeremiah was standing at the register, purchasing a small television. I have no idea where he took it, where he plugged it in, or what he planned to watch on the thing. But the look on his face when he saw me, and then looked at the television, and then back at me—it was almost confusion."

"I think I know what you mean," Emma said. "I was a teacher before I married George. Only for a couple of years. When the children would see me in town, they'd look confused, like they couldn't understand why I wasn't in the schoolhouse."

"Exactly. I'd stepped into his world, and he seemed puzzled by that."

"I don't doubt that what Grayson said is true. After all, they found proof of the airline tickets on Jeremiah's phone." Ruth sipped her cold coffee and grimaced. "But I'm not sure he'd have actually gone. So what if he had an airline ticket. That doesn't mean he would have boarded the plane. Maybe he liked the idea of such a big change, but when it came down to it, I think he would have chosen to remain Plain."

They were quiet then, because they'd never know what Jeremiah would have decided. He'd never have that opportunity.

Emma cleared her throat, needing to add something to the discussion. Needing to give Ruth and Clara some hope of resolution. "Grayson will find who did this. He's a *gut* man and a fine investigator."

"Maybe so, Emma, but we both know that it was you and Henry who solved the last two murders." Ruth stood and fetched the coffeepot to refill their mugs.

"I don't know that we solved them."

"You did. The police were looking the wrong direction both times."

"*Mamm* told me about the Monte Vista arsonist and Sophia's murderer. Aren't you all a little afraid to live here?"

Emma waved that concern away. "'Course not. Monte Vista is as good a place to live as any. It's peaceful, and the *Englischers* don't put any obstacles in our path so we can live like we want to live. No nonsense about diapering horses or requiring a driver's license to drive farm equipment. You can see for yourself that the land is beautiful."

"So you're not...afraid?"

"No. In both of those other instances, they were the killer's personal vendetta, not a random act of violence. It isn't as if we need to keep our children right at our side. Those people were not healthy—spiritually or physically. And perhaps we'll find the same is true of the person who killed Jeremiah."

"It doesn't seem real. I can't...can't quite grasp that he's gone, that someone would wish him harm."

"If only Henry could..." Ruth let the thought die away into the night. They all knew Henry couldn't. He hadn't seen a thing, and though he might be a superb observer of human nature, his gift was only useful if he witnessed something.

This time, the Monte Vista police were on their own.

Seventeen

Transcript of interview between Monte Vista Sheriff Roy Grayson and Piper Cox, regarding the July 27 homicide of Jeremiah Schwartz. Audio-tapes and a transcript of the interview are included in the permanent case file.

Sheriff Roy Grayson #3604
INTERVIEW WITH Piper Cox
Case #4751.06
7:30 p.m., Monday, July 30

Sheriff Grayson (SG): Could you state your name for the recording?
Piper Cox (PC): Piper Cox.
SG: Middle name?
PC: Aiyana.
SG: And your address?
PC: 1014 Desert Drive, Del Norte, but you already know that, since you sent your officer to fetch me.
SG: Your birthdate is June 1, 1996?
PC: Yes.
SG: You were older than Jeremiah.
PC: I guess.
SG: Just to be clear, Ms. Cox, you're not under arrest at this time.
PC: Why would I be?
SG: You're free to leave or contact a lawyer at any point in this interview. We simply want to ask you some questions since you were friends with the deceased.
PC: (inaudible)

SG: I need you to verbally answer that you understand for the recording.

PC: Yeah, I understand. Can I smoke in here?

SG: No. Smoking isn't allowed in the building.

PC: Figures.

SG: How would you characterize your relationship with Jeremiah Schwartz?

PC: We were close.

SG: In what way?

PC: Jeremiah loved me.

SG: And you returned those feelings?

PC: Yes. If I didn't, then I wouldn't have gone out with him.

SG: According to other witnesses, Jeremiah had a girlfriend named Naomi Miller. Do you know her?

PC: I saw them together a few times.

SG: Did that bother you? The fact that he was with another woman?

PC: No.

SG: Can you explain that to me?

PC: He didn't care about her, not like he cared about me.

SG: Jeremiah told you this?

PC: He did. More than once. He was going to break it off with her. He promised me he was going to do it soon, and I believed him. He was just waiting for the right time.

SG: Did you know about his plans to travel to California?

PC: Know about them? I was going with him. Jeremiah and I were going to start a new life there, a better life. Not like what we have here in this godforsaken desert.

SG: So you knew about the television audition?

PC: (inaudible)

SG: I need you to answer verbally for the recording.

PC: I knew about it. He showed me the airline ticket.

SG: You were also interviewed for the show.

PC: I guess.

SG: Were you upset that you weren't chosen?

PC: No. I was still going to Los Angeles whether I was on that show or not.

SG: You planned to go with Jeremiah when he flew out on August 6?

PC: We didn't have the money for another ticket, but Jeremiah was going to send me a ticket once he got paid by the show.

SG: Do you know anyone who would want to hurt Jeremiah?

PC: Could have been any of those rodeo guys.

SG: Why do you say that? Were there problems between Jeremiah and the other competitors?

PC: They were all jealous of one another, cutthroat even. Any one of them could have done it.

SG: Anyone in particular?

PC: Nah. I didn't know their names.

SG: Were you in the arena when Jeremiah was shot?

PC: Yes. (inaudible)

SG: We can stop if you'd like a glass of water or time to compose yourself. I know this is difficult.

PC: I'd rather get it over with.

SG: All right. So you were in the arena. Did you see anything suspicious, anything that caused you concern?

PC: Only Jeremiah arguing with Justin.

SG: Justin Lane?

PC: I guess.

SG: You guess? Or you're sure? This is very important, Ms. Cox.

PC: I'm sure it was Justin, and I'm sure they were arguing.

SG: When was this, exactly?

PC: About an hour before the rodeo started.

SG: Did you hear what was said?

PC: Only a little. Something about Kennedy choosing the wrong person.

SG: Anything else?

PC: I think maybe Jeremiah owed somebody money. I don't know who, but he said not to worry about it. Said he'd square up as soon as he got his signing bonus from the television show.

SG: Can you think of anyone else who would want to hurt Jeremiah?

PC: Maybe some of the Amish kids.

SG: Why do you say that?

PC: The way they live. It's not like you read in books or see in those stupid television shows.

SG: Go on.

PC: Some of the other Amish kids were giving him a hard time, especially the boys. One said he was an embarrassment to the community.

SG: Do you know who specifically said that?

PC: Nah, but I could tell it bothered him.

SG: Did you ever use Jeremiah's phone?

PC: Why would I do that? I have my own.

SG: Maybe you forgot yours, or maybe you picked it up when he left it lying around. Maybe you snooped a little.

PC: (inaudible)

SG: The reason I ask is that we've searched Jeremiah's phone, and he'd deleted all of his history. Can you think of any reason he'd do that?

PC: No.

SG: Here's the thing, Ms. Cox. Any information deleted from a phone isn't really deleted. The provider still has a record of those calls, texts, even Internet usage, and now we have submitted a warrant to see what was deleted.

PC: So?

SG: So it's going to take a little time. If there's anything you could tell me about that phone, about who he called or what he did online, you'd help speed up the process, and we'd stand a better chance of catching the person who killed Jeremiah.

PC: I caught him once scrolling through and deleting everything. I asked him about it.

SG: And?

PC: And he told me you never know who you can trust, and that it was better to be careful.

SG: Is there anything else you'd like to add?

PC: Only that when you catch the person who did this, the person who killed Jeremiah and our dreams, killed my chance of leaving this place...well, I hope they stay in jail for the rest of their life.

SG: Thank you for coming in tonight.

PC: Like I had a choice.

SG: If you think of anything else, especially the names of any persons upset with Jeremiah, please call me, and I'll be in touch if we have additional questions.

Eighteen

Henry couldn't do anything else at Ruth's, so he'd gone home, seen to his horse, fed his dog, and eaten a sandwich made from the widows' bread and leftover deli meat. The funeral would be the next day, and he suspected it would be a difficult one. He intended to use the time this evening to relax, pray, and listen for God's still, small voice.

He carried his cup of coffee out to his front porch and watched the sun continue its westerly descent. The day was still thirty minutes away from darkness, and he enjoyed watching the birds swoop back and forth between the feeder he'd set up near his workshop and the flowers planted in his garden. He was thinking of the different types of sustenance for the birds, and how God provided for them in myriad ways, when he spied Grayson's police vehicle turning down his lane.

He waited as the sheriff parked the car, looked around as if he'd lost something, and then proceeded to the porch.

"Why are you sitting out here?" Grayson asked as he walked up the steps.

"Enjoying the sunset."

"You're facing east."

"Enjoying the evening."

Grayson sat down in the rocking chair next to Henry, removed his officer's hat, and balanced it on his knee. "Where's that cur dog of yours?"

"She's a beagle...mostly."

"Usually meets me at the car."

"I have new neighbors, as I guess you've noticed, and Lexi has taken to sneaking through the fence to visit them. Apparently scraps are involved."

"You could fix the fence."

"I've thought about it, but they like her."

Grayson set the rocker in motion, tapping his fingers against the arm of the chair. He didn't seem inclined to jump into the reason for his visit.

"Can I get you something to drink?"

"No. I've had so much coffee I probably won't sleep again until next week."

"Investigations are always difficult."

"That they are." Grayson finally turned to glance at Henry. "This used to be a quiet town. Biggest thing I had to deal with was kids breaking into the liquor store, not even smart enough to pull the videotape. I'd talk to their parents, have them do some community service and pay for what they stole, and everyone was happy."

"Problem with Jeremiah's case?"

"Yes and no."

"What do you mean by that?"

"It seems Jeremiah wasn't who he appeared to be—or rather he was different things to different people." When Henry didn't interrupt him, Grayson continued. "To his grandmother, he was a hardworking young man headed back to the righteous path."

"Ruth cared about him deeply."

"To his father, he was a wayward son, and his mom seemed stunned about his other life."

Henry didn't contradict him. The boy had been on the cusp of either turning back to a Plain life or leaping into an *Englisch* one.

"Other life? I guess you mean the television show."

"Yes. That as well as his plans to go to California. Plus, there's the fact that he had two girlfriends, which apparently Naomi didn't know, though I'm not sure that's so unusual at his age or with his generation."

Henry allowed all of that to sink in. "I appreciate your sharing this with me, but it's a bit unusual. You're normally quite closemouthed about ongoing investigations."

When Grayson gave him an offended look, Henry laughed. "*Ya*, you've shared details of an investigation before, but usually after you have it all wrapped up."

"With your help."

"Those times were different. You're not here because you think I can—"

"No. You explained that. I know you can't draw anything to help us this time."

"Then why are you here? No offense."

"None taken." Grayson put his hat back on his head and sat forward, his elbows propped on his knees. "I've tried to talk to a few of your youth. They're polite but not particularly forthcoming."

"Do you think they're hiding something pertinent to the case?"

"I think they could be. This young woman from Del Norte, the one who was apparently dating Jeremiah too, thinks he owed someone money or someone owed him money."

"You think he was killed for money?"

"No. I doubt whatever was owed was all that much, but I have to follow every lead."

"I'll see what I can find out."

"Sometimes one lead will take us to another. Pull on the right string and the entire thing will unravel."

Grayson stood as Lexi bounded across the field and toward the front steps, stopped to sniff his feet, and then collapsed on the porch.

"She looks full."

"Scraps."

"There's one more thing, Henry. This girl also suggested that some of the Amish boys were giving Jeremiah a hard time about leaving the faith."

"But they wouldn't shoot him for wanting to leave."

"No. I agree that seems a little far-fetched."

"I'll ask around. See what I can find out. Any other suspects?"

"Yeah. I seem to add one or two each day."

As Grayson drove away, Henry remembered one of the proverbs his mother was fond of quoting. *Go far from home, and you will have a long way back*. It would seem that, for Jeremiah, that sentiment had proved fatally true.

Nineteen

Emma was pleased that the funeral for Jeremiah was well attended. The only person from the Plain community of Monte Vista who didn't show up was Bethany Kauffmann, Leroy's wife. The doctor had confined her to bed because of a cold threatening to turn into pneumonia. More *Englischers* than normally found at an Amish funeral also attended. Emma thought there were two reasons for that—Jeremiah's involvement with the rodeo and the fact that Monte Vista was at its heart a close-knit community. Though Jeremiah hadn't lived there long enough to know most people in the area, Ruth certainly had. The buggies and cars lined up and down her driveway were a testament to how well liked she was.

Or perhaps people were curious.

Usually a viewing lasted for three days, but because the authorities had kept Jeremiah's body for an autopsy and his parents had traveled in from out of state, the family had made the decision to have the viewing in the morning with the actual funeral service after a brief lunch. Then they would all return to Ruth's for a full dinner. Emma stood in Ruth's kitchen, accepting dishes for the luncheon and separating casseroles from salads from desserts.

Franey and Nancy had provided plenty of fresh bread, including their famous light-as-air biscuits, buttermilk whole wheat milk bread, and honey whole wheat bread.

Emma was thinking that maybe she'd try just one slice of the honey bread when Franey nudged her with an elbow. "Here's another one who has never seen a body laid out in a home before."

The young man who had reached the front of the line and stepped through the front door looked to be about Jeremiah's age. He'd probably competed in the rodeo if the clothes he wore were any indication— starched blue jeans, a crisply ironed Western shirt, boots, and a large belt buckle. He glanced over at Jeremiah's parents and grandmother, who were sitting in straight-back chairs that had been placed just inside the room. The person in front of him offered their condolences and then moved on.

"At least he knows to remove his hat," Emma said.

"And he's saying something to them, though from the look on Gideon's face, it's not the right thing."

"I'm not sure there is a right thing to say today."

The young man stepped farther into the room and glanced over at Jeremiah's body laid out at the opposite end. Most of the furniture had been removed and placed in the barn. The benches they used in their church service lined the walls of the room and had also been placed on both the front and back porches. They were filled with people who came to sit with the Schwartz family, to be near to them in their hour of need.

The women took turns escorting people over to Jeremiah's body. When Susan Graber walked up to the *Englisch* teenager and said something to him, he blushed red but nodded in the affirmative. Then she walked him over to the coffin.

Emma knew what he would see as she'd already been through the line, and she'd attended many funerals in her lifetime.

The coffin was hinged, wooden, and simple.

The top portion was open, and the bottom half was closed.

Jeremiah's body, which had been dressed in white clothes, was also covered with a white sheet. Susan said something to the teenaged boy, who nodded again, and then she pulled back the sheet. The funeral director in town had taken care of the body, though the process was abbreviated due to their customs.

No makeup.

No hair styling.

No cosmetic reconstruction.

Jeremiah looked in death as he had in life—Plain.

The teenager began to sway on his feet and all color left his face. Emma feared he might keel over. Fortunately, Henry stepped forward, in between the young man and Jeremiah, and blocked the image of the body. Turning him toward the back door, he walked the young man out, talking to him as he went.

"Leave it to Henry to show compassion," Franey said.

"And shouldn't we?" Emma asked.

"I suppose, though if Jeremiah hadn't been involved with—"

"We don't know that. Don't know that it was related to the rodeo at all."

"He was killed at the rodeo." Franey looked at her as if she'd taken leave of her senses.

Nancy thanked an *Englischer* for a box of store-bought cookies and handed them to Franey. "She has something of a point. And don't give me that look, Emma. Whoever killed Jeremiah did so at the rodeo for a reason."

"We know nothing about the person, or what his reasons might be."

"True. But we all know when the truth comes out, and it always does come out eventually, the rodeo is going to be smack-dab in the middle of it."

Emma wasn't so sure, but she didn't bother explaining that to her friends. Sometimes a thing happened that had nothing to do with another thing right next to it. Except now that she thought about it, the last murder they'd solved disproved her point. Sophia Brooks had been killed at the wildlife refuge, and her murder had everything to do with the area.

She spied Charles and Mary Yoder sitting on the benches. "Say, did you know Lloyd Yutzy is staying with the Yoders?"

Nancy nodded, her lips forming a tight line.

"What is it?"

"Not for me to stick my nose into other people's business." Nancy pulled an empty plate off the counter that had been filled with molasses nut cookies. She replaced it with a tray of cinnamon fans.

"Franey, can you tell me what Nancy isn't talking about?"

"I'm not a gossip."

"No one said you were." Emma pulled the two women away from the serving line. "What is it? What aren't you two telling me?"

"Only that Lloyd is taking advantage of Chester and Mary's hospitality, if you ask me." Franey moved to the right so she could see out the front kitchen window. "Look at him now. Standing out there sort of in between our *youngies* and the *Englisch* teens. There's something about that boy that irks me."

"How is he taking advantage of Chester and Mary?"

Nancy apparently couldn't keep quiet a moment longer. She pulled them even farther back into the kitchen so they were standing right beside the oven. Maybe that's why Emma's brow was suddenly covered with sweat. "Lloyd called Mary and Chester—"

"Out of the blue," Franey added.

"And asked if he could come and stay for a week or so—"

"Which normally would be no big deal—"

"Though Mary thought it was a little odd."

Emma's head felt dizzy from swiveling back and forth between Nancy and Franey. She wished they could sit down with a cup of coffee and talk this out, but now wasn't the time for that.

"They were neighbors in Goshen," Franey explained.

"But not close neighbors. Mary said they hardly exchanged more than a few words. Lloyd was several years younger than their boy and their girls, and Lloyd...well, they never clicked."

"Anyway..." Franey took up the story with gusto. "Since he's been here, he hasn't helped a bit. Eats her cooking easily enough, but he hasn't offered to spend even an hour in the fields—"

"He doesn't help with the buggy horses—"

"Doesn't even clean up the room he's staying in. Just leaves his clothes on the floor and the bed unmade."

"I'm just glad Mary and Chester aren't living there alone."

"Claudia and her husband are there."

"Expecting their first child," Nancy reminded them, as if they would forget such a thing.

"Between the four of them, maybe they can keep an eye on Lloyd. Make sure he doesn't take off with the silver," Franey said.

"Didn't know they had silver," Emma commented, trying to lighten the mood. But it wasn't happening. Now that she'd opened this particular Pandora's box, Franey and Nancy were pouring out all their fears.

"It's also a *gut* thing their other daughter Sally's gone to Pinecraft for the summer." Franey held up a hand in protest. "I'm not saying she would have gotten in trouble, but it wouldn't have been proper—Lloyd staying right in the midst of the house with a young unmarried woman there."

"Is that all you have?" Emma asked. "He doesn't help with chores, he wasn't close to Chester and Mary, and he didn't really click with their children?"

"He's out late, going who knows where and doing who knows what. I'm telling you, I don't like it." Nancy frowned at a loaf of bread, and then she pulled a knife from the butcher block and began slicing it. "They need to ask him to leave, and hopefully after the funeral they will."

"I heard his mother thinks he came just for the rodeo," Emma said.

"Maybe, but he's very..." Nancy waved the knife back and forth. "Vague about things."

Emma peered back into the sitting room. The line of folks coming into the house had finally ended, or at least there'd been a break in the visitors. "Think I'll go and speak with Jeremiah's *mamm*."

"Do you know her?" Franey asked.

"Not well, no, though I spent some time with her last night."

"Try to catch her when the father isn't around. If he is, prepare yourself." Without another word of explanation, Franey set about repositioning casseroles in the oven.

Emma walked into the main room and stopped next to the pinewood coffin. He'd looked peaceful, despite the fact he'd been shot in the chest with a high-powered rifle. Per their traditions, they only did minimal embalming, just what was required by law, but the mortician had done a good job of covering the damage. Jeremiah lay in the simple casket, dressed in the white clothes they'd sewn the day before, and looked even younger than his nineteen years. Emma was nearly overwhelmed with the tragedy of it, how unnecessary such a thing was.

Jeremiah might have returned to the faith.

He might have married a nice Plain girl, raised a large family, and lived a good life.

And yet those thoughts ran smack into their belief and her conviction that each person's days were numbered and that God knew that number from the moment a child was conceived. Didn't the book of Job say as much? *A person's days are determined; you have decreed the number of his months and have set limits he cannot exceed.* God had a complete plan for each life, and surely man could not distort that plan.

She was wrestling with those two opposing thoughts when she glanced up and saw Jeremiah's mother staring at her. Emma had spoken to Clara twice that morning, but both times the woman had barely nodded and answered in monosyllables. Now she sat beside her husband, whose face was frozen in a stoic mask. Emma couldn't help thinking Clara's look was a plea for rescue.

She gave one last glance at the coffin, uttered a prayer for Jeremiah's family, and walked over to his parents.

Twenty

want to again express my sympathy," Emma said. "We didn't know Jeremiah all that well, but he seemed to be liked among the *youngies* here."

"He'd left the faith. I doubt he had much to do with your community." The father's expression never changed. He stared straight ahead, not glancing at Emma, not glancing around at all.

Clara didn't speak, but her eyes seemed to implore Emma, or perhaps she was merely tired.

"It's a bit warm in here, *ya*? Would you like to step out onto the back porch for a moment?"

Clara glanced at her husband, who didn't acknowledge her at all, and then she looked across the room toward where her son lay.

"It's okay to step away for a moment," Emma assured her.

Clara stood, smoothing out the apron covering her dress. Instead of leading her directly out the back door, Emma took her through the kitchen and the mudroom and onto a portion of the porch that curved around the side of the house. No benches had been placed there, and so they could have a bit of privacy.

The funeral was being held at Ruth's because she was family, but the actual service would be at their small cemetery on Leroy's property. They would leave for it in a few minutes.

Clara crossed her arms against her chest, as if she needed to protect herself from something. "This valley is so…vast."

"It is," Emma admitted. "It's easy to get used to being able to see so far. See those clouds to the west? Rain in Del Norte."

"Will it reach here?"

"It's unlikely. July and August are our rainiest months, but that only adds up to about an inch and a half per month. Clyde checked the weather radio, and no rain is predicted for us today."

"Tell me about Leroy's place. About where Jeremiah will be laid to rest."

"It's a large piece of land. Leroy is by and far the most successful farmer in our community."

"Your place is smaller?"

"About half."

"And Ruth's?"

"About the same as ours if I remember correctly."

"It's so different from Goshen."

"That it is." Emma hesitated, and then she added, "We planted trees there, on the corner of Leroy's lot, so there would be shade when folks go to clean around the gravesites. It's a pleasant spot, Clara. I think you'll be pleased."

The valley stretched out in front of them, and Emma saw the beauty in it—the mountains in the distance, the vista that ran for miles, the lack of buildings and roads and development. But she wasn't sure Clara saw any of those things.

"Jeremiah was always precocious as a child, always asking why, always trying things that made no sense to me."

"Give me an example."

Clara was still staring out at the valley, but Emma realized that, as she spoke, she was seeing something far different, something from the past. "When he was only four or five years old, we had a swing set, a metal one. You know the kind."

Emma nodded, though the woman still hadn't turned to glance at her.

"I looked out the kitchen window, just to check on the children while I was preparing lunch, and Jeremiah was on top of the swing set, walking across it."

"Oh my."

"His little feet were so sure as he placed them on the metal beam, but my heart? It stopped." She rubbed a fist against her chest as if she could feel the fear still. "I was sure he'd fall and break his neck. I was afraid if I called out I'd startle him, so I stood there, my heart hammering in my chest, waiting and praying."

"That must have been terrifying."

"It was. Even though he was my youngest, I was still so young at the time."

"Amish experience motherhood earlier than most."

"I remember feeling old at the time—feeling tired. Now I look back and realize I was practically a child myself."

"Doing the best you knew how."

"I didn't realize having children would tear at your heart so, that there would be so many dangers you'd want to protect them from."

"We can only pray and love them to the best of our ability. I'm sure you did both of those things."

Tears slipped down Clara's cheeks, but she quickly brushed them away. "Jeremiah was a good boy, only curious."

Now she turned to Emma, as if she needed to convince someone, perhaps herself, of the truth of what she was saying.

"He'd bring me flowers when he was little, and then as he grew older, once he started leaving for days at a time to participate in the rodeo, he'd always bring me some small thing—a postcard or a cookbook or something."

"I really am very sorry for your loss."

She thought Clara might break down then, which probably would have been healthy and certainly understandable. But she didn't. Instead, she stood straighter, squared her shoulders, and again smoothed out the wrinkles in her apron. "He sent us money. Every few weeks a letter would come, and in it would be a cashier's check. Gideon may have forgotten that, but I haven't. I won't. Jeremiah might have been involved in some things he shouldn't have been, but he never forgot his family."

"Those are precious memories, good memories, and you need to hold on to them during this time."

"Was he...was he happy here? Do you know?"

Emma thought about Naomi and the television show in Hollywood.

She thought about Jeremiah having two girlfriends, news Henry had shared with her that morning, and the possibility that he might have owed someone money. She thought of him at the rodeo, before it had begun, waving at the group of Amish folks who were there to watch him, smiling and setting his hat back on his head.

"I think he was."

Clara smiled tightly and turned to go, but before she reached the back door, she reversed direction and walked back to Emma. She stopped only a few inches away, reached into her pocket, and pulled out a small notebook. It had a blue cover, and would have easily fit into a shirt pocket. "I found this in his room here."

"Did you look through it? Are you sure it's his?"

"*Ya*. It's Jeremiah's writing. He jotted some things on the pages, but they make no sense to me. Gideon told me to throw it out, to toss it into the pond or the fire and be done with it, but maybe it will help find the person who did this to him. Will you give it to the sheriff? Or perhaps Henry? Maybe he'd be so kind as to turn it in for me. I don't think...I don't think I can face the police again."

"Of course." Emma accepted the notebook, though it felt hot in her hand. She stared down at it, wondered what secrets it held, and then quickly pocketed it. "Both Henry and Sheriff Grayson will keep Ruth apprised of any progress in the case. Grayson can even call you in Goshen if he has any questions."

"*Danki.*"

And then Clara was gone, back into the house to say her final goodbyes to her son.

Twenty-One

Henry led the funeral procession, his buggy chalked with a large number one on the side.

The casket had been loaded onto a cart attached to the back of his buggy, the equivalent of an *Englisch* hearse.

Ruth, Gideon, and Clara rode in Ruth's buggy, chalked with a number two.

And so it went, a long line of procession, black buggies pulled by strong horses, snaking its way across the San Luis desert. Behind the buggies were *Englisch* cars, their headlights on, and at the crossroads, Sheriff Grayson waited with his vehicle, top lights throwing out a beacon warning traffic to stop. Another officer would move on in front of them, and in that way they would take turns at each of the roads they had to cross to reach Leroy's place. *Englisch* vehicles traveling toward them pulled to the side. He saw only two news vans, and fortunately they remained at a discreet distance. No doubt their long-range lenses were catching everything.

He hadn't taken time to consider what interest another murder might have to the local or even national media. The last time—in the wake of Sophia's murder—everything had turned into a real circus. Fortunately, they'd all soon grown tired of the story, especially once the murderer was behind bars. Henry was glad no one had intruded upon Ruth's privacy, at least before now.

Henry understood that funerals were more for the living than those who had passed. Jeremiah's grave had been hand dug by one of Leroy's sons. The casket had been made by Lewis Glick. Once they arrived at the cemetery, men from their community carried Jeremiah's coffin and gently lowered it into the grave. Henry stood before the people assembled, both Amish and *Englisch*, and he chose his words carefully. He spoke from Job about the sovereignty of God.

> *Where were you when I laid the earth's foundation?*
> *Tell me, if you understand.*
> *Who marked off its dimensions? Surely you know!*
> *Who stretched a measuring line across it?*
> *On what were its footings set,*
> *or who laid its cornerstone—*
> *while the morning stars sang together*
> *and all the angels shouted for joy?*

He longed to remind them of God's sovereignty, of how much their heavenly Father cared for them. His heart ached at the expressions of confusion and grief. He read from the book of John, reminding them of Christ's promise to prepare a place for them. He ended with Paul's assurance that, though now they saw only a reflection, one day they would see Him face-to-face. Now they knew only in part, but one day they would know fully.

They sang one of the old hymns. Jeremiah's mother had chosen "Precious Memories," which reminded Henry of other funerals he'd officiated in the past. It was part of his job as bishop to guide his flock through such things, and death was a natural part of life despite Jeremiah's ending in such an unnatural way.

Clara wept and was comforted by the women, including Emma and Ruth.

Gideon remained stoically silent.

After the funeral, when they'd returned to Ruth's for the evening meal, he was approached by Jeremiah's father.

"I want to speak with you for a moment."

"Of course."

"Privately."

Henry motioned toward a breezeway that led to Ruth's barn. Gideon didn't waste any time once they'd stepped into the shade.

"I know about your drawing."

Henry waited.

"I suppose everyone knows—even saw what was written about you in the *Englisch* magazines."

"Something I had nothing to do with."

"As far as your drawing, you should know we don't approve of such things."

"Approve?"

"It's not my place to point out the Scripture to you, what with your being a bishop and all."

"Just say what's on your mind."

"I won't have you drawing my son. I don't know what you did or didn't see, or how your ability works, but Scripture plainly says we're not to dabble in sorcery."

"I can assure you that—"

"Let me finish. I won't be judging your strange ability—"

"That's exactly what you're doing."

"We've all heard about the Monte Vista arsonist, and that other situation, the one with the waitress."

"Her name was Sophia." Henry kept his voice soft and worked to keep the anger out of it. The man standing in front of him was hurting, and no doubt in a day or a week or longer he would regret what he was saying now.

"No one in Goshen has forgotten about Betsy Troyer, either."

Henry felt the pulse at his right temple twitch. He thought of the young girl often, even after so many years. He could be weeding in his garden, and his thoughts would abruptly wander to her family and to the time he'd spent in jail for a crime he didn't commit. He was moving past those hurtful memories, but sometimes they still pricked his soul. Gideon's words brought back those times with the force of a spring thunderstorm.

"I'd like you to give me your word that you won't be using this thing you can do in connection with Jeremiah. The boy had lost his way, and he paid for that."

Which was probably what sent Henry over the edge, this man's presumption of knowledge and his quickness to judge.

"We can't know what life God had called Jeremiah to."

"He called him to a Plain life."

"I understand your pain, more than you think I do—"

"You understand nothing."

"But in your pain, be careful what presumptions you make."

"I suppose I know the condition of my son's soul."

"Do you? Had you spoken to him recently?"

"I didn't need to talk to him to know he'd fallen away."

"And did you speak to him even when he lived with you? Or did you sit back and judge—"

"What would you know of having a child, of having a son? Nothing. You've never had your heart broken the way I have."

"So because Jeremiah chose differently than you thought he should, you closed your ears to his words and hardened your heart to his needs?"

The look of contempt on Gideon's face did nothing to slow Henry. He was ready to quote Christ's Sermon on the Mount word for word. If it would soften this man's heart, he'd read the entire New Testament to him and then go back to cover the Old Testament as well.

He knew too well that Gideon's bitterness would poison not only his relationship with his other children, but also the union with his wife, and ultimately it would damage his relationship with his Lord.

Henry understood that it was his duty to speak to Gideon clearly and without anger, to guide him in the ways of their faith.

But he didn't have the chance, because there was a crash and a scream, people began to run, and then pandemonium erupted.

Twenty-Two

Emma had been watching her grandsons Stephen and Thomas, so she knew the moment they were in trouble. The children had wandered off after the evening meal, and it was no surprise that someone started throwing around a baseball. Normally such behavior was frowned upon during such a formal event as a funeral, but this funeral had been particularly difficult and somber. Grief was always present, but normally funerals also served as a celebration of life and a reminder of their heavenly reward.

The day seemed to have lasted the length of two or three. First the visitation period and then the lunch, followed by the ride to the cemetery.

The short message from Henry to the community had been poignant, but the boys had begun growing restless. Emma knew the signs—shuffling from foot to foot, bumping shoulders, picking up small pebbles and tossing them at one another.

Henry's sermon had been followed by singing and prayer.

The boys had begun to squirm on the ride back to Ruth's home, and she'd caught them tossing peas at each other and kicking each other under the table during dinner. In truth, she was glad when they asked to be dismissed and headed out to the pasture. The problem came after they'd been playing catch for a good five or ten minutes.

Emma's attention was torn between watching the boys and keeping an eye on Henry, who was talking to Gideon Schwartz. The talk seemed to be going none too well by the way Henry's posture stiffened.

On the other hand, the boys were moving perilously close to Ruth's pasture fence. Ruth kept both sheep and goats, but they were penned in two grazing areas. She was very careful to keep them separate.

"The goats are like a classroom full of schoolchildren—lots of energy and always investigating things," she'd once explained to Emma. "Sheep, on the other hand, are like infants. They like things to be quiet, and they're easily upset. Once one starts crying, they all start crying. Takes forever to settle them back down again."

Thomas threw the ball at Stephen, who lurched for it but missed. The ball rolled under the gate on the sheep's side of the pasture fence. Stephen jogged over and reached up to open the fence gate. Emma began moving toward them, and she was just about to warn him to leave the ball where it was when Stephen opened the gate and the sheep crowded forward. He jumped back, inadvertently pulling the gate open even wider. The sheep surged out of the fenced area, bleating and looking for all the world like a fluffy stampede.

At the same time, Curtis Graber began laughing so hard that he fell off the goat side of the fence, where he was perched. He landed on his backside on the wrong side of the fence, and when he stood, dusted off his pants, and then opened the gate, the goats pushed and shoved and would have climbed over him, but he jumped out of the way.

It all happened in a matter of seconds.

One of the women screamed as a goat tried to pull a piece of chicken from her hand, which alerted everyone to what had happened, and then the adults and children were all moving at once.

Emma stood under an elm tree with Franey and Nancy, watching the chaos that quickly followed. Her feet felt as if they were nailed to the ground, and she'd slapped her hand over her mouth, unsure whom to shout at first.

The sheep pushed their way through, baaing and bleating, running left and then right, moving together like a giant wave. One would stop to pull up some of the grass, and then another would bump into its back end, and off the entire group would run. They pushed their way through the guests, into the midst of the tables that had been set up.

Women jerked babies off the ground, toddlers squealed in delight, and men jumped up, grabbing their plates of food and drinks off the tables before they were knocked over.

Three of the goats peeled off and headed toward the serving table, bumping into its legs and pulling at the tablecloth. A platter of potato and vegetable scones went flying.

The sheep continued to graze on the grass around the tables, but the goats were less interested in the food as they headed for anything they could climb on.

"Never realized how fast a goat can move," Franey said.

"Never realized Ruth had so many," Nancy added.

It suddenly seemed as if goats were everywhere. They were standing on top of an overturned wheelbarrow, climbing the steps of the porch, and even hopping onto the picnic tables. Somehow three billies had climbed up onto a trampoline Ruth had never gotten rid of. They bounced and brayed and knocked one another off, but were quickly replaced by others, who alternated between jumping around and bumping into yet more goats.

Some of the *Englischers* were laughing, and a few of the teens had taken out their phones and were recording the animals' escape.

Emma was seized by a fit of laughter watching the sheep and goats. The sheep looked terrified, running from one side of the area to the other. The goats were simply delighted to be freed. No doubt they'd been thinking of getting out of that pasture for months. Now they had their chance and were making the most of it.

Henry had left Jeremiah's father standing in the breezeway and was attempting to herd the freed animals back where they belonged. Katie Ann, Silas, and their friends tried to head off the animals moving toward the parked buggies, and Ruth was standing in the middle of the entire thing shouting, "Turn them back, and catch the one headed toward the garden!"

That was all the encouragement the *Englisch* kids needed. Emma had been surprised they returned after the trip to the cemetery, not exactly mingling with the Amish, but apparently unsure if it was okay to take off yet. Now they sprang into action.

"Those kids were raised mutton busting and calf roping," Franey said.

"This is terrible," Emma replied.

"But funny." Nancy pointed toward the front porch. "Is that one standing on a rocking chair?"

And then they all fell into another fit of laughter.

One of the goats had taken a liking to Deborah King's apron, and she was attempting to shoo it away with a pot holder with one hand while clinging to her baby with the other. Claudia Yoder rushed over to help Deborah, but at that moment a fluffy ewe pushed in between the two of them, her lamb close behind. Claudia stopped so as not to bump into the ewe and ended up landing on her backside, though she was laughing as she went down.

"Hang on, Deborah!" Claudia called out, sounding anything but confident. In truth, the goat was the one who looked sorely afraid. It took a last bite out of Deborah's apron and scampered away.

Henry glanced toward Emma, raised his hands in exasperation, and lurched for a lamb. He managed to catch it and pick it up. Emma ran over to take the small thing. It had been years since she'd held a lamb in her arms, and she was surprised at how soft and vulnerable it felt. It cried like a small child and stuck its nose in the crook of her arm as if to hide its eyes.

"I'll take him back," she said.

Henry winked and scampered off after a wayward goat about to pull down Ruth's clothesline as it tugged on her bag full of clothespins. Emma turned toward the pens, where an *Englisch* girl stood on the sheep side, opening and closing the gate as needed, and Katie Ann stood on the goat side.

Emma slipped the lamb inside. It stood there forlornly, looking left and right before it raised its nose into the air and began to cry. The little guy's mom froze where she had been eating some of Ruth's potted flowers, turned toward the sound, and then began to run in the direction of her baby. The *Englisch* girl swung open the gate at the last possible second, uniting the two.

It took nearly an hour to return all of the animals to their pens and to right the mess of tables, chairs, and dishes scattered across the yard. While the men loaded up the benches, the women covered and stored the leftover food they could salvage in the refrigerator. Gideon had disappeared, and Clara was sitting on the front step with one of the small children, who was retelling how she'd climbed onto a sheep and taken a ride. It was the first and only time Emma saw a look that resembled happiness on the woman's face.

The sun was setting, and people were beginning to pack up and leave.

"We're sorry, Ruth." Stephen and Thomas stood in front of her, their straw hats in their hands and a look of real consternation on their faces.

"No harm done," she assured them.

"Except to your flowers, which the boys will be by to replant tomorrow." Clyde stood with his hands on his hips, turning in a circle to survey the damage. "If any other chores need to be done, or if you'd rather they come another day..."

"*Nein*. Tomorrow will be fine. Gideon and Clara are leaving first thing in the morning, and I suppose I'd like the company."

Stephen and Thomas nodded obediently, though when they walked away Emma thought she heard them say something along the lines of "there go our plans for fishing."

"Are you riding with us, *Mamm*?" Rachel stopped at her side. They were all exhausted, but somehow also lightened by the chaos of the last hour. Everyone would need to work the next day, and both Rachel and Ruth looked ready to fall asleep on their feet.

"I'd be happy to take you home, Emma."

She hadn't heard Henry come up behind her, but she nodded immediately. A few moments alone with Henry would help to calm her soul, plus she wanted to ask him about that conversation he'd been having with Jeremiah's father. And she also needed to give him the notebook Clara had given her.

Emma stepped forward and enfolded Ruth in a hug. "Are you going to be all right?"

"Of course, though it doesn't feel like it today. Thank you for asking."

"Please call me or send someone if you need anything at all."

But they were all aware that Ruth would have no one to send. Her son and his wife were leaving at first light. She'd once again be alone on her farm, as she'd been before Jeremiah had come to stay for the summer.

Ruth assured them both she would be fine, and perhaps she would. She was in business with Franey and Nancy, running the Bread 2 Go bakery, and the venture had been a healthy diversion for all three women. Plus, it seemed she was making good money at it.

More importantly, she'd grown close to the other two women. They would see that she wasn't left alone for too long. Emma had heard them mention that Ruth would be taking off the rest of the week before returning to work.

Henry reached for Emma's hand as they walked toward his buggy.

"Long day," she said.

"Indeed."

"It's possible I hadn't realized exactly how difficult your life could be. As a bishop, I mean."

"It's a privilege to serve."

"I know you feel that way."

"I do."

"But watching you...well, it seems that ministering to such a large group of people must be a full-time job."

Henry squeezed her hand. "I'll admit it will be easier with you by my side."

"Do you think...I'm right for it? That I'm a right fit to be a bishop's wife?"

Henry stopped in his tracks.

"Why would you wonder such a thing?"

"I laughed at the goats' escape when I should have jumped in to stop them."

"No one could have stopped them, Emma. They saw their chance at freedom and took it."

"I wasn't quick enough to admonish the boys."

"They're only children, and what happened was an accident."

"I suppose."

"Are you really worried about being my wife—Henry Lapp's wife? Or is it the idea of being a bishop's wife that makes you anxious?"

Emma shrugged. A dozen answers went through her mind—she wasn't humble enough, wasn't Plain enough, indulged selfish thoughts, had been known to have a quick temper when provoked...She could go on for some time listing how she fell short of the ideal Amish woman, but she shared none of that with Henry. Instead, she gave what was probably the most accurate answer. "I guess I'm tired."

"There are still times when I wonder if I'm right for the job," Henry admitted.

"Even after so many years?"

"Even so."

Henry's words soothed her heart. Somehow he always knew what to say, what she needed to hear. That was as much a gift as his ability to draw. Emma was thinking along those lines when they finally reached the area where Henry had parked his buggy. They glanced back one last time at Ruth's pens of animals, and then proceeded to walk toward the buggy.

Henry must have seen it the same time she did, because when she glanced at him, he was staring, his mouth agape. They both stood there, stopped dead in their tracks.

Twenty-Three

Henry blinked, sure he must be imagining the words chalked on the door of his buggy.

But when Emma pulled in a sharp breath, he knew it was real.

"You were buggy number one," Emma said.

"*Ya.* Always at the funerals."

On the side of each buggy was chalked a number, providing a sort of order as they made their way to the cemetery.

Henry's had been buggy number one.

Ruth's had been the second.

If there had been other family, they would have followed immediately after Ruth. This helped the people parking buggies to keep things in a logical order, and it also helped families to find their own buggy. Because all the buggies looked alike, the only real way to tell the difference was to peek inside—look for a sweater or toy or bonnet left on a seat. The numbers made telling the difference much easier.

Now they both stared at the words that had been chalked on Henry's buggy.

Stay Out of It

"Sounds like a warning," Emma said.

"But from who?"

"From the person who shot Jeremiah, that's who. Who else?"

"Which would mean he was here today."

Emma stomped closer to the driver's door and raised the hem of her apron as if to wipe the words away, but Henry stayed her with his hand.

"Leave it."

"But—"

"We should show Grayson."

So instead of going home, they drove to the police station.

Grayson came outside with them and took pictures with his cell phone as well as with a camera.

"Will it help you to find whoever killed him?" Henry asked.

"Can't say."

"But now you know he was at the funeral."

"Maybe, but I stopped by myself, and there had to be more than two hundred people there—Amish and not."

"*Ya*, the entire community turned out."

"It could have been someone who wasn't at the funeral."

"I'm not following," Henry said.

"Could have been someone who snuck in while you were otherwise occupied. Waited until the buggies were parked, sneaked in, left his message, and disappeared before anyone was the wiser."

"Wait," Henry said. They were missing something. Something about what Grayson said wasn't quite right. He snapped his fingers. "It couldn't have been during the service or before it—"

"Because you would have noticed," Emma said.

"*Ya*. Fairly hard to miss." The letters were written to cover the door from top to bottom. There was no way he would have walked up to his buggy, climbed into it, and not noticed.

"So it happened at Mrs. Schwartz's house after you returned from the cemetery." Grayson clasped the camera behind his back and frowned at the buggy. "I don't like it. Don't like that whoever it was had the boldness, the audacity to go to her place at a time like that."

"Best time, though. No one would have noticed. Lots of people coming and going."

"Or it could have been a prank." Emma shrugged when both Grayson and Henry turned to stare at her. "Teenagers are unpredictable at best. Maybe someone just wanted to feel closer to the danger."

"Sounds more wishful than logical," Henry said.

"I suppose. I'm ready for this to be over, for all of it to be over."

"Don't worry, Mrs. Fisher. We'll catch this person, and this time there's no need for you and Henry to be involved."

"Good," Emma said. Then she pressed her lips together as if she'd been too honest and was embarrassed by that.

But Grayson laughed. "Law enforcement isn't for everyone."

"Especially not the Amish," Henry said.

"Especially not Amish women. I've taken up crocheting again, remember?"

"And you have a wedding to plan for." Henry smiled at her, grateful she was with him, that she would be with him for the foreseeable future.

"I'm not certain this will help us to catch the perpetrator." Grayson waved at the message on the buggy. "But it will be useful once we have him in custody. We can get a handwriting sample and match it. Convictions are built on—"

"Solid evidence," they all three said together. Henry and Emma had heard it from him before.

Henry took a handkerchief from his pocket and looked to Grayson for permission. The police chief nodded once, and Henry wiped the words off the door of the buggy.

"Oh. I almost forgot." Emma pulled a small notebook from her purse. "Jeremiah's mother asked me to give this to you. I didn't look in it, but I did touch it."

Grayson took it from her but didn't open it. "What is it?"

"A notebook—Jeremiah's notebook. I'm sorry we both touched it."

"She found this in his things?"

"*Ya.*"

"All right. Thank you for turning it over to me. I'll have someone study it tonight."

"Do you think Jeremiah knew his killer?"

Grayson rubbed at his right eyebrow. "I don't think this was random if that's what you're asking."

"Please let us know if there's anything else we can do." Henry shook hands with the man, and then they turned to go.

They were on the way to Emma's house when Emma brought up Jeremiah's father.

"I saw you speaking with him. You looked...perturbed."

"Where were you?"

"By the picnic tables."

"And you could see my expression?"

"*Nein*. It wasn't so much that." Emma glanced at him, smiled, and then turned her attention out the window. "I suppose I know you that well, is all. The way you stand more stiffly if you're upset about something."

"Stand stiffly?"

"And run the thumb of your right hand under your suspenders."

"I do that?"

"Only when you're perturbed."

Henry was silent a moment, but then he smiled and said, "I suppose it's a good thing you know me so well."

"*Ya?*"

"*Ya*. You'll know when I'm upset about the laundry or cooking."

"Oh, is that so?"

Henry's laughter rang out, easing the tension in his shoulders for the first time that day. "It's a joke, Emma."

"I should hope so."

"You're going to be my spouse, my helpmate. Not my maid."

"That's a relief."

But she was smiling as she uttered those words, and Henry understood that he didn't have to explain himself to her.

They drove the next mile in silence, with the only sounds the clip-clop of Oreo's hooves against the pavement and the occasional cry of a bird.

"On a totally different subject, did you know Lloyd Yutzy is staying with Chester and Mary?" Emma asked.

"Can't say I did."

"Nancy and Franey are a bit...concerned."

"Because?"

"They're afraid Lloyd is taking advantage of their hospitality."

"In what way?"

"They weren't very specific on the matter, didn't want to gossip, but they were worried."

"I'll stop by and see them tomorrow."

The work of a bishop never ended. The thought reminded him of housework, which reminded him of his previous conversation with Emma. He found himself grinning in spite of the fact that it had been a long day with somber overtones.

"There is one thing I want to talk to you about." He held Oreo's reins loosely in his hands. The horse didn't need much direction.

"And that is?"

"Perhaps I should start to draw."

"Draw?"

"Jeremiah's murder."

"But you didn't see anything, and we're...we're not getting involved."

"I didn't see anything, at least nothing that seems important. Certainly I didn't see him get killed, but perhaps someone in the crowd was pushing out after he was shot, or someone beforehand. Perhaps there's something in here"—he tapped the side of his head—"that will help Sheriff Grayson catch the person responsible for Jeremiah's murder."

Twenty-Four

Transcript of interview between Monte Vista Sheriff Roy Grayson and Justin Lane, regarding the July 27 homicide of Jeremiah Schwartz. Audiotapes and a transcript of the interview are included in the permanent case file.

Sheriff Roy Grayson #3604
INTERVIEW WITH Justin Lane
Case #4751.06
8:15 a.m., Wednesday, August 1

Sheriff Grayson (SG): Could you state your name for the recording?

Justin Lane (JL): Justin Tanner Lane.

SG: Justin, I asked you to come back into the station this morning because–

JL: Seems like harassment to me.

SG: Because I have a few more questions about your relationship with Jeremiah Schwartz.

JL: I already told you. We didn't have a relationship.

SG: I also want to remind you that you're not under arrest at this time. You're free to leave or contact a lawyer at any point in this interview.

JL: Consider me reminded.

SG: You were seen arguing with Jeremiah before the start of Friday night's rodeo.

JL: We didn't argue. I might have raised my voice...

SG: What was it about?

JL: You have to understand...Jeremiah had a way of getting under your skin. He was so smug, so sure of himself.

SG: And so you argued, but what specifically was it about?

JL: (inaudible)

SG: Did Jeremiah owe you money?

JL: No. I wouldn't have loaned him money if I had it, which I didn't.

SG: Any idea who he might have borrowed money from? Anyone on the circuit—

JL: (laughter) You don't get it. People who ride the rodeo don't have money. That's what we're hoping to win, but even when we do (sound of snapping fingers), it's gone, just like that.

SG: So what was the argument about?

JL: This place is a real dump, you know. Looks worse the second time around.

SG: We're not too worried about interior design. My job is to catch those who break the law.

JL: So why are you wasting time with me?

SG: Tell me about your argument with Jeremiah.

JL: He was leading Piper on. I just thought it was wrong.

SG: So you did know the other girl he was dating. You were defending Piper?

JL: I guess.

SG: Were you jealous because he was dating her?

JL: No. See, that's why I didn't bring this up the first time we were in here. I knew you'd jump to the wrong conclusion.

SG: Explain it to me, then, so I can arrive at the correct conclusion.

JL: Jeremiah had no intentions of sending Piper a plane ticket. It was all fine and good when she was being considered for the show, but once she got the phone call telling her she'd been cut, you could tell he couldn't wait to put this town and her and probably that Amish chick behind him.

SG: You also failed to mention you were being considered for *Boots, Buckles, and Broncos.*

JL: (inaudible)

SG: Were you disappointed when you received the call informing you that you hadn't made the cut?

JL: No. I wasn't disappointed.

SG: Seems like you would be. A golden opportunity like that, the chance for fame and fortune slipping through your fingers. Seems you would be disappointed, maybe even angry.

JL: Yeah, but it's not about that.

SG: What's not about what?

JL: Bulldogging. It's not about looking pretty on a television screen. It's about two things and two things alone.

SG: And those are?

JL: The riding and winning. It's about the bulls and the mud and the blood and getting back up even when every bone in your body aches.

SG: So you weren't disappointed.

JL: No.

SG: And you weren't jealous.

JL: No.

SG: And...just to be clear...Jeremiah did not owe you money.

JL: No!

SG: Justin, while you are not under oath and cannot be charged with perjury at this time, you can be charged with making false statements and obstruction of justice.

JL: Which is why I'm not lying.

SG: (inaudible) This is a copy of a notebook found in Jeremiah's possessions. Take the pages and scan through them. While you're doing that, let me point out a few things for you. As you can see, there are lists of initials next to dollar amounts. Now, this looks like a bookie's notebook to me. We have initials and amounts of original bets, odds, and payouts. Your initials appear quite often on these pages.

JL: You can't prove that's me.

SG: Gaming operations must be licensed and are regulated in this state, and any wins must be reported to the IRS.

JL: I don't know what you're talking about.

SG: Was Jeremiah Schwartz taking bets on rodeo events?

JL: I don't know.

SG: Did he owe someone money, or did someone owe him?

JL: I don't know.

SG: Who all was involved?

JL: I don't know, and if I did I wouldn't tell you. I'm not a snitch.

SG: Are you a killer? Are you, Justin? Did you kill Jeremiah Schwartz with a long rifle on the evening of July 27?

JL: I'd like to stop the interview now.

SG: Do you know who killed Jeremiah?

JL: (inaudible)

SG: Answer the question, Justin. Verbally, for the recorder.

JL: You said I'm here voluntarily.

SG: You are.

JL: Well, now I'm leaving, and you can't stop me.

SG: That's true.

JL: You're just harassing me, and I don't have to answer your questions.

SG: Are you sure that's the way you want to play this, Justin? Because next time I bring you in here, it won't be voluntary.

JL: Yeah, well, next time you bring me in here I won't come alone. I'll have a lawyer.

Twenty-Five

Naomi was walking along the side of the road on her way to work and collecting wildflowers. She could have borrowed her *aenti's* horse and buggy, but the widows liked fresh flowers on the table, and she didn't mind the walk. Plus, they gave her an extra hour's pay for doing it. Walking in the bright sunshine felt good. It helped to settle her nervous stomach, which had plagued her since Jeremiah's death.

The Sangre de Cristo Mountains rose in the distance to the east. If she stopped and squinted, she thought she could make out the sand dunes. To the west, the San Juan Mountains dominated the skyline. They were taller, nearly 14,000 feet according to the website she looked at on Jeremiah's phone.

The thought reminded her of his death, and she felt her emotions plummet again. Jeremiah had been a good friend. He took her places, and she'd liked talking to him even when she didn't understand his moods.

She was thinking of that, and had stopped to snip a clump of small yellow flowers with the tiny scissors she kept in her pocket, when a buggy pulled up and stopped beside her. She was surprised to see Lloyd Yutzy driving it. She didn't know Lloyd well, though she'd talked to him a few times when she was staying with relatives in Goshen. She loved her *aenti* and *onkel*, but Goshen had made her nervous—all the tourists and photographers and crowds everywhere, which was why she'd moved on to stay with her *Aenti* Abigail. She sometimes thought about returning home to her parents in Missouri. She missed them, but she liked life in the valley. It was quiet and peaceful. She might enjoy look-ing up *Englisch* things on a cell phone, but she preferred living where life was Plain and simple.

"Get in. I'll give you a ride."

Lloyd was her age, the same age Jeremiah had been. Jeremiah had been a regular-looking guy—certainly not ugly, but nothing to write home about either. It was his personality, his energy, that had been so appealing. Lloyd, on the other hand, had unusually good looks. He could be a cover model for an Amish romance novel—blond hair, blue eyes, tall, broad-shouldered, and muscled up from having worked on a farm all of his life.

"Hi, Lloyd. Actually, I'm walking to the bakery so I can pick flow-ers for the tables."

"Looks like you have plenty."

Naomi glanced down at her basket. It was true. She'd collected more than she needed, but she'd been enjoying the walk and the quiet. Still, she didn't want to seem rude, so she climbed into the buggy and placed the basket on the floor.

"Mary and Chester let you use their horse and buggy?"

"I didn't actually ask." When he saw the look on her face, he shrugged. "They're old, Naomi. They rarely go anywhere."

"It's proper to ask."

"Chester was already in the fields when I left, and Mary was in the kitchen. I doubt they even realize they're gone."

She didn't know how to respond to that, so she changed the subject. "How has your visit been?"

"That's what I want to talk to you about. I'm going back to Goshen soon, and I want you to go with me."

"What?" The word came out at a higher pitch than she'd intended. Naomi swallowed, lowered her voice, and said, "Why would I do that? I live here."

"You live here now, but you have family in Goshen."

"I have family here too—my *Aenti* Abigail and *Onkel* Daniel. Plus, there's my cousin Sam."

"It's hardly even a community."

Which was true, so she didn't argue with him. She did feel mildly defensive. Who was he to judge their community, to look down his nose at it? Her heartbeat pounded in her ears, and her mouth went suddenly dry, but she didn't rise to the bait. They were nearly to the bakery, and she could be done with Lloyd Yutzy.

"Why would you want to stay here?" he asked more softly.

"I don't know. It's beautiful. I like it."

The mare clomped along the road. That and the sound of the buggy wheels against pavement helped to fill the awkward silence. They'd entered the outskirts of town, and she tried to see the area as Lloyd must see it. Monte Vista was a rural community, with little to do, and a relatively small group of Amish families. On the plus side, the local stores had what they needed, and everyone got along well.

At least everyone except for Jeremiah and his killer.

"I think you should come back."

"Perhaps I will come to visit sometime, but for now the widows need me in the bakery."

Lloyd's scowl deepened, but he didn't speak again until he'd pulled into the parking lot of Bread 2 Go. Already it was filled with customers' vehicles, which made Naomi proud. She didn't begin her day as early as the widows, who came to work before the sun was up. By the time she arrived, they were usually at the height of their rush hour, and today looked like no exception.

"I'd best be going." She reached for the handle of the buggy's door, but Lloyd grasped her other hand. She looked down at his fingers encircling her wrist, surprised that he would take such liberties. "Lloyd. You're hurting me."

He let go, set the brake on the buggy, and turned to look directly at her. "Maybe you don't understand what I'm saying. I want you to come back to Goshen with me. I want to court you, and I can't do it when you're here."

"That's very sweet, but—"

"Think about it, Naomi. Think about it before you say no." And then he dismissed her with a wave of his hand.

She snatched up her basket of flowers, practically jumped out of the buggy, and hurried into the restaurant. A line of customers greeted her, most by name, as she made her way toward the back of the store.

"Are you okay?" Nancy asked. "You look rather frazzled."

"*Ya*, fine, I guess." She put her purse on the shelf where they kept personal items and moved over to the counter where the small glass vases were awaiting her flowers.

"How is Ruth?" she asked when Franey came into the room to retrieve another tray of cinnamon rolls.

"*Gut*. She wanted to come back to work today, but Nancy talked her into waiting until Monday."

"*Ya*, probably she needs a little time off."

"Her son and his wife already left," Nancy said as she popped another tray of bread into the oven. "I think she gets a little lonely at her place."

"Was that Lloyd Yutzy who dropped you off?" Franey asked, standing next to her and helping with the flowers.

"It was. He just...appeared out of nowhere, slowed down his buggy—or rather Chester's buggy—and told me to get in."

"You don't have to accept every ride you're offered, you know." Apparently realizing how gruff that sounded, Franey touched her on the shoulder and added, "I only mean that it's okay to say no if it's someone you'd rather not ride with."

Those words bounced round and round Naomi's mind as she carried the tray of flowers out into the dining area and began placing a vase on each table.

Was Lloyd someone she'd rather not ride with?

Why did his ways irritate her so much?

Or maybe it was simply that she'd rather be alone right now.

That felt more accurate. She'd always been a bit of a loner, and she needed time to process Jeremiah's death. Though she'd suspected they were growing apart, she would miss him. She certainly wasn't ready to begin stepping out with someone else, and she had absolutely no intention of moving back to Goshen, Indiana. As she went about her work, she became more convinced that Lloyd had simply jumped to the wrong conclusion. Maybe she'd smiled at him at the funeral, or maybe he was remembering the times they'd attended singings together in Goshen.

She'd been a young girl then, but she now felt like a much older, much more experienced woman. She'd been through the death of a friend. She had a job. She had a life she liked here in the valley. Lloyd wasn't unusual in thinking she would drop everything and join him thirteen hundred miles to the east. She knew it was that far because she'd taken the bus to visit, and the ride had seemed to last forever.

Amish boys often thought Amish girls were just waiting around to be swept off their feet. She supposed the same might be true of *Englischers*. She couldn't really say. But she did know Lloyd would have to learn to take no for an answer. It wouldn't break his heart. She suspected many girls in Goshen would be interested in courting him. He'd just have to set his sights on someone else.

Twenty-Six

Henry was late getting home that evening. He'd gone to town to pick up more dog food for Lexi. Then he'd visited Ruth, who seemed to be doing all right, though of course she was still grieving. Henry knew it would take time for the despair to work its way from her heart. Fortunately, Emma's grandsons were there, repotting the flowers the goats had torn out and helping Ruth with her garden. Everyone seemed to be getting on well, so he promised to visit again toward the weekend and climbed back into the buggy with Lexi.

Sometimes he took her with him, and other times he didn't.

Today she rode on the box he kept for her in the back of the buggy. She preferred that he set it in the front passenger seat, which he'd done, and she liked to sit up on it, looking out the window. Well, who didn't enjoy looking out the window on a beautiful summer day?

Though it was nearly dinnertime, he'd decided to stop by and check on Mary and Chester Yoder. They'd insisted he stay for a meal. He carried a little extra dog food in the buggy for just such situations, so he excused himself, fed his dog, and Mary brought out a little dish of water. Full and more than a little sleepy, Lexi waited patiently on the porch while Henry enjoyed Mary's delicious cooking.

She'd made chicken casserole filled with carrots, potatoes, celery, and peas. The entire thing was, of course, topped with cheese. The casserole would have been plenty, but she'd heated some leftover potato and vegetable scones to go with it, and for dessert she served shoofly pie.

Henry insisted on only a small piece. His buttons already felt as if they were about to pop.

"I heard Lloyd Yutzy is staying with you. Is he still here?" he'd finally asked.

"*Ya*, I suppose he is." Mary jumped up to refill his coffee cup.

"You suppose?"

"We don't really know what the boy is up to." Chester sat back and pushed his plate away. He reached out to brush a crumb off the table and finally added, "To be honest, we don't really know why he's here, although he said it was for the rodeo."

"How did it come about that he ended up staying with you?"

"He left a message at the phone shack." Mary set the coffeepot back on the stove and then sat down across from him. "I was surprised, because though I was friends with his parents, I never really knew Lloyd that well. He was still quite young when we lived in Goshen. But it seemed only polite to offer him a place to stay, and we had the room."

"So he came down for the rodeo, not the funeral?"

"*Ya*, that's what he said." Mary ran a thumbnail across the tablecloth, scratching at a small stain. "He came before the funeral. Came on..."

"A week ago," Chester said. "He's been here a week, arrived the day before the rodeo—the day before Jeremiah was shot. And I don't mind saying it's time for him to go back now."

Henry let that sit between them for a moment.

When neither Chester nor Mary spoke, Henry asked, "Would you like me to have a word with him?"

"Not necessary," Chester said. "He's barely unpacked his things—though the clothes he wears are scattered across the room. The rest of his bag...well, he hasn't unpacked it that I can tell. I suspect he'll be gone in a few more days. Not much to keep him here that I can see."

"Where is he now?"

Mary shrugged, and Chester pretended to be interested in something outside the window.

Finally Henry accepted that they weren't going to share any additional details about the ways of Lloyd Yutzy. Because the lad was leaving, it wasn't really his place to question or correct him about his manners.

Perhaps he'd send a letter to the Goshen bishop, suggesting he meet with Lloyd and counsel him about showing respect to elders, especially those you were asking favors from.

The sun was beginning to set by the time he headed home. He was nearly to his lane when he noticed the bright lights of a police cruiser on the side of the road. Oreo shied from the blinking lights, but Henry held the reins firmly and directed her off the pavement and onto the grassy shoulder well behind the police vehicle.

"Stay, Lexi." He jumped out of the buggy and hurried up to the accident.

Seth Hoschstetler was speaking to Officer Moore, who seemed to be taking down his statement.

Seth's wife, Roseann, was sitting in the police cruiser, the door open and an ice pack pressed to her forehead.

Henry wanted to know what Seth was saying in his statement, but he needed to check on Roseann first.

"Is everyone okay?" He squatted down in front of Roseann.

"Henry. I didn't realize you were here." She smiled slightly and then winced. She pushed the ice pack more firmly against her head.

"Can I..." He gestured toward the ice pack, and Roseann nodded once, allowing her hand to slip down and into her lap.

He held the cool first aid compress against her skin. In the strobe of the police vehicle's lights he could read the words *Instant Cold Pack*. Finally he dared to pull it away.

"You've a goose egg here."

"I was turning toward the window when it all happened. It's a bump, is all."

"Having any dizziness?"

"Same question the police officer asked me, and the answer is no." She laughed. "I'm feeling a bit feisty because he wants me to go to the hospital, and I want to go home."

"Would you like me to have a word with him?"

"*Danki.*"

"*Gem gschehne.*"

He made sure she'd reapplied the ice pack before he stepped away.

Lexi looked as if she was on point, standing on her box in the buggy. He thought he heard a whine coming from her, but she'd have to wait. More pressing matters and all.

Seth's horse was cropping weeds on the side of the road, down in the ditch where the buggy had come to rest. The hitch between the buggy and the horse was clearly broken, and the buggy sat at a lopsided angle. No doubt there was also damage where the wheel attached to the buggy.

"Officer. Seth."

Both men looked up as if surprised to find him there.

"How did this happen?"

"Fool in a pickup truck ran me off the road, that's how it happened. Pulling a horse trailer, if you can imagine that. At least there weren't any horses in it at the time—not that I had a chance to see much before he sped away."

"Wouldn't be our first hit-and-run accident, though it's the first auto-buggy incident since I've been here." Officer Moore closed his notebook and stuck it back into his pocket. "Unfortunately, the vehicle you've described sounds pretty standard for these parts. We'll do our best, though. If he's from around here and hasn't already left the valley, we at least have a chance of finding him."

"I'm sorry I didn't notice the license plate. It all happened pretty quickly."

"Most people don't. I'm going to call this in and then check on your wife."

Which reminded Henry of his promise to Roseann. "She'd rather not go to the hospital."

"Standard procedure. An ambulance is already on the way."

"If the paramedics find her vitals are good and no signs of a concussion, would you release her to Seth? They live right there." Henry pointed to the farm across the road. "And I'm next door if they need anything."

"Can't require anyone to go to the hospital, but trust me, you don't want to mess around with head injuries."

"She's a stubborn woman," Seth cautioned.

"And she seemed quite aware of what had happened." Henry pulled off his hat and turned it in his hands. "I don't think there's a concussion. Plus, she'll rest better in her own home."

"Are Amish folk always this bullheaded?" Moore asked, but then he held up a hand. "Don't answer that. I think I know what you're going to say."

Someone on the radio alerted him that the ambulance's ETA was two minutes. Moore walked away to speak to the dispatcher and check on Roseann.

"Give me the short version of what happened."

"Someone ran me off the road."

"You think it was intentional?"

"Yes, I do."

"Because?"

"He sped up, waited until he was beside me and Cocoa was tossing her head like wild, and then he pushed into our lane. There's no doubt in my mind at all that it was intentional."

"And the description of the vehicle?"

"Battered pickup. The strangest thing was that the fool had a horse trailer attached. Who would do such a thing while pulling a trailer?"

"No animals in it?"

"Not that I could see."

"And you didn't get a look at the driver?"

"Too busy trying to maintain control of my own horse."

"I'm sorry this happened to you."

"Not your fault."

"It's rare for us to have this sort of trouble."

"No worries, Henry. We don't regret our decision to move here."

The response pleased Henry. They were a small community and needed new members to thrive. They needed members like Seth and Roseann, who were good, hardworking, faithful people. "We'll hitch your horse to the back of my buggy, and I'll give you a ride home."

"What of my buggy?"

"Hitch is broken. You can call someone out to fix it tomorrow."

Seth nodded in agreement.

Then it was only a matter of waiting for Officer Moore to finish his paperwork and clear Roseann. Seth went off to speak with the officer, and Henry remained near the broken buggy and grazing horse. He pulled on his beard and looked out over the road, as if he could discover some clue as to what had happened and why it had occurred. But all he saw was the desert floor and a sky darkening as night slipped across the valley.

Twenty-Seven

Emma was having trouble grasping what Henry was telling her. Accidents happened—sure and certain they did. But someone intentionally running Seth Hoschstetler off the road? That made no sense. "Should I go and visit Roseann?"

"I checked on her only an hour ago," Henry said, assuring her.

"Still, it might be better for a woman to go by."

"All right, but not until you've had coffee and some of those cookies with me."

They traipsed into the house, where Henry set the coffee to heating while Emma pulled out two cups and the milk from the refrigerator. She liked how easily they did things together—simple things like pulling together a midmorning snack. She liked how the silence between them was comfortable.

Once they were sitting at the table, she noticed Henry seemed disarmingly chipper—especially for someone describing an accident.

"Why are you grinning at me, Henry?"

"I was just thinking that by this time next month we'll be wed."

"The weeks are flying by."

"Would you slow them down?"

"I would not." Emma broke off a piece of cookie. Why she bothered pretending she wasn't going to eat a whole one, she couldn't say. Maybe it was as she'd read on a sign at the widows' bakery—"Free cookie pieces. No calories." If only that were true, she could enjoy the snack and stop worrying about her waistline. Why was she worried anyway? She wasn't a nineteen-year-old bride, and Henry seemed to love her exactly as she was.

That contented thought calmed her nerves for a moment, but only a moment. "It's only that I feel like a storm is brewing."

"A storm?"

"Summer storm. You know, when you can feel the electricity building up in the air."

"As far as I know, severe weather isn't predicted."

"I'm not talking about the weather."

"Ah." Henry waited, which Emma loved. Sometimes it took a few minutes to put her thoughts into words, and silence helped with that.

"First Jeremiah was killed."

"A tragedy for sure."

"Then the funeral with his parents, who were understandably out of sorts, but...well, if I were to be blunt, his father seemed like a very difficult man."

"We must continue to pray for the whole family."

"Ruth's goats and sheep on the loose during the dinner."

Henry only smiled at that.

"The warning chalked on the side of your buggy."

"A prank, I would imagine."

"And now this! Seth and Roseann run off the road, right outside their own place!"

"Actually, I think the accident began outside my place, but by the time the horse stumbled to a stop in the ditch, they were outside Seth's place."

Emma choked on the piece of cookie she was swallowing. She coughed for so long that Henry hopped up to fetch her a glass of water, and then he stood behind her patting her on the back. She waved him away, but he didn't sit down again until she pulled in a good, solid breath.

"Don't choke to death before I have a chance to marry you."

Emma could tell he was trying to add levity to the situation, but her ears were ringing and her pulse was pounding in her temples. She forced herself to calm down, took a long sip of the water, and then carefully placed the glass back on the table.

"Henry, did you say it happened outside your home?" She pointed toward the road. "That the accident started there?"

"Yeah."

"And your buggy looks the same as Seth's."

"You know all of our buggies are nearly identical."

Emma closed her eyes, determined to wish away the thought dominating her brain, but the effort was futile. "You both have beards, you're about the same height, and basically you wear the same clothes."

She opened her eyes, leaned forward, and said, "What if they meant to run *you* off the road?"

"Say again?"

"What if the person who did this thought they were running you off the road? They could have thought they were following you home, or maybe they were aware of your address, and the buggies look the same..."

"Why would someone do that?"

"Which scenario is more likely? That someone is cruising down a country road, minding their own business, and suddenly decides to run Seth and Roseann into the ditch, for no reason at all—"

"Could have been an accident."

"You admitted Seth said it seemed intentional."

"He could have been mistaken."

"So we have three options." Emma ticked them off on her fingers. "Seth is confused, and it was an accident. It was not an accident, and the person intended to run Seth and Roseann off the road—"

"Maybe he simply doesn't like Amish buggies."

"Or it's our killer, and he thinks you know something. He's warning you away."

"That's ridiculous," Henry said, but the expression on his face told her he was worried.

"First there was the warning on your buggy, and now a near-fatal accident."

"Could be a coincidence."

"Henry, we need to figure out who did this."

"Grayson is figuring that out. We don't need to be involved this time."

"You told me you were going to start drawing. That you felt the need to try to help."

"And I meant to, but I've been rather busy of late." He sipped from his coffee mug, and she knew he was considering what she'd just said. Finally, he leaned forward and tapped the table. "I will try to draw the night of the rodeo, but as far as involving ourselves, I think this investigation is best left up to Sheriff Grayson."

"I agree with you. Or I did, but now I'm not so sure."

"You feel strongly about this."

"We can't just sit back and wait."

"Actually, we can."

"Not if you're in danger. Not if this person isn't finished yet."

"But, Emma, I don't know anything."

"I know that. You know that. But Jeremiah's killer? Something tells me he's worried, and that his biggest worry is you."

Twenty-Eight

Grayson stopped by Henry's house later that afternoon.

Before he could update him on any new developments in the case—or the lack thereof—Henry shared Emma's concern that he might be the recipient of the killer's attention.

"I was made aware of the accident, but thinking the person intended to harm you seems like a jump in logic to me." They were in Henry's workshop. Grayson picked up a birdhouse made from old barn lumber. Henry had fashioned a roof from an old license plate and bent a discarded spoon to provide a bird perch. A sticker with the price of ten dollars was affixed to the top. "There's nothing in Seth's statement to suggest the person was aiming for you, though I'll admit that sort of intentional aggression is out of the ordinary in this community."

"It's certainly never happened here before, not to my knowledge."

"There was the fatality...What was the family's name? Weaver?"

"Terrible tragedy, but the driver was intoxicated. It wasn't intentional in any sense."

Grayson sighed, pulled ten dollars out of his wallet, and handed it to Henry. "My wife will love this."

"*Danki.*"

"How about in Goshen? Did your community experience any type of harassment there?"

"*Nein.* The occasional accident happened, but it was mostly a case of distracted drivers. They'd speed up on a buggy, not realizing how close they were until they'd bumped into them."

"You do look alike."

"He's twenty years younger."

"Can't tell that when you're following a buggy, and they do look identical."

"So you think Emma has a point?"

"I think she could have a point, which isn't quite the same thing. I don't know how it will change our investigation, but maybe we should heed her warning. Maybe you should heed it."

"What does that mean?"

"Keep your nose out of things. Lay low for a while. Don't you bishops ever go on vacation?"

Henry laughed at the frustrated look on Grayson's face. "Emma and I will be traveling over to Westcliffe a few weeks after we're married."

"That's not a vacation. That's a day trip."

"For *Englischers* maybe..."

"Seriously, Henry. Would you like me to have an officer put you on their route? Wouldn't hurt to have someone passing by here every few hours."

"And see what? Oreo cropping grass in the field and Lexi chasing squirrels?" He put the money in an old cigar box he kept on a shelf behind him. "Sounds like a misuse of resources to me."

"At least promise me you'll be extra vigilant."

"Of course."

"Maybe we should run a piece in the paper, declaring the police department is at a loss because Henry Lapp didn't see a thing."

Henry didn't answer that. He had no desire to see his name in the newspaper again.

"There is one other reason I stopped by." Grayson pulled a piece of paper from his pocket, unfolded it, and laid it on the table between them. "This is a copy of one of the pages in Jeremiah's notebook—the one his mother found. We think he was running a gambling operation on the side."

"Gambling?"

"That's the only logical explanation we can come up with given what you see there, and it would explain Piper Cox's comment that Jeremiah was arguing with someone over money."

"It's just hard to imagine. Surely I would have heard something if a gambling ring was in my own district." Henry pulled on his reading glasses and peered more closely at the sheet of paper. "What's this column?"

"Initials of the person who placed the bet."

"This?"

"The amount of money wagered."

"And this?"

"The odds."

"So this is the payout."

"Correct. It's small-time stuff, as you can see, but it adds up to a fair amount of money."

"I'm sorry I didn't know. I would have intervened. This reflects badly on our community, plus it's illegal. I had no idea Jeremiah had strayed so far."

"I'm not saying you should have known. People are good at hiding their real feelings as well as activities they're ashamed of."

"Indeed."

"We've already figured out who the highlighted initials belong to, but these other ones...well, there isn't exactly a directory of Amish youth."

"You think these are Amish names?"

"There's a good chance. Anyone you recognize?"

"Well, maybe...but then it could be anyone."

"If you could take a guess, I could go and speak with them." He held up a hand to stop Henry's protest. "I won't accuse them of anything, but it's possible they know who could have been upset with Jeremiah. Who could have killed him. This list is as good a place as any to start."

So Henry gave him the names that might coincide with the initials, though he prayed it wasn't true.

MG—Mahlon Graber

NK—Nathan Kline

JK—Jesse Kauffmann

LY—Lloyd Yutzy

It was only four of their *youngies*, but still it pierced his heart to think they might have been involved.

"Don't look so devastated. I've seen bigger gambling operations at the local high school."

"High school?"

"Sure. We had this one kid who would bet on anything—how many people would pass the science final, who would get a date with Joanna McBride, when the gym teacher was going to have her baby..."

"Who would bet on the birth of a child?"

"You'd be surprised." Grayson's eyes had taken on a decided twinkle.

"I'm missing the joke."

"It was me, Henry."

"You?"

"I thought I was hot stuff when I was seventeen, smarter than the rest, definitely above the law."

"You took bets from other students...in high school?"

"I even had some of the teachers in on it." Grayson slapped his hat on his head as they walked back outside into the afternoon heat. "Fortunately, the principal who caught me put me on the straight and narrow, which is why I'm the upstanding citizen you see before you today."

When Grayson was back at his vehicle and Lexi had dashed off after a rabbit, Henry remembered what Chester had told him the day before.

"If you're planning on interviewing those boys in person, best get hold of Lloyd Yutzy tonight. He's staying with Chester Yoder, but Chester told me Lloyd is probably headed back to Goshen by the end of the week."

"As in tomorrow?"

"Yeah. I believe the bus for Goshen comes through early in the morning."

"Then I'll see him tonight."

"Would you like me to come along?"

"Not necessary. If I need you, I'll send someone to pick you up."

"Would you mind if I spoke with them, in a group, and encouraged them to be open and honest with you?"

"Actually, I'd appreciate it."

"Consider it done, then."

He'd been planning on starting a project for a garden bench an *Englischer* had hired him to do. After that he was going to begin drawing scenes from the rodeo, but the boys took precedence over that. He'd go to the phone shack, leaves messages for them, and then he'd spend some time in the Good Book. Because, honestly, he had no idea what to say to boys—young men, actually—who seemed determined to turn their backs on their faith.

Twenty-Nine

Transcript of interview between Monte Vista Sheriff Roy Grayson and Lloyd Yutzy, regarding the July 27 homicide of Jeremiah Schwartz. Audio-tapes and a transcript of the interview are included in the permanent case file.

Sheriff Roy Grayson #3604
INTERVIEW WITH Lloyd Yutzy
Case #4751.06
8:15 p.m., Thursday, August 2

Sheriff Grayson (SG): Could you state your name for the recording?
Lloyd Yutzy (LY): Lloyd Yutzy.
SG: Middle name?
LY: No, sir. Most Amish don't have middle names, at least not in Indiana where I grew up. We use initials instead. Mine is Y. Lloyd Y. Yutzy. I know that sounds strange, but we use our father's last name for our middle initial.
SG: Lloyd, I asked you to come into the station this evening because I have a few questions about your relationship with Jeremiah Schwartz.
LY: Absolutely. I'd be happy to answer any questions I can.
SG: I also want to remind you that you're not under arrest at this time You're free to leave or contact a lawyer at any point in this interview.
LY: I'm sure that won't be necessary.
SG: Let's start with the gambling records. Are these your initials referred to in Jeremiah's notebook?
LY: Yes, sir. They are.

SG: So you placed bets with Jeremiah.

LY: I did. Seemed harmless enough, though some might consider it a waste of money.

SG: How much money would you say you've gambled with Jeremiah in the last year?

LY: Oh, not much. I'm pretty careful with my money. Pretty frugal. It's one of the things about Amish I suppose you know, since there's a community here. We're a bit tightfisted with our money.

SG: So you'd be surprised if I told you that you'd lost nearly two thousand dollars in the last year?

LY: I would be surprised. Yes, sir. Those were mostly fifty-dollar bets, so I'd be surprised to hear they'd added up to so much.

SG: Can you tell me how this worked?

LY: This?

SG: The gambling. How did you place your bets? Or know what there was to bet on?

LY: Oh, that. Well, Jeremiah would call and leave a message at a phone shack—didn't really matter which one, because word would get around. Maybe he'd say *Friday night's rodeo*, and we'd all know what that meant. He'd go on to list the events and the odds.

SG: And how would you place a bet?

LY: That's what his cell phone was for. Now, technically we're not supposed to have cell phones, but this was for work—at least that's the way I believe Jeremiah thought of it, and so it was okay.

SG: So you'd call his cell phone.

LY: Yes, sir. We'd call him back and leave a message, like what we wanted to bet on and how much.

SG: How did you pay up?

LY: When Jeremiah was in Goshen, that was pretty easy. Once he'd moved here, it was a bit harder. If I'm to be honest, that's part of the reason I came down. Quite a few people owed Jeremiah money, so I offered to bring it down to him.

SG: Why would you offer to do that?

LY: Probably had more to do with Naomi than with my kindheartedness.

SG: Naomi Miller?

LY: I took a liking to her last time she was in Goshen visiting, and I was hoping to begin courting her proper.

SG: It's my understanding that Naomi was dating Jeremiah.

LY: Well, that may be, but Jeremiah told me he was moving west, and that he planned to do so alone.

SG: What did you think of his involvement in the rodeo and of his plans to be on a television show?

LY: Can't say as I gave it much thought.

SG: You didn't feel that Jeremiah needed to be corrected, to be set on the straight and narrow?

LY: Why would I think that?

SG: Apparently some in your community, some of the Amish young men, felt Jeremiah had strayed. They were giving him a hard time about it.

LY: I'm not aware of any trouble Jeremiah had with others.

SG: So you didn't feel the need to correct him in some way?

LY: No, sir. That would be the bishop's job.

SG: Back to the girl...

LY: Naomi.

SG: Jeremiah told you he was moving west.

LY: He did.

SG: What was your thought process when you found that out?

LY: My thought process?

SG: Did you see it as your opportunity to swoop into town and catch the girl?

LY: I suppose you could see it that way. Yes, sir. I like to think that God was opening a door I'd prayed for long and hard. He was making it possible for me to court Naomi.

SG: When you arrived in town, did you deliver the money to Jeremiah, the money from Goshen?

LY: I did. When I first arrived here.

SG: And when was that?

LY: Before the rodeo...I think it was a Thursday. Yeah, the Thursday before the rodeo.

SG: July 26.

LY: Sounds right.

SG: And you gave Jeremiah the money.

LY: I did. He met me at the bus station. I gave him the money, and then he drove me out to Mary and Chester Yoder's place, where I'm staying.

SG: Do you know anyone who would want to harm Jeremiah?

LY: No, sir.

SG: Were you angry with Jeremiah?

LY: No, sir.

SG: Lloyd, do you know who shot Jeremiah Schwartz on the night of July 27?

LY: I don't. I wish I did, wish I could help you, but I don't have any idea who would do such a thing.

SG: Is there anything you'd like to add?

LY: No, sir. I can't think of anything that would be relevant.

SG: That's all the questions I have for now. If you think of anything else, especially the names of any persons who might have wanted to harm Jeremiah, please call me.

LY: Yes, sir. I certainly will.

SG: I understand you're headed back to Goshen soon.

LY: I haven't quite decided when I'll go back. The Yoders are real friendly people, and I'm enjoying my stay with them.

SG: All right. Thank you for coming in. I'll be in touch if we have any follow-up questions.

Thirty

Naomi was sitting in her room, copies of the *Budget* spread out across her bed, when she heard a light tap on her door.

"Come in."

"Am I bothering you?" Katie Ann popped her head around the edge of the door, but she didn't come into the room—not yet. She wouldn't until Naomi said it was okay. They had that kind of friendship, where it was perfectly acceptable to say you didn't feel like visiting.

"Of course you're not bothering me."

So she slipped inside, quietly shut the door, and perched on the edge of Naomi's bed.

"Whatcha doing here?"

"Just looking at the articles I wrote over the last six months. I guess I'm trying to get an idea for this month, but my mind is having trouble focusing on any one thing."

"Hard to believe you've been a scribe for nearly a year."

"Six months."

"Which is a few months short of a year."

Naomi squirmed backward so that her back was resting against the wall and Katie Ann did the same. She drummed her fingertips against her notebook and asked, "Did you hear about Sheriff Grayson calling in Mahlon and Nathan and Jesse?"

"And Lloyd. Don't forget Lloyd."

Naomi tried to freeze her features, but there was no use attempting to keep anything from her best friend. Katie Ann knew her too well.

"What happened now?" Katie Ann asked.

"It was no big deal."

"Tell me. All of it."

So she described how she'd been walking along the side of the road, and then Lloyd had practically insisted she get into the buggy with him, and then the awkwardness of the conversation that followed.

"He asked you to move back to Goshen?" Instead of looking alarmed, Katie Ann dissolved into a fit of giggles.

"He didn't exactly ask. It was more a statement of what he thought I should do and an expectation that I'd jump right to it—which wasn't funny at all."

"No, but I can imagine the look on your face, and that must have been funny. You hated living in Goshen. You said it made you feel like a hamster in a cage."

"It is a bit more crowded than here."

"So how did Lloyd take it when you told him you weren't interested?"

"He kind of scowled at me, and then he told me to think about it before I said no."

"Thinking won't change how you feel."

"You and I know that." She traced the bruise on her left wrist with the tips of her fingers.

"Did he do that to you, Naomi?" Katie Ann's voice was suddenly serious. "Did Lloyd hurt you?"

"He didn't mean to. I was about to leave, and he pulled me back into the buggy. I don't think he knows his own strength."

"He should. And he should treat a woman with more care. Maybe we should tell your *aenti* or speak to Henry."

"I don't want to talk to anyone about Lloyd Yutzy."

"Yes, but—"

"He'll be gone in a few days, and I can forget about him."

"I guess. In my opinion, he can't leave too soon. I'm anxious to be rid of him, and I've barely spent any time around him at all."

"Patience is a virtue, right?"

"Maybe. *Mammi* is always saying things like *adopt the pace of nature; her secret is patience.*"

Katie Ann began laughing again, and this time Naomi joined her.

It wasn't very funny, so she didn't know why she was laughing. It felt good, though, and allowed the tension in her shoulders to ease. Finally, Naomi wiped her eyes and asked, "Do you have any idea what she means?"

"None." Naomi picked up a copy of the *Budget*. "Let's look at these articles and see what you haven't written about yet."

They spent the next thirty minutes looking over the previous six months' issues. As a scribe, Naomi wasn't paid, but she did receive copies of the publication for free. Also, paper and postage were provided, so sending in her column didn't cost her anything. She loved writing, and the fact that more than seventeen thousand people read the *Budget* always inspired her. To think that you could pick it up and know what was going on in Goshen or Sarasota or Lancaster...She'd once seen a letter written by a scribe in Romania.

People wanted to know what was happening in other places, other Amish places, and that was the main reason she wrote—that, and she loved putting together sentences in a clever way, describing a scene so someone who had never visited their valley could imagine it, and writing about people. She enjoyed sharing the unique characteristics of people more than anything else, maybe because she found folks fascinating. But in life she was often somewhat shy. When she was writing, she could hide behind the pen. The best part was that if she said something wrong, or used a word that didn't quite fit, or left something out, she could always pull out a fresh sheet of paper and start over. The last piece she'd written and mailed in was before Jeremiah's death—she'd felt young and happy and carefree then. Now it seemed the days were gloomy even when the sun was shining.

She pulled out her last article, and Katie Ann scooted closer so they could read it together.

MONTE VISTA, COLORADO

July 18—Days are warming up in the San Luis Valley.

We experienced heavy rains last week, a real delight here in the valley. Local farmers say the crops are coming along well and expect a good harvest next month.

Susan Graber hosted a sew-in at her place. Attending were Franey Graber, Rachel Fisher, Katie Ann Fisher, Emma Fisher, Nancy Kline, Mary Yoder, and myself. We worked on three quilts for the upcoming school auction—including a center diamond, log cabin, and double wedding ring.

Deborah King's newborn baby shows no signs of the colic, which her first child suffered from terribly.

The church service on Sunday was well attended, with only Josephine Glick missing, owing to morning sickness.

Leroy Kauffmann hosted the evening hymn singing, which lasted late into the night. We had four visitors. Three cousins of the Grabers traveled all the way from Shipshewana to spend a month in the valley. Jeremiah Schwartz has been visiting all summer. Jeremiah's from Goshen, but spending a few months with his grandmother, Ruth Schwartz. Jeremiah will ride in the Ski Hi Rodeo later this month. He's done well competing this season and continues to excel at his favorite event—steer wrestling.

The widows' bakery, formally known as Bread 2 Go, continues to draw visitors from all over the valley. Franey Graber, Nancy Kline, and Ruth Schwartz say they might need to expand by the end of the summer to keep up with demand. Seems Amish and *Englisch* alike enjoy a fresh loaf of bread or sweet snack.

It's a sure sign of summer if the chair gets up when you do (Walter Winchell).

Naomi Miller

"Where did you get this last line?" Katie Ann asked. "It's clever."

"From a book the librarian gave me. I was returning a novel your *mamm* asked me to carry to the library last time I was over."

"It's crazy how much she reads."

"I think it's sweet. Anyway, the book the librarian gave me was about gardening and summer and such. It's in perfectly good shape, but she said they had to purge their collections—whatever that means. I like the book, though. It has short quotes and such, and I enjoy ending my pieces on a light note."

Katie Ann's fingers traced down the page again. "I like the way you write. It's conversational. I can imagine you saying these things."

"No use in using a three-syllable word if a one-syllable word will do." Katie Ann reached up to adjust her *kapp*, which had slipped toward the back. "Do you remember hearing that in school?"

"I do. I guess school here in the valley isn't much different from school in Goshen."

"Don't laugh, but I miss it some days."

"Me too. Though other days, like when my *bruders* bring home math homework, I don't miss it at all." Katie Ann picked up the paper and studied it more closely.

"What?"

"I was just thinking."

"Thinking what? You're going to stare a hole through the paper."

"This came out a week and a half before the rodeo, before Jeremiah was killed, right?" She pointed to the July 18 date in the top left corner. "What if someone read your article, and...I don't know...didn't like the thought of Jeremiah being in the rodeo?"

"So they came here and killed him? That doesn't sound likely."

"*Nein*. You're right. Guess I'm grasping at straws here."

"Sounds to me like it has more to do with his gambling, which by the way explains why he was always clearing his phone history. I guess he didn't want me to know about it. Plus, now I understand why he took so long in the phone shack when I was waiting in the buggy."

"So you think his killer was someone who owed him money?"

"I think if our boys owed that much—"

"I heard it totaled four thousand dollars."

"I heard five. But regardless of the amount, if an Amish boy can get in that deep, then think how much an *Englischer* could have owed."

"Or been owed."

"Exactly."

"What should we do?" Katie Ann folded the newspaper and tossed it back on the bed.

"Nothing. We should stay out of it."

"*Ya. Gut* idea."

"Sheriff Grayson will handle it."

"I hope so. Now let's come up with some ideas for what you can write about this month."

They spent the next hour going over the insignificant happenings in their small community during the last few weeks. That felt good and proper to Naomi. She was tired of thinking about murder and killers and gambling rings. But writing about the goats and sheep that escaped during Jeremiah's funeral? That brought a smile to her lips, and she was pretty sure that if Jeremiah were still around, he'd be smiling too.

Thirty-One

Henry woke on Friday morning with the overwhelming urge to do something.

It had been a week since Jeremiah's death, and it didn't seem to him as if they were any closer to catching the killer. He knew from his experience in Goshen that such investigations usually took months, not weeks—and yet he was impatient to have the situation resolved.

As Henry let Lexi outside, made his breakfast, and watched the sun rise over the valley, he fought the impulse to jump into the investigation. It wasn't his place to nose around. He wasn't a sleuth or a detective of any sort. Perhaps he understood a little about human nature, but then what bishop or pastor didn't? The same could be said for nurses or teachers or waitresses. If you worked with people and you paid attention, you learned some things.

For instance, he knew from the meeting he'd had with Mahlon, Nathan, Jesse, and Lloyd the day before that the boys weren't being completely honest with him, though they were hardly boys. They were men, and it was important that they learn to act responsibly. He'd called the meeting after Grayson left and caught most of them as they'd come in from the field and before they'd had dinner. They'd done it at Abe's place, which was central to where the four lived. Apparently, none had been approached by Grayson yet, so he hoped he'd accomplished something good when he reminded them of their responsibility to be honest and help in the investigation.

Still, he was worried.

Sometimes dishonesty wasn't a matter of telling a lie. Sometimes it was as simple as not volunteering the truth.

He didn't know Lloyd well, but he'd known Mahlon, Nathan, and Jesse since they were born. They had been good children. Their *rumspringa* had been marginal at its worst. They were still relatively young and hadn't been baptized into the church yet, though Mahlon and Jesse had both come to him and announced their intentions to do so.

No, they weren't the type to be in trouble—hard workers every one of them, which made the gambling all the more surprising. What else were they hiding?

He couldn't know.

He saw no obvious reason to involve himself further, and yet the itch to do exactly that plagued him.

He knew what that meant. It meant his ego was getting in the way. So instead of jumping up and *doing something*, Henry fetched his Bible from where he'd left it on the kitchen table, refreshed his coffee, and spent the next hour in prayer and meditation of the Scriptures on the front porch. Henry didn't consider himself more spiritual than any other man. He made mistakes same as everyone else. The difference was that over the years he'd come to expect to see God's hand in all things. Guiding a flock could do that to a man, make him sensitive to the voice of the shepherd.

So what was God urging him to do, if indeed this restless feeling was more than frustration?

As he opened his Bible, he prayed God would guide his reading.

> *The word of God is alive and active. Sharper than any double-edged sword, it penetrates even to dividing soul and spirit, joints and marrow; it judges the thoughts and attitudes of the heart.*

He could count on the lines he was reading, the Word of God, to judge the thoughts and attitudes of his heart. Encouraged by the words from Hebrews, he turned to Galatians.

> *Carry each other's burdens, and in this way you will fulfill the law of Christ.*

He'd been trying to solve this mystery on his own, but that wasn't what the Bible admonished him to do. Rather, he was to carry the burdens of others, and they were to carry his.

"That's it!"

Lexi jumped to attention.

"We're trying to do it alone again when we should be asking for help."

Lexi cocked her head to the side as if she were wondering why it took him so long to reach that conclusion.

"Care to go for a walk, girl?"

That was all it took for Lexi to bound off the porch steps. Henry wasn't absolutely sure about the scope of his beagle's vocabulary. He'd read that dogs could understand as much as two hundred and fifty words. He didn't know about that, but he did know she understood the word *walk*, and the fact that she was waiting at the bottom of the steps, tail wagging and butt wiggling, proved it.

They were at the phone shack within twenty minutes, and three phone calls later he'd scheduled a meeting with his deacons. They might not know what to do either, but they'd pray with him. And at this point, that was something Henry sorely needed.

✠

That afternoon Abe, Leroy, Clyde, and Henry spent the first thirty minutes in prayer, and then Henry stood and poured coffee for everyone. Nancy Kline had brought by a platter of snickerdoodle cookies, so he put that in the middle of the table. Sugar and caffeine were exactly what they needed to solve this thing.

"I don't mind saying I'm quite upset that Mahlon is involved in this." Abe frowned into his mug. "I have him doing extra chores and also finding direction from the Scripture, where we're told to be good stewards of all we have."

"Nancy mentioned that Nathan's parents are upset as well," Henry said.

"And who wouldn't be?" Leroy stared at his cookie and then stuffed it into his mouth. Once he'd washed it down with coffee, he added, "I'm beside myself about Jesse's involvement. Never saw it coming. Never suspected a thing."

"It's important to remember they are relatively young." Clyde sat back and crossed his arms.

"Young?" Abe shook his head. "You and I had a wife and child by that age."

"It does seem as if *youngies* are waiting a few years longer to marry, to commit to a Plain life," Henry admitted. "Some say the young adult years are extending nearly to thirty now."

"Thirty?" Leroy shook his head in disbelief.

"Well, that's in the *Englisch* community. Apparently, it's a mark of the millennial generation."

"What's a millennial?" Abe asked.

"Someone born between 1995 and 2005. Something like that."

"Sounds like foolishness to me." Clyde's smile belied the seriousness of his tone. "A twenty-three-year-old is not a boy. He's a man."

"It proves a point, though. The fact that our boys, or rather men, are waiting until twenty-two or twenty-three to begin a family...well, it isn't such a terrible thing."

Clyde said, "I would be upset too if Silas were involved. The only reason he wasn't, I suspect, is that he spends every extra dime courting."

"Still hasn't settled down?" Abe asked.

"*Nein.* If anything, it's worse. Last week he was out four different nights. I don't know how he manages to get up at four thirty in the morning, but he does. And as long as he does, I feel I have no reason to reprimand him. Still, it bothers me."

"I think our gamblers understand the error of their ways," Henry said, turning the conversation back to the matter at hand. "Knowing that the money won't be returned to them, even if they did *win*, should help to change their attitudes about gambling."

"What happened to the money?" Leroy asked.

"Lloyd says he gave the money from Goshen to Jeremiah. Each of our boys say they paid what they owed, but..." Henry pulled on his beard. "Grayson mentioned that Jeremiah had less than twenty dollars in his wallet, and Ruth has found nothing at her house."

"So the money's missing?" Leroy reached for another cookie, changed his mind, and clutched his coffee mug.

"Apparently."

"How much are we talking about, Henry?" Clyde stood up, fetched the coffeepot, and refilled their mugs.

"Hard to say exactly. Grayson is thinking close to ten thousand."

"That's more money than most of us see in a year." Leroy shook his head. "I'm still in shock, to tell the truth."

"It's a lot of money when you add it all together, but you have to remember it's not all Amish money. Grayson says more than half of it came from *Englischers*—people in the rodeo as well as their friends. Jeremiah was running quite an operation, taking bets from both Amish and *Englisch*."

They all fell silent at the thought of that. The clock ticked, and Lexi yipped at something in her dreams.

Finally, it was Clyde who sat forward and asked, "Why did you invite us here? It's a *gut* idea, don't get me wrong. It helps to discuss these matters as a family of believers, but what did you hope we could accomplish?"

"That's the thing. I don't know. I feel that we should be doing something, but I'm at a loss as to what."

"Have you thought about..." Abe made the motion of holding a pen and drawing.

"I have, but as you know, I didn't see the murder."

"It's possible you saw something else, though."

"I hardly know where to begin."

"Then that's where we start." Leroy slapped the table and sat up straighter. "We pray that *Gotte* will show you what to draw, that He will guide your hand. *Gotte* gave you this talent, Henry. It makes sense that you're to use it."

Henry was humbled by his friends' faith in him, by their acceptance of his odd ability. But he was also comforted, knowing they were on his side, as they had always been.

"There is something else we can do," Clyde said. "We ask for the *youngies* help. We want them to be responsible, to act like men, so we give them a chance to do that. We give them a chance to make this right."

"What exactly do you have in mind?" Abe asked.

"They know the *Englisch youngies* and we don't. They know how the operation worked. Maybe they can find the missing money."

Leroy stood and rinsed out his mug, and then he turned back toward them, leaning against the counter and crossing his arms. "Wouldn't that be putting them in harm's way?"

"It would seem to me that the killer is long gone," Clyde said.

"I don't know." Henry told them about the message on his buggy, about Seth being run off the road, and Emma's theory that the killer might have been targeting him.

"But why would the killer stick around? That would be terribly dangerous and stupid." Leroy shrugged his shoulders. "We all know *Englisch* motorists get frustrated when our buggies slow them down. I'm sorry about what happened to Seth, but I don't see its connection to this."

Abe nodded his head in agreement. "The chalking on your buggy sounds like a prank, though one done in very poor taste."

Clyde returned the discussion to his idea. "We could start by looking for someone who has conspicuously left the area."

"Which I'm sure Grayson is doing," Henry pointed out.

"True, but this is a big area if you include Alamosa. He can't check every person who has left town since last Friday. Our *youngies*, though, they..." Clyde seemed to be gaining steam, more certain as he spoke that his idea would produce results. "Our *youngies* know who the *Englischers* involved were. They can give us a list of names, maybe even tell us who the high rollers were."

Abe had just devoured one more cookie. "They wouldn't want to rat out their friends."

"The jig is up," Clyde said. "We're on to them, so they won't be making any more bets. Besides, it's the *Englischer* names we want. We already have the Amish ones."

"Let's not be too quick to assume an *Englischer* did this thing. We can't know." Henry didn't believe it was an Amish person, but he felt the need to add a word of caution nonetheless.

"Our sons—and daughters—want to be treated like adults." Clyde studied each person around the room. "I'm not saying put them in danger. There's no need to send them out looking for this person, but they need to face the fact that they became involved in something more sinister than they bargained for."

"If the killing had to do with the money..." Henry wasn't sure that was right, but he had to admit it was a possibility. What other motive could there have been?

"So no one is opposed to including them?" Clyde asked. "*Gut*. We'll speak to them tonight. Our *youngies* worked their way into this situation. Let's see if they can figure a way out."

Thirty-Two

Emma sat in her rocker in the sitting room, crocheting a baby blanket. When she was younger, she used to crochet and knit quite a bit, but then her life grew busy with grandchildren and farm work and real-life murder mysteries. Silas had challenged her to find a normal hobby after the incident on the sand dunes when she and Henry were being chased by Sophia Brooks's killer. A nice, quiet, safe hobby had sounded like a good idea, and so she'd searched in the bottom of her sewing box for the crochet needles. She'd finished half a dozen baby blankets and countless baby caps since then.

Now she was working with a variegated color—a pale yellow and green. She could just imagine a newborn baby snuggled in it. She wasn't the fastest person at crocheting, and she knew many Amish women preferred knitting, but she was learning to enjoy the process—the feel of the needle pulling the yarn, the way the stitches formed tidy rows, the repetitive motion that soothed her nerves.

And three of the reasons for her nerves were sitting in front of her—Clyde, Silas, and Katie Ann. Rachel had gone to bed early with a headache, which was code for she was tired and would rather be reading. Clyde had already explained the situation to her, and although she wasn't particularly fond of the idea, she understood the reasoning and offered her prayers and blessings for success.

The younger boys—Stephen and Thomas—were already in bed, though occasionally Emma heard laughter drift down from upstairs.

"*Mamm*'s okay with it, *Mammi*. Why aren't you?" Silas asked.

"I think I can answer that." Katie Ann plucked a throw pillow from the couch and wrapped her arms around it. "*Mammi* was with me and Henry when we caught the Monte Vista arsonist. She doesn't want us involved in that sort of thing again."

"You're absolutely right." Emma kept her eyes on her crocheting, but she nodded her head vigorously.

"And then there was that mess at the top of the sand dunes." Clyde's voice was teasing.

"You're not taking this seriously enough. We could have been killed up there, catching Sophia Brooks's killer."

"I'm not taking it seriously enough?" Clyde laughed out loud now. "You're the one who keeps stumbling into these situations."

"But Henry thinks we should do this," Silas reminded her. "If he agrees it's a *gut* idea, and he's our bishop and all..."

"Not to mention he's about to be our *grossdaddi*..." Katie Ann grinned broadly when Emma pierced her with a stare.

"You know, I haven't really talked to you all about that. How do you feel about my marrying Henry?"

All three stared at her as if she'd stuck the crochet needle into her prayer *kapp*.

"What I mean is, I don't want you to think I'm being disrespectful."

Clyde's voice was gentle, and his smile melted all the worry in her heart. "It's been nearly six years, *Mamm*. And you know we all care for Henry."

"And it isn't as if he'll be replacing *Daddi*." Silas crossed his right foot over his left knee. "He was *Daddi*'s friend. I remember how they'd play washers together."

"We're happy that you're happy," Katie Ann added. "And while Henry isn't my grandfather, he's the next best thing. It's as if...as if *Gotte* knew how much we miss *Daddi* and is providing someone else in our lives to help fill the void. Did I say that right?"

"You said it perfectly," Clyde assured her.

Finally Emma sighed and dropped the crochet project into her lap, giving her family her full attention.

"So you're okay with our idea?" Silas asked.

"I'm not going against my bishop, or my soon-to-be husband..."
Emma shook her head when Silas and Katie Ann high-fived. "I just
don't know what you hope to accomplish, what good you could possibly do. You know Grayson is working hard on the investigation, and
he's a very capable man."

"Didn't help with the Monte Vista arsonist," Silas reminded her.

"Or Sophia's killer." Katie Ann's expression grew somber at the
memory.

"I understand your concerns, *Mamm*." Clyde crossed his arms and
stuck his thumbs under his suspenders. He stared at the darkness that
had fallen outside the window, carefully choosing his words. "We often
ask our *youngies* to act responsibly, to consider the repercussions of anything they do. We remind them of the importance of the *Ordnung*, and
that its rules are to help prevent them from straying, to keep them on
the path of living a godly life, a simple and humble life. But then when
it's time to trust them with these decisions or allow them to feel the consequences, we falter. We're no better than the *Englisch* in this respect,
encouraging children to remain children long past the time it's proper
for them to do so."

"A little harsh, but basically I agree with you." Silas looked pleased
with himself until Clyde pointed a finger at him.

"Don't think you are exempt, son."

"Didn't say I was."

"Your easy way with the girls borders on disrespect."

"It doesn't. I mean no harm."

"It's possible to mean no harm and still inflict harm."

Silas had no answer for that, choosing to pick at the dirt under his
fingernails instead.

"Back to this meeting..." Emma didn't want a fight about Silas's dating habits. They needed to stay focused.

"We're not asking you to find a killer," Clyde clarified. "You chose to
be involved in gambling—"

"*We* didn't," Katie Ann and Silas said in unison.

"As a community, our *youngies* chose this path, so as a community
perhaps we can find a way back from it."

"Which would involve what, exactly?" Emma was growing tired. She pulled off her reading glasses and rubbed at her eyes.

"*Gut* question." Clyde turned his attention to Silas and Katie Ann. "The way we—the church leaders and Henry—see it, you could provide a list of names, *Englischers* and Amish if we missed any, who were involved in this thing. You could get some sense for who the high rollers were and who was just dabbling in it."

"We won't snitch on one another," Silas said.

"You shouldn't have to. You should volunteer the information, and lastly, we need to know where the money is. Did Lloyd turn it over to Jeremiah as he said he did? If he did, then where is it? Did the killer steal it from Jeremiah?"

"How?" Katie Ann asked. "The person shot him from the other side of the arena."

"I've been thinking about that," Emma admitted. "Whoever planned to kill Jeremiah—and it had to be planned—could have done so any number of places, but instead the person chose a public venue. He must have been making a statement, but what was it?"

Silas put his hand over his mouth, stifling a yawn. "I see *Dat*'s point, though. Find the money, and we'll probably find the killer."

"Maybe he stole it before the murder took place." Clyde frowned now, as if that didn't quite make sense even to him.

"If he'd stolen it beforehand, there would have been no need to kill Jeremiah—if the money was the reason he was killed." Katie Ann sighed and began plucking at the pillow in her arms.

Clyde thought on that a minute. Emma knew he was carefully considering what each person said, and she appreciated that about him. Clyde wasn't one to make a proclamation and expect everyone to follow it. He believed in the importance of gathering a family consensus whenever possible. "Perhaps our murderer stole it afterward, then. Has anyone seen anything suspicious around Ruth's house? Did someone break in and take the money before she returned home? Who suddenly has a large bundle of cash?"

They continued discussing different aspects of the case and what information they needed. Katie Ann hurried to the kitchen, rummaged in a drawer, and found a piece of paper and pen. She wrote down the most pressing questions. Then Silas and Katie Ann agreed they would meet with the others the following evening, without adults, and learn as much as possible.

Emma realized the *youngies* wouldn't necessarily be in danger if they did what Clyde asked. They wouldn't be setting a trap for the culprit or chasing him down. Their children might sometimes push the boundaries of the *Ordnung*, but they were good at heart. They were pacifists at heart. They wouldn't harm anyone.

And their information could be of benefit to Sheriff Grayson.

The only question was what would happen if the killer caught wind of it all. And if the killer was still in the vicinity, would he feel pressured to act again?

Thirty-Three

The young people in the Monte Vista Amish community met on Saturday evening. They sat in a semicircle inside Leroy Kauffmann's barn. Soft light lingered outside, enough that they could see one another without the help of lanterns or flashlights. Naomi sat clutching a notepad and pen, with Katie Ann on her right and Albert Bontrager on her left. She didn't know Albert very well. She knew he was farming his parents' land, that his family had moved out of the valley when the Monte Vista arsonist was still on the loose, and he was in his early twenties. He was also shy and kept stealing glances at Katie Ann.

Katie Ann was watching a mare in an adjacent stall and had no idea Albert was checking her out. The Kauffmanns' barn was considerably bigger than most. Leroy also had more buggy horses, workhorses, and livestock than anyone else in their community. His was a big operation, though he did nothing to draw attention to that fact. It was just something they all accepted. Leroy Kauffmann and his family were the wealthiest among them.

The gathering resembled a Sunday evening singing, but without the youngest of their group present. Someone had decided only those seventeen and up would be involved, and only those unmarried—the logic being that anyone married wouldn't have the time or funds to participate in something as risky as gambling.

All told, a dozen or so were present, including most of the boys who had been questioned by the police. Lloyd Yutzy was conspicuously absent. Naomi hoped that meant he'd returned to Indiana. She knew most of the boys and girls, though not all. She should, but she'd never been good at remembering names. Because she hadn't been raised in the valley, she didn't let that concern her. If she were to stay—which she hadn't yet decided to do—she would eventually know everyone's name. The community wasn't so large, which was one thing she liked about it.

When it seemed that everyone who was going to arrive had, Silas Fisher started the meeting.

"Guess everyone knows what this meeting is about."

There were several grunts and groans, and some nervous laughter. Naomi thought she heard someone in the back of the barn, maybe someone coming in late. She tried to focus on what Silas was saying.

"Hope you all aren't in too much trouble with your parents. I wasn't involved with Jeremiah's scheme, but only because I had my attention elsewhere." His words brought scattered laughter, but to Naomi it looked as if Silas was embarrassed about his reputation, as if he wanted to apologize for something. Instead, he shook his head and continued. "They need our help, is what it boils down to."

"Who is *they*?" Someone on the far side of the circle threw out the question.

"The police haven't asked, if that's what you mean. Our parents, though, think it's the right thing to do. More to the point, our leadership—Henry, Abe, Leroy, and my dad—they think it's the right thing to do. Anyone who doesn't agree is free to leave."

He waited a moment, during which no one moved.

"*Gut.* Since we all care about this community, we all want to see it continue and thrive, then I say we do what we can to bring this situation to a quick resolution."

"What do you have in mind, Silas?" This from Mahlon Graber, whose father was a deacon. Mahlon had always seemed more serious than most to Naomi. She was surprised he'd been involved in Jeremiah's scheme. "Because if you're asking us to rat one another out..."

"Not at all. I say we share what we know, personally. We volunteer the information—no ratting involved."

"Sounds fair enough," someone to Naomi's right murmured.

"We get a clear picture of what happened and what happened before it happened. Naomi has offered to write down what's said so we have something to analyze. Anyone have a problem with that?"

No one did, by their silence, and Naomi breathed a sigh of relief. She didn't mind recording the details of the meeting, but she didn't want anyone to resent her because she did.

Silas glanced at her and smiled. He was awfully cute. Too bad he smiled at every girl he saw. "We decide as a group what information is useful. Then one of us can take that to Henry, who will share it with the police."

There was a marked silence at that. Naomi could hear the horses moving in their stalls. Finally, Mahlon pulled off his hat and slapped it against his trousers. "I was pulled in. No one to blame but myself, though you have to admit Jeremiah was a fast talker."

Several murmurs of agreement followed his remark.

"I lost nearly five hundred, and those were hard-earned dollars too. I hated to see them go. Jeremiah convinced me I could see a good increase from what I gave him. He said it was practically a sure thing. Hard not to fall for that. Suppose I learned a lesson, though, without the grief from my parents—that was additional."

Now there was open laughter. Nearly everyone there had been lectured by their parents. Naomi's aunt had even give her a long talking to, and Naomi had never even considered gambling what little money she had.

Mahlon wrapped up with, "That's about it. Oh, and I paid Jeremiah what I owed on the Thursday before he was killed. No idea what happened to it."

Mahlon looked embarrassed but also relieved. Naomi supposed confession was good for the soul in most cases. She made a note of his name, amount owed, and date his money was paid to Jeremiah. She couldn't think of anything else to add to that. Seemed like precious little information.

Nathan Kline sat forward, elbows propped on knees. "I'll agree that Jeremiah was a fast talker, but the truth is, I was too eager to hear it. Thought I was onto something good. Thought I'd come away with double the money I started out with. Didn't happen, though."

He stared at the ground, as if he might find the answers to his dilemma there. "I didn't owe as much as you, Mahlon...only two hundred, but it was all I had. Now I'm starting over. Most of the money we earn goes into the family pot. You all know how it is. Oh, and I settled up with Jeremiah the day before the rodeo started."

Naomi added Nathan's information below Mahlon's.

Perhaps because it was his father's barn, Jesse stood and walked up to stand next to Silas.

"I was the biggest fool of the three of us—owed Jeremiah nearly eight hundred dollars, and I paid it all when I went by to see him on Thursday night. Saw him put it into his wallet, and I don't understand why it wasn't there when the sheriff searched his things. What could he have done with that much money that quickly? Didn't appear to me that he spent it on anything."

Naomi thought of the Jeremiah she had known versus the person who was coming to light now that he had passed. She was surprised when she heard the sound of her own voice. She hadn't expected to say what she was thinking. "Jeremiah was good at hiding things. By now you all have heard of the television show *Boots, Buckles, and Broncos*. I never actually thought he'd go through with moving to Hollywood. I had no idea he was involved in this gambling enterprise. So the money...well, I guess there's no telling where it is."

Katie Ann reached over and squeezed her hand, and when Naomi looked up, Silas was watching her intently, encouraging her with his eyes.

"All I'm saying is that you three shouldn't feel embarrassed about what you did. Jeremiah was good at talking, at convincing people of things. He fooled a lot of people, myself included."

The group was silent for a moment, and then Katie Ann hopped up and began pacing back and forth behind the wooden crate she'd been sitting on. "What about the *Englischers*? I don't know many by name. Is anyone aware of specific people who owed him money?"

Mahlon scratched at his jaw. "Jeremiah once told me several of the *Englischers* owed him over a thousand each. Said they weren't too good at making their bets, so it was an excellent opportunity for him."

"Any names?" Silas asked.

"Todd somebody."

"And a Roger Clemore." This came from Albert. "I remember him throwing that name around as if I should remember it, but it meant nothing to me. Jeremiah showed up at planting time, and by then I was pretty preoccupied with putting in my crops. Didn't really have time to talk to him."

"He stopped by your place?" Katie Ann asked. "To ask you to gamble?"

"*Ya*. The way he put it, I'd be investing my money, but you all know I have very little of that hanging around. I told him no thanks and sent him on his way. It's not that I was any smarter than you who did *invest* with him. I was just a little strapped for cash, which I guess turned out to be a good thing."

A girl Naomi didn't know well spoke up. She looked a year or two older than Naomi, and even in the dim light Naomi could tell she was wearing a little makeup. Who was that for? One of the boys among them? Naomi had heard rumors she was fully enjoying her *rumspringa* and thought she stepped out with *Englischers* more than Amish.

"A few of the boys I went out with—"

"*Englischers*?" Silas asked.

"*Ya*. They would ask me about Jeremiah. Seems he had quite a reputation among them, and I wouldn't doubt at all that one of them killed him and took all the money."

"Anything specific to add to that?" Silas asked, again glancing at Naomi and smiling weakly, before he turned his attention back to the first girl and attempted to look serious.

"Let's see. I heard someone say he'd better be *good for it*, whatever that means."

Jesse Kauffmann looked surprised. "Means he'd better have the money to cover the bets placed with him if the person betting won. As far as I know, that was never an issue. The few times I won, he paid quickly enough, which might be why I was so willing to risk more."

"Anything else?" Silas asked.

"Only that, as I guess you all know, Jeremiah was dating more than one girl." She tossed a look at Naomi. "No offense, but he was stepping out with an *Englischer* too. Some girl named Piper."

Naomi shrugged as if it didn't matter, but it did. The knot in her stomach tightened, and she knew her embarrassment must have shown on her face.

"It's not such a big deal," the other girl added. "*Englischers* date more than one person at a time. Unless you've agreed to be exclusive, there's no harm in it."

"There's harm in the fact that Naomi didn't know." Silas put his hands behind his head and stared up at the ceiling, and then he allowed his gaze to travel around the circle. "And I know you all think I was doing the same thing, but every girl I stepped out with knew I was also seeing others. At least I thought they knew, which is still a very poor excuse."

A couple of girls across from Naomi put their heads together and said something, but she couldn't hear what.

"I know two other names I don't think Naomi has down yet—two *Englischers*." Nathan Kline walked over to a calendar tacked to the wall in Leroy's work area. "Saw the three of them in a booth at the diner, heads together, thick as thieves."

"Names?" Naomi asked.

"Justin Lane and Daisy Marshall. They're a couple, I think. And that's not all. The three of them began to argue after a few minutes. I was about halfway through my burger when their conversation became somewhat heated. Justin said something to the effect that Jeremiah would *live to regret*...I couldn't hear what. He stormed out, and then Daisy told Jeremiah not to mess with Justin because he could be mean. I heard that clearly enough."

"What was Jeremiah's reaction?"

"Unperturbed. Jeremiah didn't seem to think anything or anyone could touch him. Maybe that was his biggest mistake."

When no one else offered any additional information, Silas called the meeting to a close. "We'll meet here again in a week, same time. If you think of anything before then, let me or Naomi know. Meanwhile, we'll take what we have to Henry, and he can decide what's important enough to share with the police."

No one seemed to want to leave, though. It was better to sit in the barn, put the matter of Jeremiah behind them, and pretend it was any other Saturday night.

Someone pulled out a transistor radio and tuned it to a local country music station.

A cooler appeared, filled with soft drinks, bottled water, and a few beers.

Katie Ann took off to check on the mare she'd been watching, and everyone else wandered into smaller groups of twos and threes.

Naomi didn't know what to do. She didn't want to join the other girls—or the boys, for that matter. She tucked her notepad and pen into her backpack, tugged it over her shoulder, and stepped out into the evening.

Thirty-Four

Naomi walked out to the pasture fence, crossed her arms across the top rail, and watched the sun set over the San Juan Mountains. A dazzling display of colors swept across the desert floor even as the first of the evening stars began to appear. It was a beautiful sight—majestic and humbling all at the same time. She was thinking of that, of the way something so simple could be made so beautiful, when Silas stepped up beside her.

He didn't say anything at first. He just stood there beside her, mirroring her pose, standing close enough to make her pulse jump but not so close as to make her uncomfortable.

When the sunset's grandeur had passed and darkness had settled enough that she could only see the outline of him, Naomi turned toward her best friend's brother. She did her best to give him a schoolmarm look, a *what are you doing* look.

"What?" he asked, widening his eyes—no doubt trying to look innocent.

She only shook her head.

"Can't a guy come out and stand beside a pretty girl to watch the sun go down?"

"Really? That's the line you're going to use?" She laughed, bumped his shoulder with hers, and turned her attention back to the creeping darkness.

For a moment she thought he wouldn't say anything else, but finally he sighed deeply and began talking. "You think I'm just out here to pick you up."

"Pick me up?"

"Flirt with you."

"Are you flirting with me?"

"You think you're just the next girl on my list."

"You have a list?"

"I don't blame you."

"And I never said—"

"I have a reputation now, and I suppose I deserve it."

"That's a start, I guess." She aimed to keep her tone light. It wasn't her place to judge Silas Fisher, but she would do well to remember his history of tossing girls aside after a couple of weeks—or less.

"I'm aiming to change my ways. Honest I am. My *dat* convinced me that what I was doing…playing the field or whatever…that it wasn't right."

"But?"

"But then lines like that about you being a pretty girl just come out of my mouth. You are a pretty girl. Don't get me wrong, but when I say it, I realize I'm acting like I did before. The only difference is that I feel bad about it now, about saying such foolish things."

"Well, maybe you can't help that you're a smooth-talking guy."

"Did it sound smooth?"

"Maybe you should be a poet or write romance books."

Silas's laughter was deep and rich. "An Amish man who is a romance writer?"

"It could happen."

"And Leroy Kauffmann could find gold in that pasture, but I doubt he will."

"So what are you doing out here, Silas? Other than trying to sweet-talk me?"

"I was worried about you, is all. That couldn't have been easy on you back there, listening to folks talk about Jeremiah."

"I guess."

"You two were…close?"

"Not as close as you might expect." She thought about telling him that she was about to have the *let's be friends* talk with Jeremiah, or maybe he was about to have that talk with her. Now they'd never know, but admitting it aloud felt disloyal. So instead she said, "I guess we'd grown apart."

"Now, that sounds like a line in one of my *mamm*'s books."

"Do you think we did any good tonight?"

"Maybe. I don't know. Seems that the field of suspects is widening, when what we need to do is narrow it down."

"Where do you think the money is?" Naomi shifted from foot to foot.

"Maybe he hid it."

"Where?"

"Maybe he had a bank account or a safety-deposit box."

"His *mammi* hasn't found a key to one. I stopped by to see her today. She didn't find anything of surprise when she cleaned his room." She hesitated before adding, "Maybe he owed it to someone. Maybe he gave it to someone."

"Too many possibilities."

"*Ya.*"

Naomi thought they were done, so she turned to go back into the barn to find Katie Ann. Silas reached out and touched her arm.

"I had another reason for coming out here, other than to see how you were doing. I also wanted to tell you to be careful."

"Be careful?"

"Whoever killed Jeremiah...well, if that person is still around, they might want to tie up some loose ends."

"You think I'm a loose end?"

"I don't know, but I think you knew him better than most."

"I'm realizing I barely knew him at all."

"If this person is trying to cover his tracks, he might think getting rid of you would do it."

"Getting rid of me?"

"Repeating what I say won't change anything."

Naomi smiled up at Silas, who had stepped closer, and then she realized it was dark and he couldn't see her smiling. He didn't know if she was terrified or teasing. "Don't worry so much. I don't think anyone's after me. If they were, there's been plenty of time in the last week to take me down."

"Don't say such things."

"You brought it up!"

"True."

He reached out and ran his fingers down her cheek. She thought he might kiss her, and her pulse quickened as her breath caught in her throat, but instead he linked his arm with hers and turned them back toward the barn. "Come on. Let's go listen to some music."

"*Englisch* music."

"It's not forbidden, not now during..."

"Our *rumspringa*? Is that what you were about to say?"

"*Ya*, I guess I was."

"So you're still trying out *Englisch* ways, testing the waters, getting into mischief..."

"That's a lot of words."

"I'm a writer."

"So I heard."

"You heard?"

"Okay, I read your piece in the *Budget* every month. Is that what you wanted to hear?"

They'd stopped outside the barn door, and Silas had moved closer. She sensed him in the dark, leaning toward her, and it occurred to her again that he was going to kiss her. Did she want him to kiss her? Before she could decide, his lips met hers.

Tingles shot down her spine.

Tiny lights exploded behind her tightly closed eyes.

Sweat slicked her palms.

She relaxed, maybe for the first time since the shot that killed Jeremiah rang out. She stopped worrying, stopped thinking, and let go of the urge to *do something*.

It was just her, a nice boy, and a kiss like she'd read about in the *Englisch* romance novels.

Then a cow lowed in the distance, pulling her back to her senses. A relationship with notorious playboy Silas Fisher was not what she needed. Maybe he had changed. Maybe he hadn't, but she wouldn't be the one who would find out. She had enough going on in her life at the moment. So she put her hands against his chest and took a step back. "Slow down, cowboy."

"Slow down?"

And then it happened. The puzzle pieces clicked into place.

She stepped back from Silas, pressed her fingertips to her lips, and turned in a circle.

"Something wrong?"

"I just remembered…"

"What?"

"I just remembered…Oh my goodness!" She clutched Silas's arm. "We have to tell someone. We have to do something."

"Now who's the one who needs to slow down?" He ran a hand up and down her arm, which didn't help her to focus one bit.

"You don't understand. Jeremiah…he told me."

"Told you what?"

"Where to look. I think I know where he stashed the money."

Thirty-Five

Henry wasn't aware of the setting sun or the little dog who lay at his feet, eyeing him occasionally. He didn't realize he'd skipped dinner. He wasn't conscious of the fact that the evening was cooling or that the solar light on the outside of his workshop had come on.

Then Lexi jumped to her feet, and a shadow passed over the sheet of paper he was drawing on.

He glanced up to find Seth Hoschstetler standing in the doorway of his workshop, his head cocked to the side and a look of concern on his face.

"Seth. I didn't hear you walk up."

"*Ya.* That much is obvious."

"Is something wrong?"

"Only that we were worried about you."

"Worried?"

"Roseann and I. Because you didn't show up for dinner."

Henry leaned his head back and closed his eyes, pinching the bridge of his nose. "I forgot. Totally forgot. I'm so sorry. I've been preoccupied..."

The words slid away as he realized Seth was looking around in amazement, looking at the pieces of paper that littered his desk. He stepped closer and peered down at a drawing that showed the mass of people exiting the rodeo in a panic, minutes after the shooting.

"You drew these?"

"Yes."

Henry didn't defend himself.

He'd told both Seth and Roseann about his ability to draw before they'd moved to Monte Vista. He'd explained how he could render in elaborate detail anything he'd seen, how the way his memory worked had changed so many years ago when he was a lad and had been hit by a baseball.

He'd told them all of it before they'd joined the community.

He told all potential members.

While the Monte Vista community of Plain folk had all accepted his strange talent, Henry was aware many in other communities wouldn't—people who shared the opinion of Jeremiah's dad, though few would go so far as to call what he did sorcery. Still, Henry allowed for each person to be convicted by God's Spirit in their own way, and he didn't hold it against anyone who was uncomfortable with his ability.

Seth was aware of what Henry could do, but knowing something and witnessing it were two different things.

"Have a look," he said, gesturing to the haphazard pile of drawings.

"You drew all of these from memory?"

"I did."

Seth picked up one sheet after another—each depicting a different scene from the rodeo. He carefully studied each one and then set it neatly in a pile. Henry hadn't realized until that moment how long he'd been at it. He was suddenly aware that his hand ached, the muscles in his shoulders felt tight, and he was terribly hungry.

"How long did this take you? How many days have you been working on these?"

"Not days. Hours. I started late this morning."

Seth squared up the sheets and looked his bishop straight in the eye. "It's amazing, Henry. It's a *wunderbaar* thing you can do. A real gift from *Gotte*."

A wave of relief crashed over Henry. He didn't need man's approval, didn't actively seek it, but it helped when those in his congregation embraced him fully despite his unusual ability.

"*Danki*," he said simply. Then his stomach rumbled.

"Would you like to go to the house with me? I hadn't realized it was dinnertime, and Lexi...well, I haven't fed her yet."

"Past dinnertime for both of you."

"Yes, past dinnertime."

Seth held up a sack he'd set on the bench when he walked in. "Rose-ann sent this over."

"Is it what I think it is?"

"Chicken potpie, bread, squash casserole, and dessert."

"Sounds delicious, especially with a fresh cup of coffee."

Henry picked up the stack of drawings, and Seth carried the bag of food. They didn't speak as they walked the short distance from the work-shop to the house. Darkness had fallen, which meant it was nearing nine in the evening, and they had church the next morning. He'd been foolish to become so caught up in what he was doing, and he'd pay for it when he had to get up before sunrise.

He set the drawings on the table, went straight to the dog food bin, and scooped out Lexi's dinner—adding a little extra to ease his own con-science. She fell on it as though she hadn't eaten for days. Well, he was late. Had she tried to get his attention? He couldn't remember.

Seth sat quietly at the table as Henry set a fresh pot of coffee to boil-ing on the stove.

"Won't that keep you awake?" Seth asked.

"It's decaf."

Henry pulled out the containers of food, offered some to Seth, who shook his head, and set out mugs for their coffee. "At least have some of the pie."

"*Ya*, all right. It's blueberry."

"One of my favorites."

"Mine too." And with that they seemed to settle upon a comfortable footing again. They enjoyed the pie and the coffee. When Henry refilled their cups, he finally broached the subject of the drawings.

"I realize it might have been startling to see those drawings."

"*Ya*. I suppose it was." Seth sat back and studied him over his raised coffee mug. Finally, he set it down on the table and said, "You told us before, but I don't think I fully appreciated what you were talking about. Can you explain to me how it works?"

"I can try. My mind seems to record everything I see. Which isn't a problem because I don't actually remember it all. Some of the doctors theorized that everyone's mind does what mine does, but none of us is aware. We don't realize the ability inside of us until something happens, something like my accident with the baseball."

"Which happened many years ago."

"When I was twelve."

"Do you decide what you're going to draw?"

"Maybe the general idea, but I don't know what's going to come out—what came out—until later. I don't...I'm not completely aware of what I'm drawing even as I draw it."

"Or that you're hungry or tired."

"No. I'm not conscious of that either."

"Those drawings have a lot of detail, and they were all centered around the rodeo."

"I met with Clyde and Abe and Leroy yesterday. They suggested, as Emma had, that I at least try drawing the events of that night, the night Jeremiah died."

"What did you hope to find?"

"I'm not sure."

"You're looking for the killer."

"I'm looking for a clue, anything I can give the police that might help them."

"We could study them together."

Henry's fatigue fell away. "Yes. Yes, that's a good idea. Let's take a look."

As the darkness deepened across the valley, Henry and Seth pored over his drawings. "These are remarkable, Henry, but I don't see any clues as to Jeremiah's killer."

"I agree."

"You captured the reaction of those in the stands."

"Quite a few people."

"Nearly all of Monte Vista from the looks of it."

"You weren't there?" Henry asked.

"*Nein*. We'd thought about it, but then Roseann came down with a headache. I was tired and ready to put my feet up, maybe read through the *Budget*."

"You've been working hard to get the place into shape."

Seth nodded and tapped the stack of drawings. "It was good of you to try."

"Not sure I'm finished."

"Hopefully you are for the night."

"*Ya*. Indeed."

Henry rinsed out the now-empty dishes Roseann had sent over. "Thank your wife for me."

"I will."

"And convey my apologies."

"No need at all. I can see how you could immerse yourself in such a thing and forget all that's going on around you."

As Henry prepared for bed, he thought about that. The ability to focus was a good thing, but he'd forgotten to feed Lexi, feed himself, go to his neighbor's. Even now he felt the urge to go back to the table and draw more. Their community was being pulled into a dark situation, and he didn't want that. He didn't believe it was God's intention for them to be preoccupied with such things.

In other words, he wanted this latest incident solved. He wanted the investigation over. He wanted his community to return to their simple life.

"Might not be up to us, though."

Lexi had no answer for that.

"Perhaps God is teaching us patience."

Lexi stretched and yawned.

"Could be that we'll learn to trust His providence and wisdom even more."

Lexi flopped over onto her side at the foot of Henry's bed.

"Still...if I could hit on the right thing and find a clue, perhaps it would move Grayson in the right direction. Tomorrow afternoon we'll try once more. We could carry the alarm clock over to the workshop so I don't get carried away again."

But Lexi's stomach was full. She'd forgotten Henry's earlier transgression and certainly wasn't worried about tomorrow's meals. She was content, and Henry understood there were some things that he, a sixty-six-year-old bishop, could learn from one of God's smaller creations.

Thirty-Six

Naomi and Silas had gone in search of Katie Ann, but it took them a while to find her. They were stopped several times by people in their group. When they asked about Katie Ann, they were told she was still back with the horses. They searched each stall but found no sign of her.

Finally, they went out the back door and surveyed the pens attached to the back of the barn.

"She's over there—in the pigpen." Silas laughed as he said it. Obviously, he was used to his sister's love of animals.

Katie Ann was squatting inside the pigpen, though at least she wasn't in the mud. It didn't surprise Naomi at all that Albert was nearby. He'd been sending her clear signs of interest during the meeting, but Katie Ann hadn't noticed.

"We thought you were checking on the horses," Naomi said.

Katie Ann glanced up and waved. "I was, but then I heard these little guys."

"She's fussing over a sow," Albert explained. "She seems to have recently given birth to eight piglets."

A battery-powered lantern sat between Katie Ann and Albert, who was watching her as if he'd spotted the moon for the first time.

"Naomi thinks she knows where Jeremiah stashed the money." Silas blurted it out as soon as they were sure no one else was around. They'd decided, the two of them, not to involve anyone but Katie Ann, and now Albert as well, as he seemed determined to be by her side for the evening.

Both Albert and Katie Ann stared at Naomi as if she were wearing a polka-dotted *kapp* on her head.

"You know where the money is?" Katie Ann asked.

"Why didn't you say so earlier?" Albert stood and dusted off his hands.

"And where is it?"

"And can we get it now?"

"Slow down." Silas laughed when the piglet Katie Ann was holding wormed its way into the crook of her arm. "Put the piglet down, and we'll explain."

Naomi could still hear the music from the transistor radio playing in the barn, the faintest strains of guitar and a woman singing, and if she wasn't mistaken, a fiddle. Jeremiah had loved country music. She'd always thought it was because of his interest in the rodeo. She'd wondered, even then, if he would decide he preferred *Englisch* things to Plain. She pushed the memory away and focused on explaining her revelation.

"Silas and I were outside, and we were talking, and then we turned to walk back into the barn."

"And then I kissed her." Silas grinned when she batted at his arm. "Well, I did, and I'm not ashamed of it."

"I was so surprised I stopped thinking, and that's when it popped into my head—what Jeremiah said the last time we were out together, other than seeing him for a moment at the rodeo."

"When was this?" Albert asked.

"Thursday afternoon, and then we went to eat at the diner. *Ya*, I'm sure of it because I had to get up early the next day to be at the bakery, and I'd told him I had to be home fairly early."

"Tell them the rest," Silas said.

"We were driving away from Vernon's, and Jeremiah said, 'I like this place. I trust it, like I trust you.'"

"How do you trust a place?" Katie Ann asked.

"Vernon Frey's house?" Albert peered at her. "You're sure that's where you were?"

"I know where we went to have some private time, and yes, I'm sure that's where we were the last time we were together."

Albert had pulled off his hat and was rubbing his hand back and forth across the top of his head. "As far as I'm aware of, no work has been done there since the fire...since Vernon died."

"Which was two years ago," Katie Ann pointed out.

"We used to go there nearly once a week. There was no harm in it." Naomi plopped down onto an overturned milking pail. "We'd drive over in his *mammi*'s buggy and sit and talk."

"That house is about to fall in on itself," Silas said.

"But we didn't go to the house. At the back of the property was an area for *kinner*."

"Vernon never had children." Albert sounded as though he were arguing with her, but his expression told her he was more confused than argumentative.

"I think the playground stuff was from the family who owned the house before him. The area is all grown up with weeds and such. There's an old tire swing and a jungle gym and a...a..." Her words stuttered to a stop. She didn't know how to explain the rest. "I think I should show you."

"Tonight?" Albert's voice rose in surprise.

They would all need to be up early to complete chores before church, but Naomi felt a sudden sense of urgency. "*Ya*. I think it's important."

"You rode here with me and Katie Ann," Silas said. "We can take you by Vernon's, check this thing out, and see if it's worth telling anyone else about."

"We'll all go." Albert plopped his hat back on his head. "Wouldn't want to miss out on the fun."

What was left unsaid was what Naomi was thinking, what she knew they all were thinking. Four was safer than two or even three.

"Take both buggies?" Katie Ann asked.

"We should," Albert agreed. "Then I can take Naomi home, and you two can head back to your parents' place."

But that wasn't what Silas had in mind. "I'll take Naomi home," he said gruffly.

She remembered the kiss, his awkward confession that he was turning over a new leaf, and the way his hand felt on her arm. Naomi couldn't suppress a smile when Katie Ann rolled her eyes, though she apparently remained clueless as to Albert's interest. Her best friend noticed very little unless the thing in front of her had four legs and a tail.

"Silas and I will ride together, and you can ride with Albert," Katie Ann said, returning the piglet to its mother.

"Actually, I want to ask you about my mare." Albert cleared his throat and rubbed at his jaw as if he'd just remembered something important. "She's suddenly putting on weight, and I'm wondering if it's healthy for her."

"*Ya*, that's something you want to be careful about." Katie Ann walked away with Albert, and Naomi heard the words *feed* and *overweight* and *conditioning*. Albert was probably getting way more information than he needed or wanted.

Silas reached for Naomi's hand and pulled her away from the pigpen and toward his buggy. "Sounds like Albert is making excuses to spend time with my sister."

"Does it bother you?"

"Are you kidding? Anyone who can snatch Katie Ann's attention from a horse stall or a piglet or a wounded bird has my vote, and Albert is a good guy."

Naomi thought he might kiss her again as he opened the buggy door for her. For a moment he leaned in close. He reached out and touched her face, and her heart seemed to stop beating. But then he stepped back and the moment passed.

Did she want him to kiss her again?

Shouldn't she still be mourning Jeremiah?

But in truth, she and Jeremiah hadn't kissed in a long time.

They waited for Albert to pull out in his buggy, and then Katie Ann waved to the two of them, indicating they should go first.

"Tell me about you and Jeremiah," Silas said as he directed the mare toward the road.

So she did. She told him about the things weighing heavily on her heart, the thoughts that circled round and round in her mind each night and stole her sleep. She told him about Jeremiah's growing fascination with the *Englisch*, how he loved the rodeo, that he often sent money home to his family.

Silas was a good listener. He waited until she finished before commenting. "It's a lot for you to deal with, Naomi. And you think he may have hid the money at Vernon's? Why? Why would he do such a thing?"

"I don't know for certain, but he wanted to go there nearly every time I saw him—as I said, at least once a week."

"You said he sent money home."

"He did, but perhaps he put it at Vernon's until he could get a money order. Or he had to keep the money he owed people somewhere. Maybe he didn't want to keep it at his *mammi*'s."

"Might have wanted to protect Ruth from any trouble, assuming he was aware there might be trouble."

"I think...I think he might have been using me for cover."

"Huh?"

"If someone saw us out, they would just assume we were courting."

"But you weren't?"

"Maybe the first few weeks. After that, though, it felt as if we were friends—good friends—but I think we both knew nothing would come of it."

She thought of Silas leaning toward her in the dark as they'd approached the buggy, of hoping he would kiss her again, of her disappointment when he hadn't. She felt none of those things with Jeremiah. Now that she looked back on it, she'd considered him to be more of a cousin who needed a friend.

"I didn't have romantic feelings for him, the kind a woman should have for a man she's stepping out with. And I don't think he felt that way about me either."

Silas reached over and squeezed her hand. "Which isn't your fault. That's what stepping out is for, to see if you share those sorts of feelings."

"Is that why you've dated so many girls? Were you trying to find someone you shared those feelings with?" She immediately wished she could pull back the words. Just the week before she'd heard Franey say at the bakery, "Think before you speak, but don't speak all you think." At the time she'd giggled, but now she understood what the proverb meant.

"I guess that was why." Silas blew out a big breath. "Honestly, I was just being stupid, not even considering anyone else's feelings. It was a game, and I thought everyone knew it. My *dat* helped me to see otherwise."

The night had grown dark except for the light of the quarter moon, making his confession all the more intimate.

Naomi remained silent. She didn't know how to answer him. She did know that some of the girls Silas dated and dropped had been hurt and confused. Perhaps they hadn't known he was dating others at the same time. Maybe they thought it was their fault that the relationship ended. If she were to step out with him, would she be nursing a wounded heart a week or month later? She wasn't sure it was worth it. Perhaps she should keep her distance.

"I believe I have some apologizing to do," he added, though she couldn't tell if he was speaking to her or to himself.

"Apologize to whom?"

"The women I hurt. Those I may have misled."

Which could mean he really had experienced a change of heart.

To Naomi it seemed a sign of maturity. Could someone's ways change so quickly, though? Silas seemed sincere, but he had a reputation to overcome. She supposed time would tell. Until she knew for certain, she would do well to guard her heart.

Thirty-Seven

Emma was wiping down the kitchen counter one last time. She'd turned out most of the downstairs lights and was about to head to bed when she heard the boys hollering. She rushed to the back door, arriving there the same time Stephen and Thomas did.

"They're out." Stephen leaned over, bracing his hands on his legs and pulling in deep, shuddering breaths.

"All of them."

"We tried to stop them."

"Couldn't, though. Too late."

"What's this about?" Clyde asked, straightening his suspenders as he walked into the mudroom.

"The horses, *Dat.*" Thomas, as the oldest, stood up straighter. "They're all out. They're all loose on the road."

Clyde owned six draft horses and three buggy horses, if you counted Emma's mare, Cinnamon. It was every farmer's nightmare that the animals would get loose and be hit by a passing motorist. Horses were the gears that made an Amish farm run. They were also a significant monetary investment.

"Which direction?" Clyde asked.

"North. I think they fled to the north." Thomas looked to Stephen for confirmation.

"*Ya.* North. At least they were."

By this time Rachel had come to see what was wrong. She'd already removed her *kapp* and brushed out her hair, preparing for bed, but she'd thrown back on her day clothes.

"Go," she said. "We'll bring more lanterns."

"And oats. Bring some buckets of oats." Clyde and the boys took off at a jog.

"We'll catch them," Emma said, and then she saw Rachel reach for the doorframe.

"*Ya. Ya*, I know we will. It's just...all of the horses? How did they all get out? They're in two separate pastures. Even if the boys had left one gate open..."

"Let's figure out the *how* of it later."

Which seemed to be what Rachel needed to hear. She reached out, squeezed Emma's hand, and then said, "I'll get the oats."

"And I'll fetch the lanterns."

They met in between the barn and the house and then rushed as fast as they could out to the two-lane road. It crossed Emma's mind that maybe they should worry about the boys standing in the middle of the road, but they were in a valley. They could see a car coming from miles away—if it had its lights on.

Emma handed a lantern to each boy. "Stephen, go to the south and stand in the middle of the road to warn off any approaching cars or buggies. Thomas, you stand near the entry to our place. The horses might see the light and come back toward you."

She could hear Clyde hollering and whooping, trying to scare the horses back their direction, but she couldn't see him. The quarter moon didn't provide enough light for that.

"I'll take one of the buckets."

Rachel kept the other, and they moved off in different directions. Emma took the right side of the road and moved closer to Clyde. Rachel took the left, and held back in case one of the horses sprinted past Emma.

It was a fact of nature that horses ran when they were spooked. It was their best defense. The question was, what had frightened them? Because Emma didn't believe for a minute that an open gate would have resulted in this chaos. The horses were well trained, well fed, and preferred the safety of home. Not to mention the boys were careful. They never would have left a gate open.

Clyde continued to whoop and holler. He'd worked his way behind the horses, far down the lane, and Emma could hear him only sporadically. Looking back toward their place, she could see the boys' lanterns, but she couldn't see Rachel. Occasionally she heard a snort and the sound of hooves coming toward her in the darkness, but then they would shy away again.

The first to turn was Big Boy, Clyde's lead workhorse. He was eighteen hands high and weighed in at 1,700 pounds the last time Doc Berry had checked. Big Boy had a warm brown coat with an even darker mane and tail. Though he was the largest, he was also the gentlest. He stepped out of the darkness and toward Emma, tossing his head and stomping, but the look in his eyes? It seemed to her he was asking to go home.

"*Ya*, come now, Big Boy. We have some *gut* oats for you." Emma held the bucket out, and when she had his attention, she began to walk backward toward the house. Once she was sure he was following, she turned and faced the right direction. The last thing Clyde or Rachel needed was to tend to an old woman's sprained ankle.

She felt more than saw the rest of the workhorses following Big Boy. When she passed Rachel, Emma said, "Go help Clyde find the mares."

The buggy horses would be grouped together, probably a bit farther down the road since they were used to traveling away from the farm.

Stephen held up a lantern and walked with her toward the pasture—the draft horses now following docilely in their wake.

"What do you think happened?" Stephen asked.

"Any chance you left the gate open?"

"*Nein.*"

"I didn't think so."

"It was shut when we got there to do the nightly check, and I remember closing it behind me when we went inside the pasture to look for them."

"I don't know what happened, then, but your *dat* will figure it out."

Which seemed to satisfy Stephen. He jogged ahead, opened the still-closed gate, and Big Boy led the team into the pasture. "Give them each some of the oats," Emma said. "I'm going back out to help with the mares."

By the time she reached the front gate, Rachel was leading the mares in with her bucket of oats. Emma's heart stopped for a minute when she saw only two of the buggy horses, but then she remembered that Silas and Katie Ann had taken Cinnamon.

Within ten minutes the mares were safely in their pasture.

"All present and accounted for," Rachel said, collapsing onto the front porch.

But Clyde still hadn't returned after the boys had gone up to bed, and Emma was beginning to worry that something else was wrong when she spied him trudging toward the front porch. Rachel hurried inside, returning with a towel, a glass of water, and a plate of cookies.

"*Danki*, but just the water." He first took the towel and wiped the sweat off his face and neck.

"You look as if something terrible has happened." Rachel didn't glance away, didn't show any of the fear that had seized her earlier. She perched on the edge of a rocker, waiting for her husband to explain. Emma took the other rocker, grateful to sit after the evening they'd had.

"Someone cut the fence."

"Are you sure?" Emma asked.

"*Ya*. I'm sure. The new *Englisch* neighbor on the east side heard all the ruckus and came out to see if he could help. We were closer to his house than ours, so he went back for tools, and we were able to patch it back together. First thing Monday, I'll repair it properly."

"Will it hold until Monday?" Rachel asked.

"*Ya*. It will." Clyde drained the glass of water and then sank onto the porch floor. "That's not our problem. Our problem is figuring out why someone would cut our fences. Not just one, either. Whoever it was had to have cut the interior fence as well, since the mares and the work-horses escaped."

"I can't imagine," Emma said, but then, suddenly, she could.

"There's more. They didn't just cut the fence. Whoever did this went into our pasture and spooked them. It's the only explanation."

That sat between them for a while.

Finally, Emma spoke what they were all thinking. "Is it him? Do you think it's the person who killed Jeremiah?"

"I don't know. Don't know why he'd be interested in us anyway. We barely knew Jeremiah."

"But we know Henry," Rachel said. "Not only do we know Henry, but he's about to be family."

"Henry didn't see anything!" Emma felt a profound weariness creep into her bones. She didn't want to be involved in another murder investigation. She didn't want to deal with the danger and darkness. But neither would she leave Henry to fend for himself. If he was in danger, she would find a way to help him. *They* would find a way to help him.

"They don't know Henry doesn't know anything." Clyde leaned his head back against the porch post. Finally, he sat up straighter and tapped the floor of the porch as if he'd discovered some great truth. "They don't know that, and I'm not sure they'd believe it if we told them."

"Which we can't do because we don't know who *they* are," Rachel reasoned.

"Exactly. My point is they're in a panic, so they're trying to frighten us."

"To what end?" A surging anger began to replace Emma's weariness. It galled her that anyone would attack her family, would go after their animals—their livelihood. And for what? To cover their own sins?

"Assuming it's someone in the community..."

"It can't be, Clyde. It just...It can't be." Rachel's words were more a plea than a statement.

"I didn't say Plain community. I said community. Someone from Monte Vista. Someone who knows Emma and Henry are about to wed. Maybe they think you have an influence over him, that you can convince him to leave this thing alone."

"I'm not sure I can or that I should."

"Good." And Clyde smiled for the first time since they'd learned the horses were loose. "Because when the deacons were with him yesterday, we all agreed he should try to draw what he can remember from that night. Though he didn't see the murder, he might have seen the murderer."

"Whoever killed Jeremiah didn't walk through the crowd carrying his rifle," Rachel argued.

"That's probably true, but you know how Henry can capture—"

"Emotions." Emma rubbed her fingertips across her forehead. "He can capture emotions."

"Right. More than an *Englisch* photograph. So it's at least possible that he saw the person leaving, saw an expression of anger or panic or fear on this person's face. Of course, he wouldn't remember that he saw it. Not until he starts drawing."

"What's he going to do?" Rachel stood now and crossed her arms, as if she could stand against this person intent on doing them harm. "Draw everything he saw? The entire evening?"

"I'm not sure," Clyde admitted. "We'll have to pray that the Lord directs his efforts."

"And in the meantime?"

"Get some sleep. I think we all need to get some sleep. We'll tell Henry about this before church in the morning and let him decide if the police need to know."

Though Emma was exhausted, she didn't follow Clyde and Rachel inside. She'd sit in the rocker and enjoy the evening's cooling. She'd wait until she saw Silas and Katie Ann return—until she was sure they were both fine. Though the person couldn't be here and somewhere else at the same time. The person couldn't be terrorizing them *and* threatening her grandchildren.

Suddenly she was grateful the fence had been cut. Better than damage done to a buggy—a wheel loosened, a horse collar sabotaged, another buggy run off the road. A fence could be mended, and the horses were now safe.

But what of Silas and Katie Ann?

No, she wouldn't sleep yet, and she wouldn't share her concerns with Clyde and Rachel, either. They were dealing with enough. She'd sit and she'd pray, and while she was at it, she'd petition the Lord to direct Henry's hands, his drawing, his special memory. Together she and Rachel and Clyde and the grandchildren and Henry would solve this thing.

When they did, peace would once again return to the San Luis Valley.

Thirty-Eight

The charred remains of Vernon Frey's home loomed up out of the darkness. Naomi could just make out a gaping hole in the side of the house that extended up through the roof. The windows had been blown out by the force of the fire. Vernon had died upstairs. The police arrested Sam Beiler for the murder, but in the end he was found innocent. Henry's drawings had pointed them toward the real killer. All of that had occurred before Naomi moved to Monte Vista, but she'd heard the stories.

The yard itself was filled with a bizarre collection of items—a discarded refrigerator, old car parts, some rusting farm equipment, bicycles without tires. The fact that no one had bothered to pilfer the stuff in the last two years was proof of its value.

"Why has no one bought this place?" Naomi asked.

Silas didn't answer right away. He'd slowed Cinnamon to a walk, directing her around the piles of debris. "A lot of cleanup would be involved, and the property doesn't have much land to go with it. The house would have to be completely razed and a new one built."

"In other words, too much work."

"And there are other, nicer properties to be had, so why bother?"

"Why indeed."

"Where did you and Jeremiah—"

"There's a trail of sorts around to the back of the property. That's...that's where we'd go."

The clip-clop of Cinnamon's hooves calmed the nerves in Naomi's stomach, that and Silas's presence beside her. Plus, Katie Ann and Albert were following close behind. When they'd finally circled around the house and reached the back area, Silas stopped, reached for her hand, and tugged her across the seat. She wanted to resist, to keep any feelings she might have for Silas Fisher at bay, but she found herself clasping his hand and moving closer.

"Can't believe Jeremiah brought you here," he muttered.

"It's not so spooky in the daylight."

"Not a proper place for a date, though. I'd take you out to eat or to a movie."

"A movie?"

"Don't sound so shocked. Didn't you and Katie Ann go to one last week?"

That would be another problem with dating Silas, not that she was considering such a thing. But if she did, she'd be dating her best friend's brother—which would be fine if the relationship worked out. She'd love to have Katie Ann for a sister-in-law, but it wouldn't be so fine if they broke up. It would be awkward.

More was on the line than her own feelings. She also had to consider her friendship with Katie Ann.

"Any place in particular?" Albert asked. He'd pulled a flashlight from his buggy and was shining the beam around the abandoned play area. Weeds sprouted through the jungle gym. The seesaw's board was cracked in places, and the handle on one end was missing. An old tire hung from a rope tossed over a branch on the largest of the surrounding trees, and to the left was the hidden grove she remembered so well.

Katie Ann walked over to the swing and shone her light down into the tire. "Nothing here."

"No snakes?" Albert teased. "You know it's a good place for them."

"I'm not afraid of a snake, but if you are, no worries. This tire is snake-free."

Silas tossed Naomi a look that said, *See? They're flirting*.

"I think if he'd hidden something, it would have been in there." She pointed to the trees.

"Huh?" Silas raised his eyebrows comically, causing some of the tension in her shoulders to ease.

Instead of explaining, she reached for Katie Ann's flashlight and said, "Follow me."

The way in wasn't hard to find if you knew it was there. She moved to the right, pulled back some bushes, and her flashlight revealed a well-traveled trail into the center of the grove. Making their way inside, they found that the trees had created a kind of hidden spot. In the middle were some old tree stumps someone had pulled over and the remains of a campfire.

"Wonder how Jeremiah discovered this," Silas said.

The area was plenty big enough for the four of them. In fact, it probably could have held a dozen. Looking up, Naomi could make out the sliver of moon as well as the stars. They sparkled through the canopy of leaves, creating a beautiful mosaic.

"Doesn't seem to be anywhere to hide money, though." Albert turned in a circle. "You're sure this is the place he was talking about? The place he said he could trust?"

"Yes. He said it as we were leaving on Thursday. This has to be the place. If he hid the money, this is the only place that makes sense."

"And you can't think of anywhere else?"

"He was always insistent that we come here." She bit her lip, suddenly embarrassed, but they'd come too far. There was too much on the line now. She swallowed her pride and regret and made herself continue. "He'd tell me to wait outside on the path. Said he wanted to check for snakes and such, wanted to make sure it was safe. Then, after a few minutes, he'd come back and declare the place safe. We'd laugh about that."

"So he brought you here, under the guise of a date." Silas sat down on one of the tree trunks that formed a sort of stool. "He'd effectively throw anyone off his path. If they were following him, they probably wouldn't keep following him once he picked you up."

Albert took up the story line. "He'd come here, tell you to wait, come in and hide the money, and then bring you in."

"If anyone was watching, they wouldn't see anything suspicious."

Katie Ann pulled her *kapp* strings to the front. "And he did this every time?"

"*Ya*. Practically. Every time I can think of."

"All right." Silas played his flashlight around the area. "It must be here then. Let's give it a good look."

They picked up each of the tree stumps, looked under the stump and checked the wood itself to see if something had been carved inside. Albert walked the circle, the beam of his flashlight dancing up through the trees, looking for any type of bag or box or package Jeremiah might have hidden. Katie Ann patrolled the edge of the circle, looking for evidence of digging. Naomi sat and tried to think like Jeremiah might have.

He'd obviously been worried. Why else would he have brought the money here?

Worried enough to use their relationship as a ruse. Concerned enough to tell her this was the place he could trust. He must have been aware that someone wanted the stash he had, so maybe he had owed people, maybe he'd fallen into a dilemma he didn't know how to get out of. His answer had been this place. His answer had been to use their relationship to keep himself and his money safe.

At least she'd been able to help him in some small way.

She stared at the charred remains of a fire, stared and tried to think of something, of anything that would help.

Silas, Albert, and Katie Ann joined her.

No one spoke, as if the quiet would spur her memories. But it didn't.

Finally, Silas said, "Too bad we don't have any matches."

"Or marshmallows." Albert laughed when Katie Ann gave him a pointed look. "I'm hungry. Dinner was a long time ago."

"Next time we'll have s'mores—if we ever come here again." Katie Ann stared up at the stars. "I'll admit it's a good place to get away. I bet no one would even know you're in here."

"That's it!" Naomi jumped up.

"S'mores? That's the answer?" Albert was still clutching his middle as if he were suddenly seized with hunger pains. "I can go back to town and buy—"

"We never had a fire. We must have come here a dozen times, but we never once had a fire."

Katie Ann reached out and squeezed her arm. "Maybe he came here with someone else."

"I don't think so. I know he was seeing that other girl, but I don't think he brought her here. Somehow I think this was only our place. That he was trying to tell me if something happened to him to come here, and I think the one place he could have hidden anything was beneath the remains of that fire."

"Gutsy thing to do," Silas said. "What if someone had come along and started an actual fire there? And how did he do it so quickly, while you were waiting for him outside this group of trees?"

But when they looked closely, they could see the pieces of wood were arranged a little too neatly, as if someone wanted it to look like a fire, but it wasn't. Or maybe Naomi was imagining things. Maybe she was seeing what she wanted to see.

Together the four of them removed the charred pieces of wood and ashes. They used some fallen tree branches to sweep the area clean, and then the boys took sticks and walked around, poking them into the ground where the fire had been. Albert was the one to hit metal.

The rectangular box wasn't buried very deep. They used the tree branches to dig away the dirt and ash and pull it from its hiding place.

"How did he do this while you were waiting?"

"Jeremiah usually carried a backpack. Maybe he had a small shovel in there."

"He'd need to be able to get it out quickly, put his money in it, and rebury it." Silas stared at the box and then at Naomi. "How long did he leave you waiting?"

"Five, maybe ten minutes."

"This could be it, then." He handed the metal box to her.

"What is it?"

"Old army ammunition box. He probably found it in Vernon's junk."

"How does it open?"

Silas showed her how to push down the lever and then pull up. Katie

Ann and Albert had pressed in closer, shining their flashlights on the contents. Naomi lifted the lid, afraid to look inside but knowing she had to. She had to see this through to the end.

On top were crumbled pieces of newspaper and below that a Ziploc bag. Naomi's hands shook as she pulled it from the metal container. The bag was gallon sized, and it was stuffed full of money. She could make out twenties and fifties and even hundreds.

Albert let out a long whistle. "I think we solved the mystery of where he kept his money."

They were standing in a circle, heads practically pressed together, staring at the money Naomi had removed from the bag.

"How much do you think is here?" Katie Ann asked.

"Thousands, at least." Silas glanced up and met her gaze. She saw no judgment in his eyes, no regret. His solidness calmed the fear racing through her heart. "Looks like mainly hundred-dollar bills."

"What do we do with it?" Naomi asked.

The answer, when it came, didn't come from anyone in their group. The voice was male, deep, and angry.

"You give it to us. That's what you're going to do, and you're going to do it now before we shoot you."

Thirty-Nine

Naomi had thought she was a patient person. She'd been through a lot in the past week, though not as much as poor Jeremiah. Still, she thought she'd handled things fairly well. She hadn't fallen apart at the rodeo. She'd made it through the funeral. She had even handled all of the comments about Jeremiah and how he wasn't a very good boyfriend, how he played the field. But when she turned and looked at the *Englischers* standing behind them, she almost lost her composure.

Three people made up the group, one notably shorter and smaller—probably female.

All three wore ski masks, which had to be uncomfortable in the summer heat. The masks didn't stop her from recognizing Justin and Daisy. After all, they'd gone on double dates together. But she didn't know if she should call them out. It seemed they didn't want to be recognized, so it might be safer to pretend she didn't know them.

Silas shone his flashlight on them, and she could tell by their hands that they were white and relatively young.

"Hand it over," the tallest one said. He, too, was carrying a flashlight, which he used to spotlight them one at a time, finally settling on Naomi, who was still holding the bag of money. "We all know that money isn't yours, so give it to us—"

"And no one gets hurt?" Silas practically spat the words. "You've been watching too much *Englisch* television."

"And you haven't watched enough news. Or maybe you don't realize people are willing to kill for far less than what your girlfriend is holding in her hands."

"Did you kill him?" Katie Ann stepped forward, and Albert jerked her back. "Did you kill Jeremiah?"

"The money belongs to us, so hand it over." Then he must have given the two people with him some sort of signal, because they both reached behind them and pulled out guns. Maybe they were wearing paddle holsters like she'd seen when she went to the movie with Katie Ann. Naomi had seen many rifles in her lifetime. Most Amish men hunted, and some girls did as well. She'd once shot a rattlesnake with a .22 rifle. The guns pointed at them now were handguns, and somehow they looked more sinister. Or maybe it was the fact that the people holding them were perfectly calm. Their hands didn't shake at all, as if they were used to threatening people with violence.

"Fine. You know what? It's not worth getting shot over." Silas took the bag of money from Naomi and started walking toward the *Englisch* group.

"Stop right there. Put it down on the ground."

Naomi thought Silas would argue, but instead he gently placed the bag on the ground, as if it were a carton of eggs rather than a stash of money, and stepped back.

The tall guy nodded to the shorter woman, who darted forward and snatched up the bag.

"Now what?" Albert asked.

"Now we take what's ours and leave." He switched the flashlight to his left hand and pulled a set of keys from his pocket with his right. "Don't try to follow us in one of your stupid buggies. Wouldn't want one of your precious horses to get shot."

And then they were gone.

At first Naomi, Katie Ann, Silas, and Albert were all quiet, as if they needed to guard their words. Then they heard an *Englisch* vehicle start up.

Albert and Silas dashed through the circle of trees after tossing back over their shoulders, "Stay where you are!"

"Did they say that because we're women?" Katie Ann had dropped her flashlight when Albert pulled her back, and now she had her hands on her hips. She was also using her *I've had it* tone.

"Don't know, and I don't care. I'm tired. Past tired. I'm weary."

Katie Ann and Naomi sank down onto a log, the same log she'd sat on with Jeremiah.

"Did you ever read *The Secret Garden*?" Naomi asked.

"*Ya*, when I was young."

"I always thought of this place..." Naomi glanced around the clearing, and then she looked up. She could still make out starlight winking from between the thick branches of the trees. Her eyes filled with tears and her heart hurt, as if someone had punched her there. Perhaps that was what grief felt like—an assault more violent than the one they'd just endured.

"I always thought of this place as our secret garden. We'd come here where no one could watch, and we'd just talk about our dreams or our fears or even stupid, inconsequential things. But it was our place. Do you know what I mean? It was special."

Instead of answering, Katie Ann reached for her hand.

"Should we go and help them?" Naomi asked.

"I have no idea what they're doing."

"Or where they went."

"We're here." Albert popped through the circle of trees first, followed quickly by Silas.

"It was a truck." Silas looked energized instead of tired. "We tried to get the license plate number, but it was already too far gone."

"Definitely a white Ford, though. That's something."

"This couldn't have worked any better if we'd tried."

"Practically walked into our trap." Albert stood in front of Katie Ann, grinning.

"What are you two talking about?"

"We were just robbed, or did I imagine that?" Naomi said.

"You did not." Silas tugged on Naomi's hand until she groaned and stood as well.

"I'm not following what you're trying to say," Naomi admitted.

Silas glanced at Albert, who shrugged. "Might as well tell them."

Silas crossed his arms and glanced around the clearing. "When you told us you had somewhere to show us, that you might know where the money was, we figured maybe whoever wanted that money was following you."

"But...how could you know that?"

"We didn't, but with that much money involved, it made sense that they might be watching you, might try to follow you. And now we know they're *Englischers*."

"We didn't expect the guns," Albert admitted.

"If we'd thought of that, if we'd known they were that desperate, we'd never have agreed to coming out here, especially at night. Who knows if they would have been so bold during the day—maybe."

"You *wanted* them to follow us?" Katie Ann sounded as incredulous as Naomi felt.

"We wanted this to be over, and now...well, maybe Grayson can find them with the description we're able to provide."

"I guess that makes sense." Naomi's arms suddenly felt terribly heavy. "What time is it? I have to be up at four."

"The night isn't over yet," Albert said as he slipped an arm around Katie Ann's waist.

"Not over...What do you two have in mind?" Naomi glanced at Silas, who was grinning. He stepped closer and snagged her hand.

"We smoked them out, but now we have to turn the information over to Grayson. Waiting until morning wouldn't be smart. With that amount of money, they might be out of the state by tomorrow, which I guess is today."

"Speaking of the money, I can't believe we just gave it to them."

"They were right about one thing." Albert's expression had turned somber. "It wasn't ours."

"Who does it belong to?" Naomi shook her head so that her *kapp* strings bounced back and forth. "I can't figure it out. I was so shocked to find it that I didn't really think about what to do next."

"One thing we all know is that you wouldn't have kept it." Silas bumped his shoulder against hers as they walked out of the small clearing, through the stand of trees, and back toward their buggies.

"*Nein*. I would have turned it in to the police."

"So we have to go into town? To the police station?" Katie Ann glanced down at Albert's hand, as if she didn't remember him grabbing hold of hers.

Silas stopped, pulling Naomi to an abrupt stop. "We'll go wherever you want. If you want to go to the police, then we'll go with you and stay with you. We're all witnesses to what just happened. Don't you see? We caught them. We caught the people responsible for Jeremiah's murder."

"I know who they were. Who two of them were."

"You do?"

"Justin and Daisy. Jeremiah and I went out with them a couple of times, but I don't think they are capable of killing someone. I don't know why they thought the money belonged to them—"

"Details for the police to figure out."

Naomi put both hands to her face and rubbed her cheeks round and round. It seemed to invigorate her, bring her back from the dark abyss that had threatened to consume her.

"You're right. *Ya*. We should go and tell the police all we know, and maybe, just maybe, they can catch whoever killed Jeremiah." She studied her friends, especially Silas, whom she'd barely known when the night had begun. Now he seemed like someone who had always been in her life, someone she wanted in her future. "But first we go to Henry."

Forty

It was two in the morning by the time Henry sent Naomi, Katie Ann, Silas, and Albert home. He and Grayson sat at the kitchen table, mugs of cold coffee in front of them, Lexi snoring in her bed next to the stove.

"This thing is escalating," Grayson said.

"*Ya*. Appears so."

"I don't mind saying I don't like it."

"I feel the same."

Grayson sat back and stretched his legs out in front of him. "It's an admirable thing that they came to you, Henry. They trust you."

"They're good *youngies*—well, adults really." Henry hesitated, and then he asked what was on his mind even though he knew there was a limit to how much Grayson could or would share about an ongoing investigation. "Will you bring Justin Lane back in for additional questioning?"

"That's why I stepped outside to use the phone earlier. I have a patrol car sitting outside his parents' home, and a BOLO issued as well."

"Will you charge him?"

"With the murder? Not yet. We don't have enough evidence for that, but we should be able to get him for aggravated robbery—"

"Because the two people with him had guns?"

"Yes, and I think they would have used them if it had come to that. Fortunately, your young people were wise enough to simply hand over the bag of money."

"But the ski masks. They kept Naomi or any of the others from making a certain identification."

"Naomi seemed sure enough, and the other three were able to pick Justin out from your drawings."

That drawing, the one of Justin pushing his way through the crowd, sat on top of the stack on his table.

"Naomi didn't see their faces, and the others can only know that his height and build are the same."

"Don't forget he was already considered a suspect." Grayson ticked the reasons off on his fingers. "He was involved in the gambling scheme. He might have felt slighted since he wasn't chosen for the television program. We have witnesses who saw him arguing with Jeremiah at the diner—threatening him, actually."

Grayson stared down at his three fingers. "He had plenty of motive, and because he was there that night, we can place him at the scene of the crime."

"You'll need more than that for a murder charge to stick."

"Pull on a string, and there's no telling what you'll find. He's involved in this somehow. That I'm sure of."

"He slipped up. The robbery drew your attention to him. He must have really wanted the money."

"Maybe he thought he needed it."

"It's amazing what we can convince ourselves we need."

"We can make the charge of aggravated robbery stick," Grayson assured him. "I expect he'll give up the names of his two sidekicks pretty quickly. You know how these things go. The first person to rat out the others receives more leniency from the court. Once Justin realizes he could be looking at years behind bars, I imagine he'll abandon his cohorts. Or maybe it will happen the other way around."

"You think the other two will sacrifice Justin to save themselves?"

"I do, but we have to figure out who they are before that can happen."

Henry tapped the drawing. "The thing I keep asking myself is why he was on this side of the arena. If he was participating in the rodeo events, he should have been with the other contestants."

"A question he'll need to answer."

"What will happen to the money if Justin has it in his possession?"

"It would become evidence."

"Will it ever be returned to the individuals who gave it to Jeremiah or were owed by him?"

"Hard to say. If the judge believes Jeremiah's notebook is an accurate log, then it might be. However, because gaming operations must be licensed and regulated in this state, I doubt it. In most cases, it remains with the agency that seized it. At least seventy percent will."

"Monte Vista police?"

"We can hope." Grayson smiled for the first time that evening. "We put it into a special account for community service ventures. It gives us the funds to continue school programs that warn youngsters about drugs, crime, and so on. Some of it goes into a victims' fund."

"At least it will be put to good use."

"It will, and I'm sorry about the young men in your community who lost their hard-earned money. It's a costly lesson for them to learn."

"The gem cannot be polished without friction, nor man perfected without trials."

"Bible?"

"Amish proverb, but the Bible does contain similar statements."

Grayson stood and stretched. "It's been a long night, and you have an early morning."

"I do, but if I know you, I suspect your workday is just beginning."

Grayson only grunted at that.

They walked out onto the front porch. Lexi didn't even stir, testament to the fact that there had been a lot of activity in the little house for one small dog. When Naomi, Katie Ann, Silas, and Albert had first appeared at his door, all talking at once and claiming they had been robbed, Lexi had run in circles and barked and growled, as if she might terrorize the culprit out of the darkness. Katie Ann finally calmed down the little dog. Lexi had the heart of a protector, that much was certain.

"We appreciate what you do," Henry said to Grayson. "I hope you know that."

Morning was still hours away, but a quarter moon provided enough light for them to easily see their way down the porch steps. Grayson opened the door to his vehicle, but instead of getting in, he stood there, letting his gaze move slowly across Henry's garden, home, workshop, small barn, and field where he pastured his buggy horse. All mere shadows in the moonlight, but Henry understood Grayson was seeing what they represented.

"You all have been a good addition to this community, Henry. I'm sorry you're tangled up in a web of crime again, and I'm not going to even begin to try to explain why this is the third time you've been called upon to help during a murder investigation."

"*Gotte's wille*, perhaps."

"That's possible, I suppose, but you've done enough this time."

"So you're certain the person who killed Jeremiah is Justin?"

"I intend to find out."

Henry remained sitting on the porch until he could no longer see the red glow of Grayson's taillights. He continued rocking, allowing the breeze and the evening sounds to minister to his soul. When he walked inside, the clock told him it was well past three in the morning. Should he even bother going to bed?

He'd slept a few hours before Naomi and her friends showed up. It wasn't much, but it was probably enough. He was sixty-six, not ninety. He could go one night without sleep.

He walked into the kitchen, stared at the sheets of paper, and fought the irresistible urge to sit down and continue drawing. There was no need. Grayson had warned him off the investigation. Justin Lane probably was the person who had murdered Jeremiah, or at least Grayson thought so.

Picking up the drawing, the one that showed Justin pushing through the mob, he studied it. Then he shook his head and carried the drawing into the living room. He sat down on the couch, pulled on his reading glasses, and looked at it some more. He had no memory of drawing it, but he had. The picture of Justin showed a scowl on his face, his eyes cut toward the side as if needing to look behind him and move forward at the same time.

It was the expression on his face that bothered Henry and caused him to turn the battery lantern to its highest setting, pulling the drawing even closer.

Justin looked irritated, which was an odd enough emotion to see immediately after someone had been shot. He also looked concerned, maybe even the slightest bit afraid.

Henry took off his glasses and rubbed at his temples. He allowed his mind to drift back—to see Betsy Troyer's killer, the Monte Vista arsonist, and the person who had murdered Sophia Brooks. Each of those individuals had possessed a certain arrogance about them. They'd clung to an almost innocent idea that what they'd done had been called for, had been reasonable, had been necessary.

He saw none of that in Justin's face. The young man might be a gambler, a thief, even a bad person. But when he looked at the person in the center of the drawing he held, Henry did not see a killer.

Forty-One

Transcript of interview between Monte Vista Sheriff Roy Grayson and Justin Lane, regarding the July 27 homicide of Jeremiah Schwartz and the August 5 aggravated robbery of Naomi Miller, Katie Ann Fisher, Silas Fisher, and Albert Bontrager. Audiotapes and a transcript of the interview are included in both permanent case files.

Sheriff Roy Grayson #3604
INTERVIEW WITH Justin Lane
Case #4751.06 and #4762.02
6:15 a.m., Sunday, August 5

Sheriff Grayson (SG): Please state your name for the recording.

Justin Lane (JL): Justin Tanner Lane.

SG: And for the record, you have waived the right to a lawyer.

JL: I don't need a lawyer. I haven't done anything wrong.

SG: You have been arrested for the aggravated robbery of Naomi Miller, Katie Ann Fisher, Silas Fisher, and Albert Bontrager.

JL: Put me in a lineup. Let's see if they can pick me out.

SG: Son, I think we're past that since we found the money in your truck.

JL: But that money belongs to me. It's not robbery if you take back what's yours.

SG: So you admit to taking the money from them at gunpoint?

JL: I'm not admitting anything.

SG: How long had you been following them?

JL: Not them. The girl.

SG: Naomi?

JL: I guess.

SG: This is your chance to cooperate, Justin. Don't waste it.

JL: We'd been keeping an eye on her since before the funeral. Figured she knew where he'd stashed the money, and he owed me. You have that notebook he kept, right? Look in the notebook, and you'll see that he owed me, that I only took what was mine.

SG: So you were going to turn in the rest of the money?

JL: Didn't say that.

SG: Why didn't you just ask for it?

JL: Ask for it? You think she would have just handed it over? She might be Amish, but she's not stupid.

SG: Why the guns?

JL: They weren't even loaded. We were just trying to scare them.

SG: Back to Naomi. You followed her to the Kauffmann farm?

JL: Yeah.

SG: Tell me about that.

JL: Nothing to tell. We'd been watching Naomi's place, so we followed her. Have you seen the Kauffmann farm? What a setup. Can you tell me where an Amish farmer came up with that much money? Anyway, it was easy enough to let ourselves into the back of the barn and listen in on what they were saying. Then it was just a matter of getting out without being seen and following the girl.

SG: Justin, did you kill Jeremiah Schwartz?

JL: No! I wouldn't do that. I didn't do that, even though it would have been justified, considering what he stole from me.

SG: You argued with him...at the diner.

JL: I wanted the money I'd won the week before. He kept putting me off. Why would he do that? You saw how much he had. I think he was planning to keep it, planning to take it to California with him.

SG: If you really believed that, why didn't you come to the police and file a complaint against him?

JL: For illegal gambling? Now you're just trying to trip me up.

SG: Where were you when Jeremiah was shot?

JL: I was at the rodeo. You know that. You even have the statement I filled out.

SG: Did you smuggle a rifle into Ski Hi Arena?

JL: No.

SG: Did you plan to kill Jeremiah Schwartz?

JL: No!

SG: And did you carry out that plan on July 27?

JL: I didn't do anything like that.

SG: Where were you standing when he was shot?

JL: You asked me before—both times you brought me in.

SG: You said you were standing in the chutes.

JL: This is harassment if you want my opinion.

SG: You said you were standing there with the other rodeo contestants, but that isn't true, is it?

JL: I'd already ridden when Jeremiah went out.

SG: You were watching him?

JL: Everyone watched Jeremiah when he competed. Don't ask me why. I never did understand the appeal of watching an Amish kid on a horse.

SG: This is a map of Ski Hi Arena. Can you point to where you were standing when Jeremiah was shot?

JL: What difference does it make?

SG: Just humor me. Approximately where were you when you heard the rifle shot?

JL: I've slept since then. I can barely remember where I was yesterday.

SG: We have a witness that places you here. Is that where you were?

JL: I don't remember.

SG: Because that would have been approximately where the shooter would have needed to be. To shoot Jeremiah as he came out here, the shooter had to be in this section of the stands, the same section you were in.

JL: I didn't see a shooter.

SG: What did you see?

JL: Yeah, I'd gone to the opposite side. I was hoping to find Piper, to tell her Jeremiah had to pay me that night, but I didn't see her. I was turning to go back when I heard the shot. Couldn't tell you where it came from, but I recognized it for what it was—a rifle shot, probably high caliber, and probably with a scope. That's just an opinion, because I don't know for certain. I did not kill Jeremiah!

SG: That's it? That's all you have for me?

JL: What else do you want?

SG: I want the truth. I want to know what happened the night of July 27.

JL: I've told you everything I know.

SG: Is there anything else you'd like to add to your statement?

JL: No. Nothing.

SG: All right. You are formally being charged with aggravated robbery. Your arraignment will occur within the next twenty-four hours.

JL: Arraignment?

SG: Your first appearance in court. A judge will decide if you're a flight risk, which I believe you are. The judge will then either set bail or decide you're to remain in jail until your trial.

JL: I can't sit in a jail cell waiting for you all to figure out I didn't do this. I can't miss the rest of the circuit.

SG: The rodeo is the last thing you need to worry about.

JL: The rodeo is my life.

SG: You still have one phone call. I suggest you call your parents and ask them to arrange for a good criminal defense attorney.

JL: (inaudible)

SG: If you can't afford an attorney, one will be appointed to represent you.

JL: I don't need an attorney.

SG: And Justin? We have both your friends here.

JL: My friends?

SG: Daisy Marshall and Roger Clemore.

JL: You arrested them?

SG: We did. They are also being charged with aggravated robbery.

JL: Seems like you're filling up your jail with people who didn't commit a crime.

SG: My advice is that you come clean before they do—

JL: I don't have anything to say about them.

SG: Because whoever tells us what we need to know first, whoever helps in this investigation, is going to receive a recommendation for leniency from me. I plan to ask the district attorney to prosecute the other two to the full extent the law allows.

Forty-Two

Emma arrived for their church service at the Hoschstetler place a few minutes early and was following the trail of folks into the barn. Stephen and Thomas had run ahead. She moved in front of Rachel, who was walking with Clyde, holding his hand as she listened to him telling her about the passage of Scripture he'd studied in case he was called on to preach the sermon. Katie Ann and Silas had spied other *youngies* and peeled off in their direction.

As she stepped into the barn, Emma glanced back over her shoulder and saw the top of Henry's roof. It felt strange, being this close to Henry's house but not being there. The Hoschstetler place had been owned by *Englisch* before, and Seth and Roseann were slowly changing it to meet the rules of their *Ordnung*—disconnecting the electricity, removing the ceiling fixtures, adding hooks for lanterns and shelves for flashlights, exchanging the electrical appliances for gas-powered ones. It was an arduous process, but it was usually completed within the first year of purchasing a place not considered Amish.

The Hoschstetlers seemed like a friendly couple, and Emma was glad they had joined the Monte Vista community. Amish districts, especially small ones, could always use new members, and God had provided in their time of need. Two more new couples were supposed to move into the area by the end of summer. She thought that was a good thing. More neighbors, more hands to help, more people for their *youngies* to date and even marry.

As Emma murmured hello and took her seat, she tried to focus on the church service, tried to calm the flurry of panic that had taken up residence in her heart since the moment Katie Ann and Silas stumbled through the back door. Of course she'd been waiting up. She understood *youngies* needed to have their time of *rumspringa*, but that didn't stop a grandmother from worrying. She was sitting at the table nursing a cup of coffee when they'd come in during the wee hours of the morning.

They'd told her the whole thing—about Naomi figuring out where the money might be, finding the money, and then being robbed at gunpoint. Though they'd appeared calm enough, though they'd assured her Henry and Grayson had everything under control, she'd stayed at the table long after they'd gone to bed. She'd prayed and worried and prayed some more. They'd repeated the night's events to their parents the next morning, and Clyde and Rachel had taken the news well.

But Emma hadn't.

She hadn't felt any better about it the second time she heard the telling.

Sometime in the past twelve hours, she'd allowed fear to worm its way into her heart—maybe because she'd been able to vividly imagine what they had described. She'd been held at gunpoint before. She understood the fear and the danger.

Silas and Katie Ann—threatened with a gun.

Albert and Naomi—pulled into the midst of this thing.

Someone willing to kill for money—willing to kill again.

And then there was the matter of the cut fence and spooked horses.

The situation, which she'd hoped was improving, was growing more dangerous. It caused her stomach to twist and turn. She found herself clutching her purse with her hands until they cramped, and her neck felt stiff. She should be focused on the church service. They'd already sung the *Loblied*, and she didn't even remember doing so. Henry had moved to the front of the group. He opened his Bible and began reading from 1 Peter.

"Always be prepared to give an answer to everyone who asks you to give the reason for the hope that you have."

Emma could do that. She could point to places in Scripture that gave her hope. She could tell how Christ had changed her life. She could talk about her salvation, but what she couldn't do at the moment was shake this feeling of dread. Tears blurred her vision as she stared down at her open Bible. She sat that way for some time as the service went on despite her inattention. When they sang, she stood and listened to those around her. When the sermon began, she remained quiet, though she couldn't have told you a word that was said. She bowed her head when they prayed, but as she searched her heart, she found only fear. She fought to keep her expression neutral, but before the service was over, Rachel reached for her hand and whispered, "Are you okay?"

"I will be," she assured her daughter-in-law.

But would she? Could she make it through yet more danger and drama?

The heaviness of her fear followed her to the serving line, where she helped replace empty platters of vegetables with full ones. She didn't want to eat, and she certainly didn't want to visit with anyone. As soon as she could reasonably escape, she fled to a cove of trees that bordered the property line next to Henry's place. She stood there, leaning against a tree and staring at a broken place in the fence line. From the track of paw prints, it looked as if Lexi was taking full advantage of the ability to freely visit Henry's neighbors.

She pulled in a deep breath, closed her eyes, and attempted to calm the swirling emotions in her heart.

"Care for company?"

She opened her eyes and saw Henry standing a few feet in front of her, Lexi waiting patiently at his side.

"I didn't hear you walk up." She swiped at the tears that had tracked down her cheeks, embarrassed and then wondering why she would be embarrassed to show this man her emotions. She was marrying him in less than three weeks. Surely their relationship was strong enough to handle a few tears.

"I was worried. I thought I'd come and check on you." He covered the distance between them slowly, giving her time to say she'd rather be alone.

But she didn't want to be alone. She wanted Henry to hold her and tell her everything was going to be all right. So she stepped forward, and then his arms were around her, and her head was resting against his chest, and she understood that she didn't need to rein in her emotions or hide her tears.

He let her cry, not bothering to talk her out of it with empty sayings such as *There's nothing to cry about*, or *Look on the bright side*, or *Things will be better tomorrow.*

When she'd wrung herself dry, she stepped back and brushed at his shirt. "You'll need to change now. The fabric is soaked."

"In this weather it will dry in no time. Would you like to walk?"

"*Ya*, I would."

Lexi had been watching them curiously, but at the word *walk* she bounced up on to her back legs and barked.

"You can run ahead, girl. But stay close."

As if she understood, Lexi darted a few feet in front of them and then slowed to sniff at the ground. And then they were holding hands and walking the fence line, looking at Seth's horses, seeing Henry's small garden on the other side of the fence, enjoying a beautiful summer day. Emma gradually felt better, and then when she was ready, she began to talk.

"It seems as if time is repeating itself, as if Silas and Katie Ann are in danger—all of them in danger like we were before."

"You care about them."

"Of course I do, but I know...I know the Lord can look out for them."

"He can and He will."

"It's only that...well, it feels as if my heart hurts, as if my heart is heavy with fear."

Henry nodded as if he understood, and maybe he did.

"Do you ever feel that way, Henry?"

"*Ya*, certainly I do."

"You're being honest?"

"I will always be honest with you, Emma." He pulled her to a stop, kissed her lips gently, and then smiled, studying her eyes and touching her face. "I am so fortunate to have you in my life, to have a future with you. I'm thankful for that more than you can imagine."

"*Danki.* I feel those things too, and then these worries crowd in, and I forget I have much to be thankful for. Do you think that fear, that worry, is a lack of faith?"

"If we live in perpetual fear, then yes, it could be that we need to spend more time studying and praying."

"The Bible says to *fear not.*"

"Indeed it does."

"Many times."

"Because God's plan for us is peace." He paused a moment and then began walking again. "But if you experience fear in response to a real danger, in my opinion that's a very natural emotion. It's not a fear born from disbelief, but an emotion—a reaction—to a situation."

"Like when we were hiding next to the sand dunes."

"Exactly. That sort of fear is your body reacting, not your heart or soul, and I like to think of it as a kind of warning system that God has given us, so that we are alert and aware of what is going on around us. Our reactions become faster, our vision better, even our hearing improves. We become ready to fight, metaphorically speaking."

"We have taken a vow of peace."

"Yes, our doctrine of nonaggression is very important to our Plain life." He cleared his throat and then said, "Perhaps I can ease some of your worries. You know Katie Ann and Silas were at my house last night, after—"

"*Ya.* They told me all about what happened, and they told their parents this morning."

"After the *youngies* left, Grayson told me he felt certain an arrest would occur soon."

"Of Justin and the others involved in the robbery?"

"*Ya.*"

"Does he think they killed Jeremiah?"

"It's a possibility, though he won't charge them with it yet."

"But they're in jail."

"Probably by now they are."

"At least there they can't hurt anyone else."

"And that's Grayson's goal, to keep our community—both Amish and *Englisch*—safe."

"I can't shake the feeling that there's more. That this isn't over yet."

"It's not. I agree with you there, but I believe we are a step closer."

"Why am I so worried?"

"Because you love them. Because you've had several traumatic events in the last few years that have changed your outlook. Because you're a good woman."

"I thought it was because I was a weak woman."

"Never mistake caring for weakness."

Instead of answering, she stepped again into the circle of his arms. She was a strong woman, and she was a faithful believer, but it felt good to have Henry's arms around her, to hear his assurances, to be reminded of his love.

Lexi bounded back in their direction, carrying a small stick, which she dropped at Henry's feet. They spent the next few moments playing fetch, laughing at her enthusiasm, and allowing the peace and quiet and joy of the afternoon to ease their fears.

When they finally turned to walk back toward the others, Henry interlaced his fingers with hers and said, "Now let me tell you more of what Grayson is thinking, and why I'm worried he might be wrong."

Forty-Three

When Silas and Albert had both jogged off to join the game of baseball, Katie Ann and Naomi found a place to sit under a shade tree. They could still see the action of the game, but they were far enough away to speak privately. Naomi thought it strange, that life continued as if nothing had happened, even when very dangerous, dramatic events had occurred only hours before.

"How are you holding up?" Katie Ann asked.

"Okay, I suppose. How about you?"

"Tired. I almost fell asleep during my *dat's* sermon."

"We had a long night." Naomi stifled a yawn with her hand and then dropped her head into her hands. "My *Aenti* Abigail was none too happy when I explained what happened. She thinks we were needlessly reckless."

"And your *onkel*?"

"Didn't have much to say. He's a quiet sort."

"My parents weren't happy either, but they didn't come down too hard on me or Silas. Maybe they're used to members of our family being threatened...you know, with what happened with *Mammi* and all."

"How did she take the news?"

"Not as well. You'd think she'd understand, but..."

"Maybe she does understand. Maybe that's why she didn't take it well."

"I suppose you have a point. She was awfully somber during church."

"Maybe she needs a little time. I'm sure we gave her quite a scare."

Naomi leaned back, lifting her face to the sun. "I don't mind admitting last night was terrifying. Seeing those guns pointed at us was like something out of a bad *Englisch* movie."

"I was equal parts frightened and angry. Frightened because...well, obviously because I'm not ready to die, and angry because...How dare they do such a thing? I can't stand bullies in any shape or form."

"Yeah, if Albert hadn't pulled you back, I think you would have tried to take their guns away."

"It's not that I'm brave. It's just that what they were doing wasn't right, and I'm tired of being pushed around."

"I like that about you," Naomi said. "You're spunky."

"Spunky?"

"It's a word my *aenti* uses, though she doesn't say it as a compliment."

"*Ya*. I suppose that's not the most common adjective for Amish women."

"But I like it."

"You like spunky?"

"I like a friend who has my back."

"We make a good team, the four of us, and don't think I didn't notice that you and my *bruder* were holding hands."

Naomi drew her knees up and circled her arms around them, making sure her dress reached the ground as she did so. Finally, she glanced at Katie Ann. "You're smiling, so I guess you aren't too upset."

"Do you like him?"

"I don't know. Everything's happened so fast, and it's only been a little over a week since—"

"You already said you and Jeremiah weren't that close."

"We were close. As friends we were, but it wasn't as if we were in love."

"I expect Jeremiah would want you to be happy, though I have to warn you about my *bruder*—"

"You already have warned me at least a dozen times! He's a player. He never stays with one girl more than two weeks. He's easily distracted by other girls."

"I'm glad you were listening."

"Of course I was listening. I listen to you, Katie Ann. I just couldn't understand why you were so intent on pushing me away from Silas."

"I didn't push."

"You certainly did a good job of keeping us apart."

"Not sure I remember that."

"What about the time we all went hiking at the sand dunes? You pulled me all the way to the back of the line with the little *kinner*, and I didn't even have a chance to talk to Silas."

"Because I was worried about this happening." But she laughed as she spoke, which eased some of Naomi's worries. "You know I'd love to have you as my sister."

Naomi dropped her forehead to her knees.

"Now I've embarrassed you."

"We haven't even talked about courting, let alone marrying."

"You like him, though."

"*Ya.*"

"You think he's changed."

"Maybe. People can change. I did, when I came here. Before? I wasn't the fun, pleasant, mature person you know now."

Katie Ann sighed. "*Ya.* I know we all can mature. I just don't want him to hurt you. I told him this morning—"

Naomi groaned and slapped her hands over her eyes.

"I told him if he hurts you, he's going to have to answer to me."

"Should I give the same lecture to Albert?"

"Albert?" Katie Ann's voice squeaked like a mouse.

"I saw you holding hands."

"Only for a minute, and only because he thought we were in danger."

"Katie Ann Fisher, Albert is smitten and you know it."

Instead of answering, Katie Ann jumped to her feet. "Let's go and play ball with them. I'm tired of sitting."

Which meant she was dodging the topic, but that was okay. At least they'd put their feelings out in the open. Naomi hadn't realized she was worried until that moment. Well, she knew she was worried...about the robbery, the police, Jeremiah's killers. But that was entirely different from being worried about your best friend's feelings.

The team up to bat welcomed them warmly. "We need your help," Stephen said.

Their participation equaled up the number of girl and boys on each side.

Albert was pitching and warned them he wasn't going easy because they hadn't slept much. By now everyone knew what they'd been through the night before. There were shouts of "Naomi's a good hitter! Better watch out!"

And then she was swinging the bat and connecting with the ball, laughing and running toward first, where Silas pretended to tag her out though Lloyd Yutzy hadn't managed to return the ball from the outfield yet. He stood staring up at the ball, which she had lobbed high, a borrowed glove on his left hand and his right ready to throw her out.

Which wasn't going to happen.

She felt the warmth of the sun on her arms and the breeze tickling the hair at the nape of her neck. Silas was daring her to try to steal second. Katie Ann was up to bat. Albert was playing up his position as pitcher with a bizarre windup sequence. And life was good in that instant.

Naomi was learning the moment you were in was the one you had to enjoy, because there was no way to control what happened next.

Forty-Four

Henry knew it wasn't good news when a Monte Vista police cruiser pulled down Seth's lane and Grayson stepped out. The sheriff wouldn't interrupt their Sunday afternoon unless something important had happened. A tightening in Henry's gut told him this wasn't a celebratory visit.

By the time the sheriff reached where Henry and Emma were seated, he'd drawn quite a crowd—basically everyone, including the *youngies*, who had stopped their ball game.

"Henry, could I speak with you privately for a moment?"

"Of course, but I think what you have to say probably needs to be heard by everyone here."

Grayson looked down at the ground for a moment. When he raised his gaze to Henry's and nodded once, Seth popped up out of his chair and insisted he take it.

Though it was obvious everyone was listening intently, they seemed happy to let Henry lead the questions.

"There's news on the case?"

"We made an arrest."

"Justin Lane?"

"Yes."

"But there's a problem, or you wouldn't be here."

"His bail will be set tomorrow, and I expect he'll bond out."

"He'll go free?"

"With an ankle monitor, but yes. I expect the judge to grant bail."

Henry thought about that a moment. He wasn't new to the judicial process, and he understood that bond for murder suspects was traditionally set high, especially if one was considered a flight risk. Which only meant one thing.

"You're not charging him with Jeremiah's murder."

"I'm not, and I won't unless I find more evidence."

"Do you think he did it?"

Grayson didn't answer immediately. He pulled at his ear and took his time studying the folks assembled around them, people who were intently focused on every word he said.

"I don't know if he did or not, but I can't at this point prove he did, so I won't bring the charge."

"And the robbery?"

"That's a different matter. We have a strong case there, strong enough that his lawyer might convince him to enter a guilty plea, which would improve his chances of leniency as far as sentencing." Grayson stood. "I'm sorry, Henry. I'd hoped to bring a quick resolution to Jeremiah's murder, but this case seems to become more complicated every day."

"We know you're doing your best."

"I wanted to tell you myself. Wanted you to hear it from me before you read it in the papers. Also, I'd like to remind everyone that if you see or hear anything, anything you even think might be relevant to the case, please contact me."

Clyde stepped forward. "I haven't had a chance to call it in, but my fences were cut yesterday, and my horses spooked out onto the county road."

"You're sure they were cut?" Grayson began to pull out his notebook.

"I am, but we don't want to file an official report. I took care of the damage with the help of a neighbor."

Grayson tapped the notebook against the palm of his hands. Finally, he said, "I'm trying to build a case here, and everything that happens, whether large or small, will help to convince a judge that this person is dangerous."

"What person?" Clyde asked. "We have no idea who is doing these things."

"Which is why it's important to document every incident."

Clyde shrugged good-naturedly. "I'll stop by the police station tomorrow, then."

"Thank you, and please..." Grayson allowed his gaze to travel across the group. "Anyone else who has any trouble, please let me know. Together, we can and will catch whoever is doing these things, whether or not it's the same person who killed Jeremiah. The main thing to remember is if you see something, say something."

People nodded and murmured in agreement, and then the group broke up with everyone going back to their various activities. Henry understood his congregation. They would accept such a turn of events as God's will. They weren't overly concerned about a murderer in their midst. There had been very little to indicate anyone was in danger since Jeremiah's murder, except for Seth being run off the road, which might have been an accident. Then there was the warning on Henry's buggy, and Clyde's animals being released from their pastures. Things that sounded more like a teenager's pranks than a threat from a murderer. The robbery the night before had been a clear case of greed, something most of his people thought was rampant in the *Englisch* world. Henry thought it was a stumbling block for humans in general—both Amish and *Englisch*.

He walked Grayson back to his vehicle. They stood there, their backs against the car, and studied the folks spread out around Seth's farm.

"Looks like something from a Norman Rockwell painting."

"Indeed it does."

"You've seen them?" Grayson's voice rose in surprise.

"*Ya*. I visited some distant relatives in Massachusetts when I was younger. They took me to the museum. During the time Rockwell painted, which I believe began in 1916, our lifestyle wasn't so different from mainstream America."

"Technology now reigns supreme on my side of the fence."

Henry didn't answer that. Amish struggled with advances in technology the same as *Englisch* did. It was only that the *Englisch* seemed to fully embrace it, while the Amish held back. The fact that every house in the valley, including the Amish ones, now had solar panels was testament to the fact that technological innovations affected them all.

When Grayson still didn't leave, Henry realized he'd come to say more. He turned to him with an appraising look.

"Yeah. I didn't feel comfortable going into great detail with the entire group, but I think it would be good for you to know how this morning went. Lane's friends turned on him pretty quickly, claimed the robbery was his idea. He assured them no one would get hurt. The guns apparently were empty of ammunition, at least they were when we confiscated them. Lane wanted the money, and his partners in crime didn't mind receiving part of the loot for helping him get it. It's as simple as that, but they weren't willing to murder anyone to get it."

"You no longer think he killed Jeremiah?"

Instead of answering, Grayson opened the door of his cruiser. But he stood there rather than getting in the vehicle, gazing again at the families spread out under the shade of the trees. "I was hoping for a quick resolution to this thing. I'm less convinced that's going to happen. I want you to be careful, Henry, and remind your people to be vigilant."

"You think we're in danger?"

"I don't know," he said. "Honestly? Our perp might be three states away by now."

"Or he might be here among us."

"That's a possibility too." Grayson tipped his hat, got into the cruiser, and drove away, leaving Henry staring after his friend and wondering what he'd heard in his interrogations to cause him to utter such a warning.

Forty-Five

On Monday morning, Naomi helped her *aenti* with the laundry. The bakery was closed on Mondays, as the three widows were also home doing their laundry. Most weeks, this meant Naomi had the afternoon off to fill as she pleased.

"I think I'll go visit with Katie Ann," she said as she removed the last of the laundry from the clothesline. It was amazing how quickly it dried in the summer heat, but then they did live in a high mountain desert with very little humidity. Some weeks she thought she could begin removing the laundry as soon as she'd finished putting it up, move from the end of the line to the front and back again.

Her *mamm* was fond of saying that keeping a neat house was like threading beads on a string with no knot. The memory made her smile and also brought a small pang of regret. She should write to her *mamm* more often. The letter she'd left on the table for Abigail to add a note was the first she'd written in a month. She should be a better daughter. She would be. She'd set her mind to it.

"You'll go straight there and straight back?" Abigail asked.

"*Ya.* I promise."

"No looking for missing money."

"I'm done with that."

"No traipsing into crime scenes."

"Vernon's place wasn't exactly a crime scene."

"You heard what the sheriff said yesterday. If you see something—"

"Say something. I know, *Aenti*. I'll go straight there and straight back. I promise."

Naomi's *aenti* was nearly sixty, but like many Amish women, she wasn't slowing down much. She'd gained a few pounds over the years, and Naomi often caught her rubbing a special ointment into her knees for the arthritis that plagued her. Her hair was gray, of course, but that was hardly noticeable when she wore her *kapp*. She was a pleasant person, and she and her husband, Daniel, had been kind to take Naomi in when she needed a change. They'd always made her feel welcome, and for that Naomi was grateful. Their only son, Sam, had built a home on his own small acreage, and word had it that he'd been corresponding with a woman in a Kentucky community. Naomi expected them to announce their intentions any day. She'd seen him reading one of her letters. He turned an amusing shade of red when he realized she was watching.

For the most part, Sam treated her like the kid sister he never had.

"Looks like rain over in Del Norte. Could reach here, and I don't want you out in it."

"I'll come home early if it looks like it's going to storm."

Abigail pulled at the reading glasses she wore on a beaded chain. Popping them on, she looked closely where a stain had been on one of her aprons and then turned to look at Naomi over the top of her glasses. "Remember, we've been involved with this sort of thing before when Sam was suspected of killing Vernon."

"My cousin would never do such a thing."

"Of course he wouldn't. My point is that we want to stay out of it and let the sheriff solve who did this, put the person in jail, and restore peace to our valley."

"Sounds like a hymn—peace in the valley?"

Abigail grunted at that. "I know you think I'm being silly. *Youngies* often think a person my age has a tendency to be overly dramatic, too careful, too serious."

She picked up one of the laundry baskets, Naomi picked up the other, and they both trudged toward the house.

"Your *onkel* and I care a lot about you, Naomi. It's been nice having a young person around the place."

"You have Sam," Naomi reminded her.

"Sam is rarely here between his working on his own fields and finishing his own house and barn."

"Don't forget his courting."

"*Ya*, there's that too."

Naomi wondered if now was the time to speak to her *aenti* about Silas, but he hadn't even asked her to court. He'd held her hand on Saturday night. The next evening he'd sat by her during the singing and then given her a ride home. He'd even kissed her once before walking her up to the front door. She was thinking of that, of the kiss, when she tripped over the bottom step going into the house.

"Something you want to tell me?"

"Um...no. Maybe later, that is. It's nothing. That is, it's nothing important."

"So you're talking about Silas."

Naomi could feel the blush starting at the top of her head and working its way down.

"You came in humming last night, and you set a full glass of milk in the cupboard."

"I wondered where that went. I remembered pouring it..."

"Love can do that to a person, cause them to be distracted." Abigail's voice had taken on a softer tone. "You be careful with Silas Fisher. I believe he has a good heart, but..."

"But what?"

"I doubt he even knows if he's finished sowing his wild oats."

"What does that expression mean?"

"It means doing wild and foolish things in one's youth, only some people forget that and continue right through old age. So be careful. That's all I'm saying." She reached out and ran a hand up and down Naomi's arm. "Now, get out of here before I find another chore for you."

Naomi was nearly to the door when she turned and said, "They may ask me to eat with them. Would that be all right?"

"As long as you're home before dark, and I suspect Emma and Rachel will ask you to stay for dinner. You could do worse than to have those two women in your life permanently."

"We're not even courting yet!"

But Abigail wasn't listening. She'd already turned her attention to storing the freshly laundered dish towels in the kitchen drawers.

Naomi practically skipped down the lane, feeling happy and free and forgetting completely that she was supposed to be careful.

Forty-Six

Naomi gladly accepted Emma's invitation to stay for dinner. She and Katie Ann had spent the afternoon tending to a new litter of kittens in the barn, harvesting some of the produce from the family garden, and folding the last of the Fisher laundry. With two young boys in the house plus five adults, they had more laundry than Naomi's *aenti* did. As she was folding the boys' pants and shirts, she allowed her mind to wander, to consider what it would be like to have a family of her own, to tend to their meals and a home and, yes, laundry.

"You're daydreaming again."

"I was?"

"*Ya.* You put one of *Mamm*'s aprons in the boys' pile."

That started them giggling, which felt good because the previous day's tone had turned terribly serious when the sheriff stopped by their luncheon. A sheriff at a Sunday luncheon—now there was something she could write about for her *Budget* article.

Instead of discussing that, Naomi told Katie Ann about setting the glass of milk in the cupboard. "I have no idea where my mind was."

"We both know where it was, or on whom it was, and I'm sorry Silas isn't here today. He hired Stuart to drive him over to Alamosa. He needed a special part for the plow. He tends to have a long list of things to do when he finally hires a driver. I expect he won't be back until after dinner."

"I came to see you, not your *bruder*."

"But it would have been nice."

"*Ya.* It would have."

"Did he ask you last night…to court, to step out with him, to be his one and only?"

"Not exactly, but he kissed me."

Which sent them into another fit of giggles.

Dinner was a delicious, boisterous affair, and then it was time to go home.

"I'm going to walk her back," Katie Ann told her mother.

"And who will walk you back?" Rachel asked.

"I could walk her back." Naomi started laughing when Rachel pointed a dish towel at her.

"Then you'd end up where you began."

"How about I go halfway with her and then I come back?"

"A good compromise."

So they'd set out down the lane, the summer sun lower but not yet touching the horizon. Clouds had continued to build along the western horizon and were predicted to turn their direction before morning. Del Norte must have had a good rain, because the storm had appeared to sit there all day. It was funny the way you could see it raining in another place and yet stand in sunshine.

If Naomi could have described what she felt that moment, it would have been good, relaxed, even optimistic. She thought that was progress, given what she'd been through in the last week, and she hoped everything would soon return to normal.

They were out of sight of the house, and not yet to the halfway mark between their places, when Katie Ann stopped to point out a crane standing near the irrigation canal. "Henry says they're a miracle of nature, that they return every year—the families do. The male and female mate for life."

"Like us."

"*Ya,* and the young stay with the parents for the first year and into the second, when the female gets pregnant and the cycle repeats itself."

"Again, like us." Which sounded like a silly thing to say, but it was true. Many of the women in their community seemed to be pregnant every other year. It was small wonder that most Amish families had eight to ten children. "Do you want a whole houseful of children?"

"Not at the moment," Katie Ann admitted. "But I might if I met the right person."

"Like Albert?"

"Maybe. I guess time will tell. Some Amish men don't approve of me."

"That's ridiculous and closed minded."

"It's true, though. They think I should work in a bakery."

"Then where would I work?"

"Or a dress shop."

"We don't have a dress shop."

"You're missing my point, and on purpose, it seems, given the smile on your face. The truth is, I enjoy working with animals."

"It is an unusual choice for an Amish woman."

"And yet it's my choice to make. I keep thinking that if I meet the right person, he will understand this passion in my heart and will want me to be happy."

"Has Albert said anything about it?"

"No. Like you and Silas, we're not even courting yet. We're..."

"Did he kiss you when he took you home from the singing last night?"

For her answer, Katie Ann began to hum, and then she walked farther from the road to pull a bunch of yellow wildflowers. "Give these to your *aenti*, and tell her thank you for letting you come."

"Sounds like you're avoiding the question, which I'll take as a yes."

"It's been a *gut* day. *Ya*?"

Naomi would think of that moment later, of Katie's humming and the yellow flowers and the way the sun played across the fields as the dark clouds marched toward them. She would remember the way the crane had raised its head to call out to its mate. The way the family of three looked, searching for food as they stood in the irrigation water.

A truck pulled up beside them then, an old and battered pickup pulling a horse trailer. At first Naomi didn't recognize the person driving, but then he leaned across the seat, popped open the door, and said, "Get in."

"We're actually enjoying our walk and have just a little farther to go," Katie Ann said.

"But thank you," Naomi added.

"It wasn't a request." And then Naomi saw the gun on the seat. His hand went to it, but his eyes stayed on them. "Now, get in."

So they did, because getting in seemed wiser than getting shot.

Forty-Seven

Emma didn't worry at first.

The sun dropped behind the San Juans, and she told herself girls were girls.

She finished cleaning the kitchen, set a platter of cookies in the middle of the table for their evening snack, and walked around the house turning on the lanterns.

Still no Katie Ann.

It was obvious that Naomi was taken with Silas, and Katie Ann had been brought home the evening before by Albert. They were young women, with their entire lives before them and new loves on their hearts. It made sense they would be distracted.

But then darkness fell.

The wind picked up, and a few fat raindrops struck the roof and splattered the windows. It kicked up the dust and caused the cranes to take flight. Rain was a blessing, and Emma was grateful for it, but she prayed it would hold off until Katie Ann made it back home.

She picked up her Bible, clasped it to her chest, and prayed that God would protect her granddaughter. She tried to tamp down her panic by reciting a psalm under her breath.

Emma couldn't imagine one good reason for Katie Ann to be so late. Normally they wouldn't have worried, but these weren't normal times. As she and Naomi had traipsed down the porch steps arm in arm, Emma had reminded her granddaughter to be back before dark. They'd spoken the night before and again at breakfast about being careful. Katie Ann had soberly listened and promised to be cautious, to be alert to her surroundings and any possible danger, to stick relatively close to home until Grayson caught the person responsible for Jeremiah's murder.

Emma moved to the front porch, paced back and forth, and finally asked Thomas to fetch his father from the barn. Rachel had been upstairs putting away the last of the laundry, but she arrived at the porch the same time her husband did.

"Something about Katie Ann?" Clyde asked.

"She's still not home."

"They left..." Rachel glanced down the lane, as if she might see her daughter if she only stared long enough, hard enough. The rain had turned to a steady drizzle and the wind had picked up even more, causing a loose board on the barn's siding to slap back and forth. "They left right after dinner."

"That was hours ago."

"*Ya*, and she was only going halfway." Rachel sank onto one of the porch rockers. "She promised me she would go only halfway. We...we made a joke about it."

"Should have taken twenty or thirty minutes," Emma said. "No more than an hour even if they'd stopped to talk, and they've been talking all afternoon, so that doesn't seem likely. She should have been home an hour ago."

Clyde studied his wife and mother for only a moment, and then he said, "I'll hitch up the buggy."

"I'll do it, *Dat*." Stephen stepped out of the darkness, where he'd been waiting, listening. "I'll hook up Cinnamon."

"Should I go and tell the neighbors?" Thomas asked. "Or run to the phone shack and call Henry?"

"Let's not get our buggy in front of our horse. I'll drive to Abigail's first. Could be the girls went there for some reason, even though Katie Ann told you she wouldn't." Clyde touched his wife's arm. "If they're not there, I'll stop by the phone shack and call Grayson. Rachel, you and *Mamm* wait here in case she comes back..."

He didn't add what they were all thinking. That Katie Ann might be hurt. That she wouldn't have done anything so disrespectful. That she understood the dangerous situation that currently held the Monte Vista community in its grip.

"Maybe she found a hurt animal," Rachel offered. "It's the only reason I can think of that she...wouldn't be back."

"We'll stay here," Emma said. "We'll pray."

Which they did. Emma clasped Rachel's hands, and they prayed that God would protect the girls wherever they were, that Clyde would find them and bring them home, that no harm would come to the two young women.

They prayed and they rocked.

They prayed some more and they paced.

Emma made coffee, but it tasted bitter and made her jump at the slightest sound. Or maybe fear did that. Maybe it was the memory of what could happen in a world where darkness sometimes won.

Rachel's mug sat cold and untouched on the table beside the rocker. The boys sat on the floor of the porch, pretending to play checkers, though neither had moved a piece in quite a long time. They should have all moved inside as the rain increased in intensity, but they couldn't.

Each person there loved and cared for Katie Ann and needed to be able to see the lane.

When lightning streaked across the sky, Emma jumped.

When thunder rolled, Rachel glanced at her, shook her head, and turned her attention back down the road.

When the rain turned to a downpour, Emma's heart filled with dread.

Forty-Eight

An hour later, Clyde turned back down their lane, but he wasn't alone. Henry followed in his own buggy, as did Abigail's husband in theirs.

"No sign of the girls," Clyde said as he took the front porch steps two at a time. Daniel and Henry were right behind him.

"You called Grayson?" Emma felt as if she couldn't swallow, as if her mouth were suddenly filled with sand.

"I did. He'll be here soon."

Her heart sank at those words. She wanted to burst into tears, to walk into Henry's arms as she had the day before. She wanted to allow herself to be weak. But Rachel had gone suddenly pale and begun to shake. Clyde squatted by her chair and spoke to her softly.

Emma went to Thomas and Stephen to assure them everything was being done, that their sister would be home before they woke in the morning. But the sight of their mother sobbing shattered the boys' innocence. They'd been largely unaware of the danger Emma had been in before when she was caught up in Sophia Brooks's murder. They hadn't even known her dangerous flight down the sand dunes was happening until after the fact. That event had seemed like one of the superhero comic books they sometimes hid in the barn, thinking no one knew about them. But Rachel had caught them a few times—pretending to be Spider-Man or the Incredible Hulk, saving a wounded dog, a child in a flood, their *mammi* as she fled from a killer. She'd talked to Clyde and Emma about it, and they'd agreed to allow the boys their fantasies, because childhood passed all too quickly. For Stephen and Thomas, it had passed in the last few moments.

Emma looked up at Henry, who sensed what she needed, joined her and the boys, and said, "How about we walk toward the lane and wait for the sheriff?"

"It's raining." Stephen swiped the back of his hand across his nose.

"You've umbrellas, don't you?"

"*Ya*, we do." Thomas jumped up, ran into the house, and returned with four umbrellas.

The movement helped the boys to find their equilibrium and gave Rachel a few minutes to pull herself together.

The first car that turned down the lane sent Emma's heart into a rapid rhythm. Perhaps someone was bringing the girls home. Perhaps it had all been a mistake. But the truck was Stuart's. It came to a stop, and Henry went over to explain to Stuart and Silas the situation as Emma stood with the boys, watching through the rain, watching down the road for the headlights from the sheriff's vehicle.

Ten minutes later Grayson turned into the lane and offered the four of them a ride. They piled in with their muddy shoes and damp clothes and dripping umbrellas. By the time they reached the front of the house, there was quite a collection of buggies and vehicles parked there.

Stuart had stayed, in case his truck was needed.

Daniel was staying, insisting that he could help with the search once it began.

Clyde hadn't unhitched Cinnamon, wanting to be ready if they needed to go somewhere to pick up the girls.

Rachel's face was tearstained, but her demeanor was calmer.

She was the first to address Grayson as he climbed the steps.

"Something's happened," she said with certainty. "Katie Ann knew how important it was to come straight back. Something had to have happened."

"Clyde gave me a brief summary of what led up to this. She was with the other girl...with Naomi?"

"Yes, and I specifically told them both to be home well before dark."

"Abigail told Naomi the same as well." Daniel pinched the skin at his throat. "She's a *gut* girl. She wouldn't have disobeyed us."

Grayson cleared his throat, stood with his hands on his hips, and stared out at the rain. When he finally looked up, Emma knew she wasn't going to like what he was about to say.

"They're adults. The fact that they're out after dark doesn't mean something nefarious has happened."

"What does nefarious mean?" Stephen asked.

"Bad." Thomas's voice was strained, as if he were trying to keep from crying.

"You're not saying that you won't look." Henry's voice was authoritative and confident.

"I am not saying that. I've already alerted all of our patrol officers. Clyde gave me a good description of both girls, which I shared with everyone on patrol tonight."

"So you will help." Emma hugged her arms around her waist, hoping to keep the fear at bay.

"What I am saying is that I can't put out an official BOLO until they've been missing at least twenty-four hours."

"That's too long." Rachel's voice sounded as if it was coming from the other side of the valley. As if she wasn't even speaking to them, but rather to a chasm opening in her heart. "It's too long. We have to do something now. We have to look for them tonight."

"I understand your concerns. Believe me, if I could, I'd send out that 'Be On the Look Out' right now, but it's not my decision to make. In other states..." He held out his hands, palms up. "It can be even longer in other states. It's because they're adults, and adults sometimes do things we can't understand but aren't necessarily illegal or even dangerous."

Silas had been sitting next to his brothers on the porch floor, his back against the house. Now he stood and said, "We can start looking, though."

"Yes, you can, and I suggest you do. Talk to their friends. The other girl, Naomi. Has she been seeing anyone lately? Any new boyfriend, maybe?"

"Actually, she and I have...connected, I guess you can say."

"Meaning?"

"I like her. I like her a lot." Silas crossed his arms and scuffed the toe of his boot against the porch floor. Finally, he said, "I think maybe Katie Ann and Albert are courting."

"Katie Ann?" This was news to Emma. She'd known someone brought Katie Ann home from the singing, but she hadn't asked who it was. Emma always thought Albert Bontrager was a fine young man—a hard worker and very respectful to his elders. It had occurred to her that he should have a wife, but she'd never once envisioned Katie Ann in that role.

"I can go to his house now to see if Katie Ann said anything to him."

"And I'll go back to the phone shack," Clyde said. "I'll call those who have a phone in their shops. They won't all pick up, but a few will. Enough to get the word out to the community."

Grayson nodded in approval. "I'll stop by in the morning and again tomorrow night. If we haven't heard anything by then, we'll issue the statewide alert."

He turned to go, but then he pivoted back toward them. "I hope it goes without saying that I want each of you to be very careful. I sincerely hope this is an instance of two young women becoming caught up in something and forgetting the time, but should it have to do with Jeremiah's death, should you stumble upon a dangerous situation, do not try to intervene."

No one answered. Emma knew every person there would do whatever they needed to do to bring the girls back. She had the feeling Grayson knew that too, but he wanted to impress on them the need to be extra careful.

"I'll keep my phone on and near me at all times. Our community is relatively small. Should you find something—anything—you think is pertinent, I can be wherever you are in a matter of minutes. But promise me you will not try to handle this yourself."

He waited, and when no one spoke, he took their silence as agreement.

Emma and Henry walked him back out to his vehicle. They stood there, huddled together under umbrellas as the rain continued to pelt the ground.

"What about Justin Lane?" Henry asked.

"What about him?"

"You said he'd be released today. Was he?"

"He was, and I'm only sharing that because it's public information."

"Did he do this?" Emma asked. "Would he...could he have taken the girls?"

"There's absolutely no reason for him to do such a thing. Plus, as I predicted, he's wearing an ankle monitor."

"You've been monitoring him?"

"Part of our job." Grayson gave an understanding nod. "I know you want this to be solved and solved quickly, but we can't jump to conclusions. Justin went straight home and hasn't left his house in Del Norte since. He's not responsible for whatever has happened."

"But—"

"He's not, Mrs. Fisher. He can't be. And remember, the girls could just be off doing what young adults do these days. Maybe they went to an all-night movie or shopping at one of the twenty-four-hour discount stores."

"How? Do you think they walked to a movie in Alamosa?"

"They might have boyfriends who have cars, friends they haven't told you about. I know you don't want to hear this..."

But Emma had already turned away. She was no longer listening. Though she knew Sheriff Grayson meant well, she also knew Katie Ann would never fail to tell them where she was and why she'd gone there, let alone stay out half the night.

But then the thought pushed into her mind that her granddaughter had done exactly that very thing on Saturday night.

"But that was different," she whispered.

And there was no one to answer.

Henry was still standing with Grayson beside his car, and Emma returned to the porch, alone with her thoughts and fears, praying that Naomi and Katie Ann would return home soon.

Forty-Nine

At first they'd driven west, away from Monte Vista and toward the storm, but then he changed his mind and turned south, circled around west and then back east. Or that's how it seemed, but with the twists and turns, and the growing darkness, Naomi soon lost her sense of direction.

Katie Ann had tried reasoning with him at first, but that had only caused his face to tighten and his eyes to narrow, which might have been funny, only it wasn't. It was terrifying and served to transform this person they knew into a complete stranger—a stranger who could and probably would destroy anyone who blocked his path.

As the rain pelted the roof of the truck and lightning crackled across the sky, they pulled up to an old motel—one abandoned long ago by the look of things. A rusted sign hung near the road, half of its letters faded so you couldn't see them even in the headlights of the truck. Weeds grew knee-deep along the asphalt. The building itself was L-shaped, with an office in the front and then two wings of rooms. Naomi tried to imagine families staying here back when the place was new, but she couldn't. In some places the roof had caved in. Windows were shattered. Part of a wall had crumbled. An old couch had been pulled from the office out into the parking area.

For reasons she couldn't imagine, the owners had fastened a chain across the entrance to the parking area to prohibit anyone from entering. Several signs proclaimed, "Private Property. Keep Out."

Grabbing a pair of bolt cutters from the back, their abductor said, "Don't try anything."

"What would we try?" Katie Ann asked.

"I know you two can't drive, and if you wreck my truck, you're going to make me very angry."

The door had barely shut behind him when Katie Ann asked, "Should we run for it?"

"Run where?"

"I don't know, but we can't just sit here."

"Yes, we can. And we should."

"You think we should go along with this?" Katie Ann's eyes were round and wide and incredulous. "We can't just go along with this. There's no telling what he has in mind."

They both peered out the front windshield. Even through the falling rain they could make out his form, his back to them, oblivious to the pouring rain, bolt cutters in hand. He made quick work of the chain, allowed it to fall to the ground, and then he was back in the truck, pulling it and the horse trailer into the parking area.

He hopped back out to refasten the chain, or at least make it appear refastened.

"They'll be looking for us," Naomi reminded Katie Ann. "All we have to do is sit tight. They'll come for us, Henry and the others. Grayson even. A whole string of police officers."

"But we could run—"

"Into the storm?" Naomi swallowed past the ache in her throat. She would not cry. She wouldn't give him that satisfaction. "We wouldn't make it a mile, and he might...he might shoot us. Any direction we go, he could spotlight us, and as flat as this valley is, there would be nowhere to hide."

She forced a smile she didn't feel and clasped Katie Ann's hand in hers. "We should wait."

"Okay. For now we'll do it your way. But when the storm breaks, when we get a good chance to slip away without him seeing us, or when the sun comes up...whichever comes first...we make a run for it."

It wasn't a good plan, but it was a plan.

With a prayer and a break in the weather, perhaps they could survive.

Fifty

Henry found himself repeatedly shaking his watch and then holding it up to his ear. The watch wasn't broken. It was only that time had slowed to a crawl.

For several hours, the small group searched everywhere they could think of for Naomi and Katie Ann. There was no sign of the two. No one outside of the family had seen them since the day before at church. It was if they had vanished into the desert night.

Rain continued to fall lightly, but according to Stuart the worst of it was still approaching. An app on his smartphone said it would reach them about three in the morning.

It was shy of that, two thirty to be exact, when Emma walked Henry to his buggy.

"I'll stay if you'd like."

"No. There's nothing you can do. Just keep praying."

"You know I will." Henry stood beside his buggy, his arms wrapped around Emma, his cheek pressed to hers. "We're going to find her, Emma. We're going to find both of them, and they're going to be all right."

Henry fervently believed that, and he hoped his confidence showed. In the deepest places of his heart, he trusted that God would not allow harm to come to Naomi or Katie Ann. He was convinced they would be saved.

Emma seemed to cling to his words and the hope he offered. Finally, she stepped back and swiped the tears from her cheeks.

"Get some rest. Tomorrow is likely to be long."

But Henry shook his head at that. "I need to draw."

"Draw?"

"I've missed something." He glanced back toward the house. The lanterns set up around the porch sent beams of light out into the rain, like a lighthouse sending out a navigational beam through a gathering storm. Perhaps Naomi and Katie Ann would see the light and make their way home.

"What could you have missed?"

"I don't know what, but it seems that's what I should be doing until both girls are returned home."

A soft glow from his battery-powered lantern encircled them. He'd opened the door to his buggy and set it on the seat, and now its beam spilled across them. He could see the worry and concern and love on Emma's face. He put both of his hands to her cheeks, kissed her softly, and promised he'd be back at dawn.

As he drove down the lane, Henry focused on praying for Naomi and Katie Ann, for Emma and Rachel and Clyde and the entire family waiting back on the porch, for Abigail and Daniel. He also prayed that his mind would once again do the exceptional and draw the one thing that, at the moment, could save the life of Emma's granddaughter and her best friend.

When he reached home, he went first to the back door. Lexi bounded out as soon as he opened it. She jumped into the buggy and rode with him to the barn, where he unhitched the buggy, dried off Oreo, and dumped a cup of oats into her feed bucket.

Lexi sat staring at him, well aware that this was not normal behavior for the middle of the night.

"We've work to do, girl."

But still he didn't go to his workshop. Instead, he went back into the house, brewed a fresh pot of coffee, and poured it into a thermos. He wrapped a few of the widows' cookies in a dish towel—they were forever bringing him whatever was left in the bakery at the end of the day. He'd find their gifts on the front porch, on his kitchen table, and occasionally in his mailbox.

Finally, he picked up Lexi's bed, the one next to the old stove. The rain was falling in earnest, so he grabbed an umbrella, and together Henry and his little dog made their way through the storm and over to the workshop. He could have drawn in the house at the kitchen table, but he had always been able to focus better in the little room where he worked on his birdhouses and picture frames and mailboxes.

He set the dog bed next to his workbench. Lexi hopped onto it, circled three times, and collapsed with her head on her paws and her eyes watching him closely.

He put his flashlight down on his worktable and lit two lanterns. These he placed on the corners of the table. He found a mug on the shelf behind him, wiped it clean with his shirt, and poured coffee into it. He hadn't realized he was cold until then, until he held the steaming mug in his hand. Taking a sip, he walked around the workshop and finally found an old bath towel, which he used to dry his arms and his pants legs and finally his dog.

He sat down then, but he didn't pull pencil or paper toward him. Instead he resumed what he'd been doing in the buggy—he prayed.

Here me, LORD, and answer me, for I am poor and needy. Look on me and answer, LORD my God. Give light to my eyes...
Hear my cry for help, my King and my God, for to you I pray.

The words of the psalmist poured from his heart. Henry prayed that God would use him, that God would bless his efforts, that his mind and his hand and his talent would somehow reveal what they needed to know.

Only then did he begin to draw.

If Emma had asked him what events he intended to concentrate on, he might have said the rodeo where Jeremiah was shot, or the funeral, or possibly events leading up to the fateful day when Jeremiah's life had ended. But his hand, or his mind, didn't focus on any of those.

Instead he drew their most recent Sunday service.

He drew his parishioners as they worshiped and ate and played.

He drew the crowd of folks gathered around to hear Sheriff Grayson's report.

He drew the thinning crowd gathered at Seth's for the meal as afternoon had given way to early evening.

His drawings covered one page after another. He'd pause only long enough to tack the completed sketch to the wall in front of him, and then he'd return to the workbench and pull another clean piece of paper close. He didn't pause to study what he'd done, or to question if he was focusing on the correct things, or to despair over the futility of his task.

His hand began to cramp and his throat grew dry as rain began to pelt the roof in earnest. Lightning occasionally streaked across the night sky, and thunder rumbled ever closer, but he barely noticed. Lexi slept—yipping occasionally in her sleep, stretching so that all four feet pointed toward the ceiling, rolling over and pushing her nose deep into the cushion that was her bed.

But Henry didn't let any of those things distract him.

As the storm grew fiercer and then moved on, as dawn crept up on the valley, Henry Lapp did the one thing he knew how to do better than anyone he'd ever met. He did the one thing God had especially equipped him to do. He drew.

Fifty-One

Naomi and Katie Ann were determined to run away from their captor. Their chance to escape came when he pulled the truck and trailer up to one of the tumbled-down motel units.

"There's a bathroom inside," he said. "No working plumbing, but it will do. And don't try anything."

The rain was still coming down in earnest, but they both knew they wouldn't get a better opportunity. It was the only time he'd let them out of his sight.

He'd parked the truck and trailer so close to the building that Naomi could barely open the passenger door.

She squeezed out of the vehicle, and together she and Katie Ann walked into the motel's room number twelve. The number was still visible beneath an outside light hanging from its cord. Naomi turned on the flashlight he'd given her. As they walked into the room, a rat scurried away. Trash littered the floor—fast-food wrappers, empty alcohol bottles, a pile of dirty clothes that looked like rags. Someone had used a metal pail to build a campfire in. The room smelled of wet wood and mold.

"Who left all of this stuff?" she asked.

"Homeless people, I guess." Katie Ann tiptoed through to the bathroom, and they pushed the door shut for privacy, though it wouldn't fasten. If anything, the small lavatory was more disgusting than the main room. They used the facilities, though there was no water connected to the plumbing, and then they looked around for a way out.

"Window's cranked open, but it's too high," Naomi said.

"Not if you stand on my shoulders."

"No way. Then you couldn't get out, and I'm not leaving you."

"You could run for help."

"I won't."

"Well, then maybe you could pull me up."

"I saw an old wooden crate out there." Naomi opened the door a crack and peered out into the bedroom. She didn't dare shine the flashlight that direction. Her eyes had adjusted to the dark enough to make out the shapes of the discarded items and, more importantly, the shape of a person if anyone was there.

"I don't see him."

She crept across the room, grabbed the crate, and scurried back into the bathroom. It wasn't tall enough to help them get out.

"The chair..."

Before Naomi could argue with her, Katie Ann had dashed out, grabbed a plastic office chair, and pulled it back into the bathroom.

"I can't believe he's letting us take this long." Katie Ann positioned the chair under the window, on top of the wooden crate. It wasn't steady, but if they were careful it might work.

Naomi went first, flashlight in her pocket. She climbed onto the chair and grabbed the lower edge of the window frame. Ducking her head a little, she hefted herself up and forward, and for a brief second, she feared she'd get stuck there with her head sticking out in the rain and her feet dangling in the bathroom. But Katie Ann pushed on the bottom of her feet, and then she was up and through, tumbling down onto the ground, scraping her arm in the process.

She hopped up as Katie Ann, the taller of the two, fell beside her, making a splash in the stream of water that had collected beneath the roof's eave.

They both froze, wondering if he could have heard them over the rain and wind.

Darkness stretched out in front of them. Naomi tried to fix in her mind which way they should run. She longed to use the flashlight she was holding, but she didn't dare. And she was acutely aware that the window of time when they could run was slipping away. A tremor caused her hands to shake, and she felt momentarily dizzy. This was their chance, their one opportunity. It was a now-or-never situation, and she became lost in visions of what might happen if they failed.

Katie Ann's voice in her ear brought her back.

"Hold my hand. We run as fast and as long as we can."

She had a fleeting moment of hope as they took off across the parking lot. The moment their feet hit the adjacent field, she nearly whooped for joy. And then a bright light shone in their eyes. They both skidded to a stop, unsure what to do, unsure where to run now that he'd caught them. His voice said, "I thought you'd try something like that."

He stood in the field, as if he'd been waiting for them. Of course he'd been. He'd known they'd try to escape. "Do you think I'm stupid?"

"We think it's time for us to go home." The words spilled from Naomi's mouth before she could consider if they'd only serve to anger him more.

"Not yet, it isn't. Now, turn around. This time you're going in the horse trailer."

"What are you going to do to us?" Katie Ann asked.

Naomi was impressed that her friend's voice didn't shake. They'd both been frightened, plenty frightened over the last nine hours, but one could only hold on to that emotion for so long. For her—and she felt sure for Katie Ann too—fear was quickly being replaced with a seething rage. He had no right to do this to them. There was no acceptable reason for his behavior.

They outnumbered him two to one, and although he had a gun and a skewed view of reality to fuel his actions, they had each other.

They had their faith.

They had families they were determined to go back to.

"I'm not going to hurt you." He sounded offended that they would suggest such a thing.

"You hurt Jeremiah. You killed him. Didn't you? How do we know you won't—"

"Jeremiah was a different matter entirely." His hand shook on the spotlight as he walked toward them. "I won't hurt you unless you try something stupid again. Unless you make me."

He stepped closer, pointing his large flashlight to the ground, and Naomi could just make out his silhouette even though her vision remained clouded with large black dots from the bright light. But she could see plainly enough—through the rain, and even with the fear and the residue of being nearly blinded—that in his other hand he clutched the handgun.

"Now, walk back toward where I parked."

When they made it around the corner of the building, Naomi saw he'd opened the back of the horse trailer. She could make out bales of hay, an old blanket, and a small collapsible table with a single chair pulled up to it. On the table was a sheet of paper, a pen, yet another flashlight, and a roll of duct tape.

Fifty-Two

The night passed so slowly that Naomi feared dawn would never come, but it did. The sun always rose. That was one thing you could count on.

Because of the LORD's great love we are not consumed, for his compassions never fail. They are new every morning; great is your faithfulness.

Someone had quoted those verses at their last church service. If you'd asked her, Naomi would have said she hadn't paid much attention at the time, but somehow the Scriptures had soaked into her soul, and her heart had called up exactly what she needed to hear.

She'd dozed off and on throughout the night. Whenever she woke, she'd lie there thinking of her family—her mother and dad, *Aenti* Abigail and *Onkel* Daniel, even her cousin Sam. They'd all been good to her, and perhaps she'd taken their kindness for granted. She couldn't wait to see them again. She prayed she would, and she fervently hoped she'd have a chance to tell them how much she cared.

Her thoughts turned to her *aenti's* sayings. She'd always rolled her eyes at them, but now they circled in her mind, an endless loop of tried-and-true proverbs.

> *Courage is fear that has said its prayers.*
> *Don't count your eggs before they're laid.*
> *It is better to suffer wrong than to do it.*

They were certainly suffering wrong, and Naomi didn't like it one bit. What was happening to them wasn't fair. She wanted it to be over.

She didn't think she'd ever take another day of waking up in her own bed for granted. She would appreciate normal and chores and working at the bakery.

And breakfast.

And her mother's letters.

And her *aenti*'s smile in the morning.

As the sun rose, she mulled over all those things and how much she missed them. Instead of eating eggs and fresh biscuits, she and Katie Ann sat huddled together in the back of the horse trailer.

The smells of hay and manure and horse were actually comforting, even to Naomi. Those smells assured her that life had been normal and safe in the past, and that it would be normal and safe again soon.

She'd been filled with enormous hope as the sky lightened, even before the sun's rays had begun to heat the inside of the trailer. At first that thought had been a relief, because the night had been cool and they'd had only one old horse blanket to cover up with. But soon the sun would be high in the sky, and they would both begin to sweat.

"We need a plan," Katie Ann said. Her throat was hoarse from screaming. They'd both hollered for at least an hour the night before, after he left, but it had done no good. No one had heard them.

"*Ya*, I agree."

"There's only one of him. At least it doesn't seem as though he's working with anyone else."

"And there are two of us."

"If we could just get this stupid tape off." Katie Ann held up her hands in front of her. The tape was wide and gray and shiny. It was also incredibly strong.

"He used nearly half the roll," Naomi said. "You'd need a knife to get through this."

He'd twisted the duct tape round and round their wrists and then their ankles. They both held a bottle of water, which they could awkwardly raise to drink from, but what happened when that water ran out? What happened when they needed to use the bathroom again? He'd let them out of the horse trailer only one other time, just before he left, with the warning not to try anything.

The trailer and truck had remained parked very close to the wall of the motel. There'd been no other opportunity to run, not with him standing outside the bathroom door, holding the gun.

So where had he gone? When was he returning, and what did he have planned?

"They'll be looking for us." Katie Ann leaned her head on her friend's shoulder. "I'm sure they will. Henry and *Mammi*, my parents..."

"My *aenti* and *onkel*."

"And the police. They'll be looking too."

"I don't think he means to hurt us," Naomi said. They'd been through this the night before, gone over every possibility until they were too tired to pass it back and forth again.

"He's not even bothering to hide his face. That must mean something."

"It means he doesn't plan to stay around here after—"

The sound of a vehicle passing by on the highway cut off Naomi's sentence. She glanced at Katie Ann, and then they both began screaming and rocking the trailer. They carried on for several minutes, but it was obvious the driver hadn't heard them.

Hope fled like air from a deflating balloon.

They stopped screaming, and silence once again permeated the trailer.

"One thing we know," Katie Ann finally said. "He is coming back."

"And when he does, we need to be ready."

Fifty-Three

Henry didn't stop drawing until Lexi stood, stretched, and walked to the door. She sat in front of it, head cocked, waiting patiently.

Henry also stood and stretched, shaking the cramp out of his hand. "I guess it is about that time."

He opened the door, and she bounded out into a morning so beautiful it stirred an ache deep in Henry's heart. The sky was a robin's egg blue, unblemished by a single cloud. The sun peeked over the horizon, splashing its palette of colors across the land. The desert floor had been rejuvenated by the life-giving rain.

Flowers bloomed. Cranes landed in the fields in front of him. Birds called to one another.

Henry was stunned by the beauty before him, and yet he had to fight the urge to turn his back on it and go back into the workshop, shut the door, and continue drawing.

He didn't.

Instead, he walked across to his house. Lexi beat him to the backporch steps. Together they walked inside, and he put her breakfast into her little bowl—just one scoop as Doc Berry had cautioned. "A fat beagle is not a healthy beagle, Henry."

He went into his bathroom, cleaned up, and donned a fresh set of clothes.

Glancing at his reflection in the small mirror, he was surprised to see his white hair standing straight up. "Old age has its mysteries," he said to no one as he slicked it down with water.

He didn't bother to make coffee or eat any breakfast. Instead, he spent thirty minutes feeding and caring for his horse, and this time when he hitched her to the buggy, he whistled once to Lexi. She jumped up into the front seat and patiently waited for him to finish his chores in the barn.

Ten minutes later they made their way back down the lane, onto the blacktop, and toward Emma's.

He felt painfully awake and aware of all that was going on around him, and at the same time like a man moving through a dream. The colors and sights and sounds were real enough, but a part of him was still back in the workshop. He didn't think the answer was there—not yet, but he was getting close. He could feel the revelation inching closer to his fingertips.

When he reached Emma's place, half a dozen other buggies were already in the yard.

The widows were dropping off food. "Terrible thing, Henry. We'll keep baking. If anyone needs anything at all, please let us know."

Sam Beiler had joined his father, Daniel.

"Naomi wouldn't have wandered off," he assured Henry. "She's matured a lot since moving to the valley."

Leroy and Abe were there, ready to spend the day searching.

And Emma, his darling Emma, looked like a completely different woman from the night before. She wore a crisply ironed white apron over a dark-green dress. Her *kapp* was precisely pinned and her eyes looked less anxious, if not exactly rested. The smile she gave him eased the worry in his heart. His Emma was strong. Together they would help Clyde's family through whatever lay ahead. When he walked into the kitchen, which was a beehive of female activity, she pulled him into the mudroom and out to the back porch.

"You look better," he said.

"*Ya.*"

"Did you sleep?"

"Not much, but Henry...I think, that is, I'm sure that today we will find them. That by this evening, they will be home."

"You had a revelation—a word from God."

She blew out a long breath and smiled. "Maybe. Maybe I did. I only know that when I finally looked out my bedroom window, when I saw the beauty of this place and remembered God's promise for each new day, I felt a peace that it's all going to end—and soon. More than that, I felt certain it's going to end well. That probably sounds ridiculously optimistic."

"Not at all." Henry was thinking of his own glimpse of the sunrise, of the image of a lighthouse the night before, of the drawings littering the walls of his workshop. Were they all messages from God, meant as a balm for their weary souls? Was a personal word from God a momentous, once-in-a-lifetime kind of thing, or was it something so everyday—so commonplace—that they forgot to listen?

And yet when fear had nearly consumed them, they had heard.

When grief tore at their hearts, they were comforted.

It was what God had done for Abraham and Isaac, David and Jonathan, Jeremiah and Job. The God they worshipped was full of compassion, and certainly His mercies were new every morning.

"God filled your heart with confidence for a reason," he assured Emma.

"I think so. It seems that everyone is more optimistic today. Even Rachel. She's much calmer."

"We're going to find them. This thing, whatever it is, is almost over."

"And your drawings? Did you discover anything important?"

"I'm not sure. I'm close."

"To an answer?"

"To something. Something important."

Clyde stuck his head out the back door. "Grayson's here."

All breakfast preparation stopped as they gathered around the kitchen table.

"None of my officers have seen any sign of Katie Ann or Naomi." Grayson held up his hands as everyone began talking at once. "This could be a good thing. If something had happened to them, more than likely someone in this town would have seen it and called it in."

"What's our next step?" Henry asked.

"Wait, as I said before. If we don't hear anything by tonight, we'll put out the official BOLO."

"Which means what, exactly?" Clyde wasn't challenging Grayson.

It was plain by the look of hope on his face that he hoped and believed what the sheriff was doing would help.

"It means every officer in the state will be on the lookout for the girls. We'll probably even get some news coverage, which in this case would be a good thing. Once we have everyone—"

But Grayson never finished that sentence because the sound of a horse and buggy shattered the quiet of the room. Whoever was coming down the lane was in a hurry. They all rushed to the front porch as Abigail Beiler pulled to a stop, her mare tossing its head and snorting, its tail slapping back and forth at the joy of being allowed to break into a gallop.

Then Abigail tumbled out of the buggy and rushed up the porch steps, clutching a piece of paper in her hand.

Fifty-Four

Emma sat at the kitchen table, stunned at the turn of events.

"I'd say this mystery is solved," Grayson said. "And I'm glad it's nothing more serious."

All the volunteers, all the concerned neighbors, had left after Grayson read the note aloud. There was much slapping on the back and murmurs of "God is good" and "*Rumspringa* is a difficult time." No one seemed put out that the girls' careless actions had created such a false alarm. Everyone was relieved that Naomi had left the note for her *aenti*, that the girls had at least thought to leave word.

But it didn't sit right with Emma. None of it made any sense.

The children had gone to take care of chores. Only Henry and Emma, Rachel and Clyde, and Abigail and Daniel were around the kitchen table. And, of course, Sheriff Grayson, who had accepted some hot coffee and was enjoying one of the widows' sticky buns. Three dozen eggs remained on the counter uncooked. There was no need to feed the group of volunteers. The emergency had passed.

"I just can't believe they would do such a thing. This is so unlike them." Emma's voice sounded far away, even to her own ears. She stared down at the note Abigail had brought, the note she was still holding.

"Our mailman doesn't come until later," Abigail explained again. "But I walked out to the road, just to look around. I suppose I had some foolish idea that maybe I'd see her coming up the road toward home."

"Why did you check the mailbox?" Henry asked.

"Habit, I guess. Couldn't remember if I'd checked it yesterday. She must have left it last night, only we didn't know."

"And that's where you found the note? In the mailbox?" Emma was holding the single sheet of paper in her hand, which was shaking so badly she couldn't read the words. She set it on the table and stared at it, trying to believe what Naomi had written.

> Dear *Aenti* Abigail,
>
> I hope you aren't worried. Katie Ann and I decided to go to Alamosa with some friends. We'll probably stay the night. I know I said I'd be back before dark, but I'll explain when I see you.
>
> Much love,
>
> Naomi

Only three sentences, and yet they were supposed to wipe away all of the anxiety and fear of the night before. Was this the reason for her earlier optimism? Had her heart known all was fine, that there was a logical explanation?

Grayson wiped his fingers on a napkin and took another gulp of coffee. When he'd set down the mug, he scratched his head and said, "The problem is that your family has been through so much, your entire community has, and so it's easy to jump to the worst possible conclusion."

"First the Monte Vista arsonist." Henry nodded in agreement.

Rachel tapped her fingers against the book she'd set on the kitchen table. She'd been carrying it around all night in her pocket, though she hadn't opened it once. "Then poor Sophia Brooks."

"And finally Jeremiah." Abigail sighed.

"It's been a tough three years." Daniel seemed to be struggling to speak, to find the right words. "Naomi has become like a daughter to us. She's a part of our family now, and we care for her like we would one of our own. This has been...quite the scare. I don't mind saying the last twenty-four hours has been harder than any amount of field work."

"Three murders in three years." Clyde shook his head. "Maybe we have grown in our faith, grown closer to one another, but I'll be happy to put the last three years behind us."

"More than that," Grayson said. "More than three years. Your trials go back all the way to Goshen, to Henry's involvement with the Betsy Troyer case."

"That was a terrible time indeed," Henry said.

"It changes a person, a community. It sets them on edge." Grayson seemed to warm up to his topic. "I've seen this before, mainly with officers who transfer here from a large city. They've seen so much violence that they expect to see it behind every 9-1-1 call, with every motorist stop. They're a bit twitchy."

"But we weren't expecting the girls to disappear." Emma pushed the note back across the table, toward Abigail.

"That's true. However, when they did disappear, when they did something fairly normal for a young adult to do, you immediately assumed the worst. But it's not always the worst that has happened."

Finally, Grayson stood and said, "It's been a long night. I suggest you all get some rest today."

Clyde walked him to his vehicle. Rachel began to clean up the kitchen. Daniel and Henry walked toward the side of the barn where their horses waited, still hitched to the buggies. Emma stepped out on the front porch with Abigail.

She didn't want to throw a damp towel on such good news, but she had to ask. "Do you think...Are you sure it's Naomi's writing?"

"Oh, *ya*. I'm sure. The way she slants her letters to the left, she's done that since she was a child." Abigail's forehead wrinkled as she looked down at the piece of paper in her hand.

"What is it? You've thought of something."

"Only that...well, Naomi isn't one to express her emotions."

"Her emotions? What do you mean?"

"See this line? *Much love?* That doesn't sound like her at all. In fact, usually she doesn't even sign her letters. I read the ones she sends to her *mamm*, add my own bit onto the end, and I'm always having to remind her to sign her name, to mention to her mother that she cares. She says her *mamm* knows, and I tell her mothers like to be reminded of such things."

"She's fallen into the habit, then."

"*Nein.* She left her most recent letter on the table yesterday. As usual, no signature. No *I love you, Mamm* or *Give Dat my love.* Nothing like that. She cares, I know she does, but she doesn't think to put it into words."

Emma thought about that a minute and tried not to assign too much meaning to it. Perhaps it was as Grayson said. Maybe they were twitchy.

"I keep wondering why Katie Ann didn't leave a note," she admitted. "I know girls go through their *rumspringa* the same as boys do..."

"I only had Sam, so I haven't dealt much with girls before."

"And our only girl is Katie Ann."

"Still, girls do go through a time of trying *Englisch* things."

"Like walking a friend home but deciding to leave for a movie instead? Deciding to stay out all night?" Emma shook her head. She couldn't imagine Katie Ann making that kind of choice.

"The idea that they would go to Alamosa to a movie, spend some time shopping, stay the night with friends...it's not as if they're taking drugs or staying with boys."

"They didn't even have their purses with them."

"Could have slipped a few dollars in their pocket."

But Katie Ann had no interest in shopping or in movies, and as far as Emma knew, she had no friends in Alamosa.

There was something else, something in the back of her mind since this first happened. Katie Ann was now working for Doc Berry on Tuesday, Wednesday, and Friday, which meant she hadn't shown up for work today.

She'd left Doc Berry in the lurch, shorthanded, without an assistant. And just like that, the anxiety and worry was back.

Despite Naomi's note, Emma knew something was very wrong.

Fifty-Five

Henry listened patiently to Emma. He didn't rush her or interrupt. She paced back and forth in front of him, a most uncharacteristic thing for her to do. She continually scanned the horizon, and when she turned to look at him, he saw in her eyes the depth of her misery.

"I agree with you that something doesn't sit right."

"Katie Ann loves working with Doc Berry."

"She's mentioned that to me on more than one occasion."

"Some days she goes over on her day off just to check on an animal." Emma had clasped both of her *kapp* strings in her hands and was twisting them round and round.

"And you're certain Naomi is scheduled to work at the bakery today?"

"*Ya*. Abigail said as much, though she didn't assign as much weight to it as I do."

"I don't know, Emma. What you're saying does concern me, but the note from Naomi explains what happened."

"If she wrote it."

"Do you have any reason to believe she didn't? Abigail said it was her handwriting."

She told him about Abigail's claim that Naomi never expressed her emotions. "The *much love* she wrote at the bottom? It doesn't sound like her at all. Abigail admitted that."

Henry scratched at a spot on the back of his neck. They'd walked over to where trees and brush had been cleared for their *dawdi haus*. Lexi sniffed around the foundation, as if she knew it would soon be her home as well. Some days he thought it was a dream, this life they had planned. Other days, it felt so real, so tangible, that he was surprised to wake up still in his own house. All that would change in three weeks.

"I'm scared, and I don't mind admitting it." Emma pressed her fingertips to her lips. "I know earlier I said I felt sure everything would be all right today, but now...with the note...Why would Naomi write a note like that?"

"So Abigail wouldn't worry."

"Why not go inside and tell her?"

"Maybe she was avoiding a confrontation."

"And why didn't Katie Ann write me a note?"

"Ah. Perhaps that's what is bothering you."

"Henry Lapp, this is not about my ego!"

"No. I believe it's about your heart."

"I know my granddaughter cares about me, but this disappearing act is so...so out of character for her."

"I agree. Have you spoken to Clyde about this?"

"*Nein.* I couldn't bring myself to dash his hopes upon the rocks. I thought I'd speak with you first."

"I'm glad you did."

"So what do we do?"

"We wait until tonight. It's all we can do. Grayson won't put out the BOLO now, not after seeing the note from Naomi."

"And if they don't return tonight?"

"Then I'll speak to him and ask him to reopen the search."

Emma tsked. "There never was a police search to begin with. And now no one else thinks they're missing."

"None of us slept much. Perhaps things will look better after we do."

"Things will look better when Katie Ann and Naomi are home."

Those words rang in Henry's mind as he made his way back to his place. He needed to visit some of his congregation this week. Josephine Glick had missed church because the doctor had put her on bed rest until the birth of her child. Deborah and Adam King's daughter had a terrible summer cold, so they, too, had missed the service. Chester

Yoder had been limping at the luncheon. No doubt his hip was bothering him again.

The work of ministering to people continued through the good days and the bad.

But as he turned Oreo down his own lane, he knew he wouldn't be visiting the sick today. Just the sight of his workshop caused his heart to race. Was drawing becoming an obsession? He didn't think so. He rarely felt the need to indulge his unexplainable artistic ability, and it wasn't as if he thought he alone could solve a mystery.

But Naomi and Katie Ann's behavior was a mystery. He agreed with Emma that leaving so abruptly was out of character for both girls. Not even bothering to show up for their jobs? That made no sense at all. Both girls loved where they worked and had said as much to him recently. They might shirk housework, but they wouldn't disappoint their employers.

Jeremiah was dead. The girls were missing.

The two events had to be connected, but perhaps he'd been drawing the wrong thing. Maybe instead of focusing on Jeremiah, he should focus on the girls.

Without pausing to go into his house, he pastured his horse and went straight to the workshop. Lexi flopped onto her bed without protest, and Henry picked up his pencil and a clean sheet of paper. Soon he was lost in the past his mind had recorded.

Fifty-Six

Naomi must have fallen asleep, which she hadn't thought was possible. When she opened her eyes, Katie Ann was staring up at the ceiling of the horse trailer.

"Find a way out yet?"

Katie Ann glanced toward her and smiled a little. "Not yet, but I'm working on it."

"Why is he doing this?"

"I've been thinking about that, and I can't come up with a good answer."

"What does he want?"

"I don't know."

"What are we going to do?" She tried to keep the panic out of her voice, but it was difficult. Her emotions alternated between anger and fear. At the moment, fear was winning.

"We're going to get out of this."

"Our plan last night didn't work so well."

"Which doesn't mean we're going to give up."

The trailer seemed to be getting smaller, perhaps because they'd been in it so long. Naomi had read about people with claustrophobia, and she didn't think she had an issue with it—but perhaps she would if she had to sit in the trailer much longer.

Leaning against the bales of hay had made her itchy, and she attempted to scratch at her legs with her bound hands. At least he'd left them in front of them when he'd wrapped the duct tape from their palms to their wrists. She couldn't do a thing with her hands, but she was grateful that her shoulders weren't wrenched behind her—that would have been terribly uncomfortable.

"Where do you think he went?"

"To deliver your note, I'm sure."

"That wouldn't have taken this long. He left well before sunup."

"I don't know, but this trailer is going to get awfully hot sitting in the sun."

"Why didn't he tape our mouths? I thought he was going to. I was tempted to bite him if he tried."

"Why bother? There's no one within five miles. No one to hear us."

Naomi scratched at her nose with her taped hands. "These bales of hay had better not have chiggers."

"*Mammi* makes a baking soda scrub that works wonders. I'll ask her to mix some up for you." Katie Ann sat up and scooted closer to Naomi. They sat there, shoulder to shoulder, considering their plight.

"We can't get out while we're taped up," Katie Ann said.

"I doubt he's going to keep us here for long."

"Why would he?"

"Exactly."

"And what was the second note he wrote?"

"I tried to read it, but he leveled me with that creepy stare and told me to mind my own business."

"Think it was a ransom note?"

"How do you know about ransom notes?"

"One of the books my *mamm* was reading." Katie Ann stared up at the ceiling of the trailer again. "A young girl had been kidnapped from a rich *Englischer*, and the man—the kidnapper—took the child to an Amish farm to hide her. He wasn't a bad man, but he was desperate. His daughter needed some medical procedures, and he didn't have enough money. That was the reason he did such a terrible thing, because he loved his daughter so much."

"And because he wanted the money."

"Exactly."

"No one in our community is rich."

"Except for Leroy Kauffmann."

"If that's who he was targeting, he would have kidnapped one of Leroy's children."

"Do you think...do you think he killed Jeremiah?"

"I don't know. Do you?"

"I think he might have," Katie Ann admitted.

"Did you ever suspect he was capable of such a thing?"

"*Nein.* I can't say I liked him, but I never considered he would be the one..."

"People hide who they truly are." Naomi lifted her hands in front of her and then let them fall. "Or maybe it's simply that we don't take the time to look closely enough."

"I think if he doesn't get what he wants, he might do it again."

"You're not cheering me up."

"But talking it through helps. *Ya?*"

"I suppose."

"We're not going to wait to be rescued." Katie Ann sat forward and arched her back like a cat. "When he moves us to wherever he's moving us, we're going to be ready. And this time? He's not going to expect what we're doing."

They tried to fist bump, but with their hands taped it wasn't nearly as satisfying.

"What should we do now?" Naomi asked.

"Try to rest. We're going to need our energy later, so let's try to sleep while we can."

"I'm not the least bit tired." Naomi yawned hugely and then sighed. "Maybe I am a little, but I want to be resting at home, not here."

"I think he plans for this to be over by tonight."

"Why do you say that?"

"No food. All he's given us is water. If he were planning to keep us for days or weeks, I think he'd be better supplied."

"So we need to be ready when he comes back. We need to have a plan by then."

"*Ya,* we do."

Fifty-Seven

Emma wasn't sure what else to do with her worry, so she set about cleaning house and doing the daily chores that needed to be done. Rachel was tending to Katie Ann's chores in the barn, and the boys were helping their father. Emma focused on the house. After she'd finished the breakfast dishes and laid out what they would need for lunch, Emma walked out to the mailbox. They were near the beginning of their mail carrier's route, so the mail was always delivered before noon. Emma glanced up and down the road, hoping she would catch a glimpse of Katie Ann walking toward home.

But all she saw was a two-lane blacktop stretching across the San Luis Valley.

No granddaughter.

No buggies.

No *Englisch* cars.

She pressed her hand to her abdomen, trying to squelch the fear and panic that threatened to overwhelm her. Katie Ann was fine. She'd simply gone off with a friend and forgotten to tell anyone. It was unlike her, but she was young and hadn't yet had much of a *rumspringa*. These things happened.

Emma reached into the mailbox and pulled out a small bundle of sales circulars, one letter from Goshen, and on top of that a blank envelope with the words EMMA FISHER on it. No mailing address or stamp or return address.

With trembling hands, she flipped the envelope over, slit open the flap, and pulled out the single sheet of paper.

> Who now would follow Christ in life
> Must scorn the world's insult and strife
> And bear the cross each day.
> For this alone leads to the throne
> Christ is the only way.

The words were familiar, coming from a hymn found in their *Ausbund*. Emma didn't understand what they were doing in this letter, what the writer meant. Then she turned the page over, and her knees went weak so that she stumbled backward and would have fallen if it hadn't been for the fence behind her, catching her and supporting her weight.

> If you want to see Katie Ann and Naomi again, get $10,000.
> Be at the phone shack nearest Henry's house at 3:25 today.
> No wires or police. Bring the drawings.
> Come alone—you and Henry.
> You'll receive further instructions there.

Emma read the note again, but the words didn't change. It wasn't signed, of course, and it didn't look like the letter carrier had delivered it. Whoever left it had waited for the mail to be delivered and then placed the ransom note on top. And there was no mistake about it—that was exactly what she was holding.

Someone wanted a ransom to return Katie Ann and Naomi.

She read the note a third time, her heart still hammering and her palms slick. When she reached the fourth line, she understood what she had to do. The writer's intent was clear. This was between her and Henry and the person responsible for taking the girls. Emma knew her family would never allow her to do as the note directed. If she walked back to the house, they would insist on calling the police, on going with her, on protecting her and Henry and the girls from this madman.

She stared at the note, her hand shaking as a westerly wind whipped the sheet of paper back and forth.

Come alone—you and Henry.

Henry would know what to do, and the writer of the note expected the two of them. Surely two would be better than one. She reached into the mailbox, pulled out the pencil they kept at the back, and scribbled a note on the back of a flyer. Folding the flyer carefully so they would be sure to see it, she placed it on top of the stack of mail, put it all back into the mailbox—all except for the ransom note—and closed the mailbox.

Then without looking back, she hurried down the road.

By the time she reached Henry's, fat drops of rain had begun to pepper the ground.

More rain in a valley where they rarely received precipitation two days in a row. She barely noticed.

Henry wasn't in the house, and there was no sign of Lexi, so she rushed over to the workshop. Lexi was sleeping under the porch overhang. The little dog sat up, yipped once, and then darted out toward her. Emma patted her on the head and then called out to Henry as she practically ran into the workshop.

He was standing in the middle of the room, staring at his drawings.

"Emma, I didn't expect to see you so soon."

"*Ya.* That's obvious."

"I just keep drawing, but I can't...I can't seem to find the answer. Perhaps it's not here."

There had to be dozens of them. He'd used thumbtacks to pin them around the room at eye level. They made a dizzying sort of wallpaper, and Emma was momentarily distracted by them.

Was the answer there among the sketches?

Had Henry managed to capture an image of the person who had brought such chaos and tragedy into their lives once again?

Would she recognize him for the evil person he was?

But then she remembered she was holding the answer in her hand, or at least a part of it.

"This was in our mailbox." She thrust the note into Henry's hands.

He read through it quickly the first time, muttering the words aloud as he did so. His eyes met hers, and she knew then, in that moment, that Henry would not desert her. Well, of course he wouldn't. He was their bishop, a good bishop, and moreover, he was their friend. He would soon be a part of their family. He would be her husband. He cared about her and about Katie Ann, about her entire family. Together they'd find a way through this.

Thunder crashed and the sky darkened so that she could barely make out his expression as he stepped toward her. "We'll go together."

"*Ya.*"

"Did you tell anyone?"

"*Nein*, but I left Clyde a note in the mailbox. I couldn't bear him worrying."

"What did you say?"

"Only that I had to see you, and that I'd explain when I returned."

"Good. That will buy us some time."

"But what are we going to do? We can't possibly come up with ten thousand dollars. Does the church even have that much?"

"*Ya.* The benevolence fund has been growing—no natural disaster or major illness since our last offering. But that's not really the issue..."

"The money's in the bank."

"It is, and it would look suspicious for me to withdraw so much."

"Then we have to go to Leroy and tell him we need the money."

Henry scrubbed a hand over his face. "I can't just ask him to hand over that amount of money without an explanation. Leroy is very careful about how he handles our funds. It's one of the reasons he's the perfect man for that position in our community."

"What do we do?"

"We go without the money. Whoever this is, they'll call—"

"Or shoot us as we walk into the phone shack."

"No. They could shoot us here. My guess is he really wants or needs the money, and yes, I realize I said *he*. I can't imagine a woman doing this sort of thing. Can you?"

Emma shook her head. In truth, she couldn't imagine anyone doing such a terrible thing, and for what? Ten thousand dollars?

Henry glanced at his watch. "Three hours."

"Why did he give us so long?"

"He couldn't have known when you'd find the note, and maybe he needs time on his end."

"To move the girls?"

"Or secure them somewhere so they can't run away."

"We have to find them, Henry. We have to bring them home."

Instead of assuring Emma they would, Henry put his arms around her, held her close, and began to pray.

As he petitioned God for the girls' safety, for wisdom and strength, to make clear their path and guide their decisions, the sky darkened like night, lightning streaked across the sky, and the rain began to fall in earnest.

Fifty-Eight

Henry and Emma huddled beneath the overhang of his workshop. The darkness had abated after the first fifteen minutes, leaving a dreary summer afternoon sky as rain continued to fall. Lexi lay with her head on her paws, as if she knew what they were contemplating, as if she wanted to somehow save them from this foolish act, but it was beyond the power of a dog. Finally, she sighed, rolled over onto her side, and fell asleep.

"What are we going to do?" Emma asked. "Who is doing this? Why did they take Naomi and Katie Ann?"

Henry put his arm around her, and she tucked in close to his side.

"We'll get them back."

"That's a promise?"

"Yes, Emma. I don't know how, but we will get them back." Even as he uttered those words, he thought of the dozens of drawings behind him in the workshop—covering every wall, taunting him with the fact that he'd seen nothing of importance.

That was it. He'd seen nothing of importance.

"Maybe it's not what we've seen."

"What?"

"Maybe it's not what we've seen." The idea solidified in his mind, and then it was as if he *could* see it. In the same way a blind person could imagine, accurately, the furniture placed in a home, so could Henry and Emma see this situation clearly. Because it wasn't about what they'd witnessed with their eyes, it was what they knew in their hearts.

He pulled her over to the rockers, repositioning one so that he was facing her, their knees nearly touching. "Maybe it's not what I've seen or what we've seen..."

"Because neither of us saw anything."

"Exactly. I wasn't there when Jeremiah was shot."

"And I wasn't paying attention."

"I wasn't there when Seth was run off the road."

"Thank God he wasn't hurt."

"And you weren't there when Katie Ann was taken."

Tears slipped down Emma's cheeks, but she wiped them away, and nodded in agreement.

"I believe God has placed us in the middle of this because we know something, something we don't even realize we know, something that will help the police to resolve the situation."

"We know the person is Amish."

"Not definitely. We can't prove it."

"But we don't have to prove it."

Emma stared out at the rain, pulling her bottom lip in and worrying it. Her hair had come loose from her *kapp*, and Henry reached forward and tucked it behind her ear, allowed his palm to cup her face.

"With Sheriff Grayson, it's a matter of what he can prove," Emma admitted. "But as you said, we're involved in this for a reason, and we don't have to prove anything. We only have to follow what we know, and then if we're right..."

"Grayson will wrap it up."

"Exactly."

Henry rubbed his hands together. "I agree, then. The person is Amish, for a variety of reasons."

"*Ya*. Someone who is *Englisch* might know the words of the hymns found in the *Ausbund*..."

"But the one this person chose speaks of the suffering of Christ. It's a rather obscure hymn, and one we sing only once or twice a year. An *Englisch* person wouldn't have randomly chosen that one. There's a reason whoever is doing this quoted that particular hymn in the note."

"We agree it's further proof that he's Amish."

"*Ya*." Henry set his rocker in motion, his mind focused on the details Emma was calling to mind.

"All right. We're agreed, then. The person is male and Amish. I think...that is, I feel certain he's also young. Do you agree?"

"Youngish. He uses *Englisch* words too naturally..."

"*No wires or police.*"

"Words and concepts that people from our generation barely understand. We sure wouldn't think to include them in a note."

"This is a ransom note." Emma's eyes narrowed. "He's focused on the money. Greed. That's his motive."

"I'm not even sure what *wires* refers to," Henry admitted.

"It's a microphone sort of thing they hide on your body." When Henry raised his eyebrows, Emma shrugged. "Rachel's been on a suspense kick with her reading."

"Suspense?"

"Murder, robbery, all sorts of terrible things." She added as an afterthought, "But always Christian fiction."

"Indeed."

"So no wires. Where would he think we'd get a wire?"

"He thinks, or he fears, we will go to Grayson."

"Why would we do that?"

"Because we have to."

"How? The kidnapper, who is almost certainly also Jeremiah's killer, could be watching us."

"I suspect he is." Henry tapped his fingers against the rocking chair arm to the rhythm of the rain. It had slowed to a steady drip from the roof eaves. It wasn't typical weather for August. March was supposed to roar in like a lion and out like a lamb, but it seemed to Henry that most Colorado weather fit that description. He checked his watch. "We have a little more than two hours."

"I can tell you have a plan, Henry Lapp. I hope it's a good one."

Instead of answering, he strode into the workshop, pulled out a sheet of paper, and jotted down a note.

"After..." Emma was watching over his shoulder. She pointed to the second line and said, "It should be *after* so we can give him the killer's instructions."

"*Gut* idea."

He fetched another sheet of paper and rewrote the note.

"The inside lobby is open until five?" he asked.

"*Ya*. Monday through Friday."

He finished the note and then pushed it to the middle of the table where they could both stare at it.

> Emma and I have been summoned by the girls' kidnapper. Find Grayson. Insist that he ride in your buggy but hidden from sight. Meet us at the phone shack at 3:40 exactly.

"Could be a few minutes early," she said.

"Could be a few minutes late."

"How are you going to deliver it?"

"That's the sketchy part of the plan."

"Sketchier than this?"

Henry folded the note top to bottom and then in half again, so that it was only a couple of inches wide. Turning it sideways, he wrote across the top edge EMERGENCY. Next he walked over to a block of cubbies next to the workshop's door. From one of them he removed Lexi's vest. Pulling an exacto knife from a drawer, he slit the top seam of the vest and tucked the note into it so that a good inch of the paper was hanging out. The word EMERGENCY was plainly readable.

"She's a smart dog, Henry, but I don't know..."

"We can't deliver it ourselves. As we said earlier, the kidnapper might be watching us. If he sees us go next door, he might follow through on his threat. It's an implied threat, but it's there nonetheless."

Henry squeezed her arm in reassurance and walked out onto the porch. He glanced out at the storm and wasn't at all surprised to see that the rain had stopped completely. The clouds continued to press down, and the wind occasionally gusted, but the main body of the storm had passed. He squatted beside Lexi, who stood in anticipation of a walk or perhaps even a ride in the buggy. Her tail set to wagging, and she looked at Henry with such adoration that he had a surge of confidence that she could do the thing he was about to ask of her.

She stood patiently as he fastened the vest on her, buckling it under her torso. Then she looked at him, no doubt waiting for him to clip on her leash. But Henry didn't plan on walking her anywhere.

"Go to Seth's, Lexi. Go see Seth and Roseann."

Lexi yipped, hopped off the porch, and stood waiting for Henry.

He squatted down, and she ran back up the steps.

"I need you to do this, Lexi. I need you to go to Seth's. Go straight there, okay, girl? Go to Seth's and give him the note."

Lexi reached out and licked his cheek, and then she turned and trotted away from the workshop. She stopped once to look back at him. When he waved her on, she scampered through the hole in his fence that he'd been meaning to mend.

"Do you really think she can do this?"

"*Ya*. I do." Henry turned to Emma, to the woman who would soon be his wife, and he smiled for the first time since seeing her rush into his workshop and thrust the ransom note in his hands. "*Gotte* used Balaam's donkey. My personal opinion is that a beagle is a whole lot smarter."

Fifty-Nine

Their plan would only work if they went to the phone shack first, at the kidnapper's set time. They hoped they could talk him out of his demand for money, but if not, they should still have enough time to go to the bank.

So they sat, and they waited.

Emma prayed for Naomi and Katie Ann. She prayed for Lexi and Henry's neighbors. She prayed that they would be successful, and that the person responsible would come to his senses.

A strange calmness flooded her heart and soul in the time they waited.

Henry pulled several of the drawings off the walls of his workshop. Did any of them include the killer? She didn't think so. When she looked at them, all she saw was people having a good time at the rodeo moments before tragedy struck their town.

Henry slipped the drawings into a flat paper sack. Finally, he left to hitch Oreo to the buggy. Emma walked outside to watch him, and then she turned and went back into the workshop, looked around, and spied a backpack Henry sometimes used when he went bird-watching at the refuge. Unzipping it, she found his binoculars inside. Those could come in handy. She searched for and found a flashlight in one of the cubbies and added that. There was no telling where they were going or how late they would be out. Best to go prepared.

Henry had no weapons of any sort except an old hunting rifle he hadn't used in years. "Doesn't matter," she muttered to herself. They didn't need weapons. What they needed was divine intervention. What they needed was to find Naomi and Katie Ann, help Grayson arrest the murderer, and put this entire chapter behind them. Seemed like a lot to ask, but then Henry was always reminding them that their God was mighty, compassionate, all-knowing. Those thoughts filled her mind and pushed away the last remnants of fear and doubt.

She hurried over to the house, added a can of soda she found in the fridge, filled a thermos with water, and wrapped up some of the widows' cookies in a dish towel. There was no telling where this desperate attempt to save the girls would lead them or how long it would take. She wanted to be prepared for anything they might need. As a last thought, she added a chunk of cheese and some bread.

By the time Henry pulled up, she was waiting beside the house.

"I packed us a picnic," she said, climbing into the buggy.

"A picnic?" Henry cocked his head as if he'd heard her wrong.

"I don't know what lies ahead, what this person has in mind, but I don't want us weak because we haven't eaten all day. And if he...if he kidnaps us and takes us to wherever he's hidden Naomi and Katie Ann, I want to have something to give them."

"You're an amazing woman, Emma Fisher."

Tears stung her eyes, but she blinked them away, reached across the buggy seat, and squeezed his hand. "Let's go get our girls."

Which was how she thought of both Katie Ann and Naomi. They were close friends, good girls, and would grow to be fine women. She'd do everything in her power to make sure they had the chance to live a Plain and simple life.

But Henry didn't call out to Oreo right away. Instead, he bowed his head and began to pray—for their safety, for Sheriff Grayson, for Lexi, for Seth, for Katie Ann and Naomi, for the troubled soul who had committed murder once and might do so again.

Ten minutes later they were at the phone shack.

"We're early."

They stood together at the counter, though there was a stool. Emma didn't want to sit on the stool. She wanted the phone to ring so they could do whatever this man told them to do.

They'd seen no unusual activity when they passed Seth and Rose-ann's farm, but then there wouldn't be. Not if they were following Henry's instructions. They'd already be gone and fetching Sheriff Grayson.

The phone rang, startling her out of her reverie.

"Good thing you came alone."

Henry held the phone so Emma could hear, though for her to do so their heads were nearly pressed together. The voice on the other end of the line was male, relatively young, and definitely Amish. The Pennsylvania Dutch was thick, and if Emma was right, there was a hint of Indiana to it.

"What do you want?" Henry asked.

"The money and the drawings."

Emma realized then that this person meant to kill Henry. He thought Henry had seen and then drawn a picture of him raising a rifle to kill Jeremiah. Henry could hand over what he'd drawn, but what would stop him from returning home and drawing the same thing again? This person feared what was in Henry's mind and what he could do with that information. And she understood then that they could argue all day long that Henry hadn't seen anything, but the killer wouldn't believe them because he was being driven by fear.

"I have the drawings," Henry said.

"And the money?"

"*Nein.* Not yet. It's a lot of money, but in the end, it won't satisfy you."

"I'll be the judge of that. You have one more chance to get the money. That's all, or—"

"What do we do once we have it?"

"Drive straight to the arena."

"The arena?"

"Go now, and don't stop anywhere else."

"I'll have to stop at Leroy's. He handles our finances."

"We both know he doesn't keep it under his mattress."

"*Nein.* He keeps it at the bank. I'll need to ask him to go and get some out."

"Stop playing with me, Hen-rrry." He drew out the last syllable as if this were all one big joke. Emma wanted to reach through the phone and shake him.

"We both know your name is on the signature card for the account."

"All right, but it would raise less suspicion if he were to withdraw the money."

"I'm sure you'll come up with a good story to explain yourself—"

"We want to speak to the girls."

"Well, I want a million dollars, but I didn't figure you'd have that much."

"We don't."

Emma couldn't remain silent one second longer. "Where is Katie Ann? What did you do with her? Where is Naomi? Let them go. They are not involved in this."

"But they are now, thanks to Naomi's need to blab in the *Budget*. As far as Katie Ann, that was an accident...wrong place, wrong time, and all that."

"I want to speak with her." Emma felt her emotions spiraling out of control.

Henry still clutched the phone with one hand, but he reached across and clasped her hand with his free one.

"Yes, calm her down, Henry. We don't need an emotional woman messing things up."

Emma's head jerked away from the phone. They'd suspected whoever this was might be watching them, but she hadn't realized he was. She leaned toward the window of the shack, trying to determine where he might be, which only succeeded in drawing a laugh from the young man.

"You won't see me, Emma. What fun would that be?"

"We'll go to the bank," Henry said. "And then the arena."

"Enter through the east entrance one hour from now."

"We'll need more time than that."

"One hour. Be at the east entrance. Enter into the breezeway and wait fifteen minutes exactly, and then walk into the middle of the field."

"Why?"

"It doesn't matter why, Hen-rrry."

"You're right. Just bring the girls. That's all that matters."

"I'll be watching to make sure you're alone."

The line went dead. Henry gently replaced the receiver, and then he reached into his pocket for a quarter and placed it in the can next to the phone.

"Where's Seth?" Emma asked.

"I told him to be here at 3:40 exactly. The call was shorter than I thought it would be."

"So what do we do?"

"We stall."

Sixty

They stepped out of the phone shack. Henry stumbled and then dropped to the ground.

Emma flew to his side. He winked at her and said, "Look concerned, Emma."

"I am concerned!"

"Good, because he's probably still watching."

She helped him to stand. He put weight on his left leg, scrunched up his face as if that hurt, and placed an arm around Emma's shoulders.

Then they both heard the clip-clop of a buggy horse.

Emma understood now why Henry had told Seth to come to the phone shack. It was the only way it could possibly look like a random meeting. By the time Seth had pulled his buggy up next to Henry's, Henry had hobbled over to the driver's side, leaning on Emma's arm.

"Henry, are you all right?"

"Emma and I are both fine. I didn't really hurt my leg. Is Lexi okay?"

"Roseann has her. She's good."

Emma could just make out Grayson in the back of the buggy, but there was no mistaking the man's voice.

"I don't like this, Henry. It's too dangerous."

"We received a ransom note from the person who took the girls, probably the same person who killed Jeremiah. He wants ten thousand dollars."

"So this is about money?"

"At least partially. I'm to get it from the bank and drive straight to the arena."

"It's deserted during the week. He must know that."

"His instructions are for us to enter through the east side in one hour, wait fifteen minutes, and then walk to the middle of the arena." Henry reached down to rub his left leg, and added, "He's probably still watching us now."

"I had an inkling about what we'd need when your note confirmed a kidnapping. We have a team assembled, but only local people. If you can give me more time, I can get a sharpshooter, even a hostage negotiator there before you arrive."

"He won't wait."

"Do you think this person will follow you to the bank?"

"I'm sure he will."

"I'll send my men to the arena ahead of you, then. They'll position in the breezeway on the east side."

"Why did he tell us to wait fifteen minutes before going on through?" Emma asked.

Grayson glanced left and right, as if he could see through the walls of the buggy to what lay ahead. "He's going to watch you enter, make sure you aren't followed, and then get in position."

"*Ya.* Likely you're right."

"We'll be there before you. Try to stall at the bank."

Emma didn't think either of them falling down again would work, and she didn't know how Henry was going to withdraw ten thousand dollars without suspicion, and she wasn't sure Grayson's men would be able to get in place at the arena that quickly.

But the die was cast.

She raised her voice a little and told Seth to have a good day. In a near whisper she added, "And don't forget to make a call so he'll believe that's why you came to the phone shack." Then she helped Henry as he hobbled over to his buggy.

They drove slowly to the bank.

"Do you think he bought that Seth just happened to be at the phone shack when we were leaving?" Emma worried her thumbnail, wanting to feel the peace and certainty she'd felt back at Henry's workshop, but she was caught up in the danger and precariousness of their situation. Her hands were sweating, and her heart was thudding in her chest. She wanted to be calm, but her body was reacting as if she were being chased by a wild animal—which she supposed she was.

"I think this person, whoever he is, is arrogant."

"No doubt about that."

"He considers himself more intelligent than others."

"I wish I could feel pity for him, but at the moment all I feel is anger."

"He'd have to know we could get a note to someone..."

"No one would believe Lexi capable of that. I still can't believe it."

"He would never guess that an Amish person would go to the local sheriff and entice him into hiding in the backseat of a buggy to a clandestine meeting."

"Does seem a bit far-fetched."

"There's something else. He's focused on the drawings. I think he'd planned all along to kill Jeremiah here, during the rodeo, when there would be so many people and no one would really see anything. But he didn't count on my being there. He's not that familiar with our community."

"Something else we know, then—he isn't actually from Monte Vista."

"He spent many days planning his retribution. For what, I have no idea. But he couldn't have known about my ability to draw, and convincing him I didn't see anything? I'm afraid that will be impossible."

Emma shook her head. "This time it's not what the bishop saw. It's what the bishop knows...or who the bishop knows."

When Henry cocked his head, she added, "We have a profile of the killer, but more importantly, you know the people who can help us."

"Like Seth and Sheriff Grayson."

"And you know that God will protect us."

"He promised as much."

"Indeed He did, Henry. Indeed He did."

Sixty-One

enry limped a little into the bank, pretending his leg was better but still sore. Unsure exactly what he was going to do. Emma offered to wait outside, but they were afraid the person watching them might try something. Better that they stick together. The bank was about to close, so Henry didn't have a lot of time to devise his course of action.

He walked up to the teller window and presented the woman with his identification card, though she knew who he was and greeted him. "Good afternoon, Mr. Lapp."

"And to you."

"How can I help you today?"

"I'd like to withdraw some money from our church account."

She tapped something on a computer, confirmed that he was authorized to withdraw funds, and then she reached for a withdrawal slip and penned the account number in the appropriate box.

"How much would you like to withdraw?"

Henry glanced at Emma, who raised her eyebrows.

"The thing is, perhaps one-dollar bills would be best."

"That's not a problem."

"I'm going to need a lot of them."

"Then you've come to the right place. We are, after all, a bank."

Henry smiled at her little joke, and then said, "They come in bundles, correct?"

"Yes, sir. We band them together. You can receive $25, $50, $100, $200, or $250 to a bundle."

"I'll take the $250."

"Sure thing."

"And I'll need ten of them. If that's not a problem, since you're a bank."

She smiled brightly. "No problem at all. You all must be having one of those auctions coming up. Folks are always wanting one-dollar bills for auctions and garage sales."

"Something like that."

"I'll just have to ask a manager to get that from the vault." She tapped something on her computer. "I'll be right back."

Henry was terribly proud of the way Emma was holding together. If anything, hearing from the killer, from the kidnapper, seemed to have solidified her resolve. Instead of becoming emotional, she'd turned to her practical side. The Emma who had cried on his shoulder was gone. Standing beside him was a woman determined to do whatever she had to, to see Naomi and Katie Ann safely returned home.

Good to her word, five minutes later the bank teller returned with ten stacks of one-dollar bills, each banded together with a pink paper strap. She counted them out, had Henry sign the withdrawal slip, and then asked, "Can I get you anything else today?"

"Perhaps something to put these in?"

She reached under the counter and pulled out a small canvas bag with the bank's logo printed on the side.

"Thank you very much. You've been extremely helpful."

"You have a good day." They had nearly reached the door when the teller called out, "And good luck with your auction."

They walked across the parking area to Oreo, Henry now limping so slightly he thought he could get away with walking normally at the arena. The horse was cropping at the grass near the railing where she was tied. Handing the bank bag to Emma, Henry winked and squatted down next to Oreo's front left hoof. He ran his hand down the horse's leg, and she picked up the hoof, never bothering to pause in her foraging.

"She's well behaved," Emma noted.

"Indeed."

"Do you think we're still being watched?"

"I do."

"And you're stalling?"

"I am."

Emma sighed as Henry cleared the horse's hoof of imaginary pebbles. Standing, he patted Oreo's neck. Then he nodded and said, "I can't think of any other way to postpone this."

He glanced about, but he saw no signs of Grayson or his officers or the killer.

Had he given Grayson enough time to move his officers into place? What was their plan once they arrived at the arena? How would he convince Jeremiah's killer to come to his senses, drop his vendetta, and turn himself over to the authorities?

Henry helped Emma into the buggy, shut the door, and shuffled around to his side. He wished he'd done a better job of stalling while inside the bank, but at the time he couldn't think of any other reason to stay.

But fate was on their side, or perhaps God did care about the day-to-day trials of man, because road construction was going on through the middle of town. Crews halted everyone on their side and allowed the traffic heading toward them through. They were third in line, behind an *Englisch* pickup and a person on a motorcycle. The road worker finally turned the sign he was holding on a tall pole from STOP to SLOW.

By the time they cleared the intersection, the delay had used up another fifteen minutes.

When they pulled into the arena parking area, the time on Henry's watch read twenty-eight minutes past four o'clock, and the sun was shining brightly as it descended in the western sky.

Henry allowed Oreo to slow to a stop, and they sat there looking out over the property. No cars were in the parking lot. The area where the carnival had been was now swept clean. The banner from the rodeo still stretched across the front of the arena.

San Luis Valley

Ski Hi Stampede

Colorado's Oldest Pro Rodeo

"Place looks deserted," Emma said.

"It isn't, though."

"Are you certain?"

"Grayson promised."

"He's a good man."

"I'm sure he has a plan."

"Any idea what it is?"

"*Nein.* You heard as much from him as I did."

"I suppose we'll have to take a step of faith, then."

"We're not alone on this, Emma. Grayson is here. His officers are here." Henry cupped her hands in his, marveling that they were ice cold but steady, that despite her fear Emma was holding her emotions together. "And maybe, just maybe, Naomi and Katie Ann are here as well."

Sixty-Two

They parked the buggy where they normally did when attending an event at the arena. A utility shed at the back held mowers and other equipment the city used on common areas. Perhaps that was why the gates were open, as they were most days. Oreo seemed appreciative of the shade. "Back in a few minutes," Henry assured the mare, but he wondered if that was true. Would they be back in a few minutes? No doubt Jeremiah had thought the same thing. He'd expected to be on the floor of the arena for less than two, three minutes at the most. But he'd died there.

The person who killed him wasn't stable, and there was no way to know what he would be willing to do to ensure his own safety.

Emma smiled at him weakly as she accepted the paper bag holding four of the drawings. Henry held the money bag in the crook of his right arm, and with his left hand he clasped Emma's hand.

"Looking forward to our wedding, Emma?"

The question seemed to catch her off guard.

"I had been. The last few weeks I'd been thinking of little else."

"And then?"

"Then Jeremiah was killed, Seth was run off the road, Katie Ann and Naomi were taken." She blinked several times, took a deep breath, and said, "But *ya*. I surely am looking forward to the day we are wed."

"Do you know what I'm looking forward to the most?"

She shook her head.

"Sitting on the front porch of our *dawdi haus*, watching the *grandkinner* play in the yard, Lexi chase butterflies, and Katie Ann tend to her animals."

291

And with that image in his mind, Henry's doubts fled. He could look past the present hour and glimpse the future God had for them.

Emma glanced at Henry, a knowing smile tugging at her lips.

"Stephen and Thomas mention it to me every day."

"Is that so?"

"They have it in their minds that you're going to be their fishing buddy."

"Perhaps I will."

They stepped into the east entrance and walked through the breezeway.

Sheriff Grayson stepped out of the area usually reserved for food service workers. "Good job stalling, Henry."

"The roadwork helped."

"As did your request for twenty-five hundred dollars in ones. Good thinking."

Henry started to ask how Grayson knew about that, but the sheriff had already turned to one of his officers and said, "Our fifteen-minute window begins now. Make sure everyone is in position."

To Henry he said, "Let's get you suited up."

"Suited up?"

Grayson motioned them into the kitchen area, and Henry and Emma quickly followed. Officer Ellen Cunningham moved forward and offered to hold the bag of money. Then she moved over to Emma and accepted the paper bag holding the drawings. She opened it, peeked inside, and let out a long, low whistle.

"Take off your jacket," Grayson said to Henry.

"Why do I need to do that?"

Grayson didn't answer. Instead, Officer Ricky Moore stepped in front of Henry and helped him out of the jacket. Next they placed a thin cord over his head, tucked it beneath his shirt, and taped the microphone dangling from it to the front of his chest.

Henry thought of David, going out to battle the Philistine. What was it the Old Testament writer had penned? *The Lord who rescued me from the paw of the lion and the paw of the bear will rescue me from the hand of this Philistine.*

Henry didn't realize he'd quoted the Scripture aloud until Grayson said, "No lions or bears here. Only a criminal, and we know how to catch those."

"Could you hold out your arms for me?" Officer Moore asked.

As Henry did so, they placed a thick, black vest over his shirt, tightened the Velcro straps, and then helped him back into his jacket. How did *Englischers* wear such things? It must have weighed ten pounds.

At the same time, they had been putting a microphone and black vest with the word KEVLAR across the front on Emma. Another woman officer said, "Sorry, ma'am. All we could find was this sweater."

It was hardly cool enough for a sweater, but before Emma could argue, they had put the sweater over the Kevlar vest and buttoned it up.

She glanced at Henry, sweat beading across her forehead.

"Tell me what we're doing here, Grayson."

"They're bulletproof vests, just in case. We have men stationed throughout the arena, but you're going to have to follow his instructions exactly, or he might take off before we have a chance to capture him. I don't think he'll have time to get a shot off, but we know he has a rifle with a long-range scope. No doubt it's what he used to kill Jeremiah. We also know he won't hesitate to shoot, so it's best if you're prepared. Now, the ear microphones will help us to communicate. You'll be able to hear us, and more importantly, we'll be able to hear you, as well as anything the killer says."

Emma jumped when someone pressed a device into her ear.

Henry glanced her way, jerking his head away from the man who was attempting to do the same for him.

"The money bag is a good idea. It'll look like you're carrying the full ten grand."

Henry had the sense that everything was spiraling out of control. Emma looked about to let out a holler if she didn't get out of the sweater. It was a warm August afternoon. The killer would either think she was daft, or he'd know they were up to something. Amish men—especially Amish bishops—often wore jackets even in the summer, but women in a sweater? It looked odd.

"Walk to the other side of the room and be sure you can hear us." Officer Moore was now fiddling with a radio.

Henry did as he asked, but his mind wasn't on what the officers were saying. He was remembering the seventeenth chapter of the first book of Samuel. He'd preached on it many times, on the sufficiency of God. He closed his eyes and imagined his hand drawing the words, the very scene from the Scripture.

> *Then Saul dressed David in his own tunic. He put a coat of armor on him and a bronze helmet on his head. David fastened on his sword over the tunic and tried walking around, because he was not used to them.*

"We need you to pay attention, Henry." Grayson cocked his head to the side. "Can you hear Officer Moore?"

I cannot go in these because I am not used to them.

Emma met Henry's gaze and shook her head once, just a tiny shake, one that was almost more of a tick than a conscious movement. No doubt she was barely aware that she'd done it, but that tiny gesture was enough for Henry. He pulled the plug from his ear and deposited it in Officer Moore's hand.

Grayson hurried over to where they were standing. "You need to leave that in, Henry."

As he pulled off his coat, Emma pulled off her sweater.

"We don't have time to come up with an alternate plan here."

They both removed their vests, and Emma let out a heavy sigh.

"Henry, tell me what you're doing."

Henry pulled his jacket back on over his shirt. He instantly felt better, more confident.

He turned to Sheriff Grayson, to his friend, and quoted that dearly beloved story from the Old Testament of a young man who was preparing to fight a giant. "You come against me with sword and spear and javelin, but I come against you in the name of the LORD Almighty—"

"I guess that's from the Bible, but, Henry, I need you to listen to me—"

"David told the Philistine, 'This day the LORD will deliver you into my hands—'"

"You're not going out to face a Philistine!" Sweat beaded on Grayson's forehead, and Henry felt sorry for the man. He was doing the best he could do, what he'd been trained to do.

"*Gotte* protected David. He will surely protect us."

"I appreciate your perspective, I really do. But this person who's holding the girls? He's desperate. And his bullets? They're real."

"Thank you for your help, Grayson, but we won't be wearing bullet-proof vests or ear microphones."

"Henry, now isn't the time to—"

"Actually, I think now is the time." He glanced at Officer Cunningham, who had been watching the fifteen-minute countdown. She nodded once.

"We'll be fine," he said.

Henry accepted the bag of money from Cunningham, and Emma tucked the bag with the drawings under her arm. He snagged Emma's hand, and together they walked out into the breezeway and toward the center of the arena.

"Felt like David suiting up in the king's armor in there."

"Thought I was going to suffocate."

"The look on your face was priceless."

"We'll be okay. Won't we?"

Henry stopped then, pulled Emma into his arms, and kissed her on the lips, cradling her face in his hands. Then he pressed his forehead to hers. "As with David, Emma, the Lord will be our shield."

Perhaps it was naive of them to think so. Bullets worked the same against believers as nonbelievers. But Henry thought somehow the tide had turned. He couldn't imagine how, but he knew with crystal clarity that they were doing the right thing.

He glanced back and saw the officers had stopped at a discreet distance, giving them a moment. Sheriff Grayson was simultaneously checking his watch and talking into his radio. Emma didn't seem a bit embarrassed that Henry had kissed her in public.

Life was short, and this could be their last chance.

Henry was relieved that they intended to make the most of it.

Sixty-Three

As Henry stepped into the arena, the afternoon sun shone so brightly he couldn't see anything on the far side, which was of course what the shooter wanted. He'd planned the details of this exchange down to the setting of the sun.

The only sound was their feet against the dirt floor, and Henry thought he could hear his heart hammering against his chest. It was true what he'd told Emma. God was their shield. And yet perhaps their lives were complete. Only God knew. Henry prayed it wasn't so for selfish reasons. He'd come to believe his life was just beginning, or at least this phase of it.

Together he and Emma made it to the middle of the arena, still holding hands, ready to do whatever was necessary to return the girls to safely. Suddenly a voice came over the PA system.

"Good job, Hen-rrry."

How had the killer managed that? Was he in the announcer's booth?

"Though you were almost late. We can't have that. You know how important punctuality is." He laughed as if he'd said something amusing.

The voice was familiar, but Henry couldn't quite place it. He glanced at Emma, who nodded once and then shrugged her shoulders slightly. She recognized the voice too, though she didn't seem to be able to identify whose it was yet. Maybe if they could keep him talking. Henry was sure he'd heard him before, even prior to the call at the phone shack. This was definitely someone they knew.

"Even better, you brought what I want. Now strap the bag with the drawings and the money onto the drone."

Henry glanced up and around, but the sun was shining in his eyes, and he saw only spots at first. Then he caught movement on the west side of the arena—light glinting off metal, and he was certain that the killer had them in his sights, had his specially equipped rifle trained on them.

"Attach it to the drone, Henry. And hurry. I'm running out of patience." The killer's voice had lost all amusement. He now sounded like what he was—a hardened, cold-blooded, ruthless murderer.

At that moment a square device flew in front of them, snapped a picture, and landed.

It was approximately the size of a breadbox, rectangular, with four propellers affixed to the four corners. It reminded Henry of one of the helicopters he'd seen land to pick up injured folks from a car accident—only much smaller.

"Like a child's toy," Emma whispered.

Suspended from the bottom of the box was a camera, though Henry couldn't imagine why the killer would want a picture of them.

Attached to the top of the device were several bungee cords, and under those someone had taped a note that read, "Put money and drawings here."

"We want to see the girls first."

"Do what I said, Hen-rrry."

"That's not much of a negotiation."

"Who said I was going to negotiate?"

"It's why we're here. We give you what you want, and you give us the girls."

"I'm not a very patient person. Now, put the drawings and the money on top of the drone."

Henry couldn't see as how they had any choice.

Emma handed him the bag of drawings, which he placed on top of the humming device. He could feel a mild vibration when he placed his hand on top of it, reminding him of Lexi when she was longing to dash off. Next went the bag of money, and then he fastened the bungee cords over the top. He'd barely snapped the last cord into place when the drone rose in the air chest-high, whirred, and zoomed off toward the west entrance.

"Where are the girls?" Henry asked.

"They're close by and they're fine. I'm not a liar, Henry."

"We want to see them," Emma said.

Something like a sigh came over the loud speaker, but it was too dramatic. It was as if he thought they were in a novel or on an *Englisch* television show. As if he didn't realize real lives were at stake.

"It's not for you to say, is it? You'll do what I tell you to do, when I tell you to do it. Understand?"

But at that moment screams broke out from the north side of the arena, somewhere in the upper deck.

"Run!" Naomi's voice sounded hoarse and weak and desperate.

"He's behind the hotel advertisement." Henry glanced north, toward Katie Ann's voice, and then she was screaming, "He has a rifle!"

Henry threw himself at Emma, knocking them both to the ground and rolling with her as shots began to pepper the dirt around them.

Someone heaved a steel barrel across the arena, and when it passed them, Henry saw an officer inside instead of a rodeo clown. The barrel came to a stop and the officer jumped out, gun at the ready, a strange sort of goggles covering his eyes. Henry had barely processed that when all of the arena lights came on, effectively blinding every person there, including whoever was shooting at them.

Henry heard cursing and the sound of boots against metal bleachers. Police officers seemed to pour out of every direction, more officers than were on the Monte Vista police force. Grayson must have sent out a call for help from Del Norte and Alamosa.

Emma struggled free from his embrace, hopped up, and began to run. At first he thought she was running away, running from the shooter, and he wanted to assure her the man had fled. But then he heard her calling out to someone, and a moment after that he saw them—Katie Ann and Naomi. He raced after Emma, and together they bounded up the bleacher steps, hearts racing and chests heaving and legs resisting the strain, but they pushed on. And then they were squatting beside the two girls, whom they loved so much.

They were bound to the bleacher seats with duct tape wrapped around their arms and chests.

Duct tape hung from their mouths, held their arms to the chairs, held their feet together.

Tears poured from their eyes, and they were saying over and over again, "We knew you would come. We knew you would save us."

And Henry thought they had, but at that moment the killer stepped out from behind a large billboard sign fastened to the top rail. He hadn't run away after all. He'd run toward them, determined to finish what he'd begun.

Sixty-Four

Emma's love for Katie Ann and Naomi had propelled her across the arena and up into the stands. She didn't think about the danger, or where the shooter might be, or what she would do when she reached them. She only knew she had to reach them, and so she ran, and climbed, and fell to her knees in front of the two girls. Their eyes were wide with fear, but they appeared to be unharmed.

Both were weeping, saying they knew they'd come, but then Katie Ann emitted a strangled, "He's going to kill us..."

When Emma looked up, she saw Henry had moved to stand between the girls and Lloyd.

Lloyd Yutzy. From a good family in Goshen. Jeremiah's friend. Someone who had worshipped with them and eaten with them. Someone she thought she knew. Only she realized she didn't really know him at all.

The expression on his face? Foreign.

The glare in his eyes? Unfathomable.

The sneer on his lips? Something she'd rather not see, more like the snarl of a dog.

Emma glanced behind her, back down toward the center of the arena, and all around. Officers were spaced out around them—on the dirt floor, in the stands below them, from a distance to the side. Lloyd still had an escape route to the top, but where would he go from there?

Everyone was frozen, as if Lloyd was a bomb that might go off at any moment.

"Surprise, surprise!" Lloyd sang out. He must have somehow still been patched into the arena's PA system, because his voice came from all around them. "It's me."

Emma's heart sank, and grief momentarily won out over her fear. She had known it was an Amish man. In the analytical part of her brain, she'd accepted that. When she and Henry had cataloged what they knew, the obvious answer had been an Amish person. But seeing this young man stand before them, dressed completely in Amish garb with some sort of special eyeglasses fitted over his head, broke her heart.

Lloyd stopped a few feet from them, still holding his rifle at the ready. "Surprised to see me? Yeah. I can see you are. Ha-ha-ha! I knew you hadn't figured it out..."

A frown replaced his unnatural grin. "Well, you hadn't, Emma. Henry must have known, though, because he drew me. Didn't you, Henry? And now I have the drawings." His laughter crackled across the space between them.

"Don't try any funny stuff, officers." He didn't raise his voice. He was confident the officers could see and hear him, that he still held the upper hand. "I have my drone watching my backside, and I can see whatever it sees."

He tapped the headset he was wearing, a type of visor that encircled his head and enlarged his eyes. "I can watch it and you at the same time. Some technology is *gut*!"

Emma cringed when he used the old language. The word sounded so disturbing coming out of this young man's mouth.

"We gave you what you want, Lloyd." Henry stood up taller and moved slightly to the left so that he was completely blocking all three women from the madman's sight. "Let Emma and the girls go."

"Oh, I plan to, but first we have to trade."

"Trade?"

"An eye for an eye, tooth for a tooth...all that."

"And what would you like to trade?"

"You and Emma for Naomi and Katie Ann. You both say you love them, that you care about them, that they are an important part of your community." Sarcasm dripped from his voice. "So how about it? Are you willing to take their place?"

"Of course we are." Emma's voice had taken on a defiant tone.

She was at the end of her patience. Lloyd would be wise to tread carefully. Messing with the *Englisch* police was one thing. Pushing an Amish grandmother to the end of her *kapp* strings was quite another. Both were dangerous.

Emma stood up, though she had no idea what her next move would be. She stood beside Henry. They would present a united front to protect Naomi and Katie Ann.

But Henry reached out, grabbed her hand, and squeezed it, and she knew what he wanted her to do. They needed to stall, to give Grayson's men time to lock in on Lloyd's location. She breathed a silent prayer that the boy wouldn't be hurt. That was how she thought of him, as a boy, though plainly a man stood in front of them—an unstable man.

"This is wrong, Lloyd, and you will reap the consequences of your disastrous decisions." Henry probably shouldn't bait the young man, but neither, she knew, could he stand there and fail to speak the truth. "Repent, Lloyd. Repent and turn from your ways."

If either she or Henry thought Lloyd would explode in anger, they were both sadly mistaken. Instead of voicing any regret, the young man burst into laughter. "If you could see how you look. Scraggly old beard, white hair—all you need is a staff and you'd look like Moses."

He stepped closer and thrust the end of the rifle toward them, which as they'd suspected had quite an expensive scope on it.

"Better watch it, old man. You and your lady friend."

Instead of responding to his taunting, Henry asked, "How do you want to do this?"

"Good question!" Lloyd stood with his feet slightly apart and allowed the rifle to come down slightly, and that was when Grayson and his officers burst out from both sides of the billboard.

"Put your hands up and drop the weapon!" Grayson didn't need a bullhorn. His voice came across loud and clear from the distance of twenty feet.

Lloyd went to raise the weapon, but his mistake was that he looked in the direction of the voice, only for a moment, but long enough for Henry to step forward and grab the length of the rifle. Emma put her hands on it as well and together they tugged with all their might. Lloyd must have been surprised to see them fight back, but they were only taking something away from the young man, something that could hurt someone, which didn't bother Emma's conscience one bit.

Lloyd might have held on still, but Emma raised her foot and brought it crashing down on top of his. He squealed like a pig caught in a trap and stumbled backward, nearly losing his balance.

"Get on your knees and put your hands in the air." This was followed by the sound of more officers running up the bleachers.

Lloyd didn't stay around to see what they wanted. He took off running, across the bleachers and then down the stands. And he had a good head start on the officers, but they were strategically spread out, and he didn't really have a chance. They caught him when he was less than a hundred feet away.

He must have still been patched into the PA system, because Henry and Emma could hear him clearly from where they stood. "I have my hands up! Don't shoot!"

"Freeze!" Grayson hollered.

"It ain't my fault. Don't shoot me!"

Grayson was closer now, holding his weapon at the ready. He nodded toward Cunningham, who also had her weapon drawn, and said, "Cuff him."

"You've made a mistake." Lloyd was talking fast now, determined that in some bizarre twist of logic he'd be able to squirm his way out of this situation. "You have the wrong guy."

Grayson's men had completely surrounded Lloyd. Cunningham holstered her weapon, nudged him down on his knees, pulled his arms behind his back, and cuffed him.

"Hang on," Lloyd said. "I have an alibi."

"Uh-huh." Grayson looked at the man with a mixture of disgust and pity.

"I can even...I can find a witness, someone who can testify."

"We filmed the entire thing. Not likely your word will sway a jury once they see that." Grayson nodded to Officer Moore, who stepped forward, pulled Lloyd to his feet, and took him by the crook of the arm, leading him down the bleachers. As they walked away, Emma could hear the officer reading Lloyd his rights, explaining that anything he said would be used against him in court, and that he had the right to consult an attorney, and if he couldn't afford one, an attorney would be provided at no cost.

Emma realized she didn't care about that, not really. What she did care about were the two beautiful young ladies still strapped to stadium seats.

One of the Del Norte officers had succeeded in cutting loose the tape that held them, and both Katie Ann and Naomi flew into her arms. Emma thought it was perhaps the best thing she'd ever felt, their arms around her, being nearly overwhelmed by their love.

"You videotaped him?" Henry asked Grayson.

"All of our officers wear cameras now." Grayson joined Emma and Naomi and Katie Ann. "We have a medic standing by. Can you girls walk down to the breezeway, or should I bring her up here?"

"We're *gut*," Katie Ann said. "We can walk down."

"*Ya*, it actually feels good to move around. We'd been taped to that bleacher for hours." Naomi started laughing then, but her laughter soon turned to sobs, and she fell back into Emma's arms. "I'm so sorry. It's my fault. I didn't...didn't realize how he felt, and then he was...was so angry because I'd chosen Jeremiah, only I hadn't. Not really."

Emma held her.

Katie Ann stood close, her right hand on Emma, her left rubbing small circles on her best friend's back.

And Henry? Henry stood looking on with a soft smile that assured Emma this, too, would pass.

Sixty-Five

The medic met them as soon as they walked into the breezeway and asked Naomi and Katie Ann to come with her, but Emma wasn't ready to let either girl out of her sight. They all moved back into the food service room, the same place Grayson had tried to put vests and microphones on her and Henry.

She ran her hands over their cheeks, pulled their foreheads toward hers, and repeated again and again, "Thank You, Lord. Thank You, Jesus. Thank You."

"We're okay, *Mammi.*"

"He didn't hurt us, Emma. Honest. We're fine."

But Emma couldn't immediately convince herself that was true. She touched their arms, looked deep into their eyes, and finally collapsed onto one of the chairs the same time Henry arrived.

Officer Cunningham had escorted them down, but now she stepped back to give them a moment of privacy. Perhaps she was told to stay with them in case Lloyd hadn't worked alone, but Emma knew the danger had passed. The look of relief on Henry's face confirmed as much.

And then Katie Ann threw herself into Henry's arms, and Emma thought her heart would nearly burst at the sight of the two of them. She hadn't realized until that moment how much Katie Ann had missed her grandfather and how much she was looking forward to Emma's marriage to Henry.

"I knew you'd find us," Katie Ann said. She gave him one final hug and stepped back, as if she was suddenly embarrassed by her show of affection.

"Of course we found you. Your *mammi* and I are good at finding lost sheep."

The medic was a middle-aged woman with dark hair cut in a short bob. She had a grandmotherly look to her and a practiced eye. "My name is Sandy Vane, and I'm going to give you a brief physical exam."

As Sandy spoke to the girls, she shone a light in their eyes, felt their pulse, and recorded their blood pressure. She explained each step of her exam.

Emma knew they were in good hands. Finally the medic said, "You seem in remarkably good shape. Can you girls tell me how you feel?"

"Tired," Katie Ann admitted.

"Hungry."

"Relieved and..."

"And sad. It's all so sad." Naomi looked about to burst into tears again, but instead she uncapped the bottle of water the medic had pushed into her hands and took a long sip.

"Were you hurt in any way? Did the man the officers arrested touch you or make any unwelcome advances?"

"*Nein.* He didn't do anything like that. He didn't even seem that interested in us." Katie Ann plopped into a chair next to Emma. "It was more like we were a means to an end."

"But we have no idea what end. He wouldn't tell us what he wanted."

"Money," Henry said. "He wanted money."

And then Grayson walked into the room, received a go-ahead look from Sandy, and prepared to take a statement from Naomi and Katie Ann. He set his phone on a stainless-steel tabletop, tapped something to record what they were saying, and pulled out his small notebook and pen to also take notes. Someone dragged five chairs up to a table, though Emma couldn't imagine where they came from. They were, after all, in the middle of an industrial kitchen.

"I've dispatched an officer to your parents' home, Katie Ann, and to your aunt's, Naomi. He will let them know you—and Henry and Emma—are okay and that you'll all be home soon."

Both girls nodded.

"Now, I need you to tell me what happened from the moment Lloyd first kidnapped you. Nothing is too small or unimportant, because whatever you tell me will help to build the case against him. Do you understand?"

"*Ya*," they said at the same time.

Both girls were silent for a moment, and then Katie Ann said, "We were walking to Naomi's from my house..."

Naomi took up the story. "It was after dinner, and we promised we'd go straight home. It was sort of...well, a joke that Katie Ann would walk with me and then I'd walk back with her. But we agreed to each go back home when we reached the halfway point. We promised to be careful." This last sentence was said in a whisper.

"We thought it would be safe because we were together, at least part of the way."

"And then an old truck with a horse trailer pulled up."

Katie Ann straightened her *kapp*, suddenly self-conscious about how she must look. "We would never have climbed into the truck, but Lloyd had a gun sitting on the seat, and he put his hand on it and told us to get in. We were hoping maybe he'd settle down and talk to us, I guess, take us to Naomi's—"

"I think we knew something wasn't right." Naomi cleared her throat. "That is, I'm sure we did, but we didn't know what to do. Didn't know if we should scream and run, or just go along with it and hope everything would turn out all right. We got into the truck and thanked him for the ride, but then instead of asking where I lived—as far as I know he'd never been to my *aenti*'s house—he drove west, out of town."

"We begged him to stop, to let us out, but he only laughed. And then, when Katie Ann attempted to open the door..."

Katie Ann glanced at her friend, and Emma could tell by the look on her face that she was remembering the events of the last twenty-four hours in vivid detail. Emma prayed that her remembering would be a healing thing, that she would be able to give her statement and then forget what had happened, but she feared it wasn't so. Hearts didn't heal that quickly.

"Which I couldn't open because he'd locked it. Child locks or something."

"Well, then Lloyd pulled out the gun again and started waving it around."

"He didn't seem to have any destination in mind." Katie Ann glanced again at Naomi, who shrugged. "Not that we could tell. Finally, he stopped behind an old motel, the abandoned one out west of town."

"He pulled into the back, asked us if we needed to use the facilities, which we did. It was disgusting—dirty and smelled awful."

"We escaped, then, through the bathroom window, but he was expecting us to do just that."

"Then he made us get in the horse trailer." Naomi's left arm had begun to shake, and she clasped it with her right hand. "He bound our hands and feet with the tape, and he told us to be quiet, to be good, and we would be home with our families soon. He said something about needing to write a note, and he said...he said he would need to leave but he'd be back in the morning."

"We didn't know what he was talking about," Naomi said. "But then he made me write a note to *Aenti* Abigail and told me exactly what to say. I added that last line...*much love*...because she'd reminded me to add something like that on the letter to my *mamm*. But I hadn't, and suddenly I wished I had."

"That line is what convinced me something was wrong." Emma smiled at Naomi.

Katie Ann took up the story. "After that he wrote a note—"

"The one he left for you, Emma." Henry sat forward, his hands clasped in front of him on the table.

"He seemed to get angrier and angrier," Naomi said. "Then he started hollering at me about the last column I wrote in the *Budget*."

"The one that mentioned Jeremiah." Katie Ann reached for her friend's hand.

"*Ya*. He said I told lies there, that Jeremiah was never anything more than an Amish kid with a pipe dream, and that I should have chosen him instead of Jeremiah." Naomi's tears began to fall. "I barely remembered him from the last time I was in Goshen, but he talked like...like we'd been courting or something."

"It's not your fault, Naomi." Henry waited for her to meet his gaze.

"It's not your fault at all. Lloyd's mind is confused. That doesn't excuse what he did, and the *Englisch* courts will make sure he pays for his misdeeds and that he can't hurt anyone again. But it does explain the why, and that this wasn't the fault of either one of you in any way."

Neither girl looked convinced. Grayson cleared his throat and stared at the phone, waiting. Emma pulled on her *kapp* strings until she feared she might tear them from the cloth.

Henry reached forward and tapped the table. "Katie Ann, if you purchased a new horse from an *Englischer*, and it couldn't pull a buggy because it was lame in one leg, would you blame the horse?"

"'Course not."

"Why?"

"Because its leg would keep him from pulling the buggy. A lame horse can't do those things. Maybe when it was well it could."

"And Naomi, would you blame a reader who didn't understand your column if only half of it were written?"

"*Nein*. It wouldn't make any sense until they read the end."

"It's the same with Lloyd. Something in him is broken. It needs mending. And his story? *Gotte* hasn't finished writing it yet. If he's found guilty of this thing—"

"He will be," Grayson said gruffly.

"Then he'll spend many years, perhaps the rest of his life, in prison or in a facility for those mentally impaired. But even there, *Gotte* can heal him, and it is *Gotte* who has numbered his days and will write the end of his story."

And Emma knew then that both Katie Ann and Naomi would be all right, because they understood that they hadn't done anything wrong, that there was something fundamentally broken inside of Lloyd Yutzy, and that now they were safe.

Sixty-Six

Transcript of interview between Monte Vista Sheriff Roy Grayson and Lloyd Yutzy, regarding the July 27 homicide of Jeremiah Schwartz and the August 6 aggravated kidnapping of Naomi Miller and Katie Ann Fisher. Audiotapes and a transcript of the interview are included in both permanent case files.

Sheriff Roy Grayson #3604
INTERVIEW WITH Lloyd Yutzy
Case #4751.06 and #4764.01
10:15 p.m., Tuesday, August 7

Sheriff Grayson (SG): Please state your name for the recording.
Lloyd Yutzy (LY): Lloyd Yutzy.
SG: Middle initial?
LY: Y. You already know that.
SG: And for the record, your permanent place of residence is where?
LY: Goshen, Indiana, which is a lot better place than here.
SG: While visiting in the valley, you were staying with Mary and Chester Yoder?
LY: If you already know everything about me, why are you asking?
SG: Lloyd, do you understand that you've been charged with the murder of Jeremiah Schwartz and the aggravated kidnapping of Naomi Miller and Katie Ann Fisher?
LY: (inaudible)
SG: I need you to answer verbally for the recording.
LY: I understand.

SG: Also, for the record, you have waived your right to an attorney.

LY: I don't need an *Englisch* attorney. I'm innocent.

SG: When you are brought before the judge tomorrow, an attorney will be provided for you.

LY: Or we could work this out tonight. You could let me go, and I promise to leave this godforsaken place and never return.

SG: Lloyd, where were you the night of July 27?

LY: I wasn't at the rodeo if that's what you're asking.

SG: Can you prove that?

LY: Sure. I was at the diner. Someone saw me there, that older waitress—the one with the red hair. She'll tell you.

SG: You were not in the arena?

LY: I was not.

SG: And what were you doing in the diner?

LY: Working on my computer.

SG: Do you think this is funny?

LY: I don't. I think you're incompetent.

SG: We found the footage of your drone tapes.

LY: Those are mine. You have no right to look at them.

SG: You shot Jeremiah with a drone?

LY: Genius, right? You can't place me at the scene of the crime. We both know that.

SG: You used the drone to shoot Jeremiah?

LY: Attached a modified rifle under the gear box. Found the instructions on the Internet! I had to practice a lot before I got here to be sure it would work. In the end, practice pays off.

SG: You brought all of that on the bus with you?

LY: It's not as if I was going through an airport security scanner.

SG: So you admit to shooting Jeremiah Schwartz on the night of July 27?

LY: I'm not admitting to anything.

SG: Lloyd, we have proof that you were in fact on your computer, guiding the movement of the drone, and that you sent the command that killed Jeremiah. Do you have any response to that?

LY: It's Henry, isn't it? He drew me sitting in the diner. He probably got the details right down to me pushing the button.

SG: It wasn't Henry. Henry was at the rodeo.

LY: I should have killed him before I went after Jeremiah.

SG: We have in our possession recordings from closed-circuit cameras—security footage from standard surveillance in the diner.

LY: I have nothing to say to that.

SG: How is it no one saw the drone?

LY: People rarely look up. It's amazing what they don't see even when it's right in front of them.

SG: That was a big risk for you to take.

LY: Not really. Even if they had seen the drone, there was no way to track it to me.

SG: It's still murder, even if you weren't physically present.

LY: You don't understand. Jeremiah was an embarrassment to good Amish folk everywhere.

SG: Is that why you did it?

LY: Somebody had to. *Boots, Buckles, and Broncos?* What a joke. He was making a joke of what it means to be Amish.

SG: So you had to stop him.

LY: I stood up, took responsibility, and did what had to be done.

SG: And the girls? Why did you kidnap Naomi and Katie Ann?

LY: They were gone less than twenty-four hours, hardly worthy of being called kidnapping.

SG: You held them at gunpoint?

LY: They weren't going to get in the truck. I figured that might happen, knew how stubborn they were. And that Naomi? She thinks she's too good for a regular, hardworking man.

SG: So you threatened them with a gun, forced them into your vehicle, and then held them captive.

LY: (inaudible)

SG: I need you to answer verbally, please.

LY: *Ya.* Whatever.

SG: Taking the girls was part of a plan to ransom money from Bishop Henry Lapp. You needed money. Is that correct?

LY: I was supposed to get Jeremiah's money. He owed me, and I could have just kept what I brought from Goshen, but then he'd have kept on riding the rodeo, embarrassing members of our faith, leading on Naomi.

SG: So you gave the money to him.

LY: Just like I told you before.

SG: Thinking you could retrieve the money after you killed him.

LY: I went to that lame funeral, looked around his room, and found nothing. When I heard about Justin Lane taking the money from the girls—believe me, news travels fast in an Amish community—I knew I had to adjust my plan.

SG: Is there anything else you'd like to add to your statement?

LY: No.

SG: You'll appear before a judge tomorrow morning, when you will be arraigned for murder in the first degree and aggravated kidnapping.

LY: Arraigned?

SG: Your first appearance in court. A judge will decide if you're a flight risk, which I believe you are. The judge will then either set bail or decide you're to remain in jail until your trial.

LY: What do I do until then?

SG: You'll be taken back to your jail cell.

LY: I have to stay here?

SG: Yes.

LY: But that isn't fair. I was only doing what had to be done.

SG: Maybe, during the trial, you'll have the chance to explain that to Jeremiah's family.

LY: But I can't court Naomi from a jail cell.

SG: No. You can't.

LY: You're saying I can't go home?

SG: No, Lloyd. You can't go home.

Sixty-Seven

Two days later, Henry drove Emma to Bread 2 Go. He told Lexi to stay in the buggy, and they went inside to order a cinnamon roll each and a hot cup of coffee for Henry and hot tea for Emma. It was late for breakfast and too early for lunch. The bakery was still packed with people. Apparently, it was an all-day phenomenon.

Franey asked after the girls and then walked around the counter and embraced Emma on hearing they were fine.

"We've been praying," she said, "and I knew they would be okay. I'd even heard as much from Abe, but it's good to hear it from you."

"Will Naomi come back to work here?"

"*Ya*, but we insisted she take the rest of the week off."

Henry stepped back as they talked about an upcoming sew-in. It was good to see Franey Graber smiling. It wasn't that long ago that many in their community had called her Frowning Franey, but it seemed she'd found a contented place in her life, and her expression—her entire demeanor—reflected that.

Ruth Schwartz had a question about their wedding cake. She fairly beamed as she showed Emma a drawing of what she planned to make.

"Not too fancy, though," Emma said.

"*Nein*. Of course not." Ruth paused, glanced at Henry, and then added, "But it's not every day our bishop gets married."

Nancy Kline refused to take their money when they checked out. "Your money's no good here, Henry. Not today. You and Emma solved another murder."

"We didn't exactly solve it," Emma protested.

Henry nodded in agreement. "Stumbled into things."

"Like last time."

"And the time before that."

"We're done with mysteries and murder, though."

"We plan to live out our lives in marital bliss, with the only excitement coming from birding and grandchildren."

"And Katie Ann's animals."

"Are you sure I can't pay you? You are a business," Henry pointed out. "Your goal is to make a profit."

"We're doing that just fine, thank you."

Henry glanced at the growing line behind him and decided it was best not to argue the point.

He carried their sweets and drinks out the door and to the side of the restaurant while Emma released Lexi from the buggy. She was once again wearing her vest and her leash was attached, though it was completely unnecessary—the little dog didn't stray from Emma's side. The bakery's picnic area had been transformed by Lewis's glider tables, which were each covered with a different color canvas top. Lexi spied Henry and jumped up into the glider, sitting back prettily on her haunches and waiting for him to set it into motion.

Emma gazed up at the purple canvas covering. "The bright colors were Josephine's idea."

"I feel like I know her well, even though she's been here less than a year."

"Same here. Though we started circle letters to her when they first announced their intentions—so it feels as if I've known her longer. She's been a good addition to our community, and Lewis is like a new man. Has a real spring in his step, isn't it so?"

"It is."

Flowers had been planted in colorful pots throughout the picnic area, and a small birding area had been set up to the south side.

"The widows have made a real nice place here."

"Three Amish women starting a business." Henry shook his head in mock despair. "Times are a-changing."

They enjoyed their sweet rolls, and after they'd finished their drinks, Henry brought up the topic of Lloyd.

"I spoke with Grayson last night and tried to see Lloyd, but he didn't want visitors."

"I heard his parents won't be coming for the trial."

"It's true. I reached them by phone, and they told me Lloyd has chosen his path. They said they no longer consider him a part of the family."

"Shunned?"

Henry shrugged. "I haven't spoken to their bishop yet, though I did leave a message."

"I can't imagine what that must be like. For them or for Lloyd."

Henry tapped his fingers against the table. He wasn't sure how much of what Grayson had told him he should share. He wasn't sure that Emma wanted a fine August morning marred by such dark news, but then it occurred to him that she would soon be his wife, and that it would be best to share as much of life's burdens as possible. Lloyd's confession was indeed a burden on his soul, that a Plain man could have fallen so far away from the path God had set before each of them.

"What is it?" Emma asked. "I can always tell when you're deep in thought. You start—"

She mimed rubbing one eyebrow, and Henry laughed. He realized it was true, now that she pointed it out. If he didn't watch out, he'd rub one off—and wouldn't that look odd?

"Lloyd confessed to killing Jeremiah. He said he was doing his community a favor, that Jeremiah was an embarrassment to our faith."

"And so he shot him?" Emma stared into her empty cup. "Makes no sense."

"The judge agrees and has ordered a psychiatric evaluation. Today he'll be transferred to the facility over in Alamosa and held there until his trial, which could be many months, depending on what the evaluation reveals."

"Will you go and see him...in Alamosa?"

"When he'll let me. Until then, I'll send letters."

That sat between them for a moment. Finally Emma asked, "Have you spoken to Jeremiah's parents?"

"I have—well, I've spoken with Clara."

"And?"

"Her grief is still a heavy thing. She says Gideon is grieving as well."

"I suppose he is in his own way."

"On the one hand, they were already reeling from having lost their son to an *Englisch* lifestyle, accepting that he wouldn't settle down, choose to be Plain, and work on a farm. They didn't understand Jeremiah's love for the rodeo or why he would want fame and fortune."

"Many wealthy *Englischers*, and even a few wealthy Amish, do great good with their money." Emma folded her paper napkin once and then again. "The Good Book doesn't say a person can't be wealthy, only that it makes life more difficult in some ways."

"That's true, and I think Jeremiah's parents might have come around to that point of view eventually. Now they won't have that chance. They had hoped that one day he would reconcile with them and with our faith—so their grief is doubled now, knowing that will never happen."

"But Jeremiah still had faith, only not the Plain kind. He still believed. He told Naomi as much."

"And I shared that with his parents. I think, in time, it will bring them a measure of comfort."

Lexi trotted beside them as they put their cups and plates into a bin for dirty dishes on a table near the door, and then they strolled to Henry's buggy.

It occurred to Henry that he'd spent enough time dwelling on the dark side of man's nature. First Vernon Frey's killer, then the Sophia Brooks murderer, and now Lloyd. He'd had more than his share of such things. He couldn't fathom why he'd been involved with all three, or what God had meant for him to learn. But he'd realized two things for certain, and it occurred to him that he should share them with Emma.

He helped her and Lexi into the buggy and waited until they were on the road before he glanced her way and cleared his throat.

"I believe our marriage will be calmer than the last few years."

"Whether it is or not, we'll have each other, but *ya*, I hope you're right."

"I've learned a few things from it all."

"Have you now?" Emma smiled at him prettily, and he saw in her face the young girl he'd once known back in Goshen, the friend who had always been there for him, and the gentle soul who was soon to be his bride.

"My accident..." He touched the side of his head. "It wasn't an accident after all. Maybe Atlee Stolzfus never intended to hit me with a baseball all those years ago, but *Gotte* foresaw what would happen, and He used it for good."

"So you no longer fear it's a curse?"

"*Nein*. A gift from God? Any gift is a thing to be treasured, simple as that."

Emma nodded in agreement. "And the second thing you've learned?"

"To appreciate ordinary days, the days when nothing happens at all to differentiate them from any other day, the days that when you look back, they make up your life."

Instead of answering, Emma reached across Lexi and placed her hand on top of his. The little dog looked from Emma to Henry, and then she placed her head on her paws with a contented sigh.

Oreo trotted at a steady pace down the road as the San Luis Valley stretched out before them.

Sixty-Eight

Naomi and Katie Ann waved when they passed Henry's buggy on the road.

"They're so cute together," Naomi said, squirming around in her seat to watch them. "And they take that dog with them whenever they can."

"I'd say Lexi has earned all the outings she wants. I still can't believe she delivered a note to Seth and Roseann."

"She probably saved us."

"Probably did. Who knows, maybe they'll even let Lexi be in the wedding." Katie Ann laughed as soon as she said it, and Naomi even managed a tiny smile. A beagle participating in an Amish wedding. That sounded like one of the books Rachel read.

"Hard to believe they're to be married soon," Katie Ann added.

"Are you glad? That she's marrying again, I mean."

"*Ya*, I am. I miss my grandfather, but I also adore Henry. I think it will be good for my brothers to have him around, and it'll be good for me too."

As they neared the center of town, traffic picked up, and Katie Ann focused on her driving. Naomi had been surprised and also relieved when she'd shown up at her *aenti*'s house and asked her to go to town. She figured Katie Ann would already be working with Doc Berry again, but apparently everyone thought they needed time off after what happened with Lloyd. Naomi would rather be busy. She thought less when she was busy and could push aside the nightmares that plagued her.

Going to town was the next best thing to working, so she'd immediately agreed.

They pulled into a lot at the end of Main Street with special parking for buggies. Shoulder to shoulder, they walked to the library and picked up books for Katie Ann's mother, stopped by the post office and mailed a letter, and then made their way to the general store. Both girls had lists from home. They wandered the aisles, baskets over their arms, choosing their purchases. It was rather nice to shop without being in a rush. When they'd checked out, the clerk said, "Would you girls like an ice cream cone? It's on the house."

"Are you sure?" Naomi glanced at Katie Ann, who looked as surprised as she was.

"'Course I'm sure. You two are practically heroes now. Double scoops, my treat."

Who could turn that down?

Five minutes later, they were sitting on a bench outside the store, enjoying their ice cream cones—strawberry for Naomi and vanilla-chocolate swirl for Katie Ann. The sun was warm on their faces, and Naomi thought she could at least imagine life being normal again, even if it wasn't quite there yet.

"You've been kind of quiet," Katie Ann said. "Are you doing okay?"

"I had the nightmare again last night."

"Were we on the train like in your other dream?"

"*Ya.*"

"And Lloyd was there?"

"*Nein.* This time he'd taped us to a seat and left us. He'd jumped off, but his drone thing—it remained there, watching us."

Katie Ann studied her ice cream cone, looking serious, as if she could solve this if only she concentrated hard enough. "Maybe we should buy one."

"Buy one?"

"A drone."

"Why would we do that?"

"We could learn to play with it."

"Didn't see any in the general store."

"No, but someone mentioned they have them at the discount store."

"You want to buy a drone and play with it?"

"Maybe. It might take some of the terror away."

Naomi shrugged and licked at a stream of strawberry that had nearly reached her hand.

"In the dream, we were about to crash?"

"We were. The train kept gaining speed and in front of us loomed—"

"A solid black wall," they said in unison.

They finished their ice cream, tossed their napkins into a trash receptacle, and walked arm in arm down the sidewalk toward Katie Ann's buggy.

A couple wearing *I Love Monte Vista* T-shirts and sporting cameras around their necks stopped and stared. The woman offered a little wave, and Katie Ann waved back.

"Tourists," Naomi said.

"At least they didn't ask to take a selfie with us this time." Katie Ann bumped shoulders with Naomi, and it felt so natural that some of Naomi's anxiety slipped away.

"Have you talked to Henry?" Katie Ann asked.

"Twice."

"And?"

"He thinks I should continue writing for the *Budget*."

"*Ya*. I agree."

"But what if..." They'd reached Cinnamon. Both girls put their hands on the mare's neck, leaned in, and smelled deeply. "What if what I write causes..."

Katie Ann waited. This was one of the things Naomi loved about her best friend. She never rushed a conversation, never acted impatient or as if she had better things to do.

"What if what I write causes someone else to do something crazy...hurt someone, even kill someone."

"I don't think that's going to happen." Katie Ann untied the lead rope and gave the mare a nice scratch between the ears. Cinnamon nickered softly and nudged her pockets, looking for a treat. Katie Ann pulled out a small carrot and held it in the palm of her hand. Cinnamon took it in her big, soft lips, and it seemed to Naomi that the mare smiled. She could write about that. A buggy horse with the same emotions as people.

"I think Lloyd was like a ticking bomb," Katie Ann said. "He was bound to go off if no one intervened, and he was good at hiding his craziness, his jealousy, so that no one knew to intervene."

"What are you saying? You think it would have happened whether or not I'd written about Jeremiah?"

"I do."

They climbed into the buggy. When Cinnamon had settled into an easy trot, and they were turned toward home, Naomi spoke again.

"I've been thinking about writing a piece I'd like to see in the next issue."

"*Ya?*"

"Uh-huh."

"What's it about?"

"An Amish woman who works with a local veterinarian."

Katie Ann's laughter was contagious. It felt good and right to be happy on a sunny August afternoon in the San Luis Valley. Naomi looked out across the fields, toward the mountains. She liked living on the outskirts of Monte Vista, nestled in the valley. She thought she could be happy here.

Katie Ann pulled up in front of the Beilers' house, but she reached out and stopped Naomi when she made to leave the buggy.

"Silas asked about you again. He wants to give you space, but he also wants you to know he's thinking about you...and waiting until you're ready to see him."

"I do want to see him, but I'm not ready to step out with anyone. Not yet."

"He understands."

"I hope so. What about you and Albert?"

"He's taking me to dinner on Friday. If you and Silas would like to join us..."

"I'll think about it.

"It takes time for life to return to normal, or it did for me. My parents and *Mammi* think it was the trip to Florida that helped me. I'd been dreaming about the Monte Vista arsonist for weeks. I couldn't rest or eat or laugh. Then I was at my *aenti*'s in Florida, and I still had those same problems, but slowly things improved. Took time, though."

"Like healing from an injury."

"Exactly. When Cinnamon had a leg injury last year, it took months, not weeks, before she was sound again."

"I remember your being so worried."

"I was. I took special care icing it, applied support bandages, even gave her anti-inflammatory drugs, but mostly what healed her was time. I think maybe that's the important thing when we're hurting—to allow ourselves time to heal."

Naomi squeezed her friend's hand, hopped out of the buggy, and stood watching her and her mare head toward home.

Maybe Katie Ann was right, and time was one thing she had plenty of.

Sixty-Nine

Emma fidgeted with her dress and her apron and her *kapp*.

Rachel stood beside her as they looked out the upstairs window at their friends and family gathering below. A few *Englischers*—and of course everyone in their church district—had come. The women's dresses were as colorful as the flowers that rimmed Emma's garden, and the men were wearing their Sunday best—black coats, black pants, dazzling white shirts. Tables had been set up to the side, under the shade of the cottonwood trees. On the center of each table was a glass jar filled with celery. Emma knew the young girls preferred flowers, but celery was fine with her—the old way was fine with her. It brought a measure of comfort.

Her dress was a pale blue, and the apron matched. Her *kapp* was new, starched, perfect.

"Nervous?" Rachel reached forward and pushed back the strings of Emma's *kapp*.

"About the ceremony? Yes. A little. But not about Henry."

"He's a good man, and he loves you."

"I love him." Emma turned and studied her daughter-in-law. "I never expected to be marrying again. Never even thought I'd want to."

"You had a good marriage with George."

"I did. I was happy and considered myself blessed. And when he passed, I thought that was the way of things, that others go through it, and I would come out the other side of my grief eventually."

"And then you fell in love with Henry."

"And he fell in love with me."

"*Gotte* is good."

"All the time."

Rachel put her arms around Emma, held her for a moment, and then said, "Clyde will wonder what's happened to us."

They walked downstairs, Rachel squeezed her hand, and then she disappeared outside. Emma walked into the sitting room where her son and Henry were waiting.

Emma sat down beside Henry, who reached for her hand.

Clyde was holding the family Bible, and he had it open to the twenty-first chapter of Genesis. Emma could make out the German text, though it was upside down. She knew that Bible well, had held it on her lap through many a long night.

"Now the Lord was gracious to Sarah as he had said, and the Lord did for Sarah what he had promised."

Emma glanced at Henry, whose smile now stretched wide.

"Are you prophesying that we're to have a child, Clyde?"

"*Nein.*" Clyde glanced up at the two of them, and then he looked back down at the Scripture. "The Lord did for Sarah what He had promised."

"Even in her old age," Emma said.

"He is always faithful," Henry added.

"I was thinking on what I could possibly say to you two. *Mamm*, you've raised me in the ways of our faith. You've been a good mother and have been kind to my wife and loving to my children. I know what you had with *Dat* was special, and I know that…" He glanced out the sitting room window, toward the barn. "I know how lonely you were after he passed."

"You all were there for me," Emma said. She heard the singing that had begun outside, and she basked in the knowledge that her friends and family were celebrating this time with them. "You helped me."

Clyde nodded and then focused his attention on Henry. "You have been my bishop for many years, a good bishop. You've guided me. You've been my friend, and I am honored to have you marry my mother."

"*Danki*, Clyde."

"So no, I'm not saying that God will bless you with a child, though with Him all things are possible. Wasn't Abraham a hundred years old, and Sarah ninety?"

"Indeed," Henry said.

"What I am saying, what I realized last night when I was praying about what to say to you two, is that God is faithful, and that He isn't finished with you yet."

Emma felt tears sting her eyes and blinked rapidly to keep them from falling.

Henry squeezed her hand, and Clyde said, "Now, if it's all right, I'd like to pray for you both and for your new life together."

Her son's words poured over her, washing the last remnants of grief from her soul and causing her heart to rejoice. And then they were walking outside. The sun was shining brightly, but the chairs had been arranged so they were facing to the south. A slight breeze cooled the air, and in the distance the mountains rose to touch a cloudless sky.

Abe preached from 1 Corinthians, and Leroy shared Scripture from Proverbs. They sang again, and then Clyde was standing and motioning for them to join him. Henry reached for her hand. Emma looked down at that, at her hand in his, and all the butterflies that had plagued her stomach vanished.

"Do you, Henry Lapp, and you, Emma Fisher, vow to remain together until death?"

"Yes, we do."

"Will you both be loyal?"

"We will."

"Will you care for each other during adversity?"

Emma stifled a laugh. Henry had been by her side through the worst she could imagine. He'd saved her life on at least one occasion.

"We will."

"During affliction?"

"Yes."

"And sickness?"

"Yes." Softer now, remembering the past, and praying that God would guide their future.

Clyde reached forward and covered their hands with his own. "All of those assembled here, as your friends and family in Christ, and I, as your deacon, wish you the blessing and mercy of God."

Emma did laugh then, just as Sarah must have. She laughed at the surprises life brought, at the joy still hers to claim, and at the sound of applause coming from those watching.

"Go forth in the name of our Lord." Clyde turned them to face their guests. "You are now man and wife."

The rest of the day passed in a blur, but Emma didn't worry about what she saw or what she remembered. Henry could draw the scenes for her later. She would ask him for that gift. In fact, she'd purchased him a special sketchbook so he could chronicle their lives together.

There was food and laughter; gifts for their new house, including sheets and towels and dishes; games for the *youngies*; and then more food. Sometime during the late afternoon, she was aware that the men had slipped away and were unloading Henry's furnishings and clothes in the *dawdi haus* that had been finished just the day before. They would return the next afternoon to move his workshop into the building on the back of the house.

Emma thought of Clyde's choice of Scripture, she thought of Sarah and Abraham and laughter, she thought of the goodness of God, and she experienced a happiness and contentment she'd never expected to find again.

Seventy

The next evening, Henry and Emma sat on the front porch, their new front porch, in a double rocking chair that had been a gift from Lewis Glick. They were watching Stephen and Thomas attempting to catch lightning bugs in a jar. Lexi ran between the boys, yipping each time they jumped for one of the bugs. Soon the mason jars were little beacons of light, a renewable resource free to all who bothered to pause and appreciate them.

"They let them go, you know," Emma said. "Katie Ann insists on it."

"She has a tender heart, and the boys...they're so full of energy."

"Reminds me of when I was their age."

"Oh, did you catch them too?" Henry nodded in understanding. "We did, even when we were older, and then we took them back to the pond, where we'd night fish. The jars acted like miniature lanterns."

"God's light source."

"I was thinking..." Henry set the rocker into motion and reached for Emma's hand, entwined his fingers with hers, marveled at the satisfaction he felt.

"You were thinking?"

"Oh, that. I was thinking I'd allow Albert's small wind-powered gizmos. He's the one who suggested we adopt the solar power."

"And look how well that's worked out. It's been a real blessing to families."

"Most folks find the idea of alternative energy favorable—with the restriction that we only charge those things already allowed."

"No cell phones."

"No."

"Or electric scooters."

Henry laughed. "None of those either."

"It's a good decision. A nice balance between the old way and new."

"Lanterns and weather radios, even an alarm clock. It will save people money, eventually. I like the idea of renewable energy, God's provision."

"You're a good bishop, Henry."

"How could I not be? *Gotte* has given me a fine community, and now...a family."

Rachel stepped out on the porch at the main house, waved to get their attention, and then hollered some of Henry's favorite words. "Pie's ready!"

Hand in hand they walked down the steps of the *dawdi haus* and across the yard. Stephen and Thomas continued to dart back and forth, catching lightning bugs, but Lexi gave up the chase and followed at Henry and Emma's heels.

The sun was setting across the valley, sending a riotous display of purple, blue, gray, and even pink across the darkening sky.

"It's a good life here, Emma. Plain and simple."

"No more murder mysteries."

"I believe we've had enough of those."

"More than enough."

Before they stepped into the main house, Henry turned and looked back at their new home. It was small but efficient, and the workshop added onto the back would allow him to keep working, keep contributing. Emma paused beside him, leaned in, and kissed him on the cheek.

"Is everything okay?" she asked softly.

"I didn't realize how lonely I was before...until...well, until now."

She stepped into his embrace and followed his gaze. They stood there a moment, appreciating the goodness of the bounty before them. The goodness of God.

The boys dashed past them, clambering into the house. But then Stephen turned back and stopped next to them, pushing his jar of lightning bugs into Henry's hands.

"I caught them for you. I thought you might want to take *Mammi* on a night walk later."

"That's a *gut* idea. *Danki*."

"Gem gschehne."

Stephen bounded into the house. They could hear Katie Ann describing an owl she'd helped Doc Berry tend, Thomas teasing Silas about Naomi, and Rachel and Clyde asking who wanted ice cream on their pie.

Henry snagged Emma's hand in his, held the jar of lightning bugs in the crook of his other arm, and together they stepped into their new life.

Epilogue

Excerpt from the Budget

MONTE VISTA, COLORADO

February 8–Snow covers the mountains that surround the San Luis Valley. The Sangre de Cristo and San Juan ranges have seen more snowfall than in the last seven years. Local farmers are hopeful that the spring snow melt will produce good crops this summer.

Josephine and Lewis Glick's daughter, Susie, was born on February 1. Both sets of grandparents have visited, and Josephine reports that Susie is eating and sleeping well.

The barn raising at Seth and Roseann Hoschstetler's went well. The Hoschstetlers bought a home previously owned by Englisch, and the place needed a larger barn. Though snow continued to fall in the mountains, the valley had cold temperatures but no precipitation. Bishop Henry Lapp reports that more than seventy people showed up for the workday, including families from Westcliff, who hired a driver to bring them over. Seth and Roseann seem quite happy with the results.

During our last church meeting, Katie Ann Fisher and Albert Bontrager announced their intentions to wed in the spring. Katie Ann's brother Silas and your humble scribe announced our intentions to wed as well. It seems I will finally be Katie Ann's sister! Rachel and Clyde Fisher say it's time to build an addition onto their house.

Speaking of Bishop Henry, his drawings were recently featured in a Monte Vista artist publication. When asked if he plans to give up building birdhouses and such, his answer was a simple "nein." He later mentioned he was teaching Emma's grandsons the joy of birding. They, in turn, insist that their new daddi take them fishing at least twice a month. Emma and Henry wed in August of last year.

The widows' bakery, formally known as Bread 2 Go, received a Chamber of Commerce award for most innovative business in the valley. Franey Graber, Nancy Kline, and Ruth Schwartz recently added an enclosed sun porch and solar energy to their store.

If in February there be no rain, 'tis neither good for hay nor grain. (English proverb)

Naomi Miller

Discussion Questions

1. Henry Lapp has long struggled with his "gift," his ability to accurately draw in detail anything he has seen. When Jeremiah Schwartz is killed, Henry is asked by those closest to him if he'll be able to assist in the investigation, but Henry didn't see the shooting. His unique ability in this instance is no help at all. If he's unable to draw anything relevant, how can he help the investigators? How can he help his congregation? What can any of us do to help when someone we love is grieving?

2. We learn that Jeremiah was planning to audition for a reality television show. Reality television first became popular in the late 1990s. It supposedly documents unscripted, real-life situations. What do you think explains society's fascination with these types of shows? Are they a good thing or a bad thing, or does it depend on the show? You can read Ira Wagler's blog regarding the reality show *Amish Mafia* at http://www.irawagler.com/?p=8029.

3. At the end of chapter 11, as Emma and Ruth are standing on the front porch, Ruth comments that "life is certainly full of grief and uncertainty." Emma doesn't argue with her. She does, however, think of words from Ecclesiastes. Read chapter 3, verses 1-8 from this book in the Old Testament. How do the words minister to your heart?

4. In chapter 18, Grayson lays out the contradictions in Jeremiah's life, and Henry is reminded of an old proverb—*Go*

far from home, and you will have a long way back. Unlike the prodigal son (Luke 15), Jeremiah won't have a chance to find his way back home. How do you think this applies to us today? What can we do to help others attempting to return to their spiritual or physical home?

5. By chapter 31, Henry realizes something is amiss within his community, and he can't figure it out alone. He has that itchy need to do something, anything, rather than sit and see how things unfold. Have you ever felt that way? Waiting is hard work. The Scriptures Henry finds (Hebrews 4:12 and Galatians 6:2) convince him he shouldn't wait alone, and so he goes in search of his deacons. Who can you call when waiting is hard? How can you support someone who is going through a difficult time of waiting?

6. Chapter 42 finds Emma sitting through their church service, hearing Henry quote from 1 Peter 3:15: *Always be prepared to give an answer to everyone who asks you to give the reason for the hope that you have.* Although she hears the words, and she believes she does have a divine hope in her heart, she is consumed by her worry. What are specific steps you can take when anxiety and worry threaten to overwhelm you?

7. When Henry and Sheriff Grayson are discussing Norman Rockwell, Henry comments that once *Englisch* life and Amish life were quite similar. Do you agree or disagree? What did we have in common then? What are the most obvious differences now?

8. When Henry goes home to draw, to find the answer to what has happened to the girls, he first prays, and in his prayer he remembers the words from the psalmist. Why do psalms touch our hearts when we're in a time of need? What is it about David's story that allows us to see God's protection and providence?

9. The morning after Naomi and Katie Ann disappear, Emma

tells Henry she feels optimistic, and Henry suggests she's received a word from God. Was a personal word from God a momentous once-in-a-lifetime thing, or was it something so everyday—so commonplace—that they forgot to listen? What do you think? Does our heavenly Father speak to us daily, or do we hear His voice only in our darkest moments?

10. As Emma and Henry enter the arena, they begin discussing their wedding plans. Even in the midst of their trouble, they're able to look forward to better times. We read that Henry "could look past the present hour and glimpse the future God had for them." How can we do that in the worst of times? What specific steps can we take to remind ourselves that our present trouble will pass?

Glossary

Aenti	Aunt
Ausbund	Amish hymnal
Bruder	brother
Dat	father
Dawdi haus	grandparents' home
Danki	thank you
Englischer	non-Amish person
Freind(en)	friend(s)
Gem gschehne	you're welcome
Gotte	God
Gotte's wille	God's will
Grandkinner	grandchildren
Grossdaddi	grandfather
Gut	good
Kapp	prayer covering
Kind/kinner	child/children
Loblied	hymn of praise
Mamm/Mammi	mom/grandmother
Nein	no
Rumspringa	running-around years
Ordnung	the unwritten set of rules and regulations that guide everyday Amish life
Wunderbaar	wonderful
Ya	yes
Youngie/youngies	young adult/adults

Recipes

Light-as-Air Biscuits

2 cups all-purpose flour
½ tsp. salt
2 tsp. sugar
4 tsp. baking powder
½ tsp. cream of tartar
½ cup shortening
⅔ cup milk

Preheat the oven to 450°. In a large bowl, mix together the flour, salt, sugar, baking powder, and cream of tartar. Cut in the shortening until the mixture resembles coarse crumbles. Make a well in the center and add the milk all at once; stir with a fork until the dough leaves the side of the bowl.

Turn out the dough onto a lightly floured surface and knead about 5 times. Roll or pat dough to a half-inch thickness and then cut with a biscuit cutter.

Place the biscuits on an ungreased baking sheet and bake for 15 minutes or until done.

Recipe from Georgia Varozza, 99 Favorite Amish Breads, Rolls, & Muffins

Buttermilk Whole Wheat Quick Bread

1 qt. buttermilk
4 cups whole wheat flour
3 cups brown sugar
Pinch of salt
1 tsp. baking soda

Mix together all ingredients and pour the batter into 2 greased loaf pans. Bake at 350° for 60 to 70 minutes.

Recipe from Georgia Varozza, 99 Favorite Amish Breads, Rolls, & Muffins

Honey Whole Wheat Bread

4½ tsp. (2 packages) active dry yeast
2 cups warm water (110° to 120°)
2 cups warm milk (110° to 120°)
½ cup butter (1 stick), softened, or ½ cup oil
½ cup honey
¼ cup molasses
2 tsp. salt
9 to 10 cups whole wheat flour, more or less

Preheat the oven to 375°. In a small bowl, dissolve yeast in warm water. Let it stand until bubbly, about 5 to 10 minutes.

In a large bowl, mix together the butter, honey, molasses, and salt. Add the yeast mixture and stir to mix. Gradually add the flour, stirring with a wooden spoon until the dough comes away from the side of the bowl and a soft dough forms. Turn out onto a floured surface and knead until smooth, about 8 to 10 minutes, adding small amounts of flour as needed.

Place the dough ball in a large greased or buttered bowl; cover and let rise until double, about 1½ to 2 hours. Punch down dough and let rest for several minutes; knead dough about 20 times and then divide into 4 equal pieces. Shape each piece of dough into a loaf and place in greased loaf pans. Cover the dough and let rise for about an hour or until almost doubled.

Bake for 35 to 40 minutes or until done. Cool in loaf pans for about 5 minutes, and then turn out loaves on a wire rack to finish cooling.

Note: This recipe makes 4 loaves. You can freeze what you won't eat right away. Just make sure the bread is completely cool before wrapping tightly and freezing.

Recipe from Georgia Varozza, 99 Favorite Amish Breads, Rolls, & Muffins

Molasses Nut Cookies

2 cups sugar

1 cup shortening

2 eggs, beaten

1 cup molasses

1 tsp. vanilla extract

6 cups all-purpose flour

3 tsp. baking soda

1 tsp. salt

3 tsp. ground cinnamon

2 tsp. ground ginger

2 cups sour milk or buttermilk

1 cup nuts, chopped

Preheat the oven to 375°. Cream together the sugar and shortening and then add the eggs, molasses, and vanilla. Mix well. In a separate bowl, combine the flour, baking soda, salt, cinnamon, and ginger. Add that to the creamed mixture alternately with the buttermilk or sour milk. Stir in the nuts.

Drop the batter onto greased cookie sheets by the spoonful, spaced 2 inches apart. Bake for 10 minutes until golden brown around the edges. Allow the cookies to cool for 5 minutes before removing to wire racks to cool completely.

Recipe from Elizabeth Coblentz with Kevin Williams, The Amish Cook

Cinnamon Fans

Fans

3 cups all-purpose flour
1 tsp. salt
4 tsp. baking powder
1 tsp. cream of tartar
⅓ cup sugar
¾ cup shortening
1 cup milk

Filling

½ cup butter, melted and cooled
½ cup sugar
2 T. cinnamon

Preheat the oven to 400°. Grease a 12-cup muffin tin and set aside for now.

For fans: Whisk together the dry ingredients. Cut in the shortening until the mixture resembles coarse crumbles. Add the milk and stir. Turn out onto a lightly floured surface and knead gently for a half minute. Roll the dough into the shape of a rectangle about one-quarter inch thick (the rectangle should be about 8 x 24 inches).

For filling: Spread the melted butter evenly on the dough. Mix together the sugar and cinnamon and then sprinkle that mixture over the buttered dough.

Cut the dough into four long strips, each about 2 inches wide and 24 inches long. Stack the 4 strips on top of one another, and then cut the stack into 12 equal pieces, each about 2 inches wide.

Turn the pieces on their sides in greased muffin tin cups so each treat fans out.

Bake for 12 minutes or until golden brown.

Recipe from Georgia Varozza, 99 Favorite Amish Breads, Rolls, & Muffins

Potato and Vegetable Scones

2½ to 3 cups all-purpose flour
1 T. plus 1 tsp. baking powder
1½ tsp. salt
4 ounces cream cheese
½ cup cheddar cheese, shredded
1 egg
1 cup cream
¼ cup each green, red, yellow, and/or orange bell peppers, finely diced
(using multiple colors isn't necessary, but it makes the scones prettier)
¼ cup onion, finely diced
½ large potato, peeled, cooked, and finely diced
⅛ cup fresh mushrooms, thinly sliced or diced
⅛ tsp. dried sage
⅛ tsp. dried rosemary
1 T. butter

Preheat the oven to 400°. In a medium bowl, mix together the dry ingredients and set aside.

In a large bowl, cream together the cheeses and egg. Add the cream and mix well.

On medium-low heat, sauté the vegetables and herbs in butter until soft, about 4 minutes. Add them to the cream mixture and stir well. Add the dry ingredients and stir by hand until a soft dough forms.

Place the dough on a buttered cookie sheet (or you can use a silicone baking mat instead) and pat into a one-inch-thick circle. Using a pizza cutter or knife, cut the dough into 8 equal wedges (as if you were cutting pie).

Bake for 20 to 25 minutes or until done. Remove scones from the baking sheet and set on a wire rack to cool.

Recipe from Georgia Varozza, 99 Favorite Amish Breads, Rolls, & Muffins

Company Chicken Casserole

4 cups carrots, diced
4 qt. potatoes, diced
2 cups celery, diced
1 large onion, diced
8 cups frozen peas
4 to 5 qt. boneless chicken pieces, cooked
1 tsp. salt
1 tsp. pepper
1 cup Colby cheese, grated

Place the carrots, potatoes, celery, onion, and peas in a pot and cover with water. Bring to a boil over medium-high heat and then decrease heat to medium. Cook for 20 minutes or until the vegetables are tender. Drain the vegetables and place them in a large roaster with a lid. Add the chicken and mix well. Add the salt and paper. Sprinkle the cheese on top and cover the roaster with a lid. Bake at 350° for 1 hour.

Recipe from Elizabeth Coblentz with Kevin Williams, The Amish Cook

Amish Snickerdoodles

½ cup butter
½ cup shortening
2 eggs
1½ cups sugar
2¾ cups flour
2 tsp. cream of tartar
1 tsp. baking soda
¼ tsp. salt
2 T. sugar
2 tsp. cinnamon

Preheat the oven to 375°. Thoroughly mix the butter, shortening, eggs, and sugar. Sift the flour, cream of tartar, baking soda, and salt and add to the first mixture. Combine well. With your hands, form small dough balls (about walnut size) and roll them in a mixture of the sugar and cinnamon. Place about 2 inches apart on ungreased cookie sheet. Bake for 8 to 10 minutes.

Cookies will flatten into circles as they cook. You can top with red hots or leave unadorned.

Double Good Blueberry Pie

¾ cup sugar
3 T. cornstarch
⅛ tsp. salt
¼ cup water
4 cups fresh blueberries, divided
1 T. butter
1 T. lemon juice
1 baked pie shell
Whipped cream

Combine the sugar, cornstarch, and salt in a saucepan. Add the water and 2 cups of the berries. Cook over medium heat, stirring constantly, until the mixture comes to a boil and is thickened and clear. (It will be quite thick.)

Remove from the heat and stir in the butter and lemon juice. Let cool. Place the remaining 2 cups of berries in a baked 9-inch pie shell and top with the cooked berry mixture. Chill. Serve with whipped cream.

AUTHOR'S NOTE

The Ski Hi Stampede is Colorado's oldest pro rodeo and includes both professional and amateur events. The first Ski Hi rodeo was held on August 11-13, 1919, and was called the Ski Hi Stampede. More than 10,000 people attended. You can visit the Ski Hi rodeo facility in downtown Monte Vista.

The first Amish families settled in Colorado in the early 1900s. As of 2010, the state was home to four Amish communities, with a combined population of under 100 families. In the San Luis Valley, farming has proven to be a challenge for the Amish, as the area receives an average of seven inches of rain annually. The growing season is approximately 90 days. Many families in the area have opened small businesses to provide an additional source of income.

Accidental/acquired savant syndrome is a condition where dormant savant skills emerge after a brain injury or disease. Although it's quite rare, researchers in 2010 identified 32 individuals who displayed unusual skills in one or more of five major areas: art, musical abilities, calendar calculation, arithmetic, and spatial skills. Males with savant syndrome outnumber females by roughly six to one.

Drones are now an affordable piece of equipment, with prices ranging from $39.99 to thousands of dollars. Many drones now have GPS, 4K camera, and autopilot.

I did much research and had the pleasure of visiting the town of Monte Vista. I took the liberty of rearranging sections of the town in order to facilitate the actions of and cause trouble for my characters. Any discrepancies in the description of the area were done intentionally for dramatic license.

About the Author

VANNETTA CHAPMAN writes inspirational fiction full of grace. She is the author of several novels, including the Plain & Simple Miracles series and *Pebble Creek Amish*. Vannetta is a Carol Award winner and has also received more than two dozen awards from Romance Writers of America chapter groups. She was a teacher for 15 years and currently resides in the Texas Hill Country. For more information, visit her at www.VannettaChapman.com.

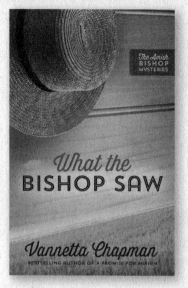

Somewhere in the Embers Lies the Truth

A fire blazes out of control in the San Luis Valley of Colorado, leaving an elderly Amish bachelor dead. Bishop Henry Lapp rushes to the scene, and he learns the fire was no accident. Someone intended to kill Vernon Frey. But who would want to kill him? Well, practically everyone—Amish and *Englisch* alike.

When the police point the finger at a suspect Henry knows is innocent, the bishop must decide whether or not to use his mysterious, God-given gift—one he's tried desperately to ignore all these years—to try and set the record straight. His close friend and neighbor, Emma Fisher, encourages Henry to follow God's leading.

Could the clue to solving the case be locked somewhere deep in Henry's memory? Will he find the courage to move forward in faith and put the right person behind bars? Is his friendship with Emma becoming something more?

What the Bishop Saw is a story of extraordinary talent, the bonds of love and friendship, and the unfailing grace of God.

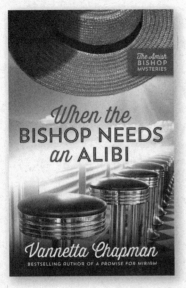

A Terrible Secret Hides in the Bulrushes

Amish bishop Henry Lapp eagerly awaits the annual arrival of 20,000 sandhill cranes to the San Luis Valley of Colorado. But his visit to the Monte Vista National Wildlife Refuge reveals more than just a miracle of God's creation. Hidden among the bulrushes and cattails is the deceased body of a young woman.

As the local authorities attempt to unravel the mystery, Henry feels God's calling to use his extraordinary talent to aid in the investigation. His ability to draw from memory in photographic detail could help solve this puzzling case.

Henry's closest friend, Emma Fisher, has always urged him to embrace his gift. As their relationship deepens, Henry realizes his involvement could put him and those he loves in the direct path of a killer, one who is willing to do anything to cover up a brutal crime, including framing the bishop.

When the Bishop Needs an Alibi is a compelling story of faith, friendship, and finding courage only God can provide.

To learn more about Harvest House books and
to read sample chapters, visit our website:

www.harvesthousepublishers.com

HARVEST HOUSE PUBLISHERS
EUGENE, OREGON